a Shetland Christmas carol

Erin Green was born and raised in Warwickshire. An avid reader since childhood, her imagination was instinctively drawn to creative writing as she grew older. Erin has two Hons degrees: BA English literature and another BSc Psychology – her previous careers have ranged from part-time waitress, the retail industry, fitness industry and education.

She has an obsession about time, owns several tortoises and an infectious laugh! Erin writes contemporary novels focusing on love, life and laughter. Erin is an active member of the Romantic Novelists' Association and was delighted to be awarded The Katie Fforde Bursary in 2017. An ideal day for Erin involves writing, people watching and drinking copious amounts of tea.

For more information about Erin, visit her website: **www.ErinGreenAuthor.co.uk**, find her on Facebook **www.facebook.com/ErinGreenAuthor** or follow her on Twitter **@ErinGreenAuthor**.

Praise for Erin Green:

'A warm, funny, uplifting writer to celebrate!'   Katie Fforde

'A lovely, heart-warming story . . . I was hooked!'
Christina Courtenay

'A delightful tale of friendship, family and love'   Jenni Keer

'Thoroughly entertaining. The characters are warm and well drawn. I thoroughly recommend this book if you are looking for a light-hearted read. 5 stars'   Sue Roberts

'Uplifting'   *Woman & Home*

'Full of humour, poignancy and ultimately uplifting this is an absolutely gorgeous read. We loved it! Highly recommended!'
Hot Brands Cool Places

'Like a scrummy bowl of Devon cream and strawberries, this is a tasty, rich and delicious summer read laced with the warmth of friendships and the possibilities of new beginnings . . . The author has the knack of making her characters spring off the pages so real that you'll care about them'   *Peterborough Telegraph*

'A pleasure to read . . . A summer breezes treat'   *Devon Life*

a Shetland Christmas carol

ERIN GREEN

REVIEW

First published in 2022
by HEADLINE REVIEW
An imprint of HEADLINE PUBLISHING GROUP

1

Cataloguing in Publication Data is available from the British Library

ISBN 978 1 4722 9503 3

Typeset in Sabon by CC Book Production

Printed and bound in Great Britain by
Clays Ltd, Elcograf S.p.A.

Headline's policy is to use papers that are natural, renewable and recyclable
products and made from wood grown in well-managed forests and other
controlled sources. The logging and manufacturing processes are expected
to conform to the environmental regulations of the country of origin.

HEADLINE PUBLISHING GROUP
An Hachette UK Company
Carmelite House
50 Victoria Embankment
London EC4Y 0DZ

www.headline.co.uk
www.hachette.co.uk

To the Ghost of Christmas Yet to Come
Stave IV, *A Christmas Carol* (1843)

There are dark shadows on the earth, but its lights are stronger in the contrast.

CHARLES DICKENS

Shetland Glossary

Peerie – small/little

Daa – grandfather

Crabbit – bad-tempered

Yamse – greedy

Chapter One

Saturday 13 August

Ebenezer's ledger

The Garrison Theatre, Lerwick – 80 years old!!! Bah humbug to you, Dickens, and your 179 years! Hopefully, my past, my present and my future – bound together as one!

Callie

'Morning!' calls the postman cheerily, unlatching our garden gate.

I slam the front door. I'm not a morning person, but there are some folks you can't readily ignore. And I can't afford to ignore his bulky size, his smiley disposition, but most importantly his regular deliveries of bad news. He's my guilty conscience, if it ever morphed into a fully fledged human being, capable of walking, talking and constantly popping up in order to irritate me.

Couldn't I live further along the street so our paths didn't cross each morning? Or could his postal route be reversed so he delivers mid-morning when I am safely out of the way? Or maybe I should move out from my parents' home? Sadly, not. Though moving out wouldn't truly solve my problem, unless I leave Shetland for ever and change my identity – which would be a bit drastic. Instead, I get to eyeball my guilty conscience square in the face on a daily basis and receive a handful of brown and white envelopes, none of which will deliver joy. Ever.

The clutch of envelopes, all slim and neatly franked, contain twisted promises which are guaranteed to ruin my day, should I open them. So, I don't. Instead, I flick through, seeking anyone's name other than my own, 'Ms C. Quinn' – which rarely happens, as my parents seem to have gone paperless.

It's fashionable to own an oversized handbag, one that can hold everything plus the kitchen sink, twenty-four hours a day seven days a week. Some women carry their make-up, their hair brushes, a spare pair of shoes, a change of tights . . . me, I carry my overdue statements and demands. All unopened, and not necessarily in the bottom of my bag. Sometimes the pile reaches the top of my bag, with my purse sitting neatly on the summit.

Without missing a step, I frantically stuff the envelopes into my shoulder bag, acting as if I'm late or too busy with my career to care. The reality is, I'm neither. I'm between jobs: waitressing. Not an ideal role, given my qualifications in beauty therapy. But beggars can't be choosers – especially when wages are vital and opportunities are scarce – so I accepted the role seven months ago. I've been kidding myself about its temporary status too; I've hugely overrun on the two-week stint I'd originally planned.

'Thank you, have a nice day!' I call in a cheery voice as I follow the postie down the pathway, hoping he's fooled by my apparent delight at receiving my mail.

I'm not delighted. I never am. It's never news of a lottery win, confirmation of a job interview or a long-lost cousin insisting on depositing a zillion pounds into my bank account before lunchtime. Instead, I receive oodles of charge card and credit card bills, notifications of additional charges, or demands for urgent payments to rectify a missed instalment. In some cases, I accidentally forgot to pay; in others, I strategically deleted the direct debit in a last-ditch attempt to delay an automatic transaction leaving my account on a particular day.

It's not that I'm trying to deny the lenders the money I owe; I acknowledge my debts. I simply wish they'd organise themselves in an orderly queue and patiently wait their turn, shuffling forward until they reach the front, much like stores make me do when I wish to purchase goods using my array of flexible friends. But oh no! Credit cards and store cards want to be served immediately, requesting automatic bank payments as the clock strikes midnight. There might just be enough funds to go around if they'd allow me to juggle my finances throughout the month. But they don't, despite me creating a password-protected and colour-coded spreadsheet tracking my payments.

As a result, I receive daily text messages from my equally unsupportive bank, kindly suggesting I might, could or *should* transfer money into my current account by two o'clock to cover today's outgoing payments. Or else! Two o'clock, why such a random time of day? Why not spread the debit payments throughout the day? Such a wasted text message, when I planned on depositing my waitressing tips later that afternoon. Yet I receive and ignore the kindly request with the same determination as I've just dodged the morning postie.

It makes for an uncomfortable start to my day. The routine of slamming the front door, turning around to utter a greeting, whilst faking a smile, and receiving my envelopes, quickly followed by a stroll towards the gallery, knowing I'll receive the anticipated daily text message en route. I suspect that our postie and the anonymous bank texter are in cahoots with each other to ruin my life. They might be one and the same person: I bet he delivers the mail before whipping out his phone to send the dreaded text message whilst I'm still in sight. It's a feasible theory, and one I'll cling to if it enables me to ignore the discomfort of my bulging shoulder bag, gaining daily in size and weight in equal proportion to my conscience.

I reach the corner of our housing estate, cross the road and look up at the newly erected brown tourist sign: 'Lerwick Manor Gallery and Hotel 1km'. I begin the trek in my sensible, flat waitressing shoes, hoping that my pristine white blouse isn't too creased or soiled on arrival. That's what I loved about my beautician's attire; a simple black tunic, leggings and ballet pumps were always pristine and smart, unless I splattered a mud mask over myself during a client's treatment.

I head out, ready to face the world: blonde bob pinned back, my painted smile in place, and a spring in my step. Living with debt, I've learnt to compartmentalise my life, which is a skill in itself; my existence is neatly separated into blocks of time or tasks. Firstly, home life alongside my parents, where I've perfected the role of solo child for the last thirty-three years. It's a hefty weight to carry, as I shoulder their kind requests, forced suggestions, hopes and dreams alone, without others to lighten the load. Over the years, I've learnt to agree, say 'mmm' and 'ahhh' in all the right places; there's no point in arguing, as it's two against one every time, so I go with the flow and then secretly please myself. The flip side is that no one grasses me up – unlike friends' siblings who break their necks to spill the beans over the Sunday roast.

I do as I wish, most of the time, which can inadvertently lead to trouble – rather like my 'shoulder bag secret' – but deep down, I'm combatting my parents' constant demands on my time and avoiding the regular chimes of 'Who else can we ask?', 'We're not getting any younger, you know' and, the worst of all, 'We've given you everything, Callie!'

Away from home, there's my current waitressing work in an artisan coffee shop connected to my cousin's arts and crafts gallery, all set within her husband's ancestral stately home. Not that I'm jealous of our Jemima, but in recent years she has had all the luck; if she fell over in goat's muck she'd stand back up wearing a new cashmere jumper. Though I don't envy her the constant sickness she's enduring with her first pregnancy. 'Blooming' and 'radiant' are the comments usually uttered about expectant mothers; most of the time she's looking pretty sallow, drained and totally fed up. And the baby isn't due until December. I appreciate that she's encountered heartache, with the untimely death of her mum and then our grandfather Tommy – but she struck lucky again there, and received a surprise legacy. Unlike me.

Perhaps it's thoughts such as these that are sullying my karma. Maybe if I took a leaf out of Pippa's book – my other, younger cousin – and pressed the 'reset' button, I could ignite a new beginning alongside a decent guy like Levi. Pippa also works for cousin Jemima, driving her mobile bread delivery van. The downside is that I'm surrounded by cousins and extended family all day at work, and smothered by my parents when I get home – another reason why I compartmentalise my existence and overindulge in retail therapy, courtesy of my credit limit.

I wouldn't say I'm spoilt exactly – despite my parents ensuring that I never wanted for anything growing up. My dad lives by the old adage 'buy cheap, buy twice'. So having always had the best, I've found it's a hard habit to break. Be it high-end make-up which promises to stay put for twenty-four hours, or extortionately priced tights which never snag or wrinkle, or my passion for hair and beauty treatments which are a future investment in the fight against visible aging. I appreciate that others can't tell the difference between my expensive, high-end purchases and their cut-price, own-brand goods, but I know. This'll make me sound like an utter bitch, but I genuinely like my colleague Aileen's Superdrug lip gloss – it's a nice shade and definitely costs less than a tenner, maybe even change from a fiver – but it doesn't stay put like my lipstick does. This morning's application of my current favourite lipstick, in the exclusive shade of Clover Dew, won't need retouching for hours, but then it did cost nearly £130 from New York via the internet! Aileen probably couldn't tell the difference, but I can.

And therein lies my problem; I'm used to the best. My spending splurges have simply become a way of life. It's not as if I'm admitting to a shopping addiction; I only have access to the local stores here in Shetland, though my purchasing prowess does include the internet and TV channels – though, sadly, they deny me the same buzz. Shopping is simply my happy place; my chosen comfort when I'm feeling a bit low, or a tad lonely, or tired, or upset – and sometimes, just occasionally, a little bit woozy after a night out.

I manage to earn a little extra at Lerwick Manor by volunteering to assist in leading the alpaca walking tours. Not your usual run-of-the-mill job, but one I love. I never imagined that alpacas could be adorable and affectionate towards their handlers. We organise a package deal offering twice-weekly treks followed by afternoon tea in The Orangery. I visit 'my boys' in their paddock or overnight stable on a daily basis after my waitressing shift has finished. The herd has a mix of fleece colours – cream, fawn, russet and black – that gallop over to greet me as I approach, and it isn't just the dried food stash in my pocket that they recognise!

My main concern is my debt. I've learnt to catalogue my worries and stack them on the bookcase inside my head. I say bookcase, it's more like a four-storey mainland city library with wall-to-wall, floor-to-ceiling bookcases, and still each shelf is jam-packed. I battle through each day as required, much as I did when I was a beautician. Whilst performing a deep-tissue massage, I thought only of the massage. Whether delivering a pedicure, a manicure or a facial, the same rules always applied and I only ever focused on the task in hand. Now, as a waitress, I apply exactly the same rule. Latte. Flat white. Wipe tables. Stack cutlery. Hot chocolate. Sprinkles. Mop floor. Make tea. Greet. Serve. Smile. Repeat. And repeat. Again. I've taught myself how to switch between tasks, knowing that each completed task earns me wages and allows the hands on the clock to move around a little faster.

I deal with my debt, and how to juggle all the demands for

repayment, once I'm alone at the end of my day. I can't afford for it to ruin my shift, or divert my attention from earning. My tips aren't great, but at least Isla, The Orangery's manager, shares out the 'tips mug' on a daily basis amongst the waitresses on duty, which is fair.

In no time, I've walked the kilometre along the lane, arriving at the entrance to Lerwick Manor. Traipsing along the driveway, passing the recently installed sculpture park and picnic tables, I can't help but admire the impressive view of the red-stone manor house, its windows glistening in the morning light. Inside, it will be a hive of activity as hotel guests occupy the breakfast room and service staff dash back and forth catering to their every need. In the private quarters on the third floor, my cousin Jemima and her husband, Ned, will be preparing for the day ahead. Meanwhile, I trek doggedly towards the decorative stone archway leading to the gallery's cobbled courtyard and The Orangery's artisan café beyond.

At this time of day, all is quiet in the converted stable yard. A couple of artists mill around, getting ready for the first visitors of the day, and Crispy duck – Jemima's pet – potters around, pecking at the cobblestones. I walk beneath the monumental arch and complete the transition between home and work life; I smarten my attitude, forget about brown envelopes and APR rates, in preparation for the busy shift ahead.

Heather

'Hello!' I holler, opening the back door of the farmhouse kitchen.

I wait on the doorstep, ear cocked, listening for the faint reply before entering; it's manners, and an old habit. They always answer with, 'Come on in!' I wouldn't want folk traipsing through my house willy-nilly, whatever stage of life I'm at. I treat my eldest sister, Iona, and her husband, Clyde, with the same courtesy.

Responding to the silence with a shout of, 'Only me!' I actually enter their kitchen. I close the back door behind me, unzip my fleece and kick off my boots, leaving them on the age-old coir doormat, before padding in stockinged feet across the red-tiled floor towards their warm lounge. Which is an understatement; as it's always roasting-toasting hot, whatever the season. My nephew, Magnus, is working single-handed to provide for his parents the best he can since their retirement from farming. He grafts all day in the fields before returning home to the farmhouse at night.

'Heather, I was just saying to Clyde, "Heather's running late!" *Are* you running late?' asks my sister, sitting cosily on the sofa with her crochet hook in one hand and a ball of wool nestled at her slippered feet.

'You know me too well. Our Pepper got herself wedged behind the sofa. I've had to shift half the lounge furniture in order to retrieve her safely. She'd chewed a section of hessian before I realised she needed help. The little sod. Our Ellie said to leave her – "She got herself stuck so she can get herself out" – but I had visions of returning home to find the insides of my couch scattered around the lounge in her attempt to struggle free.'

'Has she still not had those pups?' asks Clyde, clad in his usual russet corduroys, addressing me from his fireside chair. Remote control in hand, he's staring at the oversized plasma TV showing a rerun of a classic snooker final from decades ago.

'Not yet. She's not far off, judging by this morning's antics. I reckon she was trying to nest despite me preparing her usual whelping spot under the stairs.'

'She'll do as she pleases ... where she pleases,' adds Clyde, not averting his gaze from the drama of who will succeed in potting the black ball.

I stare at Iona, her hands working ten to the dozen, as she gazes up at me. Her wiry fringe could do with a trim and tidy. I look at the silver-grey strands sweeping the bridge of her glasses and remember when it was a vibrant auburn colour like mine – though even mine has the odd silver strand peeping through nowadays. Evidence of my so-called wisdom, as I tell my daughters.

'Did he not hear me mention under the stairs?' I ask.

'Aye, lass, he heard you alright!' says Iona, pulling a length of lemon yarn from her ball of wool before resuming her crocheting. Her hands are a rhythmical blur as the hook pokes, twists, turns and works each stitch to create the delicate garment spread across her lap. I can't knit, let alone master a crochet hook, despite the numerous demonstrations Iona's given me over the years.

'Anyway, I've brought these groceries, as your Magnus sent me a text earlier.' I retrieve several items from my shopping bag – milk, bread and fresh haddock – placing each on the coffee table, before continuing. 'And I thought you might like something a bit special for Sunday, so I dropped by the butcher's for a beef joint.'

They both abruptly turn and stare as I hold the joint aloft, wrapped in paper – which is a novel occurrence, as Clyde's gaze rarely diverts from his snooker.

'Tomorrow. Verity is coming for tea . . . you said you wanted it to be a bit special,' I gently remind them. I knew they'd forget, so I made a note on my phone last week. Magnus hadn't mentioned it in his earlier message, but he wouldn't, would he? That's our Magnus for you. My nephew doesn't expect people to chase around after him, despite the effort he shows towards others. Iona's thrilled that he's finally met someone who makes him happy; she'd given up on that happening years ago.

Tomorrow's special tea will be the highlight of my sister's week. Neither of them leaves the farmhouse much these days; I suppose that's balancing out the decades when they were rarely at home, out in all weathers, tending to sheep and lambs across their many fields. With twenty years between us, I feel like her daughter rather than her youngest sister, but that's the case when family age gaps, ailments and tragedies take hold in life. Bless them, they've been through the mill since the loss of their own daughter, Marina, as a child. Not that I'm suggesting I'm some sort of replacement, but given the four-year age gap between Marina and me, you can understand how grief altered our relationship.

Being the youngest, I wasn't old enough to care for our parents in their twilight years, so I'm repaying my eldest sister and her husband for doing the necessary back then. When you belong to a large family like mine, the generations might be blurred, with sisters acting as parents, and nephews acting like brothers, but the love and devotion shine through. I try to explain this to my daughters, Ellie and Isla. But as young adults they don't care to see – not yet, anyway.

'Is that this week?' asks Iona, exchanging a fleeting glance with her husband, who has just missed seeing who potted the black ball and clinched the deciding frame.

'Yeah. Which is why I thought we could have a little spruce-up while I'm here . . . a quick whizz round with the Hoover and a wipe down of the kitchen worktops.' It might sound tactical, but Iona won't be wanting Verity to see the true them. I'm the same when my eldest, Ellie, brings a new beau home. I want to portray the real us – us as a family of three – but without portraying the *real* us. The craziness of our family can wait until their seventh, or tenth date . . . or even their wedding day until it truly shines through.

'I thought we could make a start on the dining room; I expect you'll be eating in there?'

'Am I cooking?' asks Iona, putting aside her crochet hook, prising herself out of the armchair where she will have been sitting since breakfast. She doesn't suffer from ill health but she doesn't move as well as she ought. I reckon her joints are paying the price for all those early mornings, damp weather, and long tiring hours as sheep farmers.

'Yessss,' I reply dubiously, before adding, 'you said you wanted to make her your famous Cullen skink followed by Shetland beef.'

'Oh no, don't tell me I said that!' wails Iona, almost begrudgingly.

Has she really forgotten, or is she just acting daft, pretending certain changes to the family dynamic might not be happening in the foreseeable future? I'll play along, just for now, and see what happens.

'You did . . . so you must. This lady means a lot to our Magnus. You said you wanted to make her feel welcome as part of the family,' I declare, knowing she'll want to do her best by her lad. 'There's only half the work to do if I help out.'

'Are you not coming tomorrow?'

'No. I've got my own brood to sort and feed! And that's without a litter of new arrivals, if Pepper decides to whelp,' I retort. Honestly, enough is never enough for some folk.

'Is the haddock from the fishmonger's?' asks my sister, eyeing the supermarket packaging.

I quickly shake my head.

'And that bread's certainly not from your Isla or the baker's.'

'Nah, I'm splitting my shopping trips between the local shops and the supermarket,' I say, not wanting to explain why. 'So what's it to be – dining room or the kitchen first?'

'Kitchen. I can start making Cullen skink once you're done,' says Iona, straightening her hand-knitted cardigan and heading for the kitchen.

Relieved that the decisions have been made, Clyde returns his attention to the snooker.

As I wander around my sister's home, I envisage our Magnus laughing when I recall this conversation. The poor bloke can't win. When he was a long-term singleton, they took a keen interest in his future prospects, but now that he's courting someone special, they appear to show no interest. The man has very little support – which probably goes some way to explaining why I always try my best!

Chapter Two

Tabitha

'Thank you . . . excuse me . . . sorry,' I utter, dashing between the shoppers and tourists in Lerwick's Market Street on a busy Saturday afternoon. I hate hot-footing it towards an event, knowing I should be manning my soapery pitch at the manor's gallery instead. I've had to beg, borrow and steal favours to ensure that my business isn't affected, and all for what? A five-minute stunt, an embarrassment which many of us don't wish to participate in but feel coerced into doing. If I could get away with not attending then I'd feign forgetfulness and go AWOL. Though I'd kick myself if Ebenezer – our aged, but newly acquired, creative director – pencils a black mark in his battered ledger against my name. Why anyone would swap the bright lights of London's West End for a theatre in Shetland, at his time of life, is beyond me. But I'd best keep him sweet if I'm to be considered for future starring roles.

Why he thinks apparently spontaneous events such as these are still 'a thing' is beyond me; I'm sure they went out of fashion years ago. Our performance will hardly go viral and attract new blood to join us, given our remote location. Right now, I'd happily swap places with Aileen in The Orangery, wiping tables and serving coffee – her involvement with our little troupe purely as an enthusiastic hobbyist obviously has its advantages! I'm not knocking Aileen's lack of ambition but her participation usually peaks with the seasonal performances, regardless of whatever role she's awarded.

As I near the bastions of Fort Charlotte, I spy Kenzie lingering on the ancient rampart alongside a sturdy but silent cannon. Her thick chestnut mane is secured into coiled plaits, and her arms are heavily laden with swathes of cloth as she stands looking out across the water of Bressay Sound. She looks a picture of serenity. Maybe I should have tied back my natural flame-red locks with a hair scrunchie, but as my dad says, 'You can't tame your crowning glory, so flaunt it!'

I scamper up the grassy slope to join her elevated position. Who in their right mind would pitch me there? I need a high vantage point compared to the other actor, but has Ebenezer not thought this through? It'll be a brave soul who questions his authority.

I'm grateful for Kenzie's support, so I won't complain to her, but I'm still miffed at having to participate in another potential fiasco – yet another spectacular fail. Like last time, and the time before. After which we all vowed never to attempt such a stunt again. But here we are, with everyone having apparently forgotten the sheer embarrassment Ebenezer's enthusiasm caused us.

'Hi,' I say quietly, sauntering alongside Kenzie.

She answers without turning to look at me, as if we're on a covert mission, watching for some long-forgotten Dutch invaders appearing on the horizon. 'Hi, Tabby. Are you ready?'

'Yep. You?' Not that I doubt her preparation, but it seems polite to ask.

She gives a curt nod.

We stand pretending to admire the glistening sunlight on the choppy waves. We're not, we're simply waiting for 'the signal'; I daren't imagine the consequences if we miss it. A trillion black marks pencilled against my name in one fell swoop, I expect.

Several people are milling about the artillery fort; it's a popular tourist attraction throughout the year. I'm not into Shetland's historical heritage, though many a school trip was spent identifying features of the pentagonal-shaped construction.

I daren't look at Kenzie. I fear my nerves kicking in beforehand, and there's a good chance of me being literally sick with stage fright; I can do without buckling at the knees and hurling chunks over the tourists. I'm much better when I'm performing, when my brain can focus, and that sudden rush of adrenaline instantly dispels any last-minute panic.

I'm sure the other participants assume I haven't spotted them, but I have. Ebenezer and Freddie are below the nearest bastion, pretending to photograph each other, though their guise of revered grandfather and doting youth isn't quite believable. Ebenezer's usual combination of brocade frock coat and contrasting wild white hair, coupled with Freddie's skinny jeans and bright trainers, sets them apart by more than a few generations. I spy Rabbie lounging on the grassy bank, sunbathing without his shirt, revealing a lean and muscular frame. How I wish he were playing today's other lead role. I give him a quick glance, not wishing to be caught admiring his naked torso. Further along the approach to the fort, Deacon and Old Reg are struggling to manhandle a long cardboard box. This isn't an everyday occurrence on the fort's grassy banks, so I'm surprised Ebenezer has allowed it.

'Come on! What's the delay?' mutters Kenzie.

I'm about to answer her when a young couple, hand in hand and looking very much in love, dawdle in our direction as if intending to join us at the artillery cannon. Not what we need or practised; it'll only heighten the embarrassment for all concerned if they linger to inspect the replica relic.

'Go away, go away!' whispers Kenzie, in a harsh but audible tone.

'Shush,' I mouth, fearing the couple might overhear and disrupt the proceedings by asking what her problem is. I can do

without being dragged into a fraught situation because of feisty
Kenzie. Love her and all that, but sometimes she's a little fire-
cracker. I breathe a sigh of relief as the couple drift by; their
curiosity regarding the cannon quickly wanes after giving us
pair the once-over. Their jaded glances make me feel like a social
freak, when really what I'm about to do will secure that gold
medal in an instant. No competition.

I hate what I'm about to do. And yet, I do it. I do it because I
have dreams. Big dreams I've held dear for nineteen years, ever
since I was five years of age and played an angel in the school
nativity. My halo was a twisted wire coat hanger covered in a
strand of cheap gold tinsel, held in place with a pack of hairgrips.
I do it because . . . I believe the others will judge me as flaky or
worse . . . talentless, if I don't. I hate myself for even participating
when I should really be working at the gallery, taking care of
my day job instead of chasing my dream job. Which others say
will never happen. But I hope against hope that it does, and that
one day . . .

Oh shit!

Ebenezer is frantically waving at us in his 'Go, go, go!' manner.
He's attempting to mute his flamboyant semi-dance in order
to avoid attracting the attention of passing tourists before I'm
ready to begin.

'Go!' screeches Kenzie, as if I could miss the director's crazy
waving-not-waving action.

I take a deep breath, stand close against the parapet, and project my voice towards the blond youth in snazzy trainers who
has appeared directly beneath me on the grassy bank.

'O Romeo, Romeo, wherefore art thou Romeo? Deny thy
father, and refuse thy name. Or if thou wilt not, be but sworn
my love, and I'll no longer be a Capulet.' I focus upon my lines
as Kenzie swiftly throws her armful of fabric over my head
to dress me in a mock-Elizabethan style, complete with white

ruff, plunging neckline and corset ties. I'll give her credit, I'm transformed in one swift move, and she becomes my nursemaid seconds later with a flowing cape. Freddie is transformed too, thanks to a wide ruff and oversized feathered hat, deftly delivered by a half-naked Rabbie.

I'm not a fan of these flash-mob acting stunts – which are meant to take the public by surprise, intriguing and entertaining them with our artistic expression, caught between their mid-morning latte and a gentle stroll – but Ebenezer appears to delight in them.

There's a momentary pause before Freddie gets his act together to stare doe-eyed up at me, reciting, 'Shall I hear more, or shall I speak at this?'

I cringe, as he turns around on the grassy bank to mutter an aside to a non-existent audience. My theatrical outburst and costume change, high up on the rampart, should ensure they appear soon. Well, they usually do. I suppose I should be grateful we aren't performing the Scottish play, the unmentionable one, which is cursed to high heaven.

I deliver my practised lines. ''Tis but thy name that is my enemy. Thou art thyself, though not a Montague.' My speech spills from my lips as fluidly as it did during Wednesday night's rehearsals, and every night this week, parading around my mum's lounge and interrupting her nightly soap watching. My muscle memory takes over and away I go, my stage directions perfect; there's no way Ebenezer can complain that I didn't perform or handle the pressure of a lead part. I'm no Shakespearean fan – but needs must, especially when you've a point to prove. Fingers crossed, the director will be impressed enough to give me the role I really want in this year's Christmas special.

I fall silent, waiting for Freddie to respond, 'I take thee at thy word . . .'

I don't know how I'll hide my disappointment if Aileen or Kenzie audition and secure my desired role. No doubt I'll smile and congratulate them, as expected. Could I accept a lesser role? No! I'd rather throw in the towel. I want what I want – and if performing flash-mob skits such as this is what it takes to show my worth, then so be it.

I quickly deliver my next two lines, slightly distracted by the growing audience of tourists who have heard the commotion and have reliably drifted across to watch. Deacon and Old Reg now reveal a large wooden ladder from their cardboard box and plant it firmly against the stone wall, enabling young Romeo, aka Freddie, to gingerly climb up a few rungs and converse with me on my makeshift balcony – though he's not high enough, in my humble opinion. Two backstage guys gather at the foot of the ladder, adding their combined body weight and helping to secure it in place.

Ebenezer is shouting at Freddie, 'Higher, higher!'

As I correctly predicted, my hesitant Romeo is barely using the prop to its full potential. Freddie delivers his lines whilst nervously climbing the rungs; I can spy his white knuckles and jittering knees from up here.

That's when disaster strikes. In full flow, delivering his memorised lines, his gaze fixed on mine, Freddie begins to lean backwards. Slowly at first, the ladder moves away from the rampart, hoisting him upright above the heads of the backstage gang . . . before a mighty wobble occurs. His support gang begin sidestepping and stumbling, fighting to regain control of the ladder, which is beginning to teeter dangerously. Freddie's life is in their hands. His complexion pales to match his knuckles as he is thrust forward, narrowly missing face-planting into the parapet wall, before being snatched backwards by the manhandlers, all the while fighting to maintain his balance. The audience utter loud cries of 'ohhh' and 'ahhh' at each dramatic sway, as if viewing a pantomime with pre-planned antics. Freddie releases his grip from the top rung and clings frantically to the side rails, wrapping both arms and legs around the ladder, like a koala on a eucalyptus tree trunk.

But it's too late, the damage is done. Gravity wins.

Freddie performs a slow-motion fall backwards, in a comedic arc, taking him beyond the balance of the support act beneath. I watch as he crashes unceremoniously on to the grassy embankment, then gambols down the steep slope like a child at a ball pit, before disappearing into the astonished crowd in a parody of a well-rehearsed magician's trick. The scene could only have been made worse if he'd been catapulted from the ladder across the Bressay Sound, wailing and limbs flailing, providing a watery end to his escapades.

'Well, that's definitely jinxed the proceedings!' I whisper to Kenzie, who is nestled at my feet against the parapet wall, pretending to be within my imaginary boudoir, blissfully unaware of Freddie's antics.

I'd best not think of the consequences for either of us. Ebenezer will either withdraw his battered ledger and stubby pencil from his frock coat, delivering his dreaded black marks, or demand we repeat this performance again tomorrow!

'Wrap it up, Kenzie! Quick!' I hiss.

Having performed my script, and feeling satisfied that it was word-perfect, I'm called away from the parapet by my nursemaid, thus ending the fiasco. I wave goodbye, igniting rapturous applause from the audience below.

'They never fail us,' I mutter, appreciating the applause – which is pretty much what Ebenezer coerces us into believing each time we prepare for a performance.

It feels great to be shrugging off my costume; I need to swiftly return to my usual Saturday afternoon, back in the modern era. I'm relieved that this skit is over. Though, if there's any suggestion of repeating this farce, I'm definitely going AWOL – black mark or not!

Callie

'Callie, would you do me a favour, please?' calls Isla across the serving counter of The Orangery. She's been working in the rear prep room, and her hands are held aloft, splayed fingers covered in beige gloopy batter. 'Head across to Tabitha and ask if we can have a bar of our usual soap? She'll know which one. I meant to nip across earlier. Take a fiver out of the till – I'll account for it later.'

'A bit pricey for in here, isn't it?' I say, pressing the till buttons so the drawer springs wide open, before retrieving a five-pound note.

'The price is irrelevant, it's the quality that matters when you wash your hands as much as we do each day. The Campbells know, I've run it past them before. It actually lasts longer than you'd think.' She disappears again as I close the till drawer.

That's the atmosphere working here, efficient but relaxed, enhanced by the creative decor of mismatched couches, armchairs and chairs. An eclectic mix of patterns, textures and colours, neatly arranged around various large tables and smaller, more intimate coffee table layouts. It's a far cry from my days in the beauty salon, when the fluffy colour-coordinated towels and the all-pervading fragrance of lemongrass couldn't hide the stress we beauticians were under, fulfilling non-stop treatment bookings in swift succession, as if on a conveyer belt. I smile to myself. Waitressing might not pay as much, but I'd rather be here than back there, any day. The allure of the beauty industry can sometimes be barely skin deep; I've found there's a lot of bad blood and underlying jealousy, all of which needs exfoliating on a daily basis.

'Aileen!' I call out, attracting the attention of the nearest waitress, who is busy refilling wicker display baskets with freshly baked delights.

She looks up from where she is working, further along the serving counter.

'I'm just popping out on an errand.' I jerk a thumb towards the gallery's courtyard, visible through the huge plate-glass window.

Aileen nods and gives me a quick smile of acknowledgement.

Clutching the cash, I dart across the cobbled courtyard, which has been a hive of activity all day, heading for Tabitha's stable. The sign above her door reads 'The Goat Milk Soapery', from where she creates and sells all kinds of artisan toiletries by combining goat's milk with botanical fragrances.

Each stable is slightly different, reflecting the art or craft within, though the terracotta plastering and the historic wooden beams provide uniformity and a reminder of purpose in bygone years.

As always, a range of fragrances awaken my senses on entering: zingy lemons, tantalising limes, and a mellow undertone of lavender, I think.

I find several customers happily browsing the shelves. It's a thoroughly enjoyable process which consists of selecting and sniffing a product, reading the information label, before deciding to either purchase or replace it, then moving on to sample another fragrant delight.

'Hello, Nessie! Is Tabitha around?' I ask, spying the gallery's resident blacksmith behind the soapery counter. She looks totally out of place, dressed in her usual beige gansey and denim dungarees, though her orange pixie-cut hairstyle does match some of the soap labels.

'I'm the official babysitter, as Tabitha's had to head into town to "do her thing". She said she won't be long. So what can I do you for?'

'Mmmm, I'm looking for some soap,' I say, perusing the stocked shelving units that reach from floor to ceiling. In every direction, there's something of interest: bulbous glass jars filled with dried botanicals, rows of navy glass bottles with protruding pipettes, and a corner section filled with stainless-steel equipment similar to Isla's prep room in The Orangery.

'Seriously, I'll need a little more info, Callie. I haven't the foggiest about this kind of thing,' exclaims Nessie.

'I can't imagine it's your sort of thing.' I smile reassuringly at her, remembering only too well my beautician days surrounded by lotions and potions.

Nessie's chin juts forward. 'Oi, cheeky, I'll have you know I regularly use the lemon and bergamot bar over there.' She gestures towards a lower shelf, before adding, 'Tabby recommended it for its astringent properties and natural oils – I've bought it ever since.'

'You surprise me, that's all.'

'A blacksmith needs her luxuries too,' says Nessie, giving me a coy look. 'Isaac wouldn't be so keen on snuggling up to me if my skin was rougher than my filing rasp.'

'Or his current designer stubble,' I jest, having spied his facial hair earlier.

'Have you seen it? He's so proud of his new grooming style.' Nessie shakes her head, but her smile suggests she doesn't mind what her beau does. 'If he's hoping to match Mungo's bushy beard, he'd better look out. I'll be asking Tabby for suggestions on a shaving balm to persuade him otherwise.'

We both laugh. I've liked Nessie from the off; she's not your usual sort, but I suppose female blacksmiths never are. She's got a wicked sense of humour and an indomitable spirit – both essential attributes with which to fight her corner. She isn't going to be cowed by any shallow-minded views about a woman's place in a traditionally male-dominated industry.

'When is Tabby due back?' I ask, remembering that Isla did say 'our usual soap'. I wouldn't recognise the fragrance amongst this vast selection. In the salon, we'd only used a handful of essential oils, nothing like the huge variety on display in Tabitha's stable.

'Any time soon,' says Nessie, glancing at the wall clock.

I step aside as a young woman nears the counter, her arms laden with an assortment of soap bars and other toiletries.

'Hi, did you find everything you were looking for?' asks Nessie, in a bright and breezy tone, sounding like a true professional. She has no idea about the product but always puts her best sales face on.

'Yes, thank you. It's quite overwhelming . . . you stock such a huge range,' says the customer, glancing around at the shelves. She's certainly not wrong there.

I'll leave it for another time. If I go back with the wrong soap, Isla won't be best pleased – especially if my random selection doesn't meet with her approval.

'Hey, hey, hey! What have we here?' asks Tabitha, entering the soapery.

'Good timing, Tabby,' says Nessie, glancing up from packing the customer's goodies into one of the gallery's logoed paper bags, before announcing the till price to her customer. 'That'll be seventeen pounds twenty, please.'

The lady finds her purse while I swiftly nab Tabby and ask her about our usual soap.

'It's this one here,' says Tabitha, reaching up to a high shelf and grabbing a soap bar decorated with a spiky cactus-type plant. 'Aloe vera. Antibacterial properties, which Isla likes for The Orangery.'

'Are you sure? I'll blame you if it's wrong,' I say truthfully.

'I'm sure. Are you doubting my memory?'

'No, I'm just saying.' I fish the five pounds out, and flatten the rolled note on the nearest shelf before handing it to Tabitha.

'Thank you, do you need a bag?'

I shake my head.

'Great news – that saves the environment too,' she chuckles.

'You're in a good mood,' I say, pulling a quizzical expression.

'Ignore me. We've just floored an audience at the fort with a Shakespearean flash-mob skit. It was so embarrassing, I can't begin to tell you. But I've a funny feeling things are about to go my way, for once!'

'Ha, that's funny. To bag, or not to bag: that is the question in the soapery,' I say, showing my limited knowledge of the English bard.

'Very funny. Though it was *Romeo and Juliet* we performed, not *Hamlet*.'

'In that case, I'm off. I'm out of my depth in here with your soaps and your scripts. But thanks for this, it'll keep Isla happy.'

I stroll back across the cobblestones, unsure if my joke was verging on funny, a faux pas, or purely idiotic – whatever, I need to get a wiggle on before I'm missed in The Orangery.

Chapter Three

Sunday 14 August

Tabitha

Unlocking the stable door, I pin my 'open' sign on the doornail and sneak inside. This is my precious time, my favourite part of the day. With one flick of a switch, my tiny world springs to life beneath neon lights, revealing shelf upon shelf of creamy soap products, each one handmade by me. There's not a single item within these four walls that I haven't personally blended or mixed before curing and cutting it into individual blocks for retail. My main table is a rainbow of creamy pastel colours, with each soap featuring like a pixel in the overall display. Handwritten labels on orange cards stand to attention beside each product pile, proudly announcing the unique name of each soap above a detailed list of ingredients, benefits or comforts. Be it an astringent quality, an invigorating fragrance, enhanced with vitamins, or simply a soothing lather to ease skin irritations, my goat's milk soaps add a little luxury to the necessary routines of everyone's daily life. Whether a basic hand soap, a luxury bath soap or a shaving balm – I genuinely have a little something for every customer who enters my stable.

I remove my coat and handbag, stowing them in the storage space beneath my counter, and reach for my tabard. When I was at school, I'd have laughed at anyone who suggested a tabard would become my daily uniform. But back then, I hadn't bargained on a full-time job crafting beautiful soaps from an organic product. I also couldn't have envisaged internet sales and shipping a high quantity abroad at least three times a week, either. Though, if my science teacher could have foretold my future – donning protective goggles and gloves, and handling glass beakers of sodium hydroxide – I'd have laughed myself silly throughout my exams. Sadly, I didn't cut it; I flunked the lot, securing a full house at grade D. Not my finest hour, but an experience which forced me to rapidly hone my skill set and face up to the practicalities of life.

I quickly tie my hair back, securing it with a hair net, and don my first pair of protective gloves. I'll lose count of the number of times I change and replenish items of PPE on a production day, but it's better to be safe than sorry. Firstly, my health and well-being need protecting from the caustic chemicals, and secondly, the slightest cross-contamination of products or colourings can ruin an entire batch of soap in seconds.

I was raised playing amongst my mother's small herd of goats, so there was never a shortage of furry playmates or milk in our house. A little sideline that provided her with extra pin money by selling to the locals, nothing more. It seemed logical to produce something from the surplus milk, especially as sterilised goat's milk has a shelf life of around forty-five days; Mum didn't want to waste it by throwing it away. Having flunked my Highers exams, I took on the challenge of searching the internet and creating concoctions in the tiny shed at the bottom of our garden. From humble beginnings my venture was born, though I soon ran out of storage space – there's a limit to what can be squeezed into a six-by-four shed – hence the much-needed move to Lerwick Manor and my decision to rent this stable. Plus, it was pretty lonesome spending each day cutting and packaging soaps. Here I get to enjoy the constant flow of people, whether customers, manor guests or other artists dropping by, all of which helps break up the day.

The sweet spot in my soapery is the impressive range of shelving. It dominates the end wall, stretching from floor to virtually ceiling height, complete with a tiny ladder, which Mungo kindly made for me. One shelf houses my selection of wooden boxes shaped like treasure chests, inside which sit my vials of essential oils. They are volatile, so keeping them in a cool dark storage box prevents them from vaporising or oxidising, ensuring each soap blend is of the highest quality.

I have my favourites, just as I've heard Isla admit to having preferred ingredients for her artisan bread making. She loves poppy seeds, wholegrains and toasted almonds, while I favour lemongrass, bergamot and geranium. Though I do have to show some restraint and not select them all the time; after all, there is such a vast array of essential oils, each with additional benefits. I try not to over-complicate each blend – going 'too flowery', as I term it. I'm sure many people love a good whiff of fragrance during their morning shower. Likewise, I'm certain many don't. I have to rein in my enthusiasm at times, remembering I'm not the one who purchases and uses each product I make. I'm not making soaps for my own liking but for others.

Whatever the problem, be it a shaving rash, acne-prone skin, or troublesome eczema, I have a nourishing balm or essential oil that will ease the irritation when blended with rich goat's milk. There are times when I simply stand and stare at the paraphernalia before me and dream of creating new combinations from the dried botanicals contained within the glass jars. Alongside huge demijohns are apothecary bottles of organic oils: jojoba, cocoa, sweet almond, grapeseed, sunflower, olive, apricot, avocado, coconut and almond, all lined up like tubby soldiers. Each oil has a unique element which benefits my customers each time they use my beautiful soaps or balms.

In the corner stand my two shiny items. I'm a sucker for a bit of polished metal – and so, it seems, are many of my customers, who are drawn like moths to a flame. One item is my trusty tea urn which had a previous life serving hot beverages at the local community centre until it was refurbished a few years ago. My dad spotted the urn and saved it from being pitched into a skip by offering a couple of quid. It's pretty basic in design, just an element snaking around the bottom and a simple dial control on the outside; I had to repaint the faded dial indicators for fear of misreading temperatures. As a heat source for blending it is perfect for large quantities of a basic soap mix which I then divide into smaller batches before colouring and adding fragrance. The second shiny object, which many customers never expect to find here, is my milk fridge. And I kid you not but I lose count of the number of people who remark each week, 'So there's actually goat's milk in each soap?' I smile and nod politely. If they aren't convinced by my answer, I open the milk fridge to show the flasks of cold fresh goat's milk, though supplies tend to be running low or have run out by the weekend. I rarely make a new blend of soap during the weekend. The increased customer footfall and the extra time required to answer forthcoming questions takes up all my attention and can potentially cause a blend to be ruined, or else pose a health and safety risk when working with hot oils.

Quack! Quack!

I turn to find Crispy duck waddling through my open doorway. His emerald head feathers shimmer with accents of navy while he happily pecks the floor with each webbed step.

'No, you don't! Not in here – you're barred,' I say, quickly shooing him back outside on to the cobblestones. I've no aversion to his presence as the gallery's resident duck, but I can do without a customer finding a tiny feather in their soap bar. I'd struggle to explain away a duck's-feather-and-goat's-milk combination!

I want to make a start on a fresh batch of soap but I'd like it to be well under way before any customers come browsing. Not that they aren't welcome to watch, but there are times when the layout of each stable means customers put you off your task. I can measure out my ingredients – the botanicals, the essential oils – and at a vital moment be distracted by a customer's question. My hands switch to auto pilot, and I wonder for the remainder of the day did I add those essential oils or not? At least this morning, I can begin mixing before the gallery officially opens at ten o'clock. That'll be the best of both worlds: the important task done, releasing beautiful aromas into the air, enticing customers to venture inside. Which usually results in higher sales. Making everyone happy!

'Morning, lassie.' Dottie's voice makes me jump.

I whip around to find her tottering through the doorway. Her full-length pinny is secured with a double tie at the front, and her piercing blue eyes are twinkling bright. She's virtually a full-time fixture here at the manor, completing a little 'light dusting' when necessary. Though don't let this octogenarian's delicate bird-like stature fool you, she's as sharp as a tack.

'Morning, Dottie. Anything wrong?' I sense there is, as it's just gone eight o'clock.

'That wee lovey has been up all night with her sickness. This bairn has been a worry and a half already, and it's nowhere near its due date.'

I want to giggle but daren't; Dottie's so funny when she witters. Though Jemima's pregnancy sickness is no laughing matter – the woman looks delicate at the best of times.

'And you've come to me?' I say, sensing a request.

'These botanical things . . . anything for sickness?' asks Dottie, gesturing towards my shelf of glass jars. 'Anything at all.'

'Ginger is supposed to be very good.'

Dottie grimaces and shakes her head. 'The lass surely can't stomach any more ginger – she's been nibbling on my home-made ginger biscuits since week two – this bairn will appear swaddled in a biscuit wrapper if she consumes much more.'

'Peppermint?'

'Nah, she'll gag at the very thought. Jemima's been sucking on packets of peppermints to recover from having thrown up.'

I scan my jars and bottles for anything that might help. 'I've got raspberry leaf – but that's supposed to prepare the body for birth rather than prevent sickness. Surely her midwife or doctors can suggest something suitable?'

'They have loads of remedies. The poor wench has tried the lot, but it's not helping. She just needs a day or two to regain some strength by keeping her food down, otherwise she'll be a hospital case, I'm sure.'

'Oh, Dottie, that's awful. She's supposed to be enjoying her pregnancy.'

'Phuh! The quicker this bairn's due date arrives, the better,' says Dottie sternly, before her tone softens and she gives a little shimmy of excitement. 'I can't wait to have a munch and get my cuddles in.'

I burst out laughing. 'Oh, Dottie, you are funny.'

'Shhhh, I can't wait. Do you know how long it's been since I had a little one to coo over? Do you?'

I shake my head, taking delight in her renewed spirit.

'Too bloody long, that's how long! Ned Campbell's kept us all waiting for this honour, and I'm not about to miss out on the joy.'

'Dottie, you're a star. I'm sure they appreciate everything you do, especially at the minute with Jemima feeling so poorly.'

Dottie waves a hand as if batting my compliment away. 'Like I said, it's an honour. His own mother would have dearly loved to have seen him at this stage in his life. Bless her dear soul. And Jemima has no mother to support her, either.'

A sudden flashback from yesterday's theatrical skit invades my thoughts. Kenzie's nursemaid act is nothing compared to Dottie's true care and attention.

I'm stunned by the lump in my throat, and hastily swallow.

Why am I getting emotional? I often imagine that some folk want for nothing in life – I only have to picture Ned's stately home, or Jemima's art gallery and thriving hotel venture – when reality shows that they too have suffered loss and untold sadness. I perk up, sidestepping the change in mood.

'Here,' I say, striding towards my selection of soothing balms. 'A little gift of a chamomile balm – a little dab to her wrists might help to soothe her.' I return, pressing the small tin into Dottie's hesitant hand.

'Would chamomile tea help?' asks Dottie eagerly.

'I wouldn't try it. Not without chatting to her midwife – herbal teas sound harmless enough but you'd be surprised by some of the effects. The same goes for the essential oils.' I gesture towards my shelving supplies. 'It's better to be on the safe side, isn't it?'

'Thank you, I'll tell her you kindly sent a gift. She'll be grateful. Well, she will be once she can think of anything other than the constant nausea and the location of her sick bowl.'

'Urgh!' My gag reflex is instant.

'Exactly. It's not nice, Tabitha,' says Dottie. 'Anyway, thank you for this. And if you think of anything else . . . just let me know.'

'I will. And you take care – it isn't an easy job looking after others all the time. Would you like a little something for yourself?' I nod towards my soap bars.

'Oh no, I couldn't . . . it's Pears soap for me – nothing else.'

I give her a beaming smile; I hear that a lot from the older generation. My own gran wouldn't dream of using my goat's milk soap in preference to her trusted Imperial Leather.

Heather

I glance at the clock; I've been pacing the lounge for twenty minutes. If I do it for much longer the carpet will be threadbare and the dog will be a nervous wreck. Though at the minute she seems to be bearing up, which is more than I am.

I stand a fair distance away from Pepper's self-made nest, an undignified position wedged in the gap between and slightly behind the two armchairs. Obviously, yesterday's episode with the couch had purpose. I could scream! I spent an entire day last week sorting out her usual spot in the cupboard under the stairs where she's happily had and nursed three litters. But no, Pepper likes to surprise me.

Our Isla's in for a shock when she arrives home from work. The dog has dragged her single duvet from her bedroom, opting for a little luxury on which to lie. I only left the house for an hour – to fetch and deliver gravy granules for our Iona's special tea – and returned to find this. There's no point me trying to salvage the duvet at the moment. No doubt it'll be a 'bin it and replace it' job, as I can see Pepper's already birthed three pups on it.

After a decade of breeding Shelties – or Shetland sheepdogs, as most folk call them – you'd think I'd be used to whelping by now. My three girls, Pepper, Socks and Rosie, are very different to each other when it comes to motherhood. Pepper, a sable-and-white-coated beauty, is my most experienced, but that doesn't stop me from worrying.

'Come on, girl, tell me what you need. Is it simply more time to do as you please, or do I call the vet?' I whisper softly, her large brown eyes glancing up at the sound of my voice. She's a good mum, always has been, but you never can tell how things will turn out, so I always plan, always prepare early. And still, I find myself pacing like an expectant father. If she needs a vet, I won't hesitate – even on a Sunday, with emergency call-out fees. Any other day, I'd have phoned already, giving the local practice the heads up. Call me stupid but it always seems the right thing to do. If push comes to shove, and the vet can't attend, I'll call our Magnus if Pepper needs practical hands-on assistance. I can't imagine that birthing a sheep is much different to a dog. Well, he'd know, that's for sure. Though how our Magnus – or any fully grown adult, for that matter – is going to squeeze in between my three-piece suite, on hands and knees, to assist is anyone's guess. The cupboard under the stairs is roomy, yet here Pepper lies on a duvet licking her three wriggling babies.

I glance at the mantelpiece clock, yet again: thirty minutes gone. This isn't like her, unless she's done. Given her size and the vet's ultrasound scan, I did think there would be another two pups perhaps, but maybe I'm wrong. She's caught me out on previous occasions.

'Is three the magic number this time, Pepper?' I don't want to disturb her by getting nearer to take a closer look, but I'm in two minds; she just doesn't seem right. I'm sure she's straining every now and then, which means she's struggling. I hope I'm not wasting time by observing when I should be doing: phoning or calling for assistance.

What's it to be, Heather? Call out the emergency vet on a weekend, or phone Magnus for advice – which is it? Wait much longer and the poor dog might suffer the loss of her pups, or worse. I can't think straight. Can't decide. I don't care about the cost – only about my dog, and which intervention will arrive quicker. I can't dither, either; it'll unsettle my nerves, which in turn will spook Pepper.

I grab my phone from the coffee table, tapping the screen into life. The ringing tone goes on for ages. My knees begin to quiver as I wait for it to be answered. Maybe I'll have no choice, after all. Maybe I should end the call and dial—

A male voice answers. 'Hello, Heather.'

'Magnus, thank God for that! Any chance you could come over and take a look at Pepper? She's whelped three pups but nothing more for thirty-odd minutes, but she's straining herself. I know you've arrangements with your parents tonight, so I'll willingly call the vet, if you're busy this morning.'

'Don't be daft! Put the kettle on, grab your stash of dog towels and I'll be with you in ten minutes.'

'Thank you, Magnus. Bye.'

'Heather?'

'Yes.'

'Make sure you put the kettle on – I'll be wanting tea when I get there.'

'You cheeky bugger. I'm more concerned with my dog than making you tea. I thought you were suggesting a hot-water-and-towels birthing job.'

'I am, but I'll still want a cuppa.'

'I'm gone. Goodbye!'

'Bye, Heather.'

'Come on, little lady … let's make you comfy and see what's happening.'

I stand by, watching intently, as Magnus crawls on all fours; for a giant of a guy he's done well to squeeze himself into a fairly tight spot. Pepper gently noses his proffered hand as her three pups wriggle and squirm at her teats.

'There now, let's have a quick feel,' he reassures her.

I look away, unsure if I need to witness my nephew performing midwifery duties on my dog. It seems crazy that we're the same age, yet belong to different generations, due to the age range of my siblings. We're more like brother and sister than anything. I can breathe again, now he's here; everything will be just fine. Though the cheeky bugger asked where his cuppa was on arrival.

'I wouldn't have the nerve to check her,' I say, stupidly staring away at my skirting boards.

'It's best to feel if there's a pup stuck in the birth canal and . . . oh, yep . . . there it is. That little blighter needs to come out. If I can just . . .'

'Oh, stop with the running commentary. I don't need to know what you're doing, Magnus,' I say, feeling slightly queasy and trying not to focus on his actions at her rear end.

Magnus laughs, shaking his brown curls. 'You'd be no good come the lambing season.'

'I'd hate to think where your hands have been over the years – you've dealt with sheep, goats and my dogs.'

'Horses. Donkeys. A cow on one occasion. I'll be birthing alpacas soon, if Jemima's plans for breeding the manor's herd are successful.'

'Stop it! I don't know how Verity puts up with you.'

I sneak a peek, unsure if I wish to see, but Pepper seems content with his manhandling, so I shouldn't be complaining.

'If I can just ease . . . oh there, that moved a little way.'

'Is it alive?' I ask, my fingers crossing instinctively.

Magnus gives a shrug. 'I haven't felt it move. You might want to be ready with a towel. A bit of rubbing to stimulate it might be needed . . . if I could just . . . perfect timing, Pepper.'

'What?'

'She's contracting . . . and that's all the help we needed . . . to get this peerie pup moving in the right direction and . . . here it is!'

'How quick was that!'

I step closer, looking awkwardly down over the arms of the chairs to see a wet and withered puppy cradled in Magnus' giant palm.

'Here,' I say, holding an open towel to receive the lifeless pup.

'Don't be too gentle. Give it a firm going over, nose to tail – swing it, if you need to.'

I perch on the edge of the couch and place the folded towel, with the pup inside, on my lap. My upper hand vigorously rubs the tiny body encased beneath.

'There's another one coming. Are you doing this one on your tod, Pepper?' Magnus crawls backwards before rising to his knees and stretching his back.

I can't bear to think about the life-and-death struggle happening on my lap, so instead I take a deep breath and continue to rub.

'It's not moving,' I say.

'Check it, wipe its mouth and nose, then swing it.'

I open the towel, dabbing the corner against the pup's tiny muzzle. Four lifeless paws rest in my lap. I remember buying this towelling bale when I decorated the bathroom a decade ago – who'd have thought I'd be using one to revive a pup.

'I can't,' I say, my eyes pleading for help.

'Come here.' His hand lifts the pup from my lap, his long fingers settle along its backbone and neck, before giving the lifeless body a sharp flip with his wrist, as if emptying a ketchup bottle over my towelling lap.

'Come on, yee little bugger,' he mutters, quickly repeating the action.

I want to tell Magnus not to be so rough; don't snap its head off. But I'm being daft, the pup's in the safest of hands.

'Pass me the towel,' he says, before gesturing towards Pepper. 'Watch over her a second.' Magnus demonstrates what I should have been doing. I couldn't be so rough with a tiny creature, little limbs and head wobbling about like there's no tomorrow.

Squeak!

'That's it, peerie pup, give us another,' says Magnus, his weathered features creasing into a smile.

'Was that . . .?' I point to the towel.

He nods, just as another little squeak comes from inside the towel. 'Let's make sure, though, before we stop rubbing.'

I don't know whether to laugh, cry, or both, at the sheer relief.

'Heather,' says Magnus, nodding towards Pepper's nest as a fifth pup appears naturally and mum begins to lick the newborn.

'Pup four was stuck!'

Magnus opens the towel and the pup wriggles inside, its tiny mouth wide open, revealing a rosy tongue.

'Is it a boy or a girl?' I ask.

'Does it matter?' asks Magnus, nestling his pup alongside the new arrival and not bothering to look. 'Here you go, Mum. Do your job.'

Pepper instantly licks both pups as Magnus sits back on his haunches and I burst into tears.

'Would you have cried this much if the vet had attended?'

'Probably. After I'd paid the emergency weekend rate,' I mutter through my tears.

'You're a soppy-head, aren't you?'

'And you're not, I suppose.' I sniff, not bothering to wipe away my tears of joy.

'Get ready, number six is on its way,' urges Magnus, ignoring my remark and focusing on my dog.

Chapter Four

Callie

I stride along the manor's driveway, heading past the stone archway, complete with its Crispy duck weathervane, and follow the gravel path towards the large alpaca barn. I always feel self-conscious walking past the manor house, knowing every occupant – owners, service staff and guests – can clearly see my approach, but there's no other route. I've nothing to hide but it's eerie seeing that many windows peering down at you.

I love bright summer days, especially Sundays when our postie has the day off. More so, when I'm not waitressing but spending a few hours with my favourites on an alpaca excursion so I get to have a lie-in until mid-morning. I've got my waitressing uniform neatly folded for a shift later. But first, I get to don jeans and sweatshirt along with a head mic and mini speaker system. It is the weirdest thing in the world, talking whilst simultaneously hearing your voice emerging from the speaker strapped to your waistband. I focus on that joy whilst niftily passing the ornate stone lions decorating the entrance to the manor house-cum-hotel.

The alpaca paddocks stretch as far as the eye can see on the opposite side. Two paddocks, separated by robust fencing, prevent any mixing between the ten neutered males and the ten newly arrived females. Initially, we had six boys for walking tours, but that was back in February. Thankfully, the newer arrivals have settled in well; the animals are calmer and biddable, providing us with the perfect specimens for the public to walk and pet. I'm amazed that Ned has allowed Jemima to increase the herd as much as she has, though I suspect their trust in Magnus' animal husbandry helps to alleviate any worries. From what I see and hear, Magnus knows his stuff where animals are concerned, so a herd of twenty is probably small fry to him.

I cross the driveway and walk alongside the wooden fencing of the paddock, tapping my hand along the top. If the herd was out roaming and frolicking, I'd be clicking my tongue. It might seem ridiculous to others, but they hear me coming. And if I watch my herd of walking boys, all busy grazing or frolicking, I can see the precise moment when they register my presence as they stop, look and listen – extending their necks like telescopes, ears pricked – before dashing over to greet me.

I walk past the paddock housing the female herd. I don't distract them with my fence tapping, as they're enjoying the sunshine. My favourite fellas remain inside the large barn, awaiting my arrival.

Finally, I enter the newly erected barn. It's a luxury home compared to the old barn in the cobbled courtyard, which is where the original alpacas had their overnight pen. The warm, welcoming smell greets me; a combination of outdoor animals, used straw and urine, all mixed together and giving off a unique aroma I've come to love.

These creatures make me laugh every day when they greet me from the comfort of their two straw-strewn pens, either side of the entrance door. Trotting to the tubular fencing, they stretch their necks to greet me. I'm not supposed to, but I have my favourites.

'Hello, my boys. Pleased to see me?' I dig into my pocket, retrieving a bag of treats. Ten quivering top lips with protruding teeth do battle to snaffle the dry food as I switch position, hopping across the adjoining aisle from one pen to the other. 'Hey, yamse boy,' I say to Karma, my favourite of the lot, as his raucous behaviour knocks the handful of treats to the ground. I replenish the food before continuing to stroke and fondle their cute ears as they eagerly nudge for more treats.

'No more. There's work to be done,' I say, brushing crumbs from my hands. I have thirty minutes to select and check over the chosen six animals for today's booking. I can't rush, otherwise it'll unsettle the alpacas, which is unfair on them and on the accompanying adult who is paying for a relaxed trekking excursion.

'Callie?'

I turn to find Verity standing in the doorway, dressed in a floral tunic and leggings combo. She's usually busy in The Yarn Barn, giving customers advice about needle sizes, knitting tension and Shetland yarn, but obviously not today. She's friendly enough but she rarely wants me for my own sake; our conversations usually revolve around the whereabouts of others.

'Yeah!'

'Have you seen Magnus in the last hour?' she calls, stopping short of the alpaca pens. Her phone is in one hand, the other tucked inside her tunic pocket. She's always dressed simply but stylishly for her age. That might sound catty, but given that she's probably a decade older than me, I'd take it as a compliment. I'm in my early thirties and I know I don't scrub up as well.

I shake my head, adding, 'Not today. I've only just arrived.'

The alpacas stand watching our exchange, their top lips fluttering in case Verity has more hidden treats.

'Thanks. Have a good trek,' she says, swiftly turning around to retrace her steps.

I don't take offence; she's one of the harmless sorts who would willingly help anyone. Which is probably why she can't find Magnus – he's cut from the same cloth, so to speak.

There's a small office space created a little further along from the barn's entrance, furnished with an old desk, piled high with spare paper and pens. Above this hangs a series of hooks with various notebooks and clipboards, each displaying the details of booked walking parties. I grab today's clipboard, checking that no alterations have been made since yesterday.

Six adults for trek and afternoon tea – booked. Paid in full. No allergies. Hen party!

That's what I like to see. Hen party is underlined – twice – so this session should be fun. No last-minute faffing around for me or the waitresses in The Orangery. Hopefully, this trek will run like clockwork – unlike last Sunday's trek, when it all went pear shaped thanks to cancellations and last-minute notifications about a nut allergy. We coped, and even delivered a lovely experience for our guests, but it takes all the pleasure out of the day when you feel like you're chasing your own tail.

Within minutes, the alpacas drift away to continue their fun amongst the straw bales. I can't complain, I'd do exactly the same if companionship were calling. But it rarely does.

'Afternoon, are you waiting for me?' says Mungo, appearing unexpectedly at the desk.

'I wasn't, but if you're willing to help, I'm happy,' I say, knowing that many hands make light work, especially where these creatures are concerned.

'Good, I'll fetch the wheelbarrow,' offers Mungo, his greying beard dancing with each word, before disappearing to the far end of the barn where our equipment is stored. We keep the leading reins in a wheelbarrow, making it easy for everyone to assist and support, if extra hands are needed. I've been pleasantly surprised by the multitude of people who have volunteered to accompany me over the weeks.

Mungo returns, pushing a wheelbarrow containing a neat pile of rope leads from which we'll pluck the six we're going to use today. Each has a shiny metal clasp with a snappy trigger release, making light work of securing a lively alpaca.

'Do you know which ones are on the rota for today?' he asks gruffly, eyeing both pens.

'Yep. Karma, Carpe Diem and Be Happy from this side. By the Grace of God, This Too Will Pass and Let It Be from the other pen.'

'The originals then?' mutters Mungo, pulling six rope leads from the tangled pile.

'You make them sound like a cheesy boy band.' I laugh, securing my biro into the clipboard spring and gesturing for him to hand over three reins.

'They've got bloody ridiculous names, if you ask me. Everyone knows who you mean when you say "the originals".'

He's referring to the name tag attached to each animal's bridle, which clearly states the full name. Our paying guests take much delight in knowing who is who be it Bramble, Fern or Ginger. Mungo doesn't like the idea. Surprise, surprise.

'Our guests like to know the individual names, and that's what counts, Mungo.' I hear this same protest every time he helps out. 'Are you staying to help out during the trek, or just waving us off and then coming back for afternoon tea?' I ask, sensing his pattern won't change.

'All hands on deck at the beginning and the end, that's how it appears to me.' Mungo busies himself by opening the gate to the first pen and avoiding my glare in the meantime. Before remarking, 'Time's ticking, you know?'

He's the only one that disappears off, then shows up again at the end of the trek; knowing full well that Isla will pass him a warmed bannock or two, if he drops by when afternoon tea is being served.

'I know.' I enter the second pen to collect my chosen boys. 'The guests will be arriving as we speak. I'm expecting The Orangery to text me any minute.'

Bang on cue, my phone buzzes.

'That'll be them, so hurry up!' mutters Mungo. He has already clipped reins on to two of his animals, and is busily checking the name tag for his third alpaca.

I'm yet to secure any of mine, having been distracted by his constant chattering.

Heather

'Isla, is that you?' I call out on hearing the front door open.

I'm crouching on the lounge carpet; my usual behaviour from day one of newborn pups. I daren't take my eyes off them. You'd think I would mellow as I get older, but I haven't yet. I still wonder at the miracle of squirming little bodies, Pepper's fabulous nature, and the pups' rapid rate of growth. The only difference this time is the location – I'm usually lying on the hallway carpet, peering under the staircase.

'Yes,' comes her tired reply.

I hear her arrival routine: dropping her handbag down, hanging her jacket up, kicking off each shoe, then the *thud*, *thud* as they bump against the skirting board. She might be twenty, but that sound has occurred every day since she started school.

'Where are you?' she calls, her voice nearing the lounge door.

'In here,' I reply. 'But calmly and gently, please – Pepper's whelped.'

'Her puppies are here!' Isla exclaims.

Regardless of age in this house, thankfully we all react in the exact same manner. Every time.

Isla's head slowly appears as she cautiously peers around the edge of the door, assessing my position as I gesture between the armchairs.

'Really, Pepper?' she says, stooping to crawl nearer for a better but rather awkward look.

'It's your prerogative, isn't it, Pepper? Yes, it is.' My voice changing to sickly sweet.

'Mum, seriously, no baby talk!' snipes Isla in a hushed tone.

There's nothing worse than your daughter correcting something that you've done for a lifetime.

'How many?' she asks, sensing my inner thoughts.

'Six – five girls and a boy. Though number four was a little bugger. He got stuck, so Magnus had to . . .' I pinch my fingers together like a naked puppet action.

'Ewwww, spare me the details! *La, la, la, la, la, la, la,*' she intones, covering her ears and singing.

'Good job you weren't here then. Magnus had no choice. He performed a swinging action, letting gravity unblock the airways, before towel-rubbing the little thing. Only then did the pup squeak. I thought . . . well, I'm not saying, but I thought the worst.'

Pepper's eyebrows twitch as she stares up at us, having finished her current cleaning duties.

'She understands every word you're saying, Mum.'

'Bless her, she's a great mum. I shouldn't worry, but I do.'

'Is it three sable and three tricoloured?'

'Possibly. It's hard to tell, this early.'

'Are you keeping any?' she asks, looking over at me all doe-eyed.

'Surely three dogs are enough for anyone, Isla.'

'I suppose. Have Socks or Rosie shown any interest?'

'I haven't let them in yet. It was a job and a half, last time, if you remember. I've confined them to the rear of the house, but they aren't stupid, they know.'

Any minute now, Isla will recognise her dishevelled duvet; her current delight will soon change with the realisation that she's going to be sleeping under a pile of blankets tonight.

We fall silent as one of the tricoloured pups wakes up and yawns, showing the cutest tongue, before blindly snuggling down between her siblings. My heart melts every time one of my dogs delivers her pups. I only breed my three certified pedigree bitches when they've fully recovered after nursing a litter; I want to be sure they're healthy and the pups have had time to enjoy being part of our family. Other breeders have told me I could plan additional litters each year, which means I wouldn't have such a long waiting list for potential pups, but I'll please myself where my dogs' welfare is concerned.

'She's so good with them, isn't she?' I say, mooning over my girl and her babes.

'Yeah,' answers Isla. 'Mum, what's for tea?'

My jaw drops as I turn and stare at my own selfish little pup.

'What? I'm hungry!' she declares. 'I've been at work all day.'

'Unbelievable,' I mutter, dragging myself up from the carpet. 'Works with food all day and still comes home to bug me.'

'I'm only being honest.'

'Bloody hell, Pepper. You, my girl, have got this mothering role sorted. Me? Well . . . I'm still bloody useless with my two!' I glance at my younger girl, shaking my head.

'What?' says Isla, becoming defensive on seeing my reaction.

'Nothing. Don't you worry. I'll whip you up a meal. I can't have you saying I put my dogs before my daughters.'

'I would never say that!'

'Mmmm, I bet.'

Callie

It takes me all of twenty minutes to run through the close-down routine in The Orangery once the other waitresses have ensured the tables are cleared, wiped and disinfected, and the various chairs are straightened. I don't like being the last one out, responsible for emptying the till and securing the day's takings in the safe, before locking up. But I refuse to listen to the moaning I'd be subjected to if I asked another waitress to stay behind with me. I'm not scared, as such. I simply don't like being here alone. Isla would laugh if she knew how often I sing aloud to fill the eerie silence.

I close the door of the rear storeroom, then make my way through to the front of house, flicking off light switches as I go. All the appliances are switched off at the wall, the dishwasher is running, and the glass cloches stand empty, awaiting tomorrow morning's freshly baked cakes. My fingers dance along the final panel of switches. It's satisfying to plunge the café into darkness, knowing that Isla will be reversing this sequence in less than twelve hours. Though how she's managing the five o'clock starts is beyond me – and all in the name of baking.

My final duty is giving the front of house area the once-over before leaving. I wander around, checking the floor for forgotten handbags, straightening seat cushions, and making sure that nothing untoward has been accidentally dropped into the wood pile beside the log burner.

I'm content; it's been a good day, long but rewarding. It counts as a double shift, pay wise, so I'm not complaining. My alpaca trek was filled with hilarity and laughter. Only a hen party could create double entendres from every aspect of my alpaca demonstration, and then continue their jokes throughout the woodland walk. I tried to stay professional but when a wisecrack was genuinely funny – and somehow bizarrely applicable to the alpaca males – I simply couldn't keep a straight face. I was relieved to hear the women were sober and alcohol free on arrival. How embarrassing, if they hadn't been! I was touched when the Campbells sent a complimentary bottle of chilled bubbles across from the hotel so the hen party could enjoy it with their afternoon tea.

There, done. Nothing out of place, and everything ready for tomorrow. Though very few customers visit the café on Mondays and Tuesdays, as the gallery is closed to allow the artists a two-day break – a weekend, in effect.

Fumbling in my handbag for my bunch of keys, I exit the massive glazed door, before performing my final duty with a satisfying *clunk* from the lock. I give the door handle a good rattle, to prove the point. My waitressing duties are done and dusted. Now it's time to see my babies!

'I'll stand here, and you call them across,' says Mungo, leaning against the paddock's wooden fencing.

Having made my way to the grassy paddocks, ready to assist Mungo with herding the alpacas back into the large barn for the night, I expected more from him. A wheelbarrow piled with rope leads stands beside us on the driveway.

'Mungo, that's hardly fair!' I moan,

'That's life, Callie . . . get used to it!'

'Huh!' I retort, still annoyed that he didn't actually accompany the earlier trek, just chose to reappear in The Orangery at the end.

'Plus, I've got older bones than you, so there's less speed in these here legs.'

'Great! I'll do it all, shall I?' I'm dressed in my waitressing uniform, which he doesn't seem to appreciate; flat shoes and a pencil skirt are hardly the right gear for this game, unlike this morning's attire.

Mungo nods, as if my complaint was an enthusiastic statement.

When I enter the paddock, closing the gate securely behind me, the majority of my herd dash to the far side of their grassy field. Mungo gives a deep-throated chuckle, immediately thinking I'm beat. There's no way I'll fail at this. Has he forgotten it was Isla and me who trained these boys when Magnus first delivered them to the estate? Magnus might be their true master – and Ned, the big boss above him – but Isla and I are the hands-on alpaca whisperers, nobody else! I can read these boys like the back of my hand.

Mungo hands me a bundle of rope leads which I drape around my neck purely for convenience. At least my ten boys get the chance to plod around the estate twice a week, enjoying a change of scenery, interacting with various people and getting rewarded with handfuls of treats. Far more interesting, surely, than being a proven stud and getting your jollies once in a season but remaining in the same paddock, with the same view every day. Which reminds me, I hear Jemima is already researching entire males and a breeding programme.

'Tut, tut, tut, tut,' I call softly whilst walking across the grass.

Karma and Carpe Diem, the self-imposed leaders, stop grazing, lift their heads high and turn towards me. Their fawn and russet fleeces ensure they're easily recognisable amongst the herd.

When I extend my hand, both boys slowly walk in my direction. I want to turn around and grin at Mungo, but I don't. My task is far from over, but as I clip a rope lead on to each animal I gratefully make a fuss of them by scratching the base of their ears. 'Good boys, we'll show old Mungo how it's done, won't we?' I calmly lead the two creatures towards the rest of the runaway herd and then stop, stand quietly and wait.

The others take note before galloping towards us as if being silently called by their leaders to oblige and fall into line. Serendipity, a jet-black alpaca, is the first to arrive at our position, so I clip a rope lead to his bridle before triumphantly leading my trio back towards the fence. A sense of pride wells up inside; I always feel honoured when walking alongside these majestic beauties, whether around the estate or taking them to their beds for the night.

Mungo's relaxed approach of allowing me to perform the

evening round-up narks me, but I get where he's coming from; he's older, and a lot less agile, but blimey does he play that joker card all too often. I don't bother glancing behind me; I sense the other seven alpacas are following our path towards the fencing. Because that's what alpacas do: they stick together as a true herd, and they behave as expected of them by their leaders. More's the pity that some humans can't take a leaf from their book.

'There you go, Mungo. My boys are well trained. If you hold these three, I'll clip leads on the rest.'

Mungo takes the offered leads and the trio stand quietly whilst I whizz around the rest of the bunch, clipping leads on to their leather bridles as they wriggle and jostle shoulders. As soon as their leads are attached, there's a familiar clicking noise as each metal clasp gently knocks against the oblong name tag hanging from each bridle. When all ten are jiggling and clacking it sounds like a crazy alpaca orchestra.

'And that makes ten,' I proudly announce.

Mungo opens the gate, allowing me and my boys to exit, joining him on the driveway.

'Here, pass me some reins,' he urges.

I split the rope leads and, ambling companionably along together, we head towards the new barn.

I doubt Mungo's ten ladies will be as easy to catch.

Chapter Five

Tuesday 16 August

Tabitha

'Afternoon, Tabby, how's it rolling?'

I look up to see my friend Melissa trundling her bulky push-chair across The Orangery towards my couch. Instantly, I close the script notes I've been studying, eager to give her baby son, Noah, a cuddle.

'It's all good with me. And you?'

She looks well, her mass of blonde hair tied back and her tall frame dressed in a floral-print cotton dress.

'Sleep deprived, with his lullaby as an earworm, and annoying myself with my overuse of baby talk, so yeah – it's all good for me too!' she giggles.

I raise my hands, comically twitching my fingers towards the content blue bundle.

'Are you sure? He has a tendency to puke over people.'

'I'm sure, just gimme, gimme, gimme!' I say, as Melissa begins unclasping his pushchair straps. 'Have you ordered your coffee?'

'Nope. I thought I'd settle this little one alongside you, then experience the luxury of browsing the counter as a solo, with both hands free to open my purse and collect my coffee. Do you want a refill?' she asks, lifting the baby from his cosy-looking seat.

She gently lays him in my arms. I get a whiff of his warm milky scent as his big blue eyes stare up at me. Not a grumble or a frown ruins his bonny features. My heart melts; he's such a cutie in his tiny sailor suit and matching shoes. My index finger gently strokes his tiny chubby cheek; a minor miracle, considering he was premature, with such a tiny birth weight.

'Please. My usual, Isla will know,' I say, momentarily lifting my gaze from the baby's face.

'Two minutes,' says Melissa, gesturing towards the counter where Isla has reappeared from the rear prep room.

Melissa looks well, despite the struggle she's been through since the surprise early arrival of her baby. I'm sure she's still dabbling with her textiles and ceramics, even if it's simply planning future projects inside her head whilst juggling the demands of motherhood. Melissa is one of the most together women I know – alongside Jemima, that is. I glance at my abandoned script notes; I need to give this my all. Neither Jemima nor Melissa would hesitate to audition for the part they truly wanted rather than accepting a lesser role. Very few customers visit the café when the artists' stables are closed, so I've spent the last twenty minutes of my coffee break brooding in silence and doubting my own ability. But in the blink of an eye I know what I need – to up my game and go for gold to impress Ebenezer.

Melissa returns within minutes, delivering a fresh coffee.

'Thank you. Everything you dreamt it would be?' I ask, gesturing towards the contented baby cradled in my arms.

'Everything, plus more. But I need to talk about something other than baby stuff, and you've just been collared for today. So let's hear it. What's this all about?' She points to my script notes.

'Are you serious?' There's a giggle in my voice, unsure if she means it.

'Yep, let's hear it. Just imagine that I've been deprived for five months, so I need creative stuff, gallery gossip, and even an update on my old mucker Mungo!'

I don't need a second invite. '*This* is my chosen audition script. Our am-dram company is holding open auditions, so I've selected a monologue to perform. The director will assess this performance alongside a set piece he gives us. I'm chasing a specific part in this year's annual Christmas play, so I figured I'd better get in early and start preparing.'

'It's August!'

'Yep, but the auditions will be soon. I'll be gutted if he awards me a supporting role. Ebenezer has a habit of noting our commitment and performance in his ledger book. I'm sure he'll refer to it alongside the audition pieces. I've spent an entire year attending every rehearsal night, throwing myself into acting workshops, and even performing in weekend skits, purely to—'

'Be embarrassed in public!'

'My God, have you heard about last Saturday?'

Melissa begins to laugh. 'Who hasn't?'

I can't hold back any longer and start laughing at the recall of Freddie's expression as he fell backwards off the ladder. 'I kid you not, it was the funniest thing I've seen in ages. His body fell in a straight line, like a rigid plank of wood – he couldn't have done that if Ebenezer had asked him to. The crowd were so amazed they thought it was part of the skit, so they applauded for ages. I wanted to die.'

'I can imagine, a definite "smile and wave" moment from the parapet.'

'Exactly. Kenzie and I simply carried on as if nothing had happened, which made it even funnier for us when the audience erupted. I hear on the social media grapevine that Ebenezer wasn't impressed, but he willingly accepted the praise afterwards. I bet we'll get a lecture and a half on Thursday night at our weekly meeting.'

'Surely you can sit pretty, knowing you did your best,' says Melissa, stirring her coffee.

'Maybe. My aim is to not put a foot wrong between now and the auditions, though Freddie has definitely blotted his copybook with his ladder incident.'

'Not leading man material then?'

I shake my head, as a blush rises to my cheeks.

'Oh, look at you, lady. Suddenly hot in here, is it? I assume there must be another stud waiting in the wings for the main Christmas role.'

'Stop it. It's not like that. We all muck in together at our am-dram company,' I say hastily.

'There's so few of you, I guess there's little choice. Is it true that some actors have to perform two roles, with quick costume changes?'

'Sometimes, if you've a minor part to play. That's what I want to avoid this year. You should join us! You'd be invaluable backstage with your artistry, photography – and sewing skills, from what I've seen of your mini scarecrows on the allotment.'

Melissa grimaces. 'No can do, my lovely. I've only just returned to my allotment plot since having this little lad. The weeds were up here . . .' She gestures to her shoulder before continuing. 'I'd prefer to concentrate on that, as we both get fresh air, plus I get some exercise from digging the plot. I might be growing a little something ready for next month's annual allotment festival.' Melissa takes a sip of her coffee.

'Ooooo, sounds interesting. Carrots, by any chance?'

Melissa laughs, spitting her coffee down her front as she remembers her first attempts to produce something fit for the judging panel. 'Hey, now that's not called for!' she says, frantically grabbing for a paper serviette to mop her clothing. 'My God, when I think back to that day, with Mungo up to his tricks. Awarding me the wooden spoon for the worst bunch of carrots in the show!'

'He's a bugger, isn't he? But he's currently keeping Jemima happy with supplies of frozen pumpkin stored from last season, so I think we can forgive him any previous misdemeanours.'

'Is she still craving pumpkin?'

'Yep, it's a good job she's filling up on that. There's very little else she's keeping down. She's puking left, right and centre, around the clock, from what Dottie says.'

'I've arranged to visit her today, after her pre-natal check-up.'

'She's looking drained and lethargic . . . Verity reckons she'll be a hospital admission soon.'

'They'll be keeping a close eye on her. But still, it's not nice, is it?'

'It can't be,' I agree. 'Though you'll cope just fine visiting her – especially if little Noah here has the same tendency.'

Heather

I hold my phone between the pair of us, tapping the icon for the 'Shetland Singles' app. It's a new online venture recently launched by a local computer whizz-kid to assist islanders in our search to secure our happy ever afters. No mean feat when many folk are turning their backs on our isolated communities and heading for the mainland in search of a loving partner and a new life. Immediately, my screen bursts into life. The opening images – which I'm sure are supposed to entice, enthral and make you eager to greet your beloved – burst into life with a colourful flourish. Sadly, those youthful feelings pass me by, having been cajoled by my elder daughter to sign up a few weeks ago. I'm an old romantic at heart; I'm not certain this new-fangled form of social introduction is truly for me.

'I love this,' squeals Ellie, excitedly rubbing her hands together.

'What? Potentially helping me to select the man you'll argue with over the Christmas turkey, refuse to invite to your wedding because "he's not my dad", and finally sit across from whilst crying over my deathbed!'

'Mum!' exclaims Ellie, horrified by my remark. Her mock outrage is a natural reaction from my daughters; we might joke, but they love me dearly.

'Sorry. Weren't you thinking that far ahead? More like a drink in town and a slow walk home. Right you are, Ellie. Yay! I love this too,' I say, feigning interest.

'And you wonder why you're single!' is her only retort.

'Excuse me, but I need binoculars to locate my past love life within my own history.' Given that I've only had one true boyfriend – Jimmy Creel, who dated and repeatedly dumped me throughout both my pregnancies, until I finally saw sense in my mid-twenties – I can't claim to be an expert on relationships.

'Phuh! You're as young as you feel, Mum.'

'Am I now? That's bloody worrying then.'

Ellie snatches the phone from my palm. 'Password?'

'The usual code: three, four, six, five.'

'Are you serious, the same entry code number as Harmony Cottage?'

'How else do you think I'll remember it?' Surely, it's wise to use memorable numbers? I'm not likely to forget the code to the rental cottage next door that I manage on behalf of my nephew.

My daughter shakes her head in disgust as her fingers dance across the screen, tapping with lightning speed. How she hasn't got RSI with rapid texting is beyond me. I'm sure the next generation will wear their fingers out years before their hips and knees give way.

'Right, so let's have a look, shall we?' she coos, snuggling in beside me.

'You're actually enjoying this, aren't you?' I say, taking in her smiley face.

'Yeah. Why wouldn't I? I reckon I could match you up with a decent guy in no time.'

'Mmmph, I doubt it.' I watch as she begins to swipe the screen again, causing the men's faces to blur with the speed at which my daughter discards them. 'Hey, not so fast, I can't see.'

'Trust me, Mum – you didn't want to.' Her index finger swipes a few more.

'Ellie, I was trying to look then. That man was—'

'Too old, Mum.'

Her remark needles me. How does she know what age group I am going for? When I was her age, I thought anyone out of their twenties was old. And anyone above forty was living on borrowed time and should be grateful for reaching another birthday. Having reached that advanced age myself, I don't feel like that nowadays.

'What's wrong with him?' I point at the screen as another man disappears.

'Did you see his cardigan?'

'Ellie, I am supposed to have some input regarding my choice.'

'Don't be daft, Mum. If I leave it to you, you'll be dating someone like Uncle Clyde.'

'I'll have you know Uncle Clyde has been a very reliable husband and father – he's never shirked his responsibilities. I wouldn't go far wrong with a dependable man, young lady. And if I wished anything for you, it would be a reliable Uncle Clyde sort.'

'Err, Mum. I meant as in vegging in his armchair, Saturday night wash and brush-up for the social club, and an obsession with snooker.'

'Oh, I thought you meant . . . oh, it doesn't matter. Uncle Clyde's got a good heart.'

'Mmmm. Yeah, I want that in a bloke.' She swipes her finger again. 'What a ridiculous hairstyle. Ooo, that's a dangerous pose. Nope, he's all about his bits.'

'What?'

'Don't look, Mum, you don't need to see. Now he looks nice, though that beard needs attention.'

I lean in to view a smiling male face, sporting a bushy beard. I'm not really into beards. But still, he has a nice smile and looks like a decent sort.

Ellie holds the phone beside my face and stares hard. 'Nah,' she says, abruptly whipping it back into her palm.

'What do you mean "nah"?'

'He makes you look much older.'

My mouth drops open; I'm going to need nerves of steel to survive this. My younger daughter, Isla, who's busy upstairs working on her cookery book project, would be kinder than Ellie, somewhat gentler with her remarks and selection of potential dates. But I wouldn't contemplate involving her. Not after the stalking episode with the Lachlan Gray boy. I shake my head, deleting the very thought of him from my head, much like an Etch A Sketch toy from my childhood. I hear on the local grapevine that his trial is starting soon and, fingers crossed, my Isla can rest easy when that low-life disappears for a while, courtesy of Her Majesty's pleasure.

'Niven,' I mutter.

'What?'

'Eh?'

'You just said "Niven",' says Ellie, staring hard at me.

'Sorry, I was just thinking. No one deserves to die like that, in a hit and run. Bless him, anyway . . . you know.'

'Yeah, I know. But seriously, Mum . . . I'm not sure you should be feeling so sorry for him. Because if he did what folk now reckon he did, well . . . your little cousin paid the price, all those years ago, and justice was never truly served.'

'Thank you, I do know. But we'll never know for sure, will we? Anyway, back to it! This is my life we're trying to sort out – so I don't become a lonely figure like the one Niven cut walking around in our community.'

'I've got to be honest, Mum . . . you are hard work. Any bloke will need a medal for taking you on. It's a good job me and Isla are grown up, because I doubt anyone would be interested otherwise. It'll be tough enough having a relationship with you as a singleton with no additional responsibilities.'

'I've got responsibilities, thank you!'

Ellie pulls a face.

'I have!' I protest.

'Three adult dogs and a nest of puppies doesn't qualify.'

'Oh!'

'Have you put that in your bio profile?'

'I might have.'

'No wonder no one's taking your bait, Mum.'

'I. Am. Not. Bait.'

Ellie gives me a head tilt.

I snatch the phone from her grasp. 'I've had enough of this already. Thank you for your help, but I think I want to do this on my own. Cheers. Bye bye. Love you and all that, but I don't like your terminology, your rapid swiping and your instant dismissal of potentially very nice people.'

'Oh my God, Mum. You aren't supposed to browse dating sites at the snail's pace you apply to each page of the latest Argos website.'

'I quite like the Argos website,' I protest.

'Mmmm, we've noticed. If I leave you to your own devices, you'll read every single personal profile, noting hobbies and interests. Give that back here.' She snatches the phone from my hands and resumes her swiping.

She's got a point, though I hate to admit it.

'I might give your profile an entire overhaul, Mum. It might boost your attractiveness.'

Again, I'm gobsmacked. Is every sentence uttered from her mouth supposed to be so harsh?

'Your current profile's so bland, I'll be drawing my pension before you meet a decent fella!'

'Ellie! I haven't brought you up to talk like this. How would you like some bloke and his daughter to be judging my hair colour, my dowdy clothes, and swiping past like lightning? There's much more to me and my world than my appearance and choice of pose.'

'Everyone does it; it's society's hang-up, not mine.'

'I have tried my hardest to raise you with decent manners, so show some respect and politeness towards others, please. In the last twenty minutes, I've witnessed the sad fact that my beautiful daughter actually owns a heart of steel, has a mouth like a sewer, and her opinions about snapshots of men range from disgust to derision, based on beard growth, cardigans and superficial opinions about looks and aging. Now, I don't believe that's what I'm after. I want a man with a good heart, a good sense of humour, who's hard-working and responsible in his life. Regrettably, he also needs to be someone who can show my two daughters respect, despite me obviously making an appalling job at raising them single-handed. Perhaps I'm asking a bit much but I really don't care what he looks like, dresses like, or what he spends his leisure time doing, because I'm a bit long in the tooth for a pretty boy-band type who hasn't much between his ears and only thinks with what's between his legs!' I pause for a much-needed breath, having expelled that last statement in a burst of near hysteria.

Ellie goes to answer, but thinks better of it. She twists her mouth unattractively to the side, swiping her tongue slowly over her front teeth – her 'ugly mouth', as I call it – before slowly handing me back my phone.

'Thank you. Now, I'd appreciate a little "me time" with my dating app,' I say, snatching the offered phone from her palm.

Ellie peels herself from the sofa cushion and heads for the door. I watch her sullen manner, knowing she's taken every word to heart. I'm expecting her to attempt a final put-down.

'Mum?'

I hold my index finger aloft, as I used to when she was a child, signalling a 'not now' moment.

Ellie falls silent; she knows.

I then point the said finger towards Pepper's nest, filled with squirming pups, before continuing, 'The day your heart is as open and as loving as that basket of dogs is the day you can judge other people on this planet. Until then, young lady . . .' I cringe at those particular words leaving my lips, but still I continue to lecture. 'Until then, how dare you judge men by their general appearance! That's like judging a book by its cover; you've no idea what is hidden inside. Such superficial ideas don't sit well with me. Do I ever allow anyone to have one of our pups based purely on a desire for a particular coat colour? "Oooo, I dream of a blue merle, it's so unique, nobody near me owns one!"' I end the sentence in a whiney voice, mimicking a refused applicant from many years ago.

'No,' Ellie sullenly replies.

'Why not?' I ask.

'Because there's so much more to a dog than the colour of the coat it's wrapped in.'

'Exactly! Let that be a life lesson for you! You are no different to the people I refuse to deal with because they want a certain colour dog, purely for how impressive it appears to be, and not for the hidden beauty of all the love beating inside its chest.'

Ellie bites her bottom lip. She can see my anger. She can hear my disappointment. My tears are about to spill. She knows what's about to happen, but saves me with a single word.

'Sorry.' She glances towards Pepper, who plays her part perfectly by twitching her eyebrow in silent judgement of my daughter. 'Night.'

'Good night, Ellie.' I look away to focus on my phone screen.

I hear the door open and close, quietly.

The bright screen instantly blurs before my vision; I didn't know my daughter had such a side to her. Maybe raising boys would have been easier in the long run? Who knows?

Pepper makes a noise.

I look up to meet another mother's eyes, doleful and silently signalling that she understands my troubles with young pups and their behaviour.

Callie

I've enjoyed a quiet day off. I've helped my dad tidy the back garden, met up with a couple of old friends in town for a quick coffee, and tackled my dirty laundry for the working week ahead. Nothing out of the ordinary – simply one of those 'being an adult' kind of days. Sadly, as it's mid-month, I need to spend the evening tackling the twice-monthly task I dread: my finances.

From my bedroom upstairs, I can hear the muffled sound of my parents' favourite TV programme coming from the lounge. I recognise the theme tune and canned laughter, so I know they'll be entertained for an hour or two, meaning I don't have to worry about interruptions.

Sitting in the centre of my king-sized bed, I hurriedly empty the contents of my shoulder bag on to the duvet. I take my time retrieving my purse, rescuing several unused yet expensive lipsticks and glittery biros from the deluge; once the essential items are returned to my bag, I'll have no excuse but to focus on the pile of envelopes. I repeatedly stall before starting this process. Twice a month, I have to force myself to behave like a mature and sensible adult, and yet this task uncovers nothing but my childish behaviour.

I take a slug of wine before replacing the half-empty glass beside the open bottle on my bedside cabinet; a vital accompaniment for this task.

And so begins the step-by-step process I've crafted over many months. Don't think it's an avoidance tactic, it isn't – there's purpose in each stage.

First, I must separate the colours, similar to sorting my laundry earlier. I grab a handful of letters, swiftly shuffle them and deal three hands like a casino croupier, separating the letters into the three main colours: brown, white and beige. There's never any pretty pastel-coloured ones. I repeat this task several times before completion.

Once dealt, I take each pile, turning them over to view the reverse side, then complete a game of 'Snap' by matching the sender's address printed on the envelope's seal; I know each location off by heart. Namely, credit card 1, credit card 2, credit card 3, credit card 4, charge card 1, charge card 2, store card 1 and store card 2. There used to be more, but I've managed to consolidate some over the years, though I've kept a couple of extras purely for emergencies.

The downfall of the next stage would be in choosing the wrong pile to begin opening. I've previously been fooled into believing that the company who sends the fewest letters is the least angry regarding my lack of payments or 'refusal to enter into correspondence', as they like to call it. Experience has taught me that's not entirely true!

If I choose the wrong pile to open first, my nerves will be shot and I'll chicken out, stuffing the remaining letters under my bed in a vain attempt to avoid any words printed in bold black font. Or worse – in red. It's like Russian roulette, selecting each envelope from its pile and attempting to open, read, acknowledge the minimum amount payable, before opening the next envelope. It's essential not to sabotage the method by revealing a final demand for immediate payment! They always state that you must phone them, discuss numerous options, when there's only ever one: pay up! I hate those 'phone call' days the most. When I'm forced to telephone one credit card company to make an urgent payment, reading out the long number on the front of another credit card to keep them happy.

I have my favourites. I like to keep credit card 1 happy; that's my old faithful, my 'everyday go-to', which sits at the front of my purse because I earn purchase points with every tap. Not that I redeem the points for goods, but you never know – one day, I might.

I also have my nasties, the card companies who refuse to allow me to push their metaphorical boundaries by ignoring them, or underpaying the required amount; they're always threatening me with court action and bailiffs. So, I pay up and silence them for a few more weeks. Until they become irritated by my lack of regular payments, only to restart the threats of court action again. Those companies are like a pesky ex-boyfriend who refuses to listen and keeps popping up every few months just to check, are you dating yet?

The store and charge cards are the really deadly ones; their percentages are so extortionate that if I so much as sniff in the wrong direction I end up owing more than I spent in the first place, which defeats the object of this game I'm playing. They're like demanding babies who cry out for attention when I'm browsing but require constant soothing at irregular times, for no apparent reason.

I take another slug of wine before I truly get down to work. The real graft starts with the calculation of my total minimum payments. After double and triple checking, I reckon a grand total of £463 is the minimum needed to keep the wolves from the door.

Problem is, I haven't actually got that amount to send. With just £300 to keep these babies happy, this is where my array of experience and previous knowledge comes into play. Some are softies who don't mind the odd missed repayment now and then. Others are like Rottweilers; they'll rip your throat out at the first sign of reneging on the credit deal we somehow made and shook hands upon.

It takes all evening to calculate who gets what – and more importantly, when. My wages have been slightly higher since taking on the alpaca walks, but still, I'm adrift by a fair amount this month. I enter the payment details into my colour-coded spreadsheet whilst vowing not to succumb to any spending splurges – from now on, I'll only spend money on the basics of life – after which, I pour myself a final glass of wine. When all is said and done, I need to enjoy the little things in life; in the face of my atrocious debts, it's all I can truly afford.

Chapter Six

Thursday 18 August

Tabitha

I spend half the morning inside my own head whilst serving customers and giving advice about my various products. I love that customers show such interest and care about what they put on their skin. Though this morning, with my audition monologue looping inside my head, I'm surprised I didn't answer a customer in the character of Curley's wife, complete with American accent. Not that the irony is lost on me portraying a solitary, frustrated starlet hanging around the stables and filling her time whilst secretly dreaming of the bright lights of Hollywood. I can't imagine that Steinbeck ever envisaged his leading lady being relocated to Shetland – not quite Robbie Burns' native Highlands – purely to accommodate my 'best laid schemes o' mice an' men'.

'Tabby, any chance you're making a batch of the plain lemon soap sometime soon?' asks Nessie, browsing my shelves.

'Did I promise you any?' I can do that at times; it's so easy to promise, then it slips my mind.

'No. But Isaac wouldn't be seen dead using the same soap as me. I thought he could do with something a little richer in texture, to make up for the constant exposure to heat his skin receives, much like mine.'

'Duly noted,' I say, reaching for my reminders book under the counter and jotting down a few details. 'In the meantime, you could try a small piece of the frankincense and lime soap – the beige one, just by your right hand. It has a very earthy aroma, with the lighter citrus notes on top. He won't argue that it smells like yours.'

Nessie picks up a small bar. 'Perfect. I'll take one of his and another bar of mine, please.' She collects her usual, before making her way to the counter, cash in hand.

'Thank you,' I say, popping the two bars of soap into a logoed gallery paper bag and ringing the sale through the till.

'Have you seen Jemima at all this week?' she asks.

I shake my head. 'Nope. Though I can't say I've seen Ned either, to be honest.'

'He's running around like a headless chicken, trying to juggle both the gallery and the hotel, while she's attempting to sprint back and forth to a sick bowl. It's quite a worry, from what Dottie was telling me, but hopefully her sickness will stop soon.'

'I spied Mungo earlier and asked after Dottie, as she's spending more and more time at the manor supporting Jemima. He said Dottie's fine – in her element, in fact – but it must be taking its toll on everyone involved.'

'She's got another four months to go. Surely, it can't last much longer. Melissa dropped by the other day and mentioned Jemima was pretty miserable and out of sorts, even with her friends to chat to.'

'Poor woman, it can't be much fun. I recommended one of my chamomile balms, and Mungo says it helped her to relax for a little while. But you can't use such things repeatedly – it's all cause and effect, isn't it?'

Nessie grimaces, adding, 'What else can you do but trudge through each day, hoping tomorrow's brighter?'

'Well, that goes for everything, doesn't it?' I say, mulling over the prospect.

'Sure. We spend our lives lurching from one thing to another. Never-ending, really.'

Silence descends between us as I hand over her change.

'Bloody hell, listen to us sounding like Mungo,' chuckles Nessie, instantly cracking a smile.

'And this place can't support more than one Mungo, that's for sure,' I say, before laughing.

'We'd best start living it up a little – Callie just mentioned she's heading into town tonight for a drink or two. Have you any plans?'

On a school night? is my only thought in relation to Callie. It seems such a gamble, and I can't cope with the hangover nowadays, which makes me sound so old.

'Actually, yes,' I say. 'Tonight's my drama night. It's a fleeting dinner at home as I have to be at The Garrison Theatre by seven o'clock. Fingers crossed, the director is in a good mood and spills the beans concerning this year's Christmas performance.' I hold my hands up to show my actual crossed fingers.

'What's he leaning towards – a festive pantomime?'

'No. There's a rumour that he's planning A Christmas Carol – a big bonanza of a show, the full works, so to speak.'

'Oooo, that'll be interesting. I used to go every year as a child, but not so much now. Strange really, it was almost a family tradition at Christmas time.'

'Maybe you and Isaac can restart such traditions,' I add, with a coy smile.

'Mmmm, now there's an idea. I'll start with his soap. Let's see how that fares first!'

'Tiny steps, Nessie.'

'Something like that. See you later, enjoy your am-dram night.' In seconds, she's gone, heading back towards her forge across the cobbled yard.

I linger, deep in thought for a moment. She's right about what she said; we do lurch from one thing to another, so even more reason why we need to aim high whenever we get the chance.

Right, let's crack this monologue, once and for all! And see if I can get a head start on the upcoming auditions.

Heather

'Morning, Heather,' calls Verity, drawing the turquoise bike I lent her aeons ago to a halt, as we meet on the main road into Lerwick.

'Morning, lovey, how are you? Or more importantly, I hope my older sister looked after you at your Sunday tea?'

'Good, thanks. We feasted like kings! Honestly, she always makes an effort and prepared so much. But I suspect you had a hand in that, so thank you too.'

'You're very welcome. I help out where I can.'

'How are those adorable puppies doing?'

'Argh, don't! The girls are convinced that I'll be keeping the one pup, but I've got news for them, I can't. Can you imagine having a boy wanting his jollies with my girls when they come into season? When one is his mother, the other his sister from another mister, and the third is an aunty. It would be a genetic nightmare waiting to happen, wouldn't it? And that's without the Breeding of Dogs Act being cited at me from every direction. Nope, all six must have new homes by twelve weeks, even little boy blue.'

Verity's brow furrows.

'That's his current name, until he has an official one from his future family. Each pup has a coloured paper collar so we can identify who is who. Obviously, his is blue, but he's a no-name at the minute.'

'Bless him. Fingers crossed, they each find their for ever homes pretty soon.'

'I hope so, otherwise I'll be panicking. I've got a waiting list of potential owners to contact, but you never know how it'll work out; some families find their circumstances have changed, and other arrangements simply fall through for various reasons. It gives Pepper the wrong idea, that's for sure. I can do without her getting too attached to any remaining pups.'

'Have you never kept any?' asks Verity, taking a keen interest.

'No. Never. I only breed each girl once, maybe twice a year at the most. I like to promote the breed, helping to secure its future, but I'm not in it for the cash, Verity. I know other breeders have a constant flow of pups, but I don't work like that. My girls are my pet dogs, not some money-making puppy machines that can drop a litter every few months – that's not right, in my opinion. I want my girls to be healthy between each pregnancy and enjoy life. In the end, that's what produces strong healthy pups who will carry the bloodline into the future, ensuring the breed's standards are adhered to.'

'Sounds ethical and logical to me,' says Verity, holding her bike upright.

'I'm glad to see you're still using this old thing, I never got into the habit,' I say, pointing towards the bike. It seems like hardly any time at all since our Isla asked if we could lend it to Verity on her arrival in Shetland.

'I love it. It's made such a difference to my lifestyle. I'd have preferred a car, to be honest, but it seemed such a luxury and a huge outlay when I only planned to be here for the year.'

'And after the year?'

Verity's expression drops. 'Well, that's another question, isn't it? I hadn't planned on meeting Magnus and this whole scenario playing out as it has and . . . well, I'll have to see what happens in the coming months.'

'Won't you be staying?' I'm shocked to the core, and my tone conveys as much. Doesn't she know how lucky she is to have found our Magnus?

'You can understand the position I'm in, Heather. I've got

three lads at home in the Midlands, plus a house, a family and the remnants of my old life. I planned to stay here for one year and one year only.'

'And Magnus?' I sound defensive, though I didn't intend to. If I were lucky enough to experience what they've found in each other, I'd move heaven and earth to hold on to it for ever.

'Heather, you know how it is. I'm torn between the man and my boys.'

'They've coped. Well, from what I hear they have. I'm sure they've missed having their mum around, but what young man truly wants his mum on his case when he can have the run of the house and do as he pleases alongside his brothers!'

'You've got a point . . . which is what worries me. My Tom is only eighteen, which is not much younger than your Isla. Can you imagine leaving her?'

'No bloody way! The girl might be able to bake heavenly creations, but as for the state of her room – and don't even get me started on her mishaps with laundry washes. She'd be a first-rate nightmare come true! My Ellie would be pulling her hair out, that's for sure.'

I notice Verity turns pale on hearing my comments.

'Not that your lads are like that. I'm on about my girls, not your lads. I'm sure you prepared them before leaving for your gap year!'

'It's been lovely chatting, Heather. But I'm afraid I need to dash. See you another day.'

Oh bugger! I didn't mean to say that. Oh well, job done! I've no doubt she'll relay our conversation to Magnus. Our Magnus will tell her I didn't mean to put my size fives in it. He knows me better than anyone, I hope.

I watch as she scurries away, pushing her bike in a haphazard manner.

Chapter Seven

Tabitha

I stand nervously before the stage, waiting for Ebenezer to call the small group to order. Amidst the bubbly social chatter of the other thirteen attendees, I've remained schtum, anxiously watching our director flick through his battered ledger book, pencil poised in his gnarly grip. His wild white hair erratically stands on end, emphasising his eccentric nature, and his head is lowered as if absorbed in his notes. But he's pretending, acting. And listening. The group haven't realised, because they're too busy yapping, but if they watched, like I'm doing, they'd notice his gaze isn't directed to the page, but is fixed on his wristwatch. I'm sure he doesn't mean to be so forthright, scary or belittling, but his eccentric manner doesn't do anything to ease my nerves.

His brocade frock coat and the current surroundings simply add to his intimidating persona. Rows of raked seating in a rich burgundy fabric patiently await the arrival of an audience, while fancy gilt-edged plaster panels on the side walls provide a sense of finery to the dimly lit theatre. Behind me is the stage and proscenium arch, bedecked with matching burgundy drapes, masking curtain and an array of backdrops currently hidden from view. A proud little theatre that feels like a second home to me after the hours I've spent treading the boards and helping out backstage.

'Order! You've wasted five minutes of my time with your nonsense and jibber jabber,' roars Ebenezer, glaring at those before him, even me.

Two older members who've been happily socialising exchange a brief glance of annoyance at his curt manner. There's immediate silence. Rabbie gives a small cough, Aileen an uncomfortable shuffle, and a sharp sniff is heard from Kenzie, but not a word is uttered. They know he's caught them out, *again*.

'So ... last Saturday. I'd like to hear your reviews of our Shakespearean performance. Especially your views, Freddie.'

All eyes instinctively turn, witnessing Freddie's nervous gulp.

'I th-th-thought it t-t-turned out w-w-well,' he offers, glancing around at the bowed heads who suddenly don't wish to engage.

'Really? Word-perfect, was it?'

'N-n-near enough.' Freddie squirms under Ebenezer's gaze. For quite a bolshie youth that's some feat.

I can't look but I'm silently willing Freddie to address the elephant in the theatre. The longer he avoids mentioning the ladder incident the longer the lecture will be.

'Tabitha, do you agree?' asks Ebenezer, peering over the top of his wire-framed spectacles.

Noting Freddie's sigh of relief, I take a deep breath before answering. 'Not quite. I believe the performance was word-perfect, the projection clear, and our costumes and props were deftly handled, but the ladder incident distracted our audience, causing a dramatic change to the feel and focus of the performance.' I don't know why I'm using my best telephone voice to answer, but sadly, I am. Which makes me sound hoity-toity, when I'm certainly no better than the others now staring at me.

'Cheers,' mutters Freddie.

'Sorry,' I mouth, knowing my honesty will sting.

'And that is precisely why we rehearse, we follow direction, we listen, we learn. And we do not repeat such antics in the future. Do you all understand me? Because I have never been more embarrassed in my fifty years associated with theatre than when people whole-heartedly congratulated me on directing such a shambles as I witnessed last Saturday afternoon.' Ebenezer falls silent, glaring around at the assembled gathering.

I'm expecting more; that lecture wasn't nearly as long as previous ones we've endured.

'I suggest you each take a seat on the front row before I explain my plans for our Christmas performance. Not that I believe anyone's taking this company seriously after the weekend's dismal performance.'

We each quickly nip to the nearest seat, there's no lagging behind or chatting; Ebenezer means business, and I don't wish to waste a second before hearing him confirm what I've heard on the grapevine.

He paces to and fro in front of the stage whilst explaining. 'For a long time, I've wanted to direct my favourite Christmas tale. And it goes without saying that the fact my namesake comes from that very work gives me the greatest pleasure in announcing that *A Christmas*—'

'Yes!' The word escapes me without warning but with so much passion.

Every face turns to stare as I blush to my roots and mouth an apologetic 'sorry' in Ebenezer's direction. He shakes his bushy white hair and continues to pace. I stare at the lighting rigging above our heads, purely to focus, as he continues.

'Anyway, I am proposing *A Christmas Carol* for our festive performance. I intend to hold auditions next Wednesday evening – so it won't clash with our usual Thursday night – here at The Garrison, from seven o'clock sharp. I expect, and please take careful note, every actor to perform a personal piece they have practised, alongside a script read-through, the details of which I will provide on the night. Please don't ask me for any hints or clues regarding the audition reading – I won't be sharing the details with anyone. Any questions?'

My hand shoots into the air.

'Yes?'

'How long is the personal piece to be?' I know the answer from previous auditions but daren't assume anything when I'm aiming high.

'Two to three minutes. I'll stop you should you go over that time.'

I nod, confirming my understanding.

'Anyone else?'

There's a renewed silence. I think several actors remain riled by his curt demeanour. Personally, I'm not; since his arrival, I've always found him to be as prickly as a porcupine and as blundering as a bear. But then he cuts a solitary figure around town, which goes some way to explaining his disposition.

By the time nine thirty arrives, drawing our am-dram evening to a close, I'm as high as a kite. In my mind's eye, I've organised my entire week ahead into work time and audition practice sessions. Boy, am I glad I had the sense to select my speech and begin to learn my lines when I did. It'll give me a slight advantage time wise, if nothing else.

'What do you reckon old misery guts is going to choose?' asks Rabbie, helping me to tidy away a few forgotten props into the large wicker hamper.

I shrug. 'You never can tell. And it isn't worth the energy trying to second-guess him, to be fair.'

'Are you going for it?' he quizzes me.

'Sure.'

Rabbie hasn't been with the company long, less than six months, so I'm unsure if I trust him yet as a confidant. He was always chosen for the star role in our school performances, whereas I rarely was. Though I suspect he was persuaded to join this am-dram group by the anticipated arrival of Ebenezer, fresh from the West End, with a wealth of experience. It could spell trouble if I'm swayed purely by his devilish good looks and taut, muscular torso. Not that I've had much experience or luck with the opposite sex, apart from a few summer flings when I was younger. Now in my mid-twenties, I've sussed out that fellas see me more as the likeable 'girl next door' type, who they wish to be mates with, rather than pursuing me as girlfriend material. I tell myself it's their loss, not mine. But still, some genuine male attention wouldn't go amiss.

'Which part?'

I give him a coy smile, before teasing. 'Wouldn't you like to know!'

'It'll be one of the ghosts – everyone will be vying for those roles,' he quips, his dark eyes searching mine for confirmation.

'Not necessarily.' I throw a selection of costume hats into the basket.

'Come off it!' He laughs.

'Will you please hurry up – some of us have homes to go to!' Ebenezer's voice fills the empty theatre.

'Moaning old bugger,' mutters Rabbie under his breath.

'This little theatre has been begging for a successful director to ignite passion and inject interest into our stage performances. Show some respect – he must be in his seventies.'

'In his eighties, more like,' quips Rabbie, clearing the stage by pushing the closed wicker basket into the wings. 'As for igniting passion ... well, I'm eager to witness the talent around here at first hand. Be it his or the rest of this cast.'

Rabbie's remark strikes a chord with me, and I eye him cautiously; is he talking sheer talent, as in acting? Or *talent* talent, as in getting to know certain individuals? I observe him for a second, lost in thought.

'What?' he asks, before offering a wry smile, obviously noting my silence.

'Nothing. Will you grab the ghost light while you're there,

please?' I've learnt that Ebenezer is a stickler for his routines and tradition. There's no way he'll lock up the theatre without a flicker of light remaining in situ on the stage. I'm unsure if it's purely a superstition upheld in theatreland – I'd never heard of it before Ebenezer's arrival – but I've grown accustomed to it in recent weeks. I fancy it's an eternal light, waiting to greet our return to the stage, but in reality it's a practical way of avoiding unnecessary accidents. But whatever it is, I wish Rabbie would hurry up and perform the final task.

Rabbie reappears, holding the table lamp minus its shade, and trailing the coiled flex. It's not the finest of lamps, neither antique nor alluring, more like a cast-off from a long-forgotten relative some thirty years ago. The little brass detailing on the base is mottled and dingy-looking, and the bare bulb resembles a cheap attempt at a flickering candle flame, without looking even marginally like one. The amount of dirt and grime covering the glass blub must surely dull the brightness of the lamplight.

'When was the last time he cleaned this lamp, have you seen the layer of dust?' says Rabbie, placing it on the edge of the stage and unravelling the lengthy cable, before walking towards the nearest plug socket.

'Shhhh,' I say, embarrassed that Rabbie seems to have no filters or volume control.

'Don't shhhh me,' he replies, plugging the lamp in and flicking the switch. 'It's as old as the hills, and as for this flex – have you seen the exposed wiring on this plug?'

'Could you hurry up before he begins moaning? I don't question his instructions, not if I can help it. It'll do you no favours around here, I'm sure all creative directors have their quirky habits,' I whisper, unsure exactly where Ebenezer is in the auditorium.

'Is that positioned correctly then?' asks Rabbie, centring the lit lamp on the front edge of the stage.

'Yep. That's its usual spot.'

'Romantic candlelight, or what?' mutters Rabbie, raising an eyebrow in my direction.

I want to answer him, fire back some witty banter, but I've nothing; my mind is consumed by doubts. Is that his attempt at flirtation? Or am I incorrectly reading a non-existent subtext into everything this guy says to me?

'Ready?' calls Ebenezer, plunging the theatre's auditorium into near darkness.

I glance over, catching Rabbie's ghostly expression created by the light from the flickering bulb.

'Why doesn't he wait until we've joined him before doing that?' asks Rabbie, his tone etched with irritation.

Our moment has passed.

'Because then we're proving that the ghost light is actually working by using it to make our way to the exit. There's a method in his madness,' I explain, carefully making my way along the side aisle thanks to the faint flicker of illumination.

'Personally, I think there's a meanness in his madness, nothing much else,' grumbles Rabbie, following closely behind me.

Callie

'Thanks, Levi!' I call, slamming the taxi's rear door shut after a fun night out. I stagger my way along the garden path, knowing from experience that he won't drive off until I've opened the front door. That's Levi's manner, he's one of life's good guys. His behaviour hasn't altered just because he's dating my younger cousin, Pippa; nah, he's always been obliging. It's why so many of us ladies request Levi when booking with the taxi company.

I attempt to put the key in the lock three times, scratching my mother's paintwork with each go, until finally it's there. Though probably more from luck than judgement; I've drunk more than I intended to, way more. Once inside, I give Levi a wave and watch the taxi softly pull away and turn the street corner before I quietly close the door. I can do without annoying my parents; they'll be quoting me the precise time over tomorrow morning's toast and marmalade, regardless of how quiet I think I'm being. But a girl's entitled to have some fun, isn't she? It's hardly every night, just once in a while.

Kicking off my shoes in the hallway, I head straight for the lounge, which my parents will have vacated bang on the eleven o'clock chime of their favourite old wall clock. I grab the remote and make myself comfy, knowing I'll have peace and quiet for an hour or so before I feel obliged to go to bed for fear that I'll wake the household and cause a drama. Though I'd quite like some toast, purely to line my stomach and soak up a touch of this alcohol.

Why can't I simply say 'no' to people? I'd had every intention before going out of not getting into buying rounds of drinks. It's not as if I can afford to; I never usually do rounds. I always feel cheated when I stick to my usual drink all night, but others change their tipple to an expensive one when it's my shout. Always. Cheap vino on their own round, bubbles on mine – seems to be a familiar trick by which I'm stung every time. Forcing me to use my debit card – so then my budgeting goes to the wall too. Christ, I have to budget all week simply to afford a night out! And now I've buggered it up by overspending, which will force me to budget even tighter next week. When I buy my own drinks, with my own cash, I can control my spending. Urgh! I hate my life when it revolves around money in the way it does.

I throw down the remote control, then head for the kitchen, turn the grill on and wait for the element to glow red. I busy myself by making a coffee, because waiting around for anything is a danger zone moment. A temptation for my idle hands to grab my phone and surf the web looking for things I want to buy, but don't need, don't truly want and certainly can't afford. The trouble is, I always find something: a new shade of sparkly eye shadow, a trendy new tanning mousse promising flawless results, or a celebrity-endorsed product they swear they've been using for a lifetime. Sadly, my fingers dance through the screens faster than a singleton on that new Shetland dating app.

Within minutes, I'm back on the couch, flicking through the late-night TV channels and munching on hot buttered toast. There is never anything on that I want to watch at this late hour. I whizz through, find the TV planner and scroll down the list of recorded programmes my parents have decided they'd like to watch. There's the usual: the soaps, the quizzes, the trashy eighties films my mum loves to watch and reminisce over, and then the box sets my dad insists on recording but not watching, until there's enough to fill an entire day of binge watching. Nothing that interests me.

I flick to the main viewing screens and zap across the blue wall of programmes, each illuminated in gold writing in a poor attempt to entice me. Failed. It's not working tonight. My finger busily presses the tiny buttons of the remote control, whizzing me right, left and down past the various categories of films, sports, children TV, none of which catches my interest until I hit the late-night shopping.

I'll just see what's being offered as the star buy of the day!

I lower the volume for fear of disturbing my parents, then slowly raise it to a level that I can just hear. No one else needs to know. My parents can't stand this channel but if I dared, I'd have it allocated to my 'favourites', making for quicker access.

The shopping channel bursts to life; it might be ten past midnight but there in all her wonderful glory, looking fabulous, is Debs. And she's holding aloft a hair styling brush with a very large barrel head and torturous-looking bristles. One mishap with that and your scalp would know about it for a week!

The price appears in the top right-hand corner of the screen: £29.99 plus p&p. Not bad for a decent brush, I suppose. Though it would have to be good for that price – and create large, bouncy natural-looking curls. Anything less would be a rip-off. Though it's bigger than any of the hair brushes I own. Would my hair benefit from a brush barrel that big? I bet your hair would dry in no time with a brush that size.

Debs is giving us a demo with a hairdryer, pulling the extra-large brush effortlessly through her own glossy locks. Wow! That is a huge brush barrel, collecting and holding all her hair in one expert sweep. Amazing. What a buy!

I push my empty plate aside, lick each finger to ensure every last crumb is satisfyingly gone, and drink my coffee.

The screen changes and a list of items appears below the original price tag. Interesting, it comes as a package deal with a matching mini brush, a wide-tooth comb, an extra-wide-tooth comb, a tail comb with a metal tail, and another with a moulded plastic end . . . and a soft leatherette pouch for easy storage and super-light packing when travelling, which prevents your clothes getting snagged on the impressively strong, wide, long bristles and comb prongs.

My eyes are becoming heavy. I jump as the remote falls from my hand into my lap. My eyes immediately focus on the TV screen: wide-barrelled brush – £29.99 plus p&p.

Mmmm, I rarely use combs. Never use combs, in fact. I don't like combs, being cursed with such flyaway hair; I find they make it all staticky and super-charged. But I like that mega-barrelled brush. My hair would be dry in no time. It would save time and electricity in the long run. Debs is correct; I'd never have to buy another styling brush – or a comb, come to that – ever again.

Debs is quite right. It would make an ideal Christmas present, regardless of the fact that we're still in August. It would be better to buy now and 'store till then', rather than risk losing out and having to hunt down the supplier on the internet. A saving of time, of energy, and possibly postage too, by getting it early.

My body jolts as my head drops towards my chest. Debs is still describing, using and measuring the barrel brush. It looks good from every angle. And the measurement against the ruler is . . .

A true bargain.

Every girl needs one.

What else would I get Jemima, the girl who has everything, for Christmas? Pippa too? Mum could do with a new styling brush, though her hair is very short. And I suppose my aunty would want the same gift as Pippa, in that mother-daughter matchy-matchy manner my aunty seems to enjoy – even more so, since Pippa's moved out to live above the hotel . . .

. . .

. . . My eyelids snap open, revealing the bright glare of the TV screen. I wake up feeling cold, scrunched up in the corner of the sofa, my head lolling to the side, my neck aching and my toes turning blue. An empty plate rests on my knee, the remote control has fallen to the carpet, alongside my phone.

'Hey! That wasn't very clever,' I chunter to myself, uncurling my limbs and rolling my cramped shoulders.

How will I ever get through a full shift tomorrow? Actually, scratch that, today! Fighting the effects of alcohol and a rotten night's sleep won't be easy.

I climb the staircase and continue to berate myself with each step taken. I always have to ruin it, push it too far. I planned not to drink, and then drank heavily. Urgh! I planned an early night, and yet arrived home after midnight. Double urgh! And then stupidly browsed the TV channels in search of nothing, only to find hair brushes. Yeah, an impressive big-barrel hairbrush in a soft leatherette pouch . . . I pause on the top stair.

I did just watch, didn't I? I didn't dial in, did I? I liked them, but I didn't like them enough to phone in and place an order. An early Christmas order, or even a little workday-treat order?

Nah, I wouldn't have done that, I was far too tired.

Wasn't I?

Chapter Eight

Saturday 20 August

Heather

'Mum?'

'Yes.' Can't I ever get a minute's peace and quiet around here for an early-morning cuppa and a cuddle with one of the pups?

'What are you doing down there?' asks Isla, entering the lounge to find me in my dressing gown, sitting on the floor with a pup snuggled into my chest.

'Having some "me time" with a pup.'

She shrugs, staring over at my empty armchair. 'It's not where you usually sit.'

I reach for my cuppa, beside me on the carpet, and take a sip. The pup wriggles, as if chastising me for moving and disturbing his nap time against my warm chest.

'Anyway,' says Isla, looking down at me, 'how did your Friday night date go?'

'Is that it? You've sought me out to ask questions, take the mick and then dash out to work for the day, I see.'

'No. I'm interested.'

'In what?'

'Who, what, when, why and, maybe, if again?'

'Oh, right. So how doesn't come into it?'

'No, thanks. You can keep some stuff private. You forget that you tell Ellie everything and me nothing. So who did you spot online?'

I instantly blush, feeling the heat rise through my body. Which must feel like an electric blanket to the cradled pup.

'Like that, was it? Who are we avoiding now, the milkman?'

'You know the butcher's on Commercial Street?'

Isla's jaw drops and she stares at me, open-mouthed. 'McHaddit and Son, where you order our turkey from every year?'

I give a tiny nod.

'Oh, Mum. Not the really old chap!'

'No! The "and son" part. He bored me to tears, didn't have anything to say other than to recite his meat prices. Ask me how much they sell their beef and tomato sausages for.'

'Oh, Mum,' Isla exclaims again, a look of disbelief on her face.

'Go on, ask me.'

'How much?'

'Per kilo or pound? Which do you want?'

'You're joking me?'

'Per kilo is seven pounds forty-nine pence. Per pound is four pounds forty-nine. If you don't believe me, drop by on the way to The Orangery and see. He walked me past the window last night so I could admire their new pricing labels!' I lift the pup from my chest and kiss his tiny button nose, while my daughter stands and stares at me with a horrified expression etched across her features. 'Though I'll admit the price of their minced lean beef takes some beating, but I won't be buying from there again. In fact, I probably won't be walking past their shop window again. I'll need to take a diversion down two other side streets to avoid their shop, but it'll be a saving grace.'

'That's the fishmonger, the small bakery in town, and now the main butcher's we're avoiding.'

'I'd best cease with this online dating malarkey, otherwise

there'll be no local shops welcoming our custom other than the Tesco supermarket.'

'What if he rings asking for another date?'

'I doubt it, Isla. After three hours of butchery dirty talk, he looked quite taken aback by my refusal to show any interest in his leg of lamb – if you get my drift!'

Isla covers her face with both hands in sheer embarrassment. 'Mum, stop it! You can't talk like that! Not now, not ever!' she protests, talking through her hands.

'That's funny because McHaddit's number one son, my date, Mr One-Day-This-Entire-Butchering-Empire-Will-Be-Solely-Mine didn't stop with such lewd innuendos! Never mind, maybe I didn't fully understand his dating chit-chat repertoire.'

'I bet you did,' says Isla.

'Ah well, maybe I should stick with my fur babies and be done with men,' I say, stroking the pup's velvet fur. 'This peerie fella seems content enough in my company.'

'You'll find someone, Mum. Verity says her gran used to say "every pot has its lid".'

'Does she now. Well, tell Verity from me, I've got a cupboard full of sodding Tupperware boxes and not one bloody lid that fits whichever one I select! Tell her she's more than welcome to drop around for three hours and match 'em up if she's bored!'

'You know what she means.'

'I do, lassie. But it's not as easy as that, is it? You thought you'd found a good guy in Lachlan, and look what he turned out to be!'

Isla nods.

I hate to bring it up, because I suspect it's still painful to her. But at least she now has a barometer by which to measure future experiences.

'Apparently, he's up in court soon. Kenzie and Fiona reckon it'll be bye-bye for a short stay in prison if he's found guilty.'

'I hope so, lovey. Causing death by dangerous driving, isn't it?

Phuh! It's a matter of common decency, in my book. You can't run a man over and then drive off as if he had no worth. I know that young scallywag treated you badly when you were dating . . . and I still maintain his behaviour after so cruelly dumping you amounted to stalking, even if you didn't report it. But regardless of all that unsavoury nonsense towards you – our poor Niven paid the ultimate price. Lachlan made his bed that night, so now he must learn to lie in it.'

I don't want to raise my eyes to witness my daughter's steely gaze; I can feel her pain without needing to see the evidence written large across her face. But I look her straight in the eye, simply because it's the right thing to do. I'm not letting the likes of Lachlan Gray come between me and my girls. As my daughters frequently say, not now, not ever!

Tabitha

It's typical, isn't it? I pray for a quiet Saturday morning in the soapery – and what do I get? Run off my feet like there's no tomorrow. You'd think the world had run short of soap, the way my till is constantly ringing. Many Saturday mornings when I open up at ten o'clock, I receive a slow trickle of customers, mainly tourists mingling with a few locals, browsing my products and asking questions. Half my sales come from online purchases, so I can collate and manage those at any time in my working day. On a typical Saturday, the morning is fairly quiet until nearer midday, when there's a definite increase in footfall – and *boom!* I'm serving non-stop for a couple of hours before it begins to calm down again.

Typically, at busy times, my inner voice says, 'You could do with an assistant.' But who'd want a Saturday job for just two hours – slap bang in the middle of the day? They'd be clocking off early, by half past two, but still late enough to ruin a decent Saturday for most families. Anyway, today I brought my copy of *A Christmas Carol* into work with me, to remind myself of the cast of characters. As yet, I haven't had a minute to myself, so the dog-eared book has remained face down behind my counter.

'What's this?' asks Nessie, clocking my abandoned book during one of her coffee break drop-ins.

'Audition time for the Christmas performance. I know which character I want but thought it best to check out the rest – just in case.'

Nessie pulls a face.

'It's good fun, you should try it,' I say.

'No, thanks. I endure enough Christmas humbug from October onwards, working alongside Isaac whilst he blows a million and one glass baubles in preparation.' She picks up the book and begins flicking through the pages. 'Which role are you after then?'

'There's not that many substantial roles for females. I wouldn't want to be cast as Belle, nor the plump sister playing blind man's buff, and especially not the housekeeper, Mrs Dilber – no, thank you,' I say, screwing my nose up at the thought of a bit part.

'Who then?'

'Mrs Cratchit.'

'The clerk's wife?'

'Yeah. She's the only female with a decent amount of time onstage.'

'I thought you'd have wanted to be one of the ghosts – I could just see you as the Ghost of Christmas Present, with your long fiery locks flowing from beneath a hooded cape,' says Nessie, becoming animated with excitement.

I shake my head.

'Really? Why not?' asks Nessie, leaning on my countertop and flipping through my much-loved copy.

'I love the fact that the Cratchit family have very little in life apart from the warmth of human kindness and family ties. I want to try and show that connection onstage, portray the reality that you can be rich in life through what you share and bestow on others, even if you're utterly poor financially. Which still applies in our modern world today. Essentially, Dickens' tale is a retelling of the Christmas story where three wise men observe and pay homage, acting to secure the future of one special child.'

Nessie pauses, stares at me, before saying, 'That's a bit deep.'

I start to giggle; her quizzical expression is priceless. 'Sorry, but you did ask.'

'Note to self, don't ask in future,' chuckles Nessie.

'Stop it! You're now taking the mickey out of me. But there's one main scene where the family gather for Christmas Day, complete with a roaring hearth and candlelight, and genuine warmth is shown to every member of the family. It depicts an eternal light that will never dim or go out. I appreciate that Mrs Cratchit is frosty at first, but I want that scene as mine.'

'Based on that little speech, the part is yours, my dear!' says Nessie. Then she adds, 'Makes me want to reread it.'

'Mmmm, I don't get to give a speech to earn my part though, do I? I've opted to deliver a monologue as Curley's wife from *Of Mice and Men* for my audition.'

'Steinbeck?' she exclaims, to which I give an eager nod. 'I thought you were supposed to be having fun at this theatre stuff.'

'It is fun, in an odd kind of way. I'm trying to portray female emotion and ambition in a positive light,' I jest, hearing myself sounding quite serious.

'I believe you, thousands wouldn't. Anyway, I'm off! Otherwise Isaac will be sending out a posse of ghosts in search of me. Good luck with your audition, let me know how you get on.'

'I will, though I doubt I'll get much reading done today,' I whisper, as four more customers enter my barn.

Callie

'Callie, Jemima has just called. She's asking if you could spare a minute to drop by the office?' says Isla, as I return to the serving counter with a tray of dirty crockery. 'I'll see to that, you'll be there and back in no time.'

'Did she say what it was about?'

Isla shakes her head, then swiftly busies herself emptying the cold contents of the ceramic teapots.

I don't hesitate but immediately leave The Orangery, heading across the cobbled yard towards the tradesman's entrance, technically the back way into the manor. I push the green-painted door with some force; the bloody thing always sticks on the bottom edge. How long Dottie's been asking for that to be rectified is nobody's business. Once inside, I work my way through the warren of tiled corridors leading to the original kitchen; it has been updated as part of the refurbishment and is now used purely for serving the hotel guests. A quick jog through, avoiding the chef's impatient glare from behind the lights of his hot plate, and I'm soon heading towards the posher area of the manor where the Campbells and hotel guests reside.

Here, the standard red-tiled floors change to a classical geometric style of black and white, signifying the grand hallway. A corner section now houses the new reception desk, which represents quite a change from the olden days. And that reminds me – I really should make an effort to contact Autumn, the previous duty manager/receptionist. I faithfully promised to stay in touch when she left, a matter of months ago, to return to the life she knew best, working on the cruise ships. I shake my head in an effort to bypass my own guilt trip and hastily run up the grand staircase in search of the Campbells' office.

I'm not liking this. I feel out of place, despite it being my cousin's marital home. Our family are ordinary folk, so for her to have married into money and be living here still astounds me.

As I ascend the staircase, I can't help but glance at the ginormous chandelier hanging in the centre of the stairwell, around which swathes of burgundy velvet and Black Watch tartan hang, fighting for ceiling space. It's simply another world compared to the three-bed semi my parents bought on a local housing estate, some thirty-five years ago. I'm nearing the turn of the first landing when I lift my gaze and am greeted by generations of previous Campbells looking down their noses at me. From within their elaborate gilt frames, they retain their distinct air of respectability and poise, captured in their finery and silks. I bet the likes of them are wondering what the likes of me are even doing inside the manor. I quicken my pace and arrive at the first landing, which has recently become part of the hotel, along with the second floor. I'm slightly out of breath, but more in anticipation of Jemima's request to see me, rather than from the stair climbing.

Finally, I arrive on the third floor, taking a moment to delight in the sunshine pouring through the glazed skylight which partially runs the length of this floor before it changes to solid ceiling, signifying the beginning of the fourth, the old servants' quarters. Not a floor I've ever visited, but it's where our cousin Pippa now calls home, as well as other hotel staff who have opted to live in. I can see the advantages. But when would you ever be off-duty if you lived 'above the shop'?

I'm aware that this third landing is Ned and Jemima's private quarters, so I half expect to see him appear in his slippers, complete with his morning newspaper, though he never does. If I lived here, I wouldn't want employees seeing me first thing without my make-up. Boy, now that would be a shock for Ned – seeing me fresh faced! His ex-girlfriend was into beauty modelling so maybe he's used to seeing women who have a morning face and a day face. How he's found common ground with our Jemima baffles me, but they say opposites attract, don't they?

I make my way along, passing numerous closed wooden doors, until I reach the one opposite the ceramic jardinière with the large foliage plant.

I rap briskly on the door. I don't hesitate like other staff tell me they do; I've been summoned for a reason, so I want this done and dusted – good news or bad.

'Come in,' calls Jemima's voice.

Shoulders back, chin high, I enter the office. I'm always surprised by how modern it is after the traditional style of the hotel decor and grand staircase. It's a bright, airy space, with a large modern meeting table surrounded by matching chairs. Ned's untidy desk is positioned to one side, overflowing with paperwork. At first, I don't spy Jemima, but she's at the far end; the comfy area, with a couch and armchairs arranged in front of a decorative mantelpiece and hearth.

'Hello, I'm here,' she says, waving at me over the arm of the couch. 'My back's aching today, so a little comfort is called for.' She gently rubs her pregnancy bump and puffs out her cheeks.

'Hi, are you OK?'

'Yes, just tired and aching.'

She definitely looks it. Her dark glossy hair is pulled back into a ponytail, not our Jemima's usual hairstyle of artistic, messy bun. And her once glowing complexion, of which I'm usually so envious – how I wish I had her attractive olive colouring – has gained a waxy, sallow look.

I hesitate, taking in her appearance. My parents would be concerned if I relayed the details. My dad's not one for family fuss, but having lost his younger sister, Jemima's mum, to cancer only two years ago, he'd be right to show concern for his niece.

'You can come nearer, I promise I won't puke on you,' she says, with a giggle.

'Is that your standard line now?' I ask, striding nearer to show I have no qualms.

'No, but people's reactions make me laugh. Anyway, I wanted a quick word. Is there any chance you can do an extra alpaca walk on Monday?'

I'm relieved by her question. 'Sure. At what time?'

'We're not certain yet, but there's a party of eight tourists interested in the afternoon tea experience. We can make it a package deal on their room rate, you see, which helps everyone.'

'No worries, let me know the time and I'll organise my boys.'

I fall silent, to find her watching me.

We're now entering the awkward stage. I've been called to the office as an employee, yet the conversation is twisting and I sense family matters are about to arise.

'Are *you* OK?' she asks, turning my earlier question back on me, and looking me up and down from head to toe.

My uniform is correct, as always, so she won't spot a fault with my attire.

'Me? I'm plodding along, as I do.'

'You can take a seat, if you wish.' She gestures to one of the armchairs.

There it is. The boundary between employee and cousin has been crossed.

'I can't,' I say, quick to reject her offer. 'I've left Isla on her own. Aileen isn't due on shift for another hour.'

Jemima gives a bouncy nod of her head, and sighs loudly.

'Is there anything I can get you?' I ask, aware that company might be the thing she actually needed.

'No. Nothing. Dottie will be along in a moment to check that all is well. I'll let you know tomorrow about the arranged time for Monday's walk.' She pauses, glances away, before refocusing on me. She seems somewhat tentative. I get the impression she's hiding something or skirting around a topic, before she adds, 'Is there anything you need? You do know you only have to say?'

I nod, unsure where this is coming from. Hormones? Grief? Or a mindful Jemima, aware of family ties? Maybe she feels obliged to ask, seeing as Pippa lives here on the premises whereas I'm still at home with my parents.

'Likewise, Jemima. You too.'

She flashes me a brief smile. Suddenly, I glimpse a half-forgotten memory of my deceased aunty, resurrected through Jemima's mannerisms, from when I was a young child.

Chapter Nine

Monday 22 August

Heather

I pull the box file from the shelf and sigh heavily; this is a bitter-sweet moment when the pups morph from being ours into potentially belonging to other families. I've waited a week, ensuring that each pup is happy and healthy, thankfully confirmed by the veterinary practice, but now is the time to contact the people who've been patiently waiting for news. I'm diligent with the details I take; it might seem possessive, verging on obsessive, but I don't want any of my pups going to unworthy homes who won't treat them with the love and respect every dog deserves.

I'm sure some breeders don't give a monkey's what happens once the puppies have been sold, but I always ask that if any pup needs to be rehomed – whether as a result of family bereavement or divorce – I'm their first port of call; I'd rather negotiate a return price and welcome the pup home than risk these beautiful dogs being abandoned or gifted to rescue homes. In ten years, I've only ever had our Socks return to the fold, and that was definitely due to unforeseen circumstances.

I take a swig of my coffee before spreading the documents across the dining room table. Each family has already passed my stringent vetting criteria to join my waiting list. I make no promises, I don't supply puppies to order; my three girls and the breed standards are my priority. My heart sings at the evidence that I have such keen interest, shown from families far and wide. Each name has contact details and a brief outline of their family situation – in an attempt to meet my primary goal of providing each family with the best little dog they'll ever love. I never say 'own'; I believe the dog owns you, not the other way around. Only dog people will truly understand that.

The very thought of saying goodbye in twelve weeks to these lively bundles make me teary, but it has to happen. I can't keep them. They were bred to support and strengthen the future blood-line, preventing this beautiful breed from dying out. Another wave of emotion clogs my throat at the very thought of a world without Shelties.

'Come on! Crack on, before you talk yourself into a flood of tears,' I mutter to myself. My fingers nimbly separate the completed questionnaires into three piles – male, female or don't mind which gender – before putting each pile into completion date order. It's not a job I rush. I can't afford to, for the sake of the dogs. I swiftly write a working list:

> Pup 1 tricoloured girl
> Pup 2 tricoloured girl
> Pup 3 tricoloured girl
> Pup 4 sable boy
> Pup 5 sable girl
> Pup 6 sable girl

One peerie boy, wow! I glance at the pile of papers requesting consideration for a boy pup. It's the largest pile. Each family offering a loving home to a boy. Each awaiting a phone call asking if they're still interested or have they found their for ever dog elsewhere?

'Are you alright?'

I turn, to find Ellie lingering in the open doorway. I shrug, blubbing as big fat tears spill down my cheeks.

'You big softy!' she says, enveloping me in her arms, pressing my face into her warm shoulder. 'I thought you loved your job.'

'I do. I always act like this before calling folk. I love it, but I hate this bit; I feel I'm denying some families.'

'Yeah, but look how happy those who receive a call will be – you'll make their day!'

'I know. Every phone call brings joy to them, but a little bit of me has to say goodbye with each pup. I just wish I could keep them all.'

'Bloody hell, Mum – I'd move out if you did – this house couldn't cope with that amount of dog hair floating around!'

I start to laugh, but she's got a point. With the amount of daily grooming I have to do in order to keep just three beauties looking glamorous, our house would be covered in no time. I'm grateful that Pepper's done such a great job in the last week by keeping her pups clean, and saving me time each day.

'Come on, get these babies assigned to homes and then you'll feel happier. Do you want a hand?' asks Ellie.

'Thank you but no thanks, I need to focus. I'd hate to make mistakes and cause mix-ups.' I unfurl from her warm hug, feeling a whole lot better and slightly daft. Who cries doing a job they truly love?

'Do you want a fresh coffee?'

'Yep, it'll help to get this show on the road,' I say, settling at the table and grabbing the 'boy' paperwork pile.

Tabitha

I stand in the middle of our lounge and pause for breath for the first time in minutes.

'Done? Four minutes twenty,' says my dad, his fingers clasped around his watch face, timing my monologue.

'No way! It doesn't seem that long.'

'It bloody does when you haven't got a foggy what you're rabbiting on about,' he replies. 'Somewhat entertaining though.'

'Thanks,' I moan, begrudgingly, though I knew he wouldn't have a clue when I asked him to listen and time.

'Simply cut it in half, you'll do fine,' adds Mum, sitting along-side him on the couch.

'That's not quite the point, Mum. The woman's trying to convey a sense of . . . oh, it doesn't matter. I can't simply cut it in half and expect it to deliver the same message.'

'Does she have to do the wailing bit in the middle? That did look quite disturbing – and you said you wanted a positive portrayal.'

I bite my lower lip. I knew this was a bad idea before starting; neither of my parents have an interest in acting, but it seemed the only option. I should have asked Aileen if she wanted to meet up on our day off. I'd have received honest and trustworthy feedback, with a lot less hassle. Likewise, I'd have critiqued her practice piece.

'Why were you sitting on the floor for so long?' asks Dad, gesturing towards our hearth, where I'd started my monologue.

'Believe me, it was necessary, Dad. I wanted to show her growing in strength by standing up and finding her feet,' I say, knowing my dad doesn't do drama or interpretation.

'Oh yeah, I got that straight away,' he jests, with a bemused expression.

'I loved it. I'd give you the part straight away,' says Mum, glaring at my dad. 'Just stop before the wailing part, and I think it'll be much better. Right, who's for a cuppa?' I watch as she pushes herself up off the sofa, as if making tea can't wait. I suppose it provides a reasonable excuse to break off my performance rehearsal. They've said all they can, so it's time to crack on.

'Not for me, thanks. I'll go and give Aileen a quick call – see what she's up to,' I say, making a mental note of the official timing: four minutes twenty.

I sit spellbound in Aileen's kitchen whilst she performs her personal audition piece as Shaw's Eliza Doolittle. Why, oh why, did I think this was a good idea? I've got nothing but high praise to give – and that horrible sinking feeling in my stomach as I realise my audition piece is nowhere near as good!

Aileen freezes into a tableau to end, as Ebenezer likes us to do.

My eyes flicker up to the wall clock before announcing, 'One minute fifty-five – spot on! That was excellent, Aileen.'

'Do you think so? I'm not sure Ebenezer will like it, but then I wanted to show him I'm ready for meatier roles and not just these walk-on parts he keeps giving me. I swear if I have to be one more pedestrian walking upstage, I'll quit. Seriously, I will. Watch, this was my part in *Breakfast at Tiffany's* . . .'

I watch as Aileen strolls around me and her kitchen table, glancing at the ceiling, then casually admiring the floor tiles before taking a passing interest in the cooling teapot and walking on by. 'And this was me in *The Importance of Being Earnest* . . . simply a pedestrian walking by and ignoring a leather handbag left in Victoria Station.'

I giggle as Aileen re-enacts her difficult role before her fridge freezer.

'Which is very similar to my part as a passer-by in—'

'Stop, please! I can't cope with witnessing such an Oscar-winning performance,' I say, between giggles.

'It's only fair that I get a decent part this time, otherwise I'm history. Ebenezer can look elsewhere for his walk-on roles, because I'll be throwing off this amateur status and turning professional.'

'Aileen, you are funny.'

'Tell that to Ebenezer, please – he might even cast me in a humorous role.'

'But seriously, what are you going for?'

Aileen quickly sits down opposite me and leans across the table, excitement flashing in her hazel eyes. 'Well, between me and you . . . I don't want to tread on people's toes, but I want one of the roles as a ghost. Any of them, I don't mind which. And you?'

'Mrs Cratchit.'

Aileen sits back slowly. 'Really? I'd have thought you'd opt for something bigger.'

I shake my head.

'You know that Kenzie wants that part too, don't you?'

My heart sinks. 'Don't tell me that. I don't want there to be any bad feeling about the casting decisions.'

'Yeah, she mentioned it as we left the theatre last Thursday night.' Aileen sucks in her cheeks and purses her lips. 'Awkward when that happens, isn't it?'

'Just a tad,' I murmur, my gaze fixed on hers.

Callie

'If you'd like to follow me . . . this way,' I call to the party of eight hotel guests.

This is the part that can be slightly fractious, because many guests are slightly hyper, almost like overgrown children, after

completing their ninety-minute alpaca trek. They don't hear
instructions, can't stand still long enough to listen, want to repeat
the experience straight away, or are too busy texting friends and
family – anything other than following me.

'Through the stone archway and across the cobbled yard we
go, heading towards The Orangery for your delicious afternoon
tea.' I'm talking to myself, I know I am, but it's the norm. I've
got used to it in recent months.

The moment of calm arrives as the guests approach the large
glazed door. I've noticed that manoeuvring the weight and
holding it politely open for the person behind appears to be the
'return to normality' switch.

'Hi,' says Isla, donning a clean waitressing pinny and gesturing
towards the rear of the seating area.

I spy a selection of plates, coffee mugs and tea cups awaiting
our arrival on a low coffee table, surrounded by couches.

'Make yourselves at home, folks,' I say, waiting while they
settle, before introducing Isla. 'This is Isla, our manager at The
Orangery. She'll be taking your drinks orders. Afternoon tea
includes a hot beverage of your choice, plus a tipple from the
hotel bar. Please peruse the menus, and Isla will oblige.'

I breathe a sigh of relief once Isla steps forward. She hands
out the cream-coloured menu cards listing their choices. This is
my moment to disappear into the rear storage room, as the first
part of my duties is completed.

I close the door and pull the tiny lock across for a moment's
privacy. The system works very well. Isla entertains the guests
during my absence, with witty chat and questions about their trek
and the antics of the alpacas, while I get a few minutes to change
out of my trekking gear into suitable attire for waitressing.

When I return, I take over as their waitress. Isla prepares the
hot drinks and I take them to the table, before distributing a tray
of drinks from the hotel bar. It makes me smile when I see how

few guests notice that I've changed my outfit before reappearing to assist. A quick tidy of my hair, a slick application of lip gloss, and I'm good to go!

'I've phoned their bar order through, so it'll be delivered in a few minutes,' says Isla, as I return to the serving counter where she's busy spooning tea leaves into a row of teapots. 'They seem a bubbly bunch.'

'They certainly are. I think they've got ideas of rebooking another trek before their holiday finishes at the end of this week.'

'Impressive stuff, full marks to you!' she says, pouring boiling water carefully into each ceramic teapot.

'Maybe, but I'll need to take care which boys I select. We're already booked for treks midweek and next weekend.'

Isla fits the lid to each pot and slides them towards a waiting tray. I take the hint and begin loading, as raucous laughter erupts from the couches.

'And that's before their tipple,' I say, gesturing towards the cobbled yard as the new bell boy-cum-waiter appears at the glazed entrance.

'Good luck! I hope they leave you a decent tip,' says Isla, collecting tiny milk jugs from a nearby shelf.

'Hi there, thanks for those,' I say, wrenching open the door before standing back and allowing the dark-haired guy to pass.

'No worries. Do you know there's a duck swimming in the water trough?' he says, the glasses clinking on the tray as he gestures towards the cobbled courtyard.

'Yeah, that'll be Crispy duck – the owner's pet,' I say, realising that I barely even notice the creature some days.

'Weird, but still. Where do you want these?' he asks.

'Anywhere over there. I'll take them across,' I say, indicating the serving counter. 'If they need top-ups, are you free to bring another round over?'

'Sure. Just phone through like you did before,' he says.

I don't correct his error, as it was Isla who phoned through, but he's new to Lerwick Manor and probably finding his feet around here.

'I'm Callie, by the way, and that's Isla.'

Isla obliges us with a smile.

'I'm Rabbie. Today's my first day.'

Chapter Ten

Wednesday 24 August

Heather

'Who do I have?' asks Isla, sitting cross-legged on the lounge floor and cradling a tricoloured pup wearing a yellow paper collar.

'Let me check.' I reach for my clipboard with the pups' details. 'Yellow-collared pup is Skye, and she'll be heading to her island namesake.'

'Hi, Skye. And the orange-collared pup?'

'Isla, haven't we gone through these once?'

'We have, but I can't remember them all.'

I've spent the last few days on the telephone contacting various families. Having received confirmation of their continued interest, along with speedy deposits sent via online banking, I now have an official list of the pups' for ever home names.

'I haven't got all their names straight, either.' I peer at my vital list, knowing each family's chosen name must be memorised in the coming days. 'Orange collar is Emily, and her family will be travelling from Yorkshire to collect her when the time comes.'

'Pink?'

I love Isla's interest, but it's like déjà vu; I knew she wasn't listening last night when I read the completed list aloud.

'OK, pin those ears back, my peerie pup, listen and learn. Yellow collar is Skye, orange is Emily, pink is Marble who's staying here in Shetland – heading for beautiful Fetlar. Green is

Sheba and purple is Sherbert – the last two are staying together but going to a family in America.'

'That's nice, and the boy?'

I don't need to look for the name penned beside the blue-collared pup; there isn't one.

'Mum?'

'What?' I snap, knowing my daughter knows me better than I imagine or admit to.

Isla gives me a look.

'Don't. I'm undecided, that's all. The paperwork pile for a boy pup is massive. I just need a few more days to mull over the interested families.'

'Yeah, right,' mutters Isla, returning Skye to her mother and giving the nameless, homeless blue boy a gentle tickle. 'You're staying here, peerie boy.'

'No, he's not!' I chunter.

Isla throws me a coy smile. Bloody daughters, they think they know my every thought. Well, this time she's wrong. Totally wrong!

There's silence as the future of little boy blue is pondered by us both, even Pepper twitches her eyebrows in my direction. Admittedly, the dog probably does know what I'm thinking.

'Are you going out tonight?' asks Isla, gingerly offering me yet another coy smile.

'No. Friday, maybe.'

'Maybe? Bloody hell, my mum's actually got a date, while I'm pup sitting at twenty! Talk about role reversal!'

'Oi, don't be so bloody cheeky! You said I don't look my age.'

'You don't, but even so, I'll be stuck here learning puppy names while you're out gallivanting around Lerwick. Dare I ask who?'

I bite my lip. 'Isla, I'd prefer not to say.'

'That doesn't sound good.'

Not what I wanted to hear.

'Please, Isla.'

'Please what? Please no comment, or please don't ask?'

'Both. This isn't easy for me, you know. If I thought for one minute that I'd be swiping snapshots of available men at my age . . . argh, I'm simply not discussing this.'

'You're only forty-five!'

'Only? Listen to you – that line actually makes me sound ancient.'

'No. What you actually mean is you're not discussing it with me. I bet you tell Ellie,' she mutters, watching my stony expression. 'You tell her everything.'

She's not wrong, but the two-year gap between my girls makes a huge difference. Not that our Ellie is any more streetwise where men are concerned – her love interests seem to be fleeting, at best – but Isla didn't have the most positive first experience, thanks to sodding Lachlan Gray, so I'm overly cautious about what I mention.

'Hello, I'm right, aren't I? You'll tell her if she asks.'

'Isla, I'm wary of you getting the wrong impression of guys . . . if all you hear is bad stuff. Please don't give me attitude when I'm trying to protect you in the best way I can. Not all blokes treat women like that Lachlan lad treated you. I trusted him with my daughter, and what did he do? Treated you badly, very badly indeed. He played games and screwed with your head – that's not what dating and relationships should be about, Isla.'

Isla's expression mellows as she leans towards Pepper and selects the green-collared pup for a snuggle . . . Sheba, I think that's right. My words have hit home, I can see that. I'd happily discuss my situation if, and it's a big if, I could promise that my first date would go well and any subsequent relationship could be guaranteed to flourish healthily. But with my track record, I don't want to be introducing false or hurtful impressions of men into my younger daughter's psyche. God knows what potential damage that might cause her future relationships – and her ability to trust her heart to a man again.

'Isla, try to see it from my point of view,' I say, my voice softer than usual, rather like when I'm dealing with the pups.

'I am. I just feel as if you treat me like a little kid when it suits.'

She's got a point, but from where I'm sitting, watching a young woman cradle a pup, not unlike the ten year old she once was, it's easy to see where I'm coming from. Her birthdays may have passed in the blink of an eye, but she's still the tiny child I loved and raised.

'Are all your dates from that app?' she asks.

I nod. That app is correctly named 'Shetland Singles' and is actually the latest thing here, not that I was eager to upload my profile. But needs must, if I'm to attempt to 'get out there and mingle', as Ellie says. I still blush at the thought that I have a personal bio and a colour photograph. Men are swiping left, right – up, down, whatever! – based purely on their first impressions. For all I know, the local butcher, baker and candlestick maker might have instantly swiped me aside.

'Where are you going? Surely you can tell me that.'

'To a local bar for a drink, that's all.'

'It's not one of my old school teachers, is it?'

'Isla!'

'Oh seriously, Mum. I'm moving out if you start dating Mr Karlsson!'

'As if.' In my dreams, I think but don't say.

I still find it hard to imagine any guy would ever look in my direction. Now the girls are off my hands a little more, it feels right that I should venture out, meet new people and socialise – even if it's purely for companionship, decent conversation, and the opportunity to make new friends outside the family unit.

'Mum! I mean it.'

'You enjoyed your history classes – it was a subject you were good at.'

'I know, but there's no way I'm sharing a breakfast table with my old teacher, thanks a bunch.' Her expression says it all: she means it.

'Isla, rest assured my date is not Mr Karlsson from your old school.'

As if dating wasn't already bad enough here in Shetland! Not only am I challenged by the demographics, the rural locations and the limited population of an island community, but I must be the only woman in the local area with an 'avoidance list' of which men I'm forbidden to date, created by her daughters. Isla's list includes all her past teachers, while Ellie's list includes the unattached fathers of any young men she currently likes. Fear not, I've assured her, I can't imagine her potential beau becoming my son-in-law, having previously become a grown-up stepson! Is that correct? Given the absurd relationships in my own family, you'd think I'd have no problem getting my head around a blended family set-up. Have I thought that through correctly – stepson turning into son-in-law? My daughter marrying my potential partner's grown-up son? Too weird to think about, in all honesty; plus it makes for another source of stress come Christmas dinner, so it's a definite no-no.

Isla throws me another black look.

'Honest? A cross my heart and hope to die promise, Mum, OK?'

I see her settle back into her skin; she believes me. I'll stick to my word, I always do, but I recall how lovely Mr Karlsson was at parents' evening. He was always fully booked! My face takes on a dreamy look.

'Mum! Stop it!' Isla admonishes me.

A couple of tiny heads shoot up at the sudden noise.

'Shhhhh, please, you'll scare the pups. I assure you, tonight's date is not Mr Karlsson.'

I'm not that lucky.

Callie

'And next time you're expecting so many boxes, please let your father know beforehand,' scolds my mother, the second I walk through the front door after a long and tiring day. 'He was trying to watch the lunchtime news when the doorbell rang. He was out there so long that he missed the headlines completely.'

'Yeah, yeah, whatever . . .' My autopilot answer trails off as I'm greeted by a wall of brown cardboard boxes stacked neatly against the hallway wall. 'What are these?'

'That's exactly what your father asked when the delivery guy arrived. Not our usual parcel postie but the one who brings bulky items in a Transit van. Your father helped him unload,' calls my mother, before disappearing into the kitchen.

This isn't normal for me. My parcels are usually delivered by the Postman Pat mini-van; they are small, neat and fit easily through the letter box. Admittedly, there's usually a couple each week, but that's a drastic reduction compared to six months ago when I often had five envelopes or small parcels awaiting my arrival home. The most my parents had to do was sign on a screen, which they frequently complained about.

I peer at the first address label, to find my name clearly printed in bold type. 'Are they all for me?' I whisper, moving to the next box, quickly followed by its neighbour. Shit! They *are* all for me. What the hell have I done?

My mum appears in the doorway between the hall and kitchen. 'Birthday presents, are they?'

'Ummm, something like that.' The word Christmas swims

about my mind, chilling my heart at the very thought. We're only in August! 'Could you pass the scissors, please?' There's no point in truly panicking until I open a box and discover what's inside.

It might be something useful and prove essential to my daily life. And given the quantity, it needs to be. Or it could be an oversized box containing lots of polystyrene packaging and a tiny parcel pressed into the bottom corner. Yeah, it's probably that. Some suppliers rarely think about the environment. My heart rate settles a little, my palms cease sweating quite as much, and my brain gleefully settles on that story.

My mum passes me her favourite kitchen scissors and I open the blades before slicing through the brown tape securing the nearest box – probably one of my favourite noises. The flap springs open to reveal chunky white pasta-shaped polystyrene. Lots of packaging. Phew!

'Ah, lovely,' I utter, with a sigh, putting the scissors aside before plunging my hands into the pasta shapes. Immediately, an inch from the open top, is a second box. A big box. Ah, not as small as I'd hoped. Whatever mystery it holds, maybe the price was dirt cheap – which is what matters the most, in my circumstances.

'What the hell do you need with twenty sets of mega-barrel hairbrushes?' asks my father, peering at the boxes displaying the unique brush, alongside colour-coordinated combs, complete with a soft leatherette pouch for easy storage.

'Christmas presents,' I mutter, in an attempt to convince myself and not my father.

'We're only in August!' he rants, seeking my mother's reaction to justify his own.

'Dad, these things sell out like hot bannocks, there's no knowing how much the true price would be if I had to purchase them nearer to December,' I lie, unsure how much I've actually paid.

'My God, I don't even know twenty people, let alone buy them a brand-new brush set each!' exclaims my father, moving aside the set I'd opened to demonstrate its quality, conveniently leaving it on his sofa cushion. 'I missed the news headlines unloading this lot. Hardly worth it, was it?'

'No . . . er, no,' is my uncertain reply. Not to his question but to the one floating around my head. Can I afford these? My maths mightn't be the best, but even I can do the mental arithmetic: If Callie buys twenty hair brushes for thirty pounds each, how much change will she have out of six hundred quid? Yeah, that's right, diddly squat. I conveniently forget the additional P&P charge.

And here comes the second part of the question: How much interest will Callie be charged in subsequent months, if she pays by credit card? Lord knows, but they won't be a bargain buy. Not by the time I've paid them off!

What the hell have I done? What's the returns policy for these goods? How much will the postage be? Can I feign a stolen credit card? How drunk was I last Thursday night?

I swear, I'm never getting into buying rounds again.

Chapter Eleven

Tabitha

I stand alongside a huddle of actors in the wings, tucked behind the stage curtain, and watch as Kenzie delivers an introduction to her piece onstage. Experience has taught me that I should focus on my own audition speech before delivery, rather than being distracted by what my fellow actors have selected, otherwise I end up being a nervous wreck.

Kenzie has hinted to Aileen that she's chosen something a little different, in order to impress Ebenezer. I should have given up the ghost after witnessing Aileen's delivery on Monday, but I didn't; and having listened to her earlier tonight onstage, I'm sure she's thrilled to bits with her efforts. Round two – Ebenezer's script reading – might scupper many of us, as it's a tricky task. I'm never great at immediate delivery; I can't always project my voice or convey the intended emotion when I first read a piece. I need time to digest the meaning of the language and gestures if I'm to do it justice.

The lucky few who have already performed have taken seats in the rear of the auditorium; they're welcome to watch as long as no one interrupts or disturbs Ebenezer's focus, sitting in the front row.

I stand tall as Kenzie approaches me, collecting her guitar from behind the stage curtain.

'Good luck,' I whisper, knowing how daunting the process is. Maturity has to kick in one day when it comes to chasing my dream, but it's hard to know how to make things happen when there are so few people who take acting as seriously as I do. I'm trying to pick up some tips from Ebenezer – to learn from his illustrious career – but he's not been very forthcoming, so far. I'm not saying I'll reach the heady heights of Hollywood or the West End, but surely I can aim for a career acting somewhere? Be it small bit parts in regional productions, maybe some minor TV work, or even commercials – I'll happily start with toothpaste commercials, if that's what it takes to get a lucky break. Though it would mean leaving Shetland, the home I've always known.

I'm not boasting, or pretending I have more talent than the rest of our am-dram company, but I do have a different mindset. Others will attend every few weeks, dropping by here and there; I never do. Others are a little half-hearted when practising their lines, their stage directions, or researching their roles; I never am. If I could choose anything to spend my time doing, day after day, it would be acting. And as for all those people who suggest I'll never make it, regardless of my hard work and effort . . . well, every audition has a winner, so I need to keep chasing my dream.

Kenzie returns to centre stage, throws her guitar strap nervously over her head and shoulder, then settles in front of the microphone. She's taking a gamble, but who can blame her? Within two bars I recognise the song, 'Somewhere Over The Rainbow', and I know she's on to a winner. She's very talented, professional in her delivery, and has chosen a haunting arrangement of what is often dismissed as a cheesy anthem.

She's nailed it and, despite going way over on the timings, Ebenezer didn't cut her short. Which secretly, I'm glad about.

His decision is final – there'll be no swaying him, no cajoling – so there's little point in discussing any grievance. What will be, will be. I pray my performance secures me the role of Mrs Cratchit, not one of the medley of more minor female roles.

'Thank you. That's all,' calls Ebenezer from his position in front of the stage.

I peer around the edge of the curtain to satisfy my need to know how much I can see of him. I much prefer it when he sits midway back in the stalls. He's not, he's perched on the front row, his clipboard balanced on his knee and his pen held aloft, eager to make notes on each audition.

Kenzie turns on the spot, her big expressive eyes signalling relief, before heading down the stage steps, along with her guitar, to take her seat at the back of the auditorium.

'Freddie and Rabbie!' calls Ebenezer, glancing up from his clipboard.

There's a flurry of activity alongside me in the wings as both men appear, grinning like Cheshire cats, before stepping out on to the stage, side by side. No one said they would be auditioning as a duo; this might prove to be their downfall or a stroke of genius.

I spy one of the cast holding their phone against an off-stage mic and tapping the screen. A cheerful piano intro begins, instantly identifying the comedy duo and their signature theme tune, which our guys are attempting to emulate.

'Which one do you reckon is Morecambe?' whispers Mavis, another actor, standing beside me.

'I assume Freddie's playing Ernie Wise, given their height difference.'

'I can't imagine Ebenezer being impressed by their singing – what a racket,' says Old Reg, covering his ears.

I peer around the stage curtain again, to get a view of Ebenezer's frozen expression beneath his shock of white hair. 'He doesn't look like a happy bunny.'

'Not bringing much sunshine then?' scoffs Deacon, from our acting huddle.

'Doesn't look like it.' I admire them for thinking outside the box. But knowing Ebenezer as well as I do, they were foolish to run with the idea. You need to showcase your skills in an audition, not annoy the director.

'Cut!' cries Ebenezer after the allotted two minutes, much to my surprise. 'Thank you!'

I cringe for them both as the music ceases and they embark on what seems like a long walk from the stage to the back row of the stalls, under a shadow of regret.

'Tabitha!'

'Great! I'm supposed to follow that,' I mutter, receiving an encouraging pat on the back from the final few thespians awaiting their turn.

I take a deep breath, clear my mind of the other auditions, and walk out from behind the curtain. My footsteps echo on the empty stage. It isn't a sound I often hear, being more accustomed to the noise that usually accompanies our weekly theatre session, but tonight's different.

I crouch down and settle in a sitting position, centre stage, surrounded by darkness; I know that other hearts are beating in rhythm with mine, a short distance away in the wings. The anticipation, the sense of expectation, builds. Nerves jangle inside me like the grains in a salt shaker. I like my nerves; they don't discourage me. I've heard Ebenezer complain that some actors are 'always nervous' because they don't prepare enough, but theatre's not like an exam. The nerves don't diminish in proportion to the amount of pre-prep and study. Stage nerves are a positive attribute, a side effect of performing – or 'showtime', as others say. Yes, they're pesky, they make me doubt myself and force me to continually run back and forth to the bathroom for the hour before walking out on to the stage, but they're as necessary as the electricity that buzzes through the lighting rig.

In the school nativity, all those years ago, I was an angel, not a part I wanted, standing on the back row, beside a tea-towel-wearing shepherd. I'd have preferred to be centre stage, clutching a swaddled doll. Sadly, I wasn't. I suspect my fiery-red locks put a stop to my audition chances. My tinsel halo was askew, my dress was a bed sheet, and my bare feet were cold on the splintered wooden boards, but I have relived and returned to that first moment more times than I care to admit. The moment when I looked out across the audience, seated neatly in rows, and saw a blur of faces smudged into one. I might have spent what felt like aeons learning my one little line, 'Hark, a baby in a stable!' But I delivered it with as much feeling and depth as anyone can, aged five. I didn't know what 'hark' meant, and I was baffled by the stable location, but still I delivered my line on cue, unlike many of the other children, who mostly failed to contribute to the school festivities. The sound of camera clicks, the sight of smiling faces, and the annoying jigging of the shepherd wanting the toilet, simply ignited my sense of destiny and I knew what I wanted to be in life.

Every day since then has been tailored towards making my dreams come true: learning dance routines on the lino in my parents' kitchen; grabbing any unfortunate relative who said they had ten minutes to spare and urging them to test me on my lines; walking around reciting speeches inside my head. And all whilst missing the main events of family life. Growing up, I tried for every part that took my fancy, ignoring comments and opinions from others about casting. I memorably argued that an auburn-haired Alice was 'refreshing' amongst a gaggle of blonde actors. From primary school onwards, each year has been remembered for that year's show and nothing else.

'When you're ready,' calls Ebenezer, his face almost blotted out by the glare of the footlights.

I take a few more deep breaths, transforming into Curley's wife.

Callie

'Callie!'

I switch my hairdryer off and listen, before responding. Was that my mother calling from downstairs?

'Callie!' she repeats.

'Yeah!' I bark back. I felt I had to show willing, to cover my embarrassment about the boxes of brushes, so I've washed my hair and am now partway through styling it with my new big-barrelled brush.

'The phone. For you.'

I glance down at my silent phone beside me; the screen is blank. No text. No missed call. Someone has called the landline? That's unheard of!

'Coming down!' I yell, throwing my hairdryer on to the duvet and launching myself from my bed. This must be an emergency. One of my friends? One of their parents perhaps? A hospital job?

I dash down the staircase and take the proffered receiver from Mum's outstretched palm. This feels like a return to my teenage years when I didn't have a mobile and the landline was simply called 'the telephone'.

'Thanks.'

Mum squeezes past the boxes and shuffles back towards the lounge.

'Hello?' I say tentatively.

'Hi, Callie, Jayden here. I was wondering if you were available to cover a shift on Friday night. It's a local venue, eighteenth birthday bash, nothing too strenuous. Cash in hand, so to speak. I've had a staff member call in sick, so I thought I'd give you a call.'

Jayden? Who? Cash in hand?

'Sorry, who am I speaking to?'

'Jayden. We met last week in town – might have been Thursday night. I thought this was the perfect opportunity to offer you a shift. If you're available,' comes the guy's deep voice.

'I'm available, but for what exactly?'

'Bar work. You mentioned you were looking for extra work. I supply bar staff for private hire venues – we work the bar and serve food, depending on the requirements of the occasion.'

Did I? I have no recollection of this guy or our conversation. The pause is lengthy.

'Look, it's fifty quid for serving a few drinks. The shift won't go past midnight. I can call elsewhere if—'

'No, I'll take it. Sorry. I was just grabbing paper and pen to make a note of the details – what's the address of the venue?'

'It's the Islesburgh Community Centre – I'll need you to help set up behind the bar from six thirty, sharp.'

'Yeah, OK.' I'm still a little stunned, but I'll give it a shot. It'll be a squeeze, after leaving The Orangery, stabling the alpacas, then getting showered and changed for a six thirty arrival.

'Right you are, Callie. I'll see you on Friday. If you could wear a black and white combo you'll match with the other bar staff.'

'Sure. Thanks.'

'Cheers. Bye now.'

I replace the handset. My mind fills with countless questions, the main one being: how drunk was I last Thursday night? Still, I'm impressed that I actually remembered the landline number after a night on the town!

Chapter Twelve

Friday 26 August

Callie

'Good morning, Callie,' Isla calls out from the behind the counter as I enter The Orangery.

'Is it!' I snort. I'm definitely wearing my grumpy pants today.

She does a double take and smiles at me, obviously unsure whether to go there or not. I take my handbag and coat through to the back room, and breathe. I've been berating myself constantly since my latest spending splurge, even waking myself up in the night after dreaming about it, and now I'm stupidly bringing my troubles to work. I can't take this out on others – but sodding hell! If I've drunkenly purchased a brush set for Isla as her Christmas present then I probably have thirty quids' worth of resentment to work out of my system. Colleagues might need to put up with my sourpuss mood and earn their gift. At least that way it'll have double meaning as a Christmas present-cum-apology – two for the price of one!

'What needs doing?' I ask, returning to the front counter as if my earlier snap dragon act hadn't occurred.

'This, for a start.' Isla pushes a freshly made latte in my direction and gestures to the nearest table. 'Shall we?'

Oh shit. I hesitate before leading the way; she's obviously thought this one through.

I settle in a comfy armchair. Isla sits cosily opposite, dipping her fruit tea bag in a mug of steaming water.

'How are we?'

'We?'

'You, then.' Her tone is soft, encouraging.

'I'm . . .' I ponder my choice of word. It's kind of her to ask, but I don't wish to say too much; she works for my cousin, after all. 'I'm . . .' I should be honest and say what I'm feeling. But not so honest that I regret it. Or that it gets me into trouble. 'I'm . . . pissed off!' It's out before I can rein it in.

'OK. At what?'

'Life!' Sodding hell, how honest should I be at just gone half nine on a Friday morning?

Isla nods, dips her tea bag a few more times, before looking up and meeting my gaze. 'Yeah, I can kind of tell.' She pulls a grimacing expression.

'Not good, hey?'

'Not really. Ned received a couple of complaints last week about your curtness, verging on rudeness, to customers . . . and, well, I've spotted it myself, to be fair.'

'Who complained?' I notice she hasn't referred to Jemima; that would have been pressing my buttons, quoting her name.

'Does it matter, Callie?'

'If it's Mungo, he can talk,' I quickly say, hoping to deflect attention from my own situation. 'He's as grumpy as the Grinch. He only lightens up when he's got some gossip, or Levi is due to arrive.'

'Mungo is very sweet when you get to know him. It took me a while, but I'm there now. But this isn't about him, Callie – it's about you. You seem so . . .' She pauses.

Great, we're both playing a game of word selection whilst tiptoeing around the scattered eggshells. 'I want to say tense, but that doesn't quite cover it.'

'Tense?' I repeat.

'Uptight might be more fitting.'

'Uptight?'

Isla nods, removes her tea bag, places it on her saucer and distracts herself by stirring the tea in her mug. Her auburn hair is secured under a hairnet for health and hygiene, her freckled complexion enhanced with a touch of make-up, but she's as fresh and artless as they come.

The silence lengthens. My cue to speak, supposedly. Isla sips her fruit tea as if I wasn't present; she's not scrutinising me, not staring, not watching anything, just sipping her tea. It's a ploy I've seen our Jemima use a million times. Boy, is this one a mini-Mima prodigy, or what? She'll wait now, give me time to think, to answer, to convey whatever is troubling me. Bloody hell, I might as well have our Jemima seated before me. She'll come out with a well-chosen line any second now.

Isla's gaze flickers to meet mine. 'I know it can't be easy opening up, but we work together virtually every day, Callie. I've noticed a difference in you, these past few weeks. I simply want to offer my help and support, if I can.'

Bingo, there it is! My God, she is a carbon copy of my younger cousin. Which definitely means I'm not opening up, because our Jemima has a memory like an elephant and would remember every word I say.

I shift in my seat, take a sip of my cooling latte, before answering. 'Sorry, I'm a tad off colour. I'll make more of an effort . . . with customers . . . with staff and the artists. Do I need to speak to Ned about the complaints?'

'No, he was very sympathetic about it. Said everyone has their off days, but—'

'I have more than most . . . is that what you're saying?'

Isla chews her lip as if holding back and editing her reply. 'No, I'd say that you're caught off guard more than most. I realise the situation between you and Pippa isn't great, and maybe that colours your mood ... or your day.'

She's handed me a get out of jail card, without realising.

'Well, actually yeah,' I say. 'She rubs me up the wrong way most days. And yeah, I suppose I let it get to me, and sometimes it filters through during a shift.' Phew! Thank you, Isla.

'I see. Can you imagine a time when this ... situation, will be resolved?'

'Doubt it! Though it's better than it once was,' I say jauntily, not wishing to sound quite so stroppy.

Isla nods. 'In that case, I just wanted to touch base and say, if there's anything I can do to ease the situation then please just say. I hope your feelings towards Pippa don't affect you for much longer ... if you get my drift. Ned was understanding about the recent complaints, and asked me to have a quiet word with you, but future ones might be addressed by him and not me.'

'OK. Thank you ... I appreciate it.'

'If there's nothing else ...?' Her words linger a fraction longer than her gaze.

I shake my head.

'OK, shout if there is.'

'Sure. Thanks.'

Isla pushes her chair back and makes to stand up, before adding, 'Callie ... I'm not one for gossiping, so I will respect your privacy if you need to talk.'

'I never doubted that, Isla.'

'Good. Remember, I'm just a phone call away!' Her tone brightens, her smile too, as she collects her drink and wanders back to the counter.

I linger for a moment, sipping my latte, and feeling relieved that I didn't utter a word to Isla about my money worries. This is not the start I wanted, especially as I've a long day ahead of me, with my first shift for Jayden this evening. From today, I need to make sure that I'm on top of this role – because despite my two side ventures, if I lose my main waitressing job I'll be in serious hot water.

Tabitha

'Morning, Rabbie, I thought it was you,' I say, heading towards my soapery but diverting my route to speak to the guy I've just spotted descending the steps at the entrance to Lerwick Manor.

'Hi, Tabitha. Yeah, it's me. I started here last week as a bell boy slash waiter,' he says, sounding bright but not looking too enthused at the prospect.

'Enjoying it?'

'So far. Though I've mainly been shadowing other staff – learning the ropes, so to speak.'

'I looked out for you last night but . . .'

He grimaces as though I've touched a nerve.

'After Wednesday night, I thought I'd give it a miss. It wasn't our best performance, was it?'

I hate to agree but can't avoid a sympathetic shake of the head. 'Probably not your finest hour . . . but still, you should have shown up. Ebenezer was full of the joys of spring. He led a decent session, based around mime helping to encapsulate and portray deeper emotions.'

'Cool, though I bet it was all furrowed brows and wide eyes,' he says, with a hint of mischief.

'Yeah, it was a bit intense, but it could be useful in future, depending on the role.'

'I went to the pub.' He looks as guilty as sin.

'With Freddie?'

'Nah, with my mates. Did Fred not show either?'

'No. I imagined you were both drowning your sorrows together.'

Rabbie shakes his head. 'I shouldn't have agreed to it in the first place. But I felt sorry for him – he made a complete prat of himself with the Shakespearean skit, so I went along with it. I knew it wasn't the right audition piece for me, and yet I still did it. I was trying to be fair and support a mate, but it's well and truly backfired. The minute we started to sing, Ebenezer's expression crumpled into a frown. I just knew. I wanted to end it right there and revert back to my original piece.'

'Which was?'

'It doesn't matter.' He sounds utterly deflated, in need of a pick-me-up.

'Rabbie, I'm trying to be as supportive as you were to Freddie. Out with it!' I cajole.

He brushes the tip of his polished black shoe against the gravel of the driveway and gives me a sideways glance, before answering. 'Do you know who John McClane is?'

'As in *Die Hard*?' I say instantly.

'Yeah!' Rabbie's face lights up, causing his dark eyes to twinkle. 'I'd prepared a speech from where he does battle with the hostage takers. Basically, trying to show a mixture of acting styles and emotion in a masculine way but, well . . . then I tried to do Freddie a favour by switching acts.'

'Heck! You need to be a little selfish in this game.'

'I'm realising that now. Did Ebenezer say when the casting list would be announced?'

'Tuesday. He's going to pin the cast list on the noticeboard in the library downtown so everyone has a chance to see it before Thursday night. If you come to the meeting, that is.'

'I'll come. I can't avoid Ebenezer, though no doubt I'll be assigned to backstage duties alongside Freddie.'

'You'll have fun, whatever role you're awarded.'

'Mmmm, I hope so . . . anyway, I must get going. I've got a

full shift today, unlike tomorrow.' He shakes his head, looking deflated.

'What's with tomorrow's shift?' I ask.

'A split shift. Four hours in the morning, clock off, then back for four hours in the evening. Nothing in the afternoon, which means I can't start anything or go anywhere, as I need to be back here by five thirty, but I can't just hang around here and waste the time, either. Simply dead time on a weekend, not good.'

'And that happens every Saturday?'

'It looks that way. I seem to have drawn the short straw on the rota system. Other staff will have split shifts on other days, but a Saturday? Man, that sucks!'

'Interesting! I might have a solution for your down time.'

His ears prick up at the mention, so I spend the next few minutes outlining my own issue on a Saturday during my busy time slot. I could certainly do with a couple of hours' extra help.

'I'll speak to Ned and see what he thinks,' I promise Rabbie.

'Cool. I'm happy to help, Tabs. It does me a favour in the long run – saves me going home for a wasted afternoon.'

Tabs? I feel an instant blush creep up my neck. Oh dear, on second thoughts – how will I be able to cope in his presence for an extra two hours a week? This might prove to be the ultimate test of my acting abilities!

Callie

The doors to the Islesburgh Community Centre swing shut behind me.

'Sorry I'm late.' Not the best opening line on arriving for my first shift, but hey, I'm being honest.

Three blank faces, belonging to my new work colleagues, stare at me from behind the bar as the clock hands nudge towards quarter to eight.

'I got caught up with my previous job,' I explain, realising how lame it sounds.

Why I carry on speaking is beyond me, given that the others, two blokes and a young woman, haven't reacted or responded to my apology. There's an older chap untangling a handful of cables and leads, setting up a speaker system in the corner. He gives a sharp nod while repositioning his giant black boxes. The room has been tastefully decorated: there are coloured streamers, a 'Happy Birthday' banner, and numerous giant balloons in the shape of a '1' and an '8', with trailing curled ribbons, float around the ceiling above the long but empty buffet table.

I get that they're irritated by the newbie, instantly assuming that I'm a slacker, possibly work-shy, before I even remove my jacket, but I'm neither. If they only knew that I had to chase an alpaca, Serendipity, around his paddock for forty minutes because he stubbornly refused to follow our usual routine, maybe they'd have a little more sympathy. But they don't. So they won't.

'Nice to meet you all.' I fall silent, hoping that Jayden will appear from nowhere and save me from the silent treatment.

He doesn't. Great.

Can I spend four hours working in silence for fifty quid cash in hand? Yep, I sure can.

'Put your coat and bag in the back room,' instructs the older guy, gesturing over his shoulder to indicate an open doorway. 'Then you can polish these glasses – there's a bar towel here.'

'Fine. No worries. Right to it,' I say, hastily making my way around the bar, squeezing past the other bodies and entering the tiny room filled with barrels, pumps and a whole load of tubing snaking from each one. There are two chairs, draped in coats, so I remove my jacket, wrap it around my handbag and stuff the parcel beneath the chair legs. I return to the bar and begin the allotted task: glass cleaning.

No one says a word.

I've seen barmen perform this task many times in films: white cloth applied rapidly and swiftly around the bowl of each freshly cleaned glass, hold it up to the light, look through and check for smears, lipstick or water marks, then stack on the shelf. Easy.

Still no one speaks. The only sound behind the bar is the clinking of mixers and beer bottles as fridges are being stocked from cardboard boxes. Even I'm not adding to the noise.

'Here, another rack of glasses,' says the older chap, depositing a wire basket of upturned wine glasses.

'Are these not clean from last night?' I ask, unsure why I'd be polishing at this stage of the evening.

He turns back, eyes me cautiously before answering. 'The glasses had marks on them – we don't know how long they've been sitting on the shelf, so we've put them through the dishwasher to ensure they're clean for tonight's gig.'

Oh right, that explains it.

'How many guests are you expecting?' I ask, though he's disappeared up the other end of the bar, checking the contents of the fridges as he goes.

'Sorry?'

'I said, how many guests are expected? So I know how many glasses to polish.'

'Polish till I ask you to switch jobs. Simple.'

He's a little older than me. But he's got an authoritarian air about him, which suggests I shouldn't argue with his orders.

'OK, OK,' I mutter, selecting the next glass, holding the stem between my fingers in a delicate pincer grip, and twisting the bowl against the towel to ensure a sparkle. The young woman is working a little way further along, wiping down the bar counter and realigning beer towels. 'An eighteenth birthday party, I believe?' I say, attempting to make conversation.

'Yeah,' she says. Her tone is flat as she cold-shoulders me and moves along, completing her task.

No more, there's no point. I've apologised, but they didn't give me a chance to explain, so now I'll disappear into a world of my own and simply polish the glasses. I've worked in worse situations than being ignored all night.

'Here, another rack of clean glasses,' says the younger fella, adding a third wire rack to my current task.

I smile, there's nothing more I can do. They can ignore me all they like; I need the money, so I'll complete the shift and bugger off home fifty quid richer. My skin can be as thick as rhino hide when it needs to be.

The double doors of the hired room swiftly open, ushering in a boisterous crowd, just as the speaker guy gets his music going and a rig of spinning disco lights projects a twirling pattern on to the ceiling.

'Here,' says the young woman, stacking a fourth rack of wet glasses beside the others.

'Cheers!' I say, forcing a smile. How short is the dishwasher cycle?

Chapter Thirteen

Sunday 28 August

Heather

'Morning, my lovely. How are you?' I enter The Yarn Barn early, knowing that customers don't tend to appear as soon as the doors are opened.

Verity looks so calm and cosy, sitting in her knitting chair, her needles busily working away at a skein of pale-blue yarn. She visibly jumps on hearing me. 'Heather, you gave me the fright of my life.' Her hands lift to her chest and her knitting drops to her lap.

'Sorry, sorry. I just wanted to drop by and ask if you were OK after our conversation the other day. I felt I'd put my foot in my mouth and then turned around three times. It wasn't a dig at you or your lads – if anything, I was probably being too damned honest about my own downfall in raising my girls.'

'No, not at all . . . I . . . I . . .' She stops trying, falls silent and gives me a smile. 'Who am I kidding? Actually, yes. I was ticked off, in a way. I should have said. I can be honest with you, as Magnus would trust you with his life, but . . . I just couldn't bring myself to say what I was feeling, in case it rocked the boat.'

'I get it. Honestly, Verity, I think the world of you and truly admire what you've done for yourself – and, in turn, for our Magnus – but it wasn't a dig at you and yours. Please believe me,' I say, crossing the stable floor and standing in front of her chair.

She gives me a nod, as if accepting my good intentions, her tousled hair framing her face.

'No, seriously,' I insist. 'I'm apologising if anything I said rubbed you up the wrong way; it wasn't meant.'

Verity's face bursts into life, with a generous smile that reaches her eyes. Now, I'm genuinely forgiven.

'It's at this point after a disagreement that my girls always ask each other, "Do you wanna hug it out?" So do ya, Verity?' Why my voice goes all soppy and daft is anyone's guess.

Verity starts to laugh. 'No, because I hate that line,' she says. 'My lads would have fist-bumped or knuckle-dusted each other's heads vigorously, by now,' she adds.

'I'm up for that, if you are?'

'Later! Can't you see I'm knitting?' says Verity, with a giggle, before picking up her next stitch. 'But I'm in the wrong too. I should have known better. We're cool, don't worry.'

'Phew! And here was me thinking we could look daggers at each other over the Christmas turkey this year, which was—' I abruptly cease talking on seeing her smiley expression fall. 'Verity?'

She looks up, her smile back in place.

'What's going on?'

'Well, that's it, isn't it – you've hit the nail on the head. Will I be here for Christmas dinner this year?'

'Of course you will. Unless . . .' My words slow until they fade. 'I see. You're thinking of returning home?'

She gives a tiny nod. I really did drop a clanger, didn't I?

'I see. And Magnus?'

'That's the quandary.' Her gaze drops to her knitting and she gulps several times. 'Iona's invite to tea the other Sunday was an attempt to show what life could be like, if I stayed here and moved in with Magnus. I've no issue with how life might be, but

I don't know whether I can up-sticks from my lads and move here permanently.'

'Do you want to talk about it or not?' I ask, filling the silence.

'I don't know if I can without getting upset.'

'That's fine, it's me you're talking to. I can handle a few tears.' I quickly check my watch: quarter past ten. 'Do you get customers drifting in at this time of the morning?'

'Sometimes, which is another reason why I shouldn't start blubbing to you about my choices.'

'I agree. I'd hate to cause you any upset – which is the original sodding reason why I walked in.'

Her expression lifts and she cracks a smile. 'You're a good soul, Heather. Seriously, I don't know what Magnus would do without you in his life. He loves you to bits – which is why I wrongly assumed he'd been talking to you about stuff when we spoke the other day.'

'I get it now. No. Just me putting my foot in it, as usual. Well, keep talking, despite the tears and the pain, you never know. I'm here if you need me, so just shout!'

'I will. Though I expect Magnus might want to chew the fat with you, and he rarely discusses anything with anyone ... so it might be best if he has the chance to air his views before you hear my side of the story.'

'Hey, no way! Ellie and Isla have trained me to be piggy in the middle over the years. I rarely have the chance to put my skills to good use outside of my own four walls. I promise we'll hug it out afterwards, all three of us!'

Verity continues to laugh, which is how I want to leave her.

'Anyway, less of this chit-chat – what are you knitting?'

'A baby set for Melissa. Her little lad has come along nicely and filled out, so he's outgrown many of the premature knits I made. She's mentioned that she'd like a few hand-knitted bits and bobs that'll see him through into the winter months.' She holds up her work as she speaks. 'I thought I'd give the Lerwick Manor home-spun alpaca yarn a try.'

'It looks beautiful, I'm sure she'll be thrilled.'

'I hope so, he's growing fast – got a right pair of cheeks on him.'

'Bless him. They've been through the mill with worry. Fingers crossed, he continues to get bonnier and stronger,' I say, gesturing with both hands.

Verity nods eagerly. 'And you and your brood?' she asks.

'Verity, you wouldn't believe it if I told you,' I say, with a giggle. Not wishing to discuss my latest disaster date, I hastily add, 'Right, I'm off. I've said my bit, and we're all good, but shout if there's anything else, my lovely.'

'I will. Thank you.'

I turn on my heels, blowing her a kiss from the doorway.

Tabitha

I'm as nervous as hell climbing the manor's grand staircase, not because I've asked to speak with Ned, more at the prospect that he might refuse my idea. I need him to agree to what I think is a sensible plan.

I finally reach the third floor, briefly admiring the billowing clouds through the vast skylight, before moving along the line of closed doors. Isla gave me the hint that it's the door opposite the ceramic jardinière with its large leafy plant, which I'm relieved to see. I've never ventured beyond the reception hallway before, so this seems like another world. It reminds me of a stage set – all quaint old-world charm – but in a classic way, rather than threadbare and drab.

I stand before the office door, knowing exactly what I wish to say; I've practised it numerous times this morning. I give a hard rap on the door and wait.

'Come in,' calls Ned's muffled voice.

On entering, I find him seated at his desk, a mound of papers and account books piled before him, in a thoroughly modern office – not what I was expecting. Ned swivels his chair, turning to face me. Jemima is nowhere to be seen.

'Good morning, Tabitha, I understand you wanted a word?'

'Morning, Ned, yes, er . . . I wanted to ask you something.'

He smiles encouragingly, signalling for me to continue.

'I was wondering if you'd mind the new bell boy, Rabbie, working a two-hour shift in the soapery on Saturday afternoons? It's the busiest time of the week, and I'll happily pay the going rate for the mini-shift. It won't affect his split shift in the hotel – if anything, it makes life easier for everyone.' Just like my stage fright, any nerves disappear as soon as I begin to recite my well-rehearsed lines.

Ned listens, his head inclined, giving my suggestion due consideration. He gathers his thoughts before I've finished.

'And Rabbie is happy to assist you?' he asks.

'Yes, we've spoken briefly. It saves him returning home, only to come back to the hotel a few hours later. Serving in the soapery isn't strenuous, so it won't affect his ability to complete his evening shift.'

'And what if his work rota changes?'

'Then I'll need to rethink the situation, and possibly find someone else.'

Ned's mouth twitches, as if my answer was unexpected.

'I appreciate that you're his main employer but assisting me would help customers of the gallery.' I fall silent, there's nothing else to say.

'I think that's a feasible solution. Are you happy to confirm the arrangements with Rabbie?'

'Sure.' I'm assuming that's an agreement.

'Thank you, Tabitha. I appreciate that you've mentioned it to me before going ahead.'

'No problem, it's common courtesy more than anything,' I say, now eager to leave.

'Anything else?'

'No, just that request.'

'No worries. And thank you for the gift you sent for Jemima, we both appreciate the sentiment.'

'She's welcome. If it helps her, then all well and good. Thank you, bye.'

'Bye, Tabitha.'

I exit, hurriedly closing the office door behind me. It feels like the swiftest 'word' I've ever had. It just goes to show that when you practise your lines, then deliver them as rehearsed, the scene is soon over and done – without fuss or fear.

Callie

'Morning, lassie, how are we?' calls Dottie, as we meet by chance on the driveway.

She's heading towards the stone archway while I've just finished helping Magnus walk and unleash the alpacas into their paddocks for the day.

'So-so, I suppose.' I'm finding it hard to summon up much enthusiasm.

'That doesn't sound good.' Her piercing blue eyes peer at me as if seeking answers.

'I was booked for an alpaca walk – a group of guests wanted to repeat the experience before going home – but they cancelled yesterday, leaving me high and dry.'

'No plans to fill your day then?'

'Nope. I'm not needed in The Orangery, as Isla's got enough waitresses on shift,' I say, sounding slightly lost.

'That's good news for me, maybe you'll give me a hand with my delphiniums,' she says, a bright smile adorning her features.

'Really?'

'Phuh! I've been run off my feet of late. What with caring for Jemima, my Mungo, and the annual allotment festival looming – you'd be doing me a favour.' She doesn't wait for me to answer before declaring, 'This way!'

It takes all my energy to keep up with Dottie as she hotfoots it under the stone archway, across the cobbled courtyard, around The Orangery, leading me on to the manor's paved terrace, where several guests are enjoying their coffee. Down the ornate steps we go, across the manicured lawn to stroll alongside the flower borders, heading towards the carp pond near the wooded copse and, finally, reaching the wall with its ancient gate leading to the adjoining allotment plots.

Without a word of a lie, the elderly woman isn't even out of breath, despite talking the entire way. Whereas I'm hoping she slows the pace, or doesn't require me to answer her.

'I don't usually use this private entrance, but it saves my legs when I'm short of time. Through you go.' She twists the rusty iron ring and firmly pushes the wooden gate open.

As I stride through behind Dottie, I feel like Alice stepping through the looking glass into another world, with the car park gravel crunching beneath my feet. The large metal gate stands before us, a huge padlock securing the sliding bolt, signifying the main entrance for all other allotmenteers.

This isn't my thing, but I can't argue that I've anything more important to do today than a load of laundry and possibly tackle my end-of-month payment routine. Both of which I'll happily avoid.

'This way! Anyway, as I was saying, Jemima's looking perky today, which is a good sign, as she might manage to join us at the annual festival on Saturday. It'll be a pity if she has to stay at home. You're working, aren't you? I saw the staff list drawn up by Isla.'

I nod, conserving my breath simply to keep pace beside her.

'Anyway, we'll make light work of this task, and then I'll be free to return to Jemima. The poor lamb, she hasn't had it easy these past few months. That's where her and Ned met, right there – standing on top of a skip she was, fetching me a bundle of wire from off the top.' Dottie points to the edge of the car park just as we depart along the grassy pathway separating the allotment plots.

I've visited a couple of times previously, as a child with my granddad, but only on open days associated with the manor. The higgledy-piggledy sight before me never ceases to amaze. There are blue water butts, cane wigwams, flagpoles, mannequin heads on spikes, camouflage army nets, lopsided scarecrows, a multitude of white plastic chairs, gaudy carpets covering the earth, numerous polytunnels of various sizes, laughing garden gnomes, painted bookcases, a complete bathroom suite showcased as flower planters, and a decorative bench dedicated to one of the old boys who has sadly passed and is clearly much missed.

I smile as we reach Jemima's plot, complete with my granddad's old front door as its entrance gate. 'Are any of these plots vacant?' I ask.

'Old Bill's is at the moment. The young man who took it on stayed a matter of months but has upped and offed now. It's the best plot, yet it's going to rack and ruin. Here we are,' says Dottie, carefully unlocking a wire gate.

There's not a vegetable to be seen but a sea of tall, elegant delphiniums in a rainbow of colours – some vibrant, others in pastel shades – plus five beehives at the far end beside the polytunnel. 'Now, it's this row here I'll be showing on Saturday in the bouquet category. I need you to check each plant for any signs of damage, black marks, browning of blooms, or little visitors. I'll check the next row. Shout if you find anything.'

It seems an easy enough task. I place my feet either side of the earth mound and crouch down on my haunches to begin the inspection.

'Did you have a good start to your weekend?' comes Dottie's voice, her bird-like frame hidden by the foliage of the next row.

'Not really. I helped out on a bar shift for a party, but because I was late arriving the boss docked me a tenner from my night's wages.'

'And were you late?' she asks sharply.

'Yes, despite doing my best to leave work on time, I was waylaid by a stray alpaca refusing to be caught. Though the bar boss didn't ask me for a reason. Instead, the whole team gave me the cold shoulder all night and kept me on glass collecting duty throughout the party. It was hardly what I signed up for.'

'Is this a third job?'

'Yes, I'm afraid so. Though I doubt I'll be called on again. Turns out the older guy in the staff team was actually the boss, so my lateness caused him earache from the others.'

'Why aren't you focusing on your beauty treatments?'

I sigh heavily. 'Because I was renting a treatment room at the local salon. If I wanted to go mobile and offer a range of treatments, it would mean a huge outlay for the vast range of products. It's a massive gamble, if it doesn't pay off. And clients like the atmosphere of a salon – which is why renting a treatment room worked so well for me. I had access to all the products in return for paying a nominal rent, and the environment suited me and my clients.'

'So why quit?'

'There was a falling out between me and the salon owner. She claimed I was nabbing her clients by undercutting her prices.'

Dottie suddenly stands tall, a startled expression on her features. 'My Lord, it sounds like dog eat dog out there!'

'It is,' I mutter.

'Which is why you're waitressing, doing alpaca trekking tours and seeking bar work?'

I give her a nod.

'You know what they say – all work and no play makes Callie a dull girl!'

'I don't have any choice, Dottie. Juggling jobs has become my forte in life.' I raise my eyebrows after delivering my answer.

'At this rate, you'll be burnt out by the time you reach your mid-thirties,' she adds, with a knowing nod, before ducking down behind the foliage to continue her inspection.

She's not wrong; there are mornings when the weight of my world is heavy upon my shoulders. Though, I remind myself, it is all self-inflicted. Nobody makes me purchase the unnecessary goods. No one forces me to spend money on credit cards I can't pay back. But now that I'm in this financial bind, and it truly feels like a treadmill I can't clamber off, I need to keep chipping away at my debts.

'Have you found anything yet?' calls Dottie, after a lengthy silence.

'Nope. You?'

'Of course not, I grow the best delphiniums this side of the Forth Bridge.'

I start to giggle, she's very funny, which evolves into a hearty chuckle and, eventually, a laugh.

'Are you laughing at me?' comes Dottie's voice.

'You're simply too modest, Dottie!' I snort between my peals of laughter.

My phone rings, bringing our banter to an abrupt end. I reach inside my pocket, retrieve it and glance at the illuminated screen.

Jayden.

Do I? Don't I?

'Are you answering that thing or not?' calls Dottie.

I tap the screen.

Chapter Fourteen

Tuesday 30 August

Tabitha

'Mum, can you do me a favour, please?' I say, my hands jittering with sheer nerves at the prospect of today's casting announcement. I've come into the soapery to occupy myself, and now I'm feeling sick at the prospect of finding out Ebenezer's choice.

'Sure. What do you need?' says Mum, as expected.

'Can you drop by the library, take a look at the large noticeboard, and snap me a photo of the casting list for *A Christmas Carol*?'

'The whole list?'

'No. Just the section showing who's been cast as Mrs Cratchit. OK?' I say. I'm so nervous, I'll have to busy myself by creating a new batch of soap and checking the curing on a previous batch.

'Just the Mrs Cratchit part?' she repeats, waiting for my confirmation.

'Yep. Love you loads,' I say, knowing full well that she'll head out sharpish, rather than allow me to worry.

'And you, my darling.'

I tap the screen, ending the call. I thought I could be mature enough to wait until after work, wander into town and take a look for myself, but my curiosity has got the better of me. Now, I need to fill my time until she messages me the image. What I'll do if I'm awarded the part, I don't know. Probably scream for joy, run around the cobbled courtyard in celebration, or simply shut up shop and go home early. But it's best not to think about it. Best to pretend it's an ordinary Tuesday, when the other artists aren't in their stables, and I'm busy restocking my shelves, cleaning and scrubbing my barn, ready for another busy week of sales. But, oh … how wonderful would it be to discover I've been awarded the role I want?

Heather

'Heather, have you got a minute?' calls our Magnus as I'm halfway along Lerwick's Commercial Street on an errand for my sister.

'Yes, why?'

He crosses the road, with Floss at his heel, and is standing in front of me in a heartbeat. I can't imagine there's many folk in Lerwick or Shetland who wouldn't have the time of day for this giant of a man. He's willing to help anyone, brave enough to stand by his convictions, and doesn't take any nonsense from either god or man.

'What's up?'

'I was wondering if you could spare a minute?'

'Sounds ominous, Magnus.'

He gives a nonchalant shrug. 'Not here, I thought maybe grab a coffee and …'

'Chat?'

He nods.

'Now, this is a first. We might be a generation apart but I've got a funny feeling that all nephews turn to their aunties at some point in their life. You know the modern beliefs: aunties are similar to your own mother, but way cooler – which still applies to us, you know?'

'Does it now? You won't mind me being frank then, Aunty Heather.'

Not a name he's used often in our life together. It's always seemed strange, right from primary school days, explaining to folk that I was his aunty. But when your siblings are much older than you – and start producing when your own parents are still having babies – it's what happens. He's the brother I never had, and I'm the second little sister he never . . . bless her, our Marina. Our family set-up might be weird to others, but it's normal to me.

We walk towards Winnie's café in silence; hardly my favourite pit stop for a cuppa, but definitely the nearest.

Magnus holds the door wide open, and I walk in. Floss remains on the doorstep and settles with her head on one side, eternally vigilant where Magnus is concerned. I head straight for the furthest table. I have no idea what kind of advice he's after. I can only be honest in my response to whatever is troubling him, and give my own opinion based on the facts as I see them. Please don't let this be about sex. I might have watched him perform midwifery duties on my whelping dog, but seriously, I'm not the woman to give him advice on how to improve his bedroom antics.

Magnus raises two fingers in the direction of Old Winnie, behind her counter, mouthing 'two teas, please' – at which she nods.

'So,' I say, settling myself.

'So, yes . . . I've been meaning to have a chat for a while now.' Magnus sits down opposite me.

Here we go, poker face at the ready. Keep it straight, play it safe, and don't show surprise.

'Go on.'

'I was wondering . . .' Magnus pauses, then swiftly looks around the busy café as if noting who is sitting near us, before continuing. 'What the bloody hell are you doing on a sodding dating app, flogging yourself like a prize heifer at McAlpine's bloody cattle auction?'

My breath catches in my throat; this is not what I expected to hear.

He swiftly continues, 'I get that it must be lonely, Heather – I've been there myself – but bloody hell, gal! What the friggin' hell are you playing at? You don't need to do that. And all for what – a cheap sodding night out at the local dive on the arm of the likes of Jock McHaddit? I ask you! Know your worth, and quit the app.'

I am gobsmacked. We have never had a conversation such as this.

'Magnus, I'll have you know we had a nice evening together.'

'Aye, well, make it your last. The guy's a total sleazeball. If I cop him bragging about anything that's gone on between you, I'll be having words with him, so don't you even question it.'

'Excuse me!' My brow furrows faster than my jaw drops.

'I said . . .'

'I sodding heard what you said, Magnus! Tell me, when did I ever interfere with your love life?'

Magnus sits back heavily in his chair as my words hit home.

'Answer me that!'

We lock eyes across the tiny table.

Winnie silently appears at the edge of our table, holding two mugs of steaming hot tea. We both look up, breaking our warlike stare, politely smile and thank her before reverting to our stand-off.

I grab a mug, add a sugar sachet from the table's condiment supply and angrily stir my tea, slopping some on to the tabletop. Magnus silently sips his drink, staring at me over the rim of his white mug. We have never exchanged a cross word in our lives. Even as children, we laughed and joked, but never had a single argument or falling out. This feels strange.

Magnus is the reliable, good guy in my life. The chap who has been a role model to my daughters. The fella I have frequently extolled to my girls, saying, 'You need to find yourself a Magnus.' Hell, *I* need to find myself a Magnus! Yet here I am, fuming and speechless, because he thinks he can openly warn me that he'll be having 'words' with any man who dates me and then speaks out of turn? And, as for the instruction to remove myself from the dating app . . . well, he's delusional if he believes he can tell me what I can and can't do at this stage in my life!

Woe betide me if Magnus hears about the latest date – Irvine, the car salesman, at the big garage just up the road, complete with his bloody enormous 'big dick' watch face peeking out from beneath his buttoned cuff. Not to mention his chat-up patter. 'I love what I do, to be fair . . . it isn't the job for everyone. But I've got the gift of the gab, as they say. Today, I sold a nice little brown Mini, ten thousand miles on the clock, for the full asking price, the chap didn't even attempt to haggle. Which is unheard of, because everyone asks for a little bit to be sliced off the asking price. Guess how much for?'

I remind myself that Irvine was my choice from the online dating app, Ellie was not at fault.

'Don't you glare at me like that, Magnus.'

'Don't even think about playing the "aunty" card on me, Heather.'

'Phuh! As if.'

'You say that, but I saw it flash across your mind. I've got as much respect for you as I have for any woman, but please don't try to pull family rank on me just because you don't like my opinion. I've spent my life surrounded by women, growing up with my gran – your mother – plus my mother, your other sisters, our Marina, you and your two girls . . . there aren't many men around these parts who can say that, but I'm one of them. I love you girls to bits, but I'm not letting the McHaddits of this world spread gossip and slander about my kin.'

I get where he's coming from, I can hear the sincerity in his tone, the goodness within his heart, but . . .

'I don't need the likes of you fighting my battles, thanks!'

His chin juts forward as if I'd physically slapped him.

'I've raised two girls single-handed, held down numerous full-time jobs in the meantime, and now I manage your cottage rental, plus my dog breeding, with very little assistance, so maybe you should keep your beak out of my business and focus on your own future.' I have nothing more to say. Nothing that springs to mind, not at the moment, anyway; I'm sure I'll think of plenty at two o'clock in the morning, when I can't sleep and this entire scene will replay itself in my head.

He doesn't answer, but sits and stares: thinking dark thoughts, no doubt.

I take a sip of my tea. Why am I even drinking this? I didn't want tea; I came into town to run errands. I only agreed, thinking Magnus needed a supportive chat. I push back my seat, stand tall and take one last sip as I don't like wasting food or drink.

'Thanks for the chat, Magnus. I'll see you around.' For the first time in my life, he doesn't answer as I hastily walk away from the nicest, kindest man – the most reliable tower of strength I have ever had in my life.

The door chime sounds above my head as I wrench open the door, alerting the world to my simmering anger. I give Floss an affectionate ear rub on passing; I couldn't possibly take my annoyance out on her.

My quick walk home is powered by my inner ranting and sheer frustration. Who the hell does Magnus think he is? Shouldn't it be older brothers who act like this? Or is this because he's the only cockerel in the hen house?

The only drake in the gaggle. The only bull in the field. The only ram in the herd. The only dog in the litter.

I stop dead on reaching my garden gate, with that final lingering thought echoing around my head.

Well, that says it all!

Tabitha

My phone pings, indicating a message, just after midday. I carefully finish cutting the cured soap slab into smaller individual bars, despite every nerve in my body wanting to dash over and grab my phone off the counter. After trimming the bars, I carefully dispose of the knife, wash my hands and lock my knife away. I'm stalling. There's no doubt about it. I know that the second I open the message there will be no going back. I want this role so badly, it hurts my heart.

It's a good job there are no customers on Tuesday; they'd laugh if they saw my behaviour. I take a deep breath, collect my phone from the counter and tap the text speech bubble – a message from Kenzie.

I tap to open the text.

Congratulations xx alongside the emoji of a champagne bottle.

OK. That's nice. But keep calm. I can't read too much into it until I receive my mum's photo.

Ping!

A second text message. From Aileen, this time.

Bloody hell! Big hugs, big kisses – go you! xx

'Big hugs' could mean commiserations, I haven't got the role. 'Go you!' could mean I have! No, I can't overthink it. I need to wait. I can't let my thoughts go careering off in all directions until I see the evidence for myself, in black and white, from my mother.

How I manage to keep myself busy and sane until two o'clock, I'll never know. But finally, my mother's text message comes through.

Spotted the list. Snapped the first image but the young man reading the noticeboard said I should send this image too. Hope it helps. Love Mum x

She's sent two attached images. I tap the first, enlarging it to read a selection of names.

Tiny Tim – Little Josie
Bob Cratchit – Rabbie
Mrs Cratchit – Aileen
Ghost of Christmas Past – Mavis
Ghost of Christmas Present – Deacon
Ghost of Christmas Yet To Come – Reg (a double role)

My heart sinks. I'm thrilled for Aileen, but gutted for me. My eyes well up with hot tears. I don't attempt to stem their flow. I'm entitled to cry. To express my utter disappointment. I wanted that part so badly, I'd have given my right arm to have the casting list read 'Mrs Cratchit – Tabitha'. But it doesn't. Oh well, there's nothing I can do or say, other than congratulate the others. Wow, I'm surprised at Rabbie being given anything other than a backstage role after his hand in that truly awful rendition of 'Bring Me Sunshine'.

I'm about to reply to Kenzie ... then stop. I've forgotten to open the second image sent by Mum. Not that it'll be worth reading, but it closes that message sequence. I tap the second photo and enlarge it to read the list of names.

Scrooge – Tabitha
Marley – Reg (a double role)
Fred – Freddie
Belle – Kenzie

Sorry, does that say 'Scrooge – Tabitha'?
Scrooge – *Tabitha!*
Oh my God, go me!

Chapter Fifteen

Thursday 1 September

Heather

I enter his sheep barn two days after our last encounter. I find Magnus manually shifting straw bales from an open-sided trailer and stacking them into a large pile against the end wall. Floss lies on a pile of matting a little distance away; her head lifts, acknowledging my arrival.

'What can I do for you?' he says, looking up from beneath his mop of curls, before throwing another bale on top of his partly constructed wall.

'I just wanted to say sorry for how I reacted the other day. I assume you were doing your best and looking out for me in the circumstances, but . . .' I feel quite nervous having to apologise. I shouldn't, but I do; this is a first for me.

'Aye, but you put me in my place. Maybe it was wrong of me to presume to speak up before asking you.' He manoeuvres another bale from the trailer.

'Perhaps, but I did go off like a rocket – for which I'm sorry. Can we at least be friends again?'

'Friends? That's a backwards step where you and I are concerned, is it not?'

I shrug, a smile eclipsing my sullen features. 'I suppose.'

'I thought we were closer than that, which is why I took the liberty of airing my views in the way I did. If we were just friends . . . phuh! No way would I have ventured there, knowing I could offend a friend, or worse still, lose or damage a relationship. But you, the closest bloody thing I've got to a sister . . . nah, I couldn't cause you offence, because you know me better than I know myself.'

I want to cry. I puff out my cheeks, hoping he spots the incipient lake of emotion swimming about my eyes. If he doesn't stop talking, I won't be able to hold it back.

Magnus stops working, and stares. 'Are you OK?'

I nod, for fear of crying. There's so much I want to say in answer to his remarks. Our poor Marina, I know he misses her so much. He's been my rock, through thick and thin, yet every time he shows that so-called brotherly instinct I jump down his throat. I get that he was born to be a big brother; tiny Marina loved him dearly, and that protective instinct doesn't die when others do. Just as when we were naive teenagers, his actions today are coming from a good place, a big heart. Back then, I was a gawky kid who didn't know what was what when it came to life or men – so when I announced I was expecting our Ellie, I knew Magnus would be on my boyfriend Jimmy's case. And too right, he was; someone needed to be honest about Jimmy's new-found responsibilities in an attempt to stop his philandering ways. But this . . . this is different to how things were, back then.

He continues to throw the bales around as if they weigh nothing. I suspect it's the physical exertion he's relying on as a means of distraction.

'It's ingrained, isn't it – that need to protect?'

'Oh yeah, just under the surface. Lying dormant for the majority of the time, but then when I hear a whisper on the grapevine it springs to life and ... I don't know, what am I supposed to do? I was a big brother for long enough to have it instilled in me, "Look after your sister", "Hold your sister's hand", "Don't frighten her", "Don't let anything bad happen to her" and yet, it sodding did, didn't it?'

My hands clutch at my heart, and I hear Floss whine at the distress in his voice. It's painful to watch and hear him speaking the truth.

'I'm so sorry, Magnus. I totally misread your meaning. I know that meddling and causing drama isn't your style, but on hearing you say, well, what you said in the café ... I lost it. I felt judged, somewhat undermined by you threatening what you'd say if a man stepped out of line. Do you get my drift?'

'It's exactly what Verity said, when I mentioned it to her,' he says, throwing his straw bales one after the other.

'Did she?'

'Yeah, she said I must have worded it wrong and come across all bolshie, rather than explaining what I know about the way some guys talk to each other, running down women. That's what I was getting at, really. You know what that bunch are like – we've known them long enough, Heather!'

'I get it. Honestly, I do.'

'No worries.'

I lunge forward, catching him sideways in mid-throw, and wrap my arms around this gentle giant, knowing full well he'll act like a gruff old bugger and reject the affection, like always.

'Thank you for looking out for me and having a plan of action just in case,' I say, giving him an awkward bear hug.

'Get away with yee! How are those pups doing?'

I give him a tight squeeze before letting go; he knows I know he can't handle affection, so I don't fight him.

'Getting big now. Though the peerie boy still hasn't got a home.'

'Really? I thought you always said the boys were selected first.'

'They are. Most families want a boy dog as you haven't got the malarkey of seasons if you decide not to spay a bitch – though I always advise they should be done, in time.'

Magnus pulls a face. 'What's the problem then?'

'Me. I can't make my bloody mind up. I've got seven decent families, each wanting a boy – as long as he's healthy.'

'And is he?'

'Doh, he's one of mine. All Pepper's litters have been good and healthy pups – I make sure my girls only mate with the best stud, which is why I travel up to the same breeder in Burrafirth. It costs a fortune each time, but I wouldn't risk mating my girls with any other dog.'

Magnus gives me a coy smile. 'Protective, are we? A bit choosey about who they date and mate?'

'Fair play, I fell straight into that one,' I say, wincing. 'Anyway, it's no different with you and your sheep breeding.'

'Or the alpacas,' says Magnus, collecting the last bale and throwing it into place, before smacking the front side of his constructed straw wall to straighten and compact it. 'So what will you do, keep him?'

'No, I can't. I've got to sit down and make some hard decisions about who I should phone. I can hardly contact a potential buyer and then renege on my offer. That would be a shocking disservice to a family who've been waiting patiently for a pup. The first on the list, or the second family . . . I need to pull my finger out, because everyone likes to get photos of their pup, week by week, as they're growing.'

'Do you still do that?' asks Magnus, hitching the side of the trailer in place.

'Oh yes. And if I'm a few hours late sending out the newest

photo, I get inundated with messages just checking I haven't forgotten – which I couldn't possibly, given the constant nudges.'

Magnus shakes his head and laughs. 'See, I don't get that with my lambs, my ewes would think I'd lost the plot if I started photographing the little ones.'

'I bet Jemima will want publicity shots on the gallery's webpage if she gets a baby alpaca amongst the herd. Is it called a colt or a calf?'

'A cria, actually.'

'Mmmm, you know your business.'

Magnus taps the side of his nose. 'The Campbells are looking to purchase a herd of fine studs, believe me.'

'I've heard it all now!'

'What did you expect? Once Jemima's got an idea, she runs with it. They're on to a winner with spinning fleece and branding the alpaca yarn, trekking tours, and now the possibility of a breeding programme too. There'll be a surge of customers, mark my words – and cuteness overload – if a photograph of a newborn cria is posted on their website.'

Callie

'Hi, Isaac, would you like a slice of cake or a cookie?' I ask, gesturing towards the two food platters alongside a pile of paper serviettes.

'Cheers. I was hoping there'd be goodies,' he quips, taking a slice of cake.

'Ned couldn't call a meeting without offering a little something, could he?'

'That's a good point. Nessie will be over in a second.' He collects a coffee mug and wanders across to join the other artists settling on the couches and armchairs.

It seems strange seeing everyone gathered together after a workday, but it's the easiest way to address the main points of this weekend's annual allotment festival.

'Hello, are we late?' asks Dottie, tottering through the door arm in arm with Mungo.

'No, there's plenty of time. Would you like a slice of cake or a cookie?'

Mungo peers at each platter before helping himself to two large cookies and taking a coffee mug. I don't bother mentioning that he's only entitled to one cookie, as he's a law unto himself. Dottie selects a tiny slice of cake before waving aside the hot beverage. The unlikeliest of couples, yet somehow it works. Having spent a lifetime as just friends, namely at school, growing up in the same street and later allotmenteering, who'd have thought Mungo and Dottie would finally get it together as a couple in their eighties! Verity frequently refers to every pot having a lid, but I wouldn't have put these two together. Though Levi never doubted it; he says he's always been aware of Mungo's admiration for all things Dottie. And Levi knows the old codger better than anyone ... or rather, he's a close second to Dottie.

'How's it going?' asks Ned, appearing at the door.

'Good. A couple of others are expected, but the majority are here and tucking into coffee and cake.'

'Good show. I'll take one of those ... and one of those,' says Ned, selecting cake and coffee, before looking past me and calling across to Isla, 'We'll get going in a few minutes.'

'Ladies and gentlemen, thank you for attending. I'll keep this short and sweet, as I don't wish to keep you after hours on a busy day at the gallery.' Ned stands to address the artists, hotel staff and a couple of allotment holders. 'As you know, this coming Saturday is our annual allotment association's festival. We're providing the usual set-up – judging marquee, beer tent, evening mash-up – nothing is changing, as the allotment committee have got this down to a fine art in recent years. From tomorrow, we have teams arriving on site to erect two giant marquees on the grass alongside the driveway, so please don't be alarmed by the number of trucks and vans visiting the site. In addition, we're doing mini alpaca walks around the paddock; the artisan bread basket will be serving ice creams for the day over by the picnic area; and Isla and her team will be serving hot beverages and baked treats here in The Orangery. I just wanted to say that everyone is welcome to join in the fun, as the gallery will be closed for the day. Other than that, does anyone have any questions or suggestions?'

I'm surprised at the flurry of raised hands. Ned systematically takes each question in turn, spending ten minutes answering queries about start times, closing times, the involvement of family members, and the arrival of the judging committee. I'm impressed by the way he handles everything; my cousin Jemima isn't present, and Ned usually relies on her for reassuring glances and support. I can't help smiling to myself; I suspect he's going to have to learn to 'fly solo' a lot more often, once the baby arrives.

Chapter Sixteen

Tabitha

'Are you having a laugh?' rants Kenzie, flapping her hands at Ebenezer as her audition disappointment boils over.

If I didn't know better, I'd say this was an audition piece; she's giving a perfect rendition of a disgruntled Mrs Cratchit – albeit without her Christmas tipple for her reluctant toast. Kenzie's definitely braver than I am; our director is not to be swayed when it comes to his decision making and casting. Aileen and I exchange a brief glance. If I'd known Kenzie was going to make a show of herself before the entire cast, I would have warned her not to bother. Ebenezer stands tall and silent, his silver brocade frock coat blending with his shock of white hair to create a ghostly figure. The rest of the cast stare at our feet, all of us imagining we're invisible.

'I chose the best actor for the role, Kenzie.'

'Are you serious? No offence, Aileen,' splutters Kenzie, continuing with her drama.

I've seen reactions such as this before – never of my own doing, but from others who have received bad news – and it never goes down well. When Jenni McLeod didn't get the part of Dorothy in our last production, *The Wizard of Oz*, she protested by refusing to allow her own little dog Toto to be cast in the all-important canine role. Forcing Ebenezer, who'd only just arrived, to use an emergency substitute, Old Reg's dog – which was rather a stretch, as he has a German shepherd with a tendency to bark at crowds. It lived up to its reputation throughout the two-hour performance, totally ruining every song, every line of the script, and the finale too! I was awarded the role of Aunt Em but I'll never forget watching Jenni stomp around the stage, shouting and swearing, just wishing she'd stop. I knew she'd never play another starring role in Lerwick, Shetland or the neighbouring Hebrides, after that unnecessary performance. She was forced to quit soon afterwards and retire her Toto from the spotlight; Ebenezer banished him, with his owner's poor behaviour gaining several black marks in his ledger. Being owned by a diva possibly suggests a dog might act like one, and Ebenezer certainly wouldn't risk that happening again.

What do we do now? Pull Kenzie aside and talk her round somehow, or allow her to follow Jenni McLeod's strop by collecting her handbag and exiting stage right!

'If everyone else could take a seat, I'll be handing round the script for our festive performance. Kenzie, make your decision!' says Ebenezer, cutting her down while she's in full flow.

Aileen and I wince before taking our seats.

Rabbie is striding around the stage, saying, 'Right you are, Mr Scrooge,' and, 'Thankee, sir, most obliged.'

'Well?' I ask, watching his comedic walk.

'Well, I'm Bob. Bob Cratchit, how's it going, Scrooge?'

'You're pleased then?'

'Too right,' says Rabbie, re-emerging from his characterisation. 'Aileen's a good sort, she'll play her part to a T, so I've no complaints. And you?'

'I'm good, now the shock's worn off, but I crumbled into a blubbering mess the second I saw the cast listing.'

'Ebenezer's taken a gamble, opting for a female to play the part. If you put a foot wrong in the performance, the critics will say it was a poor casting decision. If you're brilliant, though, they'll say he was a genius for spotting your talent.'

'Please don't. I can do without the pressure. Do I play it straight, as the script suggests, or add my own flair?' I say, stupidly becoming nervous at the prospect.

'I've a feeling you'll be guided by Ebenezer on that one.'

'I'd have been happy with Mrs Cratchit, but this puts me centre stage for the whole performance . . . I can't complain.'

'Unlike Kenzie.' Rabbie grimaces, before peering across to the raked seating where she's still pondering her next move.

'I've tried talking to her, but she's not having it. I think she's praying Aileen truly breaks a leg during the performance.'

'That's too cruel.'

'How about your second role, are you as happy about that?'

'My second role?' asks Rabbie, puzzled by the question.

'I've asked Ned, and he's agreed that it's a feasible solution if you join me in the soapery on Saturdays. It'll be minimum wage for two hours each week – which is all I can truly afford. Is that still OK with you?'

'Perfect. Nice one, Tabs. I'll start this weekend, if that suits you.'

'Ah, it's the annual allotment festival, so not a typical Saturday at the gallery, I'm afraid. Though the following weekend will be here soon enough, and I'll go through the basics with you then.'

'Thankee, Mr Scrooge, you need some goat's milk soap on that there . . .' Rabbie drops his Cratchit voice, returning to his own. 'On what? What do you actually put goat's milk soap on?'

'On? You wash with it! Seriously, you'll be amazed when I run through all the benefits.'

There's a call for quiet from Ebenezer, who gestures for us all to take a seat.

'Given it's the holiday season, I propose we perform another of our scenes in Fort Charlotte. The last one raised a lot of interest from locals – and also caused a stir in the local news-paper, though for all the wrong reasons,' says Ebenezer, as we all glance towards Freddie. 'Who's available for Saturday afternoon?'

A smattering of hands are raised. I sink lower in my seat, my hand remaining in my lap, Aileen and Rabbie do the same.

'Tabitha?' His voice is icy. 'Not interested?'

'It's not that, but I've already volunteered to help out some-where else on Saturday afternoon. Sorry, but I can't do this one, Ebenezer.'

His features are pinched; he purses his mouth and narrows his eyes, giving a stare that is enough to turn me to stone.

'But you're our star player,' he mutters, as if that clears my Saturday afternoon commitments.

'It's the annual allotment festival, held at Lerwick Manor, so I've been asked to—'

Ebenezer's features twist and curl at the very mention. 'Phuh! Lerwick Manor and the mighty Ned Campbell. From what I've heard, he needs knocking down a peg or two. The way that family conducts themselves and their business, you'd think they owned the whole of Shetland.'

I'm taken aback by his response; rarely do you hear a bad word said about the Campbells.

'Sorry, but have you even met them?' I utter, feeling the need to defend them. 'They're thoroughly nice people.'

'Thoroughly nice? If you call "nice" putting local people out of business with their craft gallery, monopolising the area with their branded logo, alpaca farming, a mobile bread van, plus creating a hotel attracting the tourists away from the town centre. Greed, that's what it is! Money, money, money – lining their own pockets, and nothing more!'

'Bloody hell,' mutters Aileen, as confused as the rest of us by this sudden outburst.

Ebenezer switches his gaze to her and then Rabbie. 'And you two?'

'Same. I'm working at the manor,' answers Aileen.

'Likewise,' adds Rabbie.

Ebenezer scans the other two rows of actors. Kenzie looks up, a smirk adorning her features, but he quickly looks past her.

'Well, that's that idea squashed,' he mutters, shaking his head and turning towards the stage, before quickly addressing us again. 'Forget it. That's all for tonight.'

No one moves for a split second, before everyone jumps up in unison and scrambles to make a hasty exit.

'Not the usual close to a Thursday night session,' mumbles Aileen, out of the corner of her mouth.

'Bloody hell, he's narked. I'll catch you later, ladies,' says Rabbie, grabbing his jacket, before sidestepping along the row towards the exit.

Ebenezer stands at the edge of the stage, watching the bodies disappear like jack rabbits across a meadow.

'Stay with me,' I whisper to Aileen, before raising my voice to speak to Ebenezer. 'Would you like us to do the ghost light before leaving?'

The tiniest incline of his head suggests a 'yes', after which he moves aside and starts gathering his belongings from the front row.

'Quick, let's do it and then get out of here,' mutters Aileen.

We leave our seats and take the wooden steps up to the stage, where I quickly fetch the small lamp from the wings. I unwrap the coiled flex as I walk, in an effort to be efficient, pressing the plug into the socket and flicking the tiny switch. Rabbie's right, this lamp has seen better days.

Ebenezer continues to pack his briefcase with his script notes, battered ledger and phone, and then collects his coat. His silence is eerie. I don't appreciate his remarks, but I recognise it can't be easy relocating purely for your art. He probably thinks we don't appreciate his expertise, or value the future opportunities that may arise from working alongside him.

'Is this the centre, Aileen?' I ask, walking across the stage as far as the taut cable will allow.

'Thereabouts,' she says, judging the distance across the wooden boards.

I crouch down, position the lamp on the edge of the stage, and flick the tiny switch across; instantly, the small candle bulb illuminates beneath a layer of dust. I should bring a damp cloth one day and give it a wipe. I stand, gesturing to Aileen to douse the stage lights, and say, 'Come on, let's go.'

Our shoes echo noisily on the boards as we descend the stage's wooden steps.

'We'll be off then,' I call as we stride along the side aisle. 'You'd be welcome to attend the allotment festival on Saturday and meet some of the locals,' I add.

There's no reaction from Ebenezer. Aileen pulls a face.

I call his name. 'Ebenezer?'

He looks up. Across the rows of seats in the dimly lit auditorium, I can feel his steady gaze upon me. Aileen tugs at my sleeve, but I can't leave him like this. He doesn't look mad or sad, but utterly disappointed in me for refusing to participate in his afternoon skit and for speaking up in defence of the Campbells. I hate that feeling – knowing I didn't meet his expectations. Guilt overwhelms me like waves crashing on a beach; he thinks I should show more loyalty, and be grateful to him for awarding me the main role.

'Good night to you,' he says, his voice heavy and lifeless.

The ghost light eerily illuminates the stage behind him, imparting a circular haze to his solitary figure.

'Come on, please. He's giving me the creeps,' whispers Aileen, tugging my arm. 'Night!'

'Bye,' I say, before feeling the need to add, 'see you next week.'

His chin lifts in acknowledgement, but nothing else is said.

Heather

'It's hardly working, is it?' announces Isla, as I wash the dishes and she dries the crockery.

'That's unfair!'

'Hardly, Mum. You've been on countless dates – and not one second date.'

I wipe the excess bubbles from the dinner plate and rinse it in a dribble of cold water before handing it to her. She's got a point. Not that I want my youngest to keep such records for me, but I can't argue with her observation.

'I'm not going to venture on a second date when I haven't enjoyed the first, now am I?'

Isla stares at me, the sceptical tilt of her head saying far more than her silence. 'Come off it, have any of them called for a second date?'

I shake my head, distracting myself by scrubbing the roasting pan.

'Precisely. In other words, you're no more their cup of tea than they're yours.'

I let her words settle, before I get the point she's making. When the penny drops, I'm open-mouthed. 'You cheeky little bugger!'

'What? Had you not realised that?'

'Well, I . . . I told myself . . . I suppose . . . No! I hadn't, but now. Wow, they think I'm bloody boring so they haven't bothered to get in touch!'

'I wouldn't say boring, Mum, but . . . it works both ways!'

'Cheers, you know how to make your mother feel great!'

I circle furiously with my scouring pad, removing the congealed fats from the roasting tin.

How ridiculous am I? I've viewed it purely from my point of view and not theirs. How many times have I sat on the sofa with Ellie in recent days, unkindly picking faults with my dates, when the reality is their daughters were probably sat with a cuppa, dissecting my words, deeds and actions too, in support of their fathers? Have I been described as nondescript? Lacking in substance? Too materialistic? I blush.

'Cringeworthy or what?' says Isla.

'Will you stop with the comments, please,' I chunter, as a sobering dollop of reality is served to me by my daughter.

'Has anyone even hinted at the prospect of another date?' she asks.

'Not as such.'

'Bloody hell, Mum. You must stink at this game.'

'Isla!'

'I'm just being honest. How many dates have you been on?'

'Five . . . six, if you count . . . yeah, on second thoughts, don't. I'll say five.'

'And no second requests?'

I shake my head.

Isla sucks her cheeks in, which says it all.

We continue to wash and dry in silence. I try to take satisfaction in my gleaming roasting tin but, nah, my satisfaction has been ruined by Isla's plain talking.

'Are you this direct at work?' I mutter, unsure if I wish to know how she conducts herself with her staff.

'Sometimes. When it's necessary.'

'Glad I don't work in The Orangery then,' I mutter.

'People might not like my honesty, but I'm fair. I've learnt that from Jemima.'

I appreciate that Jemima has had a positive influence on my daughter since she joined the gallery venture, for which I'm grateful, though I'm not so sure about this evening's outspoken observations about my situation. I suppose I can't have it both ways.

'What do you talk about?' she asks.

'Isla, I'm not doing this.'

'Doing what?'

'This overanalysing everything that I say and do on a date, I get enough questions from Ellie.'

'Ah, but Ellie hasn't asked about second dates, otherwise you wouldn't be so shocked at the realisation that you are a serial one-date woman.'

I empty the washing-up bowl, swill it with cold water and shake the bubbles from my hands.

'I am done with this conversation, young lady. Maybe Ellie isn't as sharp as you when it comes to realising the bare facts, but I haven't been too canny, either. I suppose they learn all they wish to in one evening, and then . . .' I can't think of a polite way to say it, so I don't bother.

'They ignore you?'

I've had enough of this conversation. 'You really do have a lovely way with words, Isla. Lord knows how any young man is going to cope with your candidness.'

'You worry about your own affairs!'

'You're right, Isla. You'll do alright, whatever the situation – which gives me a true sense of pride.'

'Don't worry about me – just focus on getting a second date.'

'I'm not going to obsess about it. If they were interested, they'd ask. If not, so be it.'

'Mmmm,' she says, sounding unconvinced, and draping her damp tea towel over the radiator.

'What's that supposed to mean?'

'Well, if you keep confiding in our Ellie, and the two of you keep choosing such dead-end dates, what do you expect?'

And with that my younger daughter rests her case.

'Isla, I said no!'

Don't you just hate it when daughters point out the bloody obvious, and their words swim around in your brain for the remainder of the day!

'I'm just saying, let me sit with you for one look through and I promise, I won't ask again.' She slides on to the sofa cushion next to mine, trying to be all chummy-chummy, but I know what her game is. She hates feeling left out; it's so easy for that to happen in a household of three.

I stare at her eager face, those good intentions shining through. Honest and alert, that's our Isla. As a child, she was never one to shy away from new experiences, but first she'd watch, then suss out the situation, before cautiously approaching and joining in – or on many occasions, removing herself completely.

What's the worst that could happen? Is my dating experience likely to affect her that much? Now she's seen that young scallywag Lachlan for what he truly is, am I being overly cautious? A case of shutting the stable door after the horse has bolted, perhaps?

'You win!'

'Seriously?'

I pluck my phone from my pocket, swipe and then tap the dating app. The site bursts into life as if inviting me into a new exciting world of singletons. Ironically, I doubt if all the participants are truly single.

Isla snuggles up alongside, pleased to have been granted a long-standing wish. Boy, how life changes so rapidly. There was a time I'd see that little face beam as we opened the new Argos catalogue, now it's my dating app.

I flick through the screens and begin reading the profiles; many I recognise from previous visits. Isla sits quietly at my side, leaning in and reading over my shoulder. How different can two daughters be? I get to read at my own pace, without a heavy sigh for being too slow. Ellie is rarely silent when I browse. There's always a comment in my ear about a beard, a stance or pose, or the instruction to 'swipe, Mum!' – which makes me uncomfortable, as I'd happily take some time to read the mini bio for anyone I'm drawn to. Ellie doesn't stand for my loitering. She wants me to act like the younger generation, making snap decisions, swiping rapidly, fingers moving non-stop as if flicking through a glossy magazine at high speed, and making decisions based purely on first impressions. That's just not me; it doesn't appear to be Isla either, given her silence for the last five minutes.

I glance up, for fear she might have fallen asleep at my shoulder, but no.

'What?' she asks.

'Nothing.' I smile to myself. Could my younger daughter be showing a maturity of which I approve? Or has her experience at the gallery taught her about human beings and making snap judgements?

'I'm pretty slow when it comes to this process. I like to read what they've put about themselves.'

Isla nods, before saying, 'I'd probably be the same.'

It's music to my ears.

I continue to linger, swiping slowly, thoughtfully, carefully – not a speed my elder daughter would approve of. This feels right. Now it doesn't feel like a cattle market, a meat store and a cheap shot. I'm a mature woman interested in taking the first step towards the future life I wish for myself, not some game-playing cougar desperate to achieve three hours of male conversation.

'Isla.'

'Mmmm.'

'This is nice,' I say, before adding, 'thank you.'

Isla screws up her face, confused.

'You probably won't get it, but this is how I like to view this site – with a bit of respect for the men who've been brave enough to upload their profiles.'

Isla gives me a knowing nod. How wrong I was!

Nothing changes for a fair while. I tilt the screen every now and then, as if asking her opinion, but she rarely makes a comment. There's a couple of profiles I'd be interested in contacting. A man from Yell who also breeds Shelties, and a fella from Sumburgh who works at the airport – his interests include model aircrafts and wildlife photography. I've never been one for outdoor pursuits, but with the girls off my hands I need to branch out and explore more interests.

I swipe to the next profile after placing a 'save' marker on the previous two. I'll have another read in quiet, and make my decisions then.

Isla suddenly jumps to life at my side.

'My God, I know him!' she exclaims.

I turn to view my daughter's delighted face, slightly bemused at her reaction. How do you raise two babies in the same house, under the same circumstances, and with the same boundaries, yet they're simply chalk and cheese!

'Seriously, Mum. He's one of the kindest men I know,' she says, before adding, 'he came to Shetland from Estonia.'

I return my gaze to the dark features in the photograph, noting his gentle smile, his laughter lines, and feeling encouraged by my daughter's endorsement. My gaze flickers to hers, and the glint in her eye urges me to tap the 'save' marker.

Chapter Seventeen

Saturday 3 September

Callie

I lean the chalkboard against the paddock fencing and write: *Alpaca walks around the paddock – £1.50 per child, per lap. All funds donated to charity!*

I stand back to admire my scrawl. It's hardly the neatest handwriting, but it's the best I can do – though if our Jemima walks past, there's no doubt she'll want to rewrite it for me. I figure that two children per lap, with me leading and them holding a halter rein each, is worth three pounds to charity. It might mean I have to walk around the same space all day – and change my alpacas, each hour on the hour – but I think it's a feasible plan.

This morning I helped Mungo to walk and release the newly acquired herd of entire males plus our females into their respective paddocks, further along from this one. They'll provide other visitors with a fun attraction to watch and admire, though there is so much to view and enjoy around the estate today, from the huge marquees to the artisan bread van – converted for one day to sell ice creams. The Orangery will be busy, as usual, serving cakes. Jemima has even arranged for the stone archway to be decorated with a sumptuous garland of delphiniums, kindly donated by Dottie. I feel a sense of pride being part of it all, to be honest.

I adjust the strap on my money bag, making sure it's tightly secured around my waist like an apron. Not that I wanted to

wear it, but Isla said it made sense as I'll be on my own, so juggling a Tupperware full of change whilst completing walks isn't
an option. My pockets are stuffed with dried food as treats for
my alpaca boys – not that they'll need much coaxing – and each
child will be given a handful of food with which to thank them
at the end of the lap. It's a nice way to round off the experience,
plus it might entice some parents into thinking of booking a full
trek in the near future.

I've checked over each animal, as is the routine each morning,
and I've selected Be Happy, a fawn-coloured alpaca, to start the
day. With three lead reins currently attached to his bridle, all
tethered to the fence runner, he's probably a bit confused, to be
fair. Magnus said it was best to switch the animals regularly –
they're happier in a herd environment, less stressed – but I'm sure
we'll be fine. And they'll be able to see two paddocks of alpacas,
just a short distance away.

'Excuse me, are you open?' asks a woman, with two small
boys at her side.

'Yes, I'm good to go! For two, is it?'

'Please. Though my younger lad is a little nervous,' she says,
digging into her purse for coins.

'No worries. If you come through, I'll introduce you both. I
bet you'll never guess what his name is?' I say, unlatching the
paddock gate and smiling at the youngsters as they tear themselves away from their mother's side.

I traipse for an hour non-stop around the paddock, alongside
numerous children, each time returning to my never-ending
queue of patient but eager customers. I talk the entire way
around, answering questions about alpacas, their funny hair-do,
why they have protruding teeth, and the size of their droppings –
the latter being the most frequently asked question of the day!

'Ladies, gents and kiddiewinks,' I announce, 'if you'd be kind enough to wait a few more minutes, I need to go and switch alpacas as the lovely Be Happy here has done his duty for the day. If you wouldn't mind stepping back from the gate, I'll be back shortly with a new boy.'

The waiting queue obligingly shuffle backwards, freeing my exit from the paddock. Ideally, Mungo would be on hand to assist with the changeover, but he's on the allotment committee, so he's busy with the judging process at present.

It doesn't take long to reach the barn, and it gives me a little break from doing laps of the paddock. I select a russet-coloured alpaca called Let It Be. I'm conscious that if I return with another fawn-coloured alpaca, it might look suspiciously like I've nipped off for a quick jaunt and returned with the same animal!

'Hello!' I call, and give a wave to the excited children as I near the paddock. 'I'm back with a fresh boy,' I say on arrival, 'so if I could ask for someone to open the gate, we can make a start.'

Heather

'Is Ellie not coming down?' I ask Isla as we stand before the makeshift stage, listening to the annual awards being announced and handed out. 'It's a glorious day and she's missing it.'

'Nope. She said she was busy when I asked her this morning.'

'I assumed she'd meet us here.'

'I'll be clocking on for duty in a little while.'

'Great, so I need to make the most of your company before being abandoned for the day. I'll probably walk back in an hour or so, to check on Pepper and the pups, anyway.'

'She'll be fine, you worry too much about the pups.'

'Isla, Pepper will need to go outside, if nothing else. I won't leave her all day – that's not fair.'

I scan the crowd, seeking familiar faces. It's great to see Jemima looking well today – long may that continue for her. I spot Pippa and Levi, cosied up and in love, Nessie and Isaac too. Not forgetting Dottie and Mungo. It seems as if everyone is finding the lid for their pot. Ah, and there's Verity and Magnus; fingers crossed their situation sorts itself out soon.

We give a round of applause as Dottie totters towards the stage to collect her umpteenth award for her delphinium bouquet.

'She wins every year,' gushes Isla, in admiration.

'She deserves to, when you consider the time and effort she dedicates to her flowers. Oh, look at Fiona's mum's face – daggers or what?' I say, spotting a familiar face in the crowd.

'She should be pleased with second place,' says Isla, following my gaze.

'She asked me earlier if I'd got a pup she could have.'

'Have?' questions Isla, staring hard at Fiona's mum, a woman she's known all her life. 'As in . . . give?'

'I haven't a clue, I didn't venture there. I explained that they all have for ever homes with families on my waiting lists.'

'You didn't mention the boy pup then?'

I shake my head, as Ned steps forward to make the next announcement.

'Ladies and gentlemen, our next award is for the category of hanging basket,' he announces, his voice booming out across the crowd, thanks to the powerful speaker system. 'Mungo, if you'd do the honours, please?'

'Thank you.' Mungo's microphone creates an ear-piercing wailing noise before he continues. 'A glorious new category, introduced by our committee to encourage the smaller individual projects within our gardens. I'm proud to announce that the second prize is awarded to Kaspar . . . Kaspar . . . well done, Kaspar, mate!' Mungo stutters and stammers on seeing Kaspar's surname displayed on the announcement card. His embarrassment is masked by the noise of the crowd's appreciative applause, wolf whistles and chanting.

'No one can pronounce his surname!' mutters Isla, giving a sympathetic smile.

'I imagine he's used to that,' I say. Then add, 'How many Kaspars are there in Shetland?'

'Exactly. He never complains ... but it's a bit rude, isn't it?'

'Ignorant, really, not to try,' I say.

I remain silent, watching as Kaspar meets and greets the line-up of judges, before collecting his prize certificate, his red satin ribbon, and finally posing for the obligatory photograph. He is stocky and well-built; dressed in jeans and sweatshirt, his attire is simple but clean. A strong brow and jaw are offset by a light-brown crew cut. He seems jolly, likeable and well-mannered in his short interaction with the judges; that's nice.

I turn to find Isla watching me.

'Do you think he looks younger than me?' I ask her.

'No. He's definitely your age group.' Her eyebrows arch slightly as she speaks.

'What?' I say, slightly irritated that my life is never my own.

'Just looking, are we?' she whispers, before taking a sip of her iced tea.

'You, madam, need to stop it.'

'I'll get another round of these in ...' She tilts her near-empty glass, before adding, 'And then I'll introduce you later.'

'Mmmm, here you go.' I slosh back the remaining mouthful of my beetroot wine and hand her my empty glass. 'Be off with you!'

The announcements continue as my daughter heads towards the beer tent.

'First prize in our prestigious new hanging basket category is ... Levi Gordans,' wails Mungo, his excitement getting the better of him. 'Ah, mate, I'm chuffed for you.'

I automatically applaud, whilst my gaze drifts towards the

runner-up, who stands a little distance away, energetically cheering.

Tabitha

'Well, well, the costume suits you,' says Rabbie, entering The Orangery and spying me dressed as a waitress. 'Is this Act One, Scene One – or has an intermission occurred already?'

'Ah, very droll. No costume, unfortunately. I'm helping out for the day as they're a waitress down. Callie's walking the alpacas around the paddock, so I volunteered to help out. My role mainly consists of wiping tables, clearing dirty crockery and loading the dishwasher – so very little training was required,' I cheekily reply, carrying a tray of piled crockery towards the serving counter.

'I thought you'd grabbed another starring role for a moment,' says Rabbie, speaking in rather a forced, slightly unnatural manner.

'Nope, I'm just a spare pair of hands on a busy day.'

I smile.

Rabbie smiles.

I smile again.

He shifts awkwardly, before gesturing towards the counter. 'Well, I guess I should order something.'

'Yes, and I should deliver these to the dishwasher.' I head for the gap in the serving counter and shimmy through to the rear kitchen area, placing the loaded tray on a stainless-steel worktop. What was that about? Did I blush because he went all awkward? Or did he go awkward noticing my blush? Cripes, I can do without this happening every Saturday afternoon in the soapery.

I quickly busy myself, emptying cold tea from the individual teapots, draining the little milk jugs, and clearing crumbs along with crumpled serviettes into the correct waste bins. I must have caught Rabbie by surprise, he made a joke about the uniform, probably felt a bit stupid about his slightly awkward delivery and . . . but he didn't stammer or blush. Mmmm, I need to watch myself.

'Tabitha, any chance of clearing some tables?' calls Isla, from the serving counter.

'Sure. Right with it,' I reply, emptying the crockery and wiping down my wooden tray, ready to collect another load. Two more trips and I think this dishwasher will be fully loaded.

I re-enter the front of house area, only to find Rabbie sitting in the first armchair facing the counter. He smiles on seeing me. I smile back, but keep walking as I feel a flush spreading through my veins.

Focus, Tabitha. You're busy clearing tables.

It's very busy today, so there are plenty of tables in need of clearing. Isla tries her hardest to maintain the rule that no one sits down at a table still cluttered with the remnants of the previous occupant. Which is nice, but attempting to deliver her high standards is like spinning plates.

Within minutes, I'm heading back towards the kitchen with a heavy tray, dodging customers, their belongings and pushchair wheels. As I near the serving counter, I see Rabbie's gaze flick in my direction, accompanied by another warm smile.

Chapter Eighteen

Heather

'Isla, should we be doing this?' I ask, as my daughter leads the way through a wooden gate in the manor's garden wall. She twists the rusty iron ring and pushes the gate open, without hesitation or concern.

'I'm entitled to a coffee break, Mum. With a late start comes a late finish, you know?'

'I know, sweetie, you work so hard. But is this somewhere we're not supposed to trespass? Remember, it is part of their property – and it doesn't look as if it's open for public use.'

'Mum, it'll be fine. Come on, I want to show you something, that's all.'

We find ourselves on the gravelled car park of the adjoining allotments. I've been here many times in my life – though I've never ventured to take on an allotment since we have a largish back garden at home. I've never been one for growing my own veggies, either.

We sound like a little army marching swiftly across the gravel; I'm in two minds as to whether our speeding feet are down to my daughter's excitement or an attempt to take cover and not be seen where we're not meant to be.

Isla swiftly darts along the grassy pathway nearest to the main entrance gate. 'Hurry up,' she urges, beckoning me closer as I trail behind.

I quicken my pace, snatching a brief view of each plot as we march past at high speed. The plots all blur and merge into one big mish-mash of colour and bright objects as we dart by, but I spy some unusual sights: mannequin heads, cargo nets, laughing gnomes, a front door and a flowerpot man.

Isla stops walking and points through the fencing of plot number 16, where a large blue, black and white flag flutters above our heads.

'Look ... Kaspar's plot.'

I'm speechless. I've seen the bathroom suite before – when we enjoyed the scarecrow parades, and on previous open days – but I've never seen it in full bloom, with orange nasturtiums filling and trailing over the edges of the roll top bath, toilet, hand basin, bidet and a full-length urinal.

'That's beautiful,' I gasp.

'And he does it all himself, you know. Well, apart from earlier in the year when Natalia, Ned's ex-girlfriend, was here – but she could only do a bit of weeding. I think it was more like therapy for her than serious gardening. Anyway, this is Kaspar. Impressive, hey?'

'Isla, this is something else, isn't it? Can you imagine the time, care and attention he must pay to each section? There's not a blade of grass out of place, or a knocked-over watering can in sight ... unlike some of the other plots we've seen.'

'Mmmm, just imagine how well he looks after a lady, Mum. I bet he's as attentive and caring towards women as he is to the tiny seedlings he plants.'

'Isla!'

'Seriously, Mum. I told you, he's one of the nicest guys that come into The Orangery. He's friends with Levi, the taxi guy ... our Magnus hasn't got a bad word to say about Kaspar. No one has. But I think this speak volumes – much more revealing than that dating app, his profile bio or a photo.'

'Stop it. Even your sister doesn't push it this far,' I jest.

'Oi! You there!' calls a male voice.

'Oh bugger,' says Isla, turning around quickly to see who's calling. She turns back to me, with wide eyes and a cheeky smile dawning. 'It's Kaspar!'

'Bloody hell, Isla. Now we'll be in for it.'

In an instant she runs, literally at top speed, along the allotment plots and out of sight. There is not a cat in hell's chance that I can follow her, especially not after all the beetroot wine I've consumed. I might as well stand still, take the bull by the horns and act daft, saying that I've wandered in here by accident. I'll kill my younger daughter when she gets home tonight.

'Excuse me, you are not supposed to come through the wall. Mr Campbell, he only holds the allotment festival at the manor – this is private property. You need to go, quickly, before someone else sees you.'

'Hi. Sorry. I got a bit lost and ended up here,' I call back, not sure if Isla is anywhere nearby and listening.

He arrives slightly out of breath, keys in his hand, wearing a pair of bright-yellow waders.

'Madam, you can't stay here. Allotmenteers on the far side will complain to the committee, and then it causes upset and lengthy discussions at the next meeting. I'll walk you back. OK?'

'Thank you. That's very kind of you, Kaspar. Kaspar?' I linger on his name, drawing out the syllables and prompting him to respond further.

'Nikolájev,' he says, nodding softly.

'Kaspar Nikolájev,' I say. Mmmm, not that difficult to pronounce, Mungo.

His eyes widen and a smile tweaks the corners of his mouth. 'Yes, that is me.'

'Heather Henderson, nice to meet you.' I extend my hand

towards him, which he takes and shakes gently. 'Sorry, but I was just admiring this plot and . . .'

'This one is my plot. You like it?'

Callie

'Hello, what can I get you?' I ask for the umpteenth time this evening.

The man has been standing here for five minutes waiting to be served, but only now glances at the beer taps to decide. The beer tent has been swarming all day; the glorious weather has helped bring the community out for the festival.

'Three pints of Guinness and one lager,' he says, pointing at the various taps.

I grab the biodegradable pint glasses on offer and slowly pour his drinks. I'm as happy doing this as being the glass collector for the night, though there's no need to polish these empties – just pop them straight into a hessian sack for disposal.

'How's it going?' says Jayden, drifting along to my end of the bar to grab a pile of pint glasses.

'OK, so far. Busy, but that's nice to see.'

'Agreed. I'm glad you accepted my offer of another shift. You're a decent worker – and tonight you turned up bang on time!'

I place the first pint down, allowing it to settle, and begin to pour the next Guinness. 'I'm pleased you're pleased. I wasn't too impressed with having my wages docked last time, so I was in two minds when you phoned on Sunday offering me the shift, but it's been good. Plus this venue is right on my doorstep, so to speak.'

'I gathered that earlier, I saw you with the llamas.'

'Alpacas,' I swiftly correct him; it's become a particular bug-bear of mine.

'Expert, are you?'

'Not quite, but I know my alpacas from my llamas.' I set down the next pint and collect another glass.

Jayden laughs. 'Catch you later.'

As I finish serving my customer, I spy Melissa emerging from the crowd alongside Hamish, her husband. I give her a smile and they stroll towards my serving area.

'Hello, how are you both?' I ask, wiping my bar top.

'Good, good, and you?'

'Plodding along.'

'We know – we saw you earlier,' giggles Melissa. 'Around and around you went, like a good 'un, with all those children.'

'They were pretty sweet, to be honest, but obsessed with alpaca droppings – quite worrying. What can I get you?'

'A beetroot wine and a pint of lager, please,' says Hamish, perking up.

'How's the baby doing?' I ask, knowing that's probably everyone's default question for this couple. My hands are busy, reaching for glasses and working on fulfilling their order.

'He's getting bonny – thank goodness. He's outside, with my parents, while we have a wander around.'

'Congratulations on your second place in the veggie growing competition, I bet you're chuffed?'

'I'm thrilled. Especially as parsnips aren't my thing, and I came second to Mungo!'

'That's an achievement in itself,' I say, handing over the wine.

'It is – though to pay him his dues, he was delighted for me after last year's disaster and me getting the booby prize!'

'He's a sweetheart under all that gruffness,' I add.

'He is,' adds Melissa, though Hamish doesn't seem so sure.

I hand over his pulled pint and take the proffered note, before waving them goodbye. They seem content together, a solid little unit.

Tabitha

'My feet are killing me,' I proclaim as the hands on The Orangery wall clock nudge towards nine. 'Any chance we can leave the clearing up until tomorrow, Isla?'

'Not a chance!' she retorts, with a cheeky grin. 'My café is left spick and span every single night, ready for opening the next day. Seriously, you won't want to come across tomorrow morning to help me straighten the place. Plus we've afternoon teas to create and serve, as Callie has a booking for tomorrow. They've gone the whole hog and ordered champagne too – I've already collected it from the bar and popped it into the rear fridge to chill overnight. Mind the crystal glasses I've set out on the tray – I can do without those being smashed while we clean up.'

'You're a tough boss, you know that?'

'It's routine and habit – it'll take half the time if it's done tonight when we're motivated to finish up quickly and head home.'

I puff out my cheeks; it's not that I'm unused to late nights and hard graft, but running back and forth all day has been a killer. Thankfully, we got to enjoy and be involved in the main event and hear the awards being announced. Which was lovely.

I grab a wooden tray and head for the nearest group of tables. Seeing the amount of dirty crockery and cutlery, it appears I might have failed in my duties. Aileen follows suit, clearing tables further along, while Isla takes the chrome coffee machine to pieces – slightly too technical for me.

Today's work experience as a waitress has taught me there's no point overstacking each tray. You think it's an achievement when you can successfully balance a party of eight coffee mugs, teapots, milk jugs, numerous spoons and dessert forks on top of a pile of plates, but you soon come unstuck. Or rather, I have.

The tray has either been too heavy to lift or I've found myself dropping half the contents on the walk between the front of house area and the dishwasher out the back. Several times today, I've ended up doing a ridiculous speedwalk, veering on a final mad dash, before walloping the heavy tray down on the counter. Creating quite a racket when carrying rattling crockery and pots! It's much easier making two trips to the table, and walking at a normal pace. Like now, I safely deliver the crockery to the countertop, empty out the slops of coffee, milk and tea. Then I load the dishwasher, before heading back to fetch the remaining few items and wiping the table over.

I'm not entirely sure that I'm cut out for this waitressing task all day, every day, like Aileen, but ... I stop en route to the serving counter, tray in hand, my attention caught as I glance outside through the glazed frontage of The Orangery. I see an empty courtyard, with two figures underneath the decorated stone archway.

What are they up to? I stand motionless for a second. It seems very obvious – but surely not?

'Isla, here a minute,' I say, without taking my eyes from the view.

'What?' She arrives at my side. 'Oh, who's that?'

'Mungo and Dottie ... but look ... he's ...'

'What's going on?' asks Aileen, swiftly joining us.

I simply point towards the decorated archway where Mungo is slowly, with one hand resting on the stonework for support, lowering himself on to one knee.

'After all these years, he's finally asking her,' whispers Isla, as excited as I am.

'They're framed by her flowers,' I add.

'Perfect,' swoons Aileen.

We fall silent and watch.

From his lowered position, Mungo looks up into Dottie's

smiling face and takes her hand. Despite his bushy beard, I can see his lips are moving, while her gentle features melt with joy. And then, without hesitation, Dottie utters a single word. Before beaming smiles adorn both their faces.

'She said yes, right?' asks Aileen.

'She must have, otherwise he's damned happy about a refusal!' I say, astonished that she even needs to ask.

'Tabitha, can you grab the champagne for tomorrow's alpaca afternoon tea from the rear fridge, please?'

'Are you serious?' I squeal in excitement.

'Yeah. I'll explain to the Campbells, they won't mind at all. Aileen, could you grab two of the crystal flutes and a small tray. Let's help them celebrate in style.'

Chapter Nineteen

Wednesday 7 September

Heather

'Thank you, it's reassuring to know that all are happy and healthy,' I say, as Vet MacKay returns the final pup, Sherbert, to the waiting basket, after a second thorough examination.

'No worries. Will you be having them vaccinated before they're collected by their new owners?' He closes the lid before taking the weight of the puppy basket and assisting me out of the surgery.

I urge Pepper to go first but she's hesitant about her pups, so I hold the door for her. 'Of course,' I tell the vet, 'it's the usual routine for my litters. I'll make an appointment nearer the time.'

'Good, good,' he acknowledges as we walk towards my car. 'I was going to mention, knowing that you're related to the Sinclair farm, we had an injured duck brought in a few weeks ago. The veterinary nurses have been caring for it – they've done well, considering she was virtually flattened on the main road. I know the Sinclairs are primarily sheep farmers, but you wouldn't know if they'd consider rehoming it? It's a duck ... it doesn't take up much space or require much care.'

I give a gentle laugh. 'As a matter of fact, I know somewhere better than the Sinclair farm. I'll ask and come back to you,' I say, opening the rear door of my car.

'Thanks, that's much appreciated,' says Vet MacKay, placing the puppy carrier on to the rear seat of my car as I encourage

Pepper to jump in alongside. 'The duck's perfectly healthy, apart from a healed war wound that's left her with a protruding wing.'

'No worries, leave it with me.' I secure the car door and return inside to pay my bill.

Tabitha

'Morning, Mungo. Can I help at all?' I say, struggling to control my bemused expression.

His visit is a surprise, but I should be encouraging everyone to pay a visit to the soapery, not just relying on my usual footfall.

Mungo cautiously looks around at my shelving units; his gaze roves from top to bottom in a fleeting action, certainly not taking in any of my product range. 'Dottie sent me.'

That figures.

'She reckons you'll have a little something for my beard,' he says, stroking his hand the length of his greying whiskers.

'Dry and wiry, is it? Or is your skin playing you up underneath?'

'I keep scratching it. It's driving us both crazy – she keeps threatening to cut it off whilst I'm sleeping.'

'Oh dear, sounds painful,' I jest, tempted to make a Bobbitt reference. But I'm not sure that Mungo would fully appreciate it, so I save myself the embarrassment of explaining by side-stepping. Instead, I ask him, 'Have you changed any of your products lately?'

'Not for years. I swear by cold tar soap – used it since I were a peerie lad.'

My heart melts at the pride in his voice. 'Bless you, well maybe you need a little change for a while, then return to your usual routine. Fingers crossed, either your wiry beard will have softened a touch, or your skin issue will have cleared up by then.'

I quickly dash around the counter, happy to show him my 'especially for men' range, discreetly tucked away on the corner unit, which Mungo hasn't even glanced at.

'Now, this would be a good place to start. A goat's milk soap; it isn't fragranced like my other products, but it does contain aloe vera to soothe your skin irritation,' I say, handing him a soap bar, before gesturing towards the next shelf. 'Coupled with this little balm, which comes in a tin for easy use.' I quickly lift the lid to show him the creamy white contents. 'It gently melts with the warmth from your fingers, and you just stroke it through your beard. You won't need a lot, but with daily use it'll help the condition and soften the wiry feel.'

'I'm not one for such stuff.'

'I know, Mungo, but maybe a little something will resolve the issue, otherwise you'll need to think about restyling your facial hair ...' I stop talking on seeing his eyes widen.

'I think not, young lady.'

'Well, a little experiment and an open mind are needed then,' I say, getting a sense that my offering has suddenly become more urgent. 'I'll tell you what I'll do, take these as a little sample. If they don't work, you won't tell anyone but me.' Mungo's ears prick up, much like the alpacas on hearing their dry food being dished up. 'If it does work, you'll tell five other men what a great opportunity it was to try something new, and how well my products worked.'

'Five?' He says, his brow furrowing.

'Yep, five of your buddies – either here, in the hotel or at the allotment. Deal?'

Mungo's fingers begin to twitch as if he's counting to himself. After a lengthy pause, he says, 'You've got yourself a deal!' I wasn't expecting a handshake but it's what he offers.

'Which balm would you like – sandalwood or lemon?'

'Nothing flowery.'

'Sandalwood it is then,' I say, more to myself than Mungo. 'Here, let me show you how to use it.' I spend the next few minutes educating Mungo on applying a balm and suggesting how best to lather and wash with his new soap. 'You want to feel your chin and cheeks being massaged with the lather, Mungo.' He's keenly taking note, so I might be on to a winner here. 'And make sure you give your face and beard a thorough rinsing.'

I opt for a discreet brown paper bag and fold it as small as it'll go.

'And congratulations, by the way. I hope you'll be very happy together,' I add, having forgotten to mention it earlier.

'Thank you. I've known her long enough to know her ways. Dottie Nesbit's not a woman to throw the bairn out with the bathwater now she's got a ring on her finger. I can't see much changing, other than the obvious.'

Mungo stuffs the package inside his overalls.

I sensed he would, for fear that others might see him with grooming products. Boy, this will be interesting! I can't wait to see if he's pleased with the outcome.

Heather

'I don't see what all the fuss is about?' I say impatiently, as Pippa hesitates on the threshold of the vet's surgery.

'You would, if you'd seen the state of me the last time I dashed in here, carrying your Magnus' dog after she'd been hit by a car. I half expected Floss to die in my arms, I couldn't wait to pass her over to the professionals,' she says, her blue eyes wild with panic.

'That was then, this is now! Nothing bad is going to happen. Here, take this carrier,' I say, urging her through into the reception area, before speaking to the lady behind the counter. 'Heather Henderson, here to collect a female duck that needs rehoming.'

We sit waiting for ages, or rather it seems that way, for the veterinary nurses to collect the duck from the rear rooms, say their goodbyes and wish her luck for the future. I'm an animal lover but even I'm rolling my eyes and feeling impatient at the long-drawn-out farewell – and as for Pippa, she seems astonished by the affectionate display before her.

'It's a duck,' she says repeatedly, as we drive back towards Lerwick Manor.

'I know. But they've cared for it, loved it, nurtured it . . . what do you expect?'

'Not that! I can't believe you embarrassed yourself by saying, "You can visit her any time at the gallery . . ." That was a bit much.'

'It worked, though, didn't it? We'd still be there, waiting to leave, if I hadn't.'

Quack! Quack! adds the duck.

'It's definitely female, is it?' asks Pippa, as we cut through the town's traffic in the early evening.

'Yes, they should know. Plus it's a speckled brown – it'll certainly look dull waddling along beside Crispy.'

'Don't say "waddling", Jemima's getting het up by that word. Dottie reckons it's a compliment, but Jemima's not buying it.'

'She's hardly waddling; and we rarely see her out and about, due to her pregnancy sickness.'

'Well, she thinks she is, so I'm just saying.'

'There are no guarantees that these two ducks will get along, anyway – it could be the War of the Cobblestones. Hostilities before dawn,' I add.

Jemima was thrilled by my phone call earlier, and didn't need to give it much thought.

'I hope Jemima doesn't regret this after the event, and this poor duck ends up having to be rescued again and shipped to the Sinclair farm in a bid to restore peace.'

'They'll take her?'

'Oh yeah, Iona said she's welcome, if this arrangement doesn't work out.'

I indicate left, pulling on to the long driveway of Lerwick Manor.

'And this, my little feathered girl . . . will hopefully be your for ever home.' I feel a glow of satisfaction similar to when one of my pups departs for their new home.

'Mmmm, I like how you've forgotten to mention her potential mate,' jests Pippa, instantly bursting my bubble.

I've unknowingly orchestrated a blind date, without considering either party.

Chapter Twenty

Saturday 10 September

Callie

'Wake up, sleepyhead,' says Isla, as I yawn for the umpteenth time this morning.

'I'm sorry. I'm just so tired.'

'Late night?'

'You could say that.' I feel guilty, as if she's carrying me on this shift. 'I completed another shift for the hospitality guy last night.'

Her delicate eyebrows shoot up into her auburn fringe. 'It's becoming quite a regular occurrence.'

'Yeah, it gets me out of the house. You know how it is: friends are all settled, family aren't into my interests, so I thought why not? It kills two birds with one stone.'

'You're so right. Anything interesting, or just more bar work?'

'It depends on the size of the function, and where they need me. I was on cloakroom duties last night, which seemed a doddle, but boy does it go crazy at the end of the evening! Everyone arrives at once, demanding their coat, scarf and brolly.'

'I couldn't commit to anything like that now, given my early starts ... it would be a case of burning the candle at both ends if I tried; a social night with friends is pushing it for me.'

I yawn again, feeling the need to apologise. 'So sorry. It took ages for the cloakroom to be emptied, and I couldn't leave until every item had been collected.'

'I can't amend your hours, or lessen your workload, as the Campbells are pretty sharp-witted, but thanks for explaining. I wrongly suspected you'd been painting the town red.'

'Oh no, nothing like that.'

'Maybe a coffee will perk you up?'

'Maybe.'

Isla drifts off, and I immediately head for the coffee machine. The last thing I need right now is Isla or the Campbells watching my every move and suggesting that one job is affecting the other.

The café is quiet at this hour, so I stand by the serving counter sipping my much-needed coffee, absently gazing out of the window at the healthy stream of customers darting back and forth across the cobblestones.

'What's with the banging?' I ask, as my ears pick up on a clanking and hammering, very different from the rhythmical sounds of the forge.

'They're replacing the tradesman's door,' says Isla, refilling the wicker baskets with freshly baked bread.

'About time too. That bottom edge is a nuisance; whenever you try to push it open, it sticks on the tiles every time.'

'Precisely. Dottie reckons it's been like that for decades.'

I take a few steps forward to view the rear entrance of the manor, where a carpenter's wooden sawhorse is positioned and two guys are busy working.

'Out with the old and in with the new, eh?'

'Hardly,' she snorts.

I turn, surprised by her reaction.

'Do you not know?' she asks, looking slightly alarmed.

'Know what?'

'It's your daa's old front door, taken from Jemima's allotment.'

I hear the words, but they don't make sense.

Isla continues to explain. 'Ned's organising a replacement gate to be refitted on her plot.'

'Would it not have been wiser to simply shave five millimetres from the bottom edge of the existing door?' I ask, stating the obvious.

'Maybe, but that's what's happening – they're rehanging your daa's original, as a replacement for the warped door.'

'Warped, in many ways!' I add.

I don't begrudge Jemima her sentimental moments. But the question is, do I truly wish to see my granddad's front door every time I cross the yard?

'What the hell?' I suddenly exclaim, nearly dropping my coffee mug.

'What?' asks Isla, dashing across from behind her counter.

'There's another duck!' I point, unsure if my eyes are deceiving me as Crispy waddles by with a friend in tow.

'Yeah, that's Pancake. She's a rescue from the local vet's – arrived the other day. She was half flattened on one of the main roads, so Jemima's given her an appropriate name. She's got a duff wing but it doesn't seem to bother her. Nor Crispy.' Isla laughs, as the fowl peck companionably at the cobblestones. 'She seems happy enough.'

'Wow! How much is changing around here,' I mutter, before taking a sip of my coffee.

Tabitha

'Do you want to fetch a coffee before you start? I haven't got an issue, as long as you don't spill it everywhere,' I tell my new recruit, the second he arrives for his mini-shift.

'I'm good, thanks,' says Rabbie, removing his bell boy's dicky bow and stuffing it into his trouser pocket. 'What's happening in the world of goat's milk?'

I'm feeling at ease; gone are the blushing and awkwardness from the festival day.

'You may laugh, but it's all happening!' I say, eager to divulge a wealth of knowledge.

It takes me a while to give him a standard tour of my products – soap bars, balms and liquid soaps – outlining the benefits of goat's milk and its everyday uses in the beauty industry. I even touch on the use of botanicals to impart fragrance and colour during the manufacturing process, and finally end with an explanation of the curing period.

'That's mind-blowing!' exclaims Rabbie, when I fall silent. 'I never imagined you kept it in storage for – what? – four to six weeks between production and shelf stacking. Wow!'

'That's just for starters. Customers sometimes ask for a bit of background information about the item they're purchasing. I'll be here to answer any questions if they want to go a little deeper.'

'Sure, I'll happily call you for assistance if I'm out of my depth – you don't have to worry about me ad-libbing any answers purely to save face.' He falls silent, as a group of customers enter and begin browsing.

'You can interact as much or as little as you like,' I say, 'though don't crowd them while they're browsing. And never do a hard sell, it's not necessary here.'

'Do most people buy something?' he whispers, watching as a group of customers select, pick up and smell various items.

'Pretty much, yeah. I never have to push for sales like some artists do; my product sells itself.'

As if on cue, a woman from the group comes up to the counter and places four bars of soap next to the till. 'I'll take these, please,' she says.

'Thank you. A lovely selection. Have you used goat's milk soap before?'

'No, a friend recommended it to me – she's used it for years. Swears by it, in fact.'

I note that Rabbie listens and watches intently as I wrap her goods, tell her the price and tender her change. 'I'm just going to drop a little sample of balm in there for you,' I say, carefully wrapping the items in a logoed gallery bag. 'All my products are available to purchase online, if you're interested – website details are on the product label.'

'Thank you, that's sweet of you,' she says, glancing towards her friends. 'Bye.'

'Bye, take care now,' I call, before turning to Rabbie. 'See, that's it. Not a difficult role, really.'

'Look at you giving out samples … hardly a good example of Scrooge, are you?'

'No, I couldn't be that stingy if I tried.'

'Unlike Ebenezer,' adds Rabbie.

I hesitate before speaking. 'I feel sorry for him.'

'Sorry for Ebenezer? You have got to be joking?'

'No, I truly am. He's downsized, left his career and life in London, to come here to Shetland. And we've hardly welcomed him with open arms, have we? He was gutted the other Thursday when we said we were busy working here. Admittedly, I didn't like his remarks about the Campbells. But still, he doesn't know them like I do. I bet he hardly knew or spoke to any of his neighbours when he was living in London – it's different here.'

'I can't feel sorry for someone like him,' Rabbie protests. 'He's as miserable as sin, yet he's doing what he loves, still working within the arts. Why's he here, anyway? I'm told at interview he promised to transform our little theatre – making it a haven for activity, with drama groups, choirs and even stand-up comedy nights. Yet he's totally failed to provide any mentoring, or to encourage us as actors. Admittedly, he hasn't been here very long – and yeah, our tiny theatre is minuscule in comparison to the London venues. But he comes across as mean-spirited; always jotting notes in that ledger of his. Nah, I don't feel sorry for him, not one bit.'

I don't reply; Rabbie makes a fair point. But still, I think Ebenezer feels ostracised by our am-dram group, cutting a rather solitary figure within our warm community.

Heather

We have arranged to meet on the harbour front, overlooking the sea. I am bang on time but, more importantly, so is he.

'Hello, how are we?' asks Kaspar, his accent softer than I remembered.

'I'm good, thank you, though slightly shocked to realise that the allotment festival was a week ago already,' I reply. 'Thank you once again for walking me back to the walled gate,' I add.

'It was my pleasure. I hope you don't mind, but I've booked us a table.' Kaspar gestures towards the nearest restaurant overlooking Lerwick harbour. 'Shall we? I thought a quiet meal first and then, if we have plenty to chat about, maybe a quiet drink. Or if you prefer, I will call you a taxi to ensure you arrive home, safe and sound.'

Instantly, I know tonight's date is going to be different. It's not about him per se, and yet it's everything about him. The warm, open smile; the careful, slightly hesitant way he speaks; his expression of genuine interest when he listens to my replies. He isn't giving me automatic responses, filled with clichés, phrases and remarks muttered so many times before that the conversation drifts on a current of hot air. Here is a man who listens. Who watches. Reading reactions and responses before he speaks.

How wrong would it be to phone my daughter – right now, while I'm on the date – and agree with her that, yes, you are so right, he is a truly decent man. Slightly embarrassing for her, even more so for me. I focus on enjoying the date, and quietly congratulating myself on a 'mummy moment' of utter pride; I've done alright in raising my Isla. She might only be young, but I'm impressed by her honesty and integrity. I'm so glad she's mine. After the way she contrived my introduction to Kaspar, it's possible ... probable ... pretty much a certainty that her name will come up in conversation, sooner or later.

'Did he mention seeing me run away on the allotment?' asks Isla, leaning across the kitchen table, eagerly awaiting my arrival home at eleven o'clock.

'No. I'm not convinced he saw you that day. I haven't mentioned the one who got away!'

'Phew!' she jests, feigning relief. 'In that case, what did you talk about?'

'I don't know,' I say, taking the proffered mug of tea Ellie has just brewed. 'Thanks, my lovely.'

'Damn it, Mum,' she says, settling opposite, beside her sister. 'So, plenty of pauses then?' She pulls a face; I'm clearly not coming up to scratch.

It feels like a job interview, with nowhere to hide.

I sip my drink cautiously, knowing it will be red hot, and gather my thoughts. 'Err, no. We didn't stop talking, actually – no silences, no awkwardness at any point.'

'What then?' Ellie insists. 'Hobbies? Interests? Family? Jobs? Phobias? Dream holidays?'

'Bloody hell, Ellie. Let me get a word in edgeways here,' I retort, not sure I like her demanding tone.

'Don't you remember anything? What family has he got?'

Isla sits, patiently waiting.

'Mmmm, no children, no ex-partner as such, at least not in Shetland. He works on the ferries, toing and froing between

Shetland and the mainland. He did have a dog, but not since his childhood in Estonia.'

'Estonia?' screeches Ellie. 'Where the hell is that?'

'I asked the exact same thing, but with a little more decorum,' I say, feeling increasingly riled by her outbursts. 'Apparently, north-eastern Europe – jutting out into the Baltic Sea. Or so Kaspar tells me.'

'Kaspar?' Ellie rolls her eyes.

I glance between my two girls, suddenly wary. 'Do you know him?'

'No! But with a name like Kaspar, he's hardly your typical Shetlander! Dear God, what the hell are you doing?'

'Going on a date, Ellie.' Yet again, I'm not liking her tone.

'You saved the profile details for three men – I thought you'd have gone for the dog breeder bloke.'

'You're right, I did save all three. But on meeting him briefly last Saturday, I chose to contact Kaspar ... and I'm glad I did, he's smashing. So funny, witty, attentive, and smiley to everyone he meets. The waitress dropped a dirty knife down the back of his shirt as she cleared our table after the main course. I wasn't embarrassed by him. There was no shouting, no rudeness, nothing. She nearly died of embarrassment; he told her not to worry, it was just a shirt! He actually asked the young lady if she was OK.' I beam a smile at Isla, who gracefully returns it in silence.

'Why do you keep smirking at her?' asks Ellie, glancing between us.

'Isla knows him,' I say candidly.

'Do you?'

'Yep, he comes into The Orangery with his friend Levi,' explains Isla, sipping her tea.

'Levi! Now, there's a chap and a half. I still can't believe you've been on a date for an entire evening, yet can't remember what you talked about for most of that time. How bad was it? It must have been boring.'

'I think it's lovely.' Isla springs to my defence. 'It shows she was comfortable and engaged throughout; time just flies when you're happily chatting with someone.'

'It certainly did. I learnt lots about his homeland, and he was so interested in life here in Shetland. He says he feels he could live here for the rest of his days and never tire of the beautiful skies or the people. How nice is that?'

'Mmmph!' snorts Ellie.

'What's wrong with that?' I ask, bristling at her disgruntled reply.

'Ignore her, Mum. She's just jealous because her efforts to match you up with someone came to nothing,' says Isla.

'My efforts saw Mum go out on five dates,' Ellie retorts, clearly affronted. 'Whereas your efforts have resulted in one, hardly relevant and barely memorable date. And, anyway, maybe my own luck is changing.'

'And he brought me home in a taxi,' I say, suddenly registering what my elder girl has just said. I'll ask Ellie about that in a second.

'Did he?' sighs Isla, all too quickly.

'Whoopty-bloody-doo. So he pops you in a taxi and sends you away. How is that courteous?'

'Actually, he called Levi's taxi, then sat in the front seat while Levi drove me back here, and then . . . Kaspar walked me to the door!' I gush. 'He has such lovely manners.'

'I'm going to puke!' announces Ellie.

'You've missed the point, Ellie. Your efforts involved the butcher who gave Mum a rundown on meat prices, the car salesman who tested her on car parts, and the baker who cut the night short because he had to be up early in the morning. I can't even remember the other two blokes, they were so nondescript! At least she's had a lovely time on this date.'

'And . . .' I tease.

'You're going on a second date?' squeals Isla, her fists excitedly drumming the tabletop.

'No way!' scowls Ellie, thumping her mug down on the table in surprise.

'We certainly are!'

I never thought I'd be so chuffed, but I'm quite excited by the prospect.

Chapter Twenty-One

Wednesday 14 September

Tabitha

'Coffee, please,' I say, after Aileen greets me with a beaming smile. 'Are you ready for tomorrow night?'

'Now there's a question!' she says, her hands busy preparing my drink.

I know exactly what she means. It's one thing to be awarded a specific role, receive the script, then start looking at your lines and stage directions. But it's a whole new ball game learning everything off by heart.

'Has anyone heard from Kenzie?' I ask, unsure if she's decided to accept the role as Belle, Scrooge's one-time girlfriend, or throw the towel in.

'I didn't like to ask, especially after I was given the role she wanted. But I hear from Mavis that she plans on turning up tomorrow night, so hopefully it'll all be forgotten.'

'Have you started learning your lines?' I ask, knowing it's a bitter-sweet task for me. I love the intensity of practising – the study and concentration needed for a flawless performance – but I get so frustrated when I can't grasp a specific scene. If I work too hard for too long, I buckle under the pressure, incorrectly memorising a sequence of lines, or even going blank whilst in full flow.

'Some,' admits Aileen. 'Though my scene is a fraction compared to your entire performance. How are you planning to play your role?'

'I'd like to play it straight, as Dickens intended, but Ebenezer hasn't said what his approach is going to be. I'm hoping that's something he'll touch on tomorrow night.'

'Wouldn't you like the challenge of stretching the character towards a Ms Scrooge for modern audiences?'

'No. If anything, I want to highlight my acting skills by depicting a male character. I've only ever acted as a female. I'd welcome the challenge to transform myself with a walk, a swagger, a mannerism – plus hair and make-up, of course.'

'You'll be in make-up for ages, trying to tame your hair under a skull cap and cover your flawless skin in wrinkles – not to mention the old man's stubble!' she exclaims. 'There you are, one coffee to go.'

'Ha, I never thought about that. Thank you. Can you put my coffee on my tab, please?'

'Sure. I'm half expecting Ebenezer to read us the riot act tomorrow night, because he won't want a word of criticism written about his first festive production. It may only be Lerwick, but he'll be demanding West End talent on show at The Garrison.'

'You're probably right. And we'll all be scared to death and act like a bunch of wooden blocks, for fear of stepping out of line and disappointing him. Anyway, thanks for this, and I'll catch you later. Shout if you want a study buddy for your lines, I'm happy to help,' I offer, preparing to leave.

'Thanks, Tabitha. Rabbie's already arranged a couple of evenings when we can get together. Maybe you'd like to join us?'

Instantly, my stomach lurches. I attempt to cover my momentary blip with a breezy, 'That'd be great! Let me know when. Bye.' It doesn't sound genuine in my head, so I doubt it will fool Aileen, despite my cheery wave goodbye as I swiftly leave The Orangery.

What's wrong with me today? I've never encountered the green-eyed monster rearing her ugly head before. Yet one mention of Rabbie . . . and *boom!* I thought I just liked him as a mate, but this . . . this is suggesting much more. Maybe it's a good thing I wasn't awarded the role of Mrs Cratchit, if this is how I'll react between now and December.

Heather

'Look what I've got!' I say, waving a small tin on entering the kitchen, to find both daughters drinking tea at the table. 'Kaspar just dropped them round for me.'

Isla looks up, her face filled with delight at the intrigue. Ellie frowns like a sourpuss.

'Cookies?' suggests Isla, with a knowing look.

'How did you know?'

'It's Kaspar's thing. He makes them for people, mainly Dottie, but I know he likes to gift them to others when they're poorly, or feeling down.'

'That's nice!' blurts Ellie. Then she adds, mimicking a deeper male voice, 'Commiserations, but I've had time to think and change my mind. So I'll be cancelling our second date, but here, have some cookies to cheer you up when I fail to call.'

'Like that, is it? So you won't be wanting any?' I jest, lifting the lid and offering the tin to Isla.

'Well, no. I just meant . . .'

'Mmmm, I heard what you meant. Here, take one and stop being so judgemental. I didn't raise you to be so cold-hearted and Scrooge-like,' I say, giving her second dibs after Isla.

'Scrooge-like? Thanks, Mum,' says Ellie, cheering up.

I take another cookie for myself as silence descends on our kitchen.

'They're very moreish,' says Isla, licking her fingers and eyeing the tin.

'Mmmm, I agree. One's not enough, and two's not too many,' I say.

'Nah, too sickly for me,' declares Ellie.

'Wow! You do surprise me, I thought sweet was your thing,' I say, offering Isla the tin for a second time, and watching her hand dip in without hesitation.

I continue to nibble on cookies while Ellie pretends not to interrogate me about Kaspar. She thinks she's being subtle, but she's as subtle as a house brick in a blancmange.

'How old?' Ellie's jaw hits the kitchen table.

'I said . . .'

'I heard what you said, Mum . . . which means he actually sits in-between our ages. You'd go mad if I was dating someone ten years older than me.'

'I wouldn't,' I lie, not wishing to enter into this particular conversation.

I suddenly wish our Isla wasn't here; she might offer a word of wisdom, in spite of her youth, but I don't like this dissection of the dating game in front of her. I want her to hear about the positive aspects of a relationship, not reinforce negative stereotypes. Is thirty-five too young to my forty-five?

'Age is funny like that; it changes through a lifetime, doesn't it? A sixteen year old hanging around with an older man is wrong in my book, but a twenty-something with a thirty-something . . .' I fall silent. Did I just quote my daughter's age group?

'What? Is acceptable?'

'Mmmm, maybe. Whereas no one bats an eyelid when it's seventy and eighty.'

'That's because they're so old, they're so near to popping their clogs, no one has a chance to complain. But it's still ten years, Mum!'

'You know exactly what I mean, Ellie. As we mature, the age gap doesn't seem so big, does it?'

'That's nice to know. Here was me, avoiding the older guys because I thought my mother wouldn't approve, when actually you've just added a whole host of new talent to my radar.'

'Ellie!'

'Seriously, Mum, what does a thirty-something guy want with an older woman? Surely there are women his own age he could show interest in. Or is it because you're financially stable, have your own home and business and . . .'

'You make me sound ancient, Ellie.'

'You're middle-aged, Mum . . . and he's not.'

'What are you implying?' I glance towards Isla, purely to check she's OK.

'I'm not implying anything, just stating the obvious. You see it on the TV all the time – young guys honing in on older women, to cash in on the goods they can't get elsewhere.'

I stare at my mouthy daughter. Is she a realist or am I naive? I take another cookie from the tin and begin to nibble. Granted, you hear of such things, but Kaspar's not like that; he has his own home, his own income and a healthy, independent mindset.

'You wait till he starts asking to borrow money off you, Mum.'

I'm whipped out of my little daze. 'Now stop it! I don't know much about this man, but one thing I do know, he is a true gent. He would prefer to go without than ever ask me for a penny. You should have seen him when the restaurant bill arrived; he was on it, quick as a flash, despite my protests to go halves. No, Kaspar isn't like that.'

'Not yet.'

'No, Ellie! Kaspar isn't one of those sorts,' says Isla, turning a steely gaze on her sister.

Ellie raises her eyebrows. She's not listening; she thinks she has all the answers. Thinks I'll be appearing on the *This Morning* sofa next to Phil and Holly, weeping as I recall a tale of woe and self-destruction, warning other older women about my missing fifty grand nest egg.

'Ask yourself, why?' she adds, getting up and putting her empty mug into the dishwasher. 'Why you? If he's so gorgeous, why aren't thirty year olds flocking to his door? They want gentlemen too, you know.'

'You make life sound so simple, Ellie.'

'It is. You're born, you grow up, you live, you love, you have babies, you struggle like hell, then you die.'

'Such a happy prospect before me, given that I'm past all options apart from the last one!'

'You need to watch yourself, he might be wanting babies. Will I end up with a younger brother or sister, twenty-five years younger than me, just like your Iona did? History repeats itself, you know.'

I watch as she leaves the kitchen; her words are ringing in my ears.

'Do you want another cookie, Mum?' asks Isla, offering me the tin.

'Bugger it! Given Ellie's sweet-talking, I'll be needing a whole tin!' I say, taking another buttery cookie.

'I wouldn't mind a younger sibling,' says Isla.

I nearly choke. 'Isla, I'm not planning on having any more children. Pups, yes – babies, no!'

Callie

I pour myself a large glass of wine, settle on my king-sized bed, neatening the pile of envelopes before me. It's mid-month, which means only one thing: my credit card shuffle.

My routine is well established by now, so between slugs of wine, I follow the self-imposed sequence, step by step.

In an hour, maybe two, I'll have a definite payment plan for the coming days. I'll be free to do other things – anything other than purchase more goods, watch TV shopping channels, or get absurdly drunk.

Realistically, what have I got to show for all my spending? I stare about my bedroom, the room I've had since childhood. Hidden within the familiar cupboards and chests of drawers are the spoils of my addiction: celebrity-endorsed and expensive designer brands of make-up, all of which I purchased thinking the shade or application technique was exquisite – but now, they rarely see the light of day. Then there are the rewards of my previous beauty career – lashes, nails, spray tans, HD eyebrows and waxing – which I regularly accumulated with each tap of a flexible friend. Despite the 'mate's rates' offered by the salon's other beauticians, I'd hate to think how much money has slipped through my fingers over the years – and for what? To make myself happier? Feel better?

If I'd shown half as much diligence in controlling my spending as I do in keeping track of my debt repayments, I wouldn't be in this situation.

'Callie!' My mum hollers up the staircase.

'What?'

'Phone!'

I clamber from the bed, midway through my task; this will be Jayden, offering me additional shifts. He might be paying fifty quid cash in hand, but even that hasn't made much of a dent in this month's minimum payments. I take a large sip of my wine before going downstairs. And this doesn't always help, does it? One too many and I hit the shopping channel like a lottery winner on day one!

Chapter Twenty-Two

Tuesday 20 September

Heather

Despite it being a whole week since receiving the gift of cookies from Kaspar, I'm not upset that our second date hasn't happened yet. Seeing as both of us are busy with previous commitments, our diaries have clashed each time he's phoned. His calls have been far from disappointing but have provided lovely moments of insight and unexpected conversations, all of which simply add to the attraction. That is, until today's call, when we finally settled on a date and time.

'Hello, Melissa, how are you?' I say, spying the new mum strolling around town pushing her pram, as I walk Socks and Rosie.

'I'm good, thank you. I thought we'd pop out for a breath of fresh air before the next feed.'

I peer at the sleeping baby, his blankets parted to reveal a tiny plump face. 'Ah, how sweet is he?'

'He is. We've had a few scares in recent weeks, but he's going from strength to strength. Every day we can see little changes in his growth and development.'

'And Hamish, he's adapting to the nappy changes and night feeds?'

'Phuh! You'd think he'd be good at night feeds, after all the years he's switched between night shifts, twilight hours and day shifts, but nah, he's bloody useless. The whole neighbourhood would be wide awake if I waited for Hamish to get up to settle Noah. Though to be fair, he's still adjusting to working on land again – and he's very hands on during daylight hours.'

'That's a good thing, Melissa. Be grateful for the "me time" a sleeping babe allows. Drop by anytime for a cuppa and cake.'

'I will, thank you. An hour elsewhere with a change of scenery is what the doctor ordered, to be fair. I'm trying to keep in touch with all my colleagues and friends at work; maternity leave sounds great, but it can be isolating relatively quickly.'

'Exactly. I remember how I was with both of mine. I neglected myself somewhat, in the name of "baby and perfect mum syndrome", when the truth was, neither girl went without – it was purely me who suffered from that silly idea. If I'd been more chilled and sociable, they would have automatically benefited from having a happier mum.'

'I get where you're coming from, Heather. It's so easy to get into the trap of baby routines, baby talk, baby care, baby socials – baby always comes first – when actually I need to do what's right by him, me and Hamish. Together, we're carving out a family life for ourselves, and some of these rituals others are upholding, and which I am trying to aspire to, are totally absurd.'

'I agree, sweet. You're a level-headed woman who's had a baby. Yes, his early arrival was a shock, but seriously, give yourself time to get your head around that, and simply enjoy being his mummy. In fact, you need to come round to ours; my Pepper will teach any new mum a thing or two, I swear she's got it down to a T.'

'Seriously?'

'Absolutely. I sit and watch her sometimes. I start panicking from the armchair at the antics of her pups, while she happily lies back and bides her time before *boom!* She nips their behaviour in the bud. She's in charge, yet she's as relaxed as they come, and as for the pups, well … they are a dream. I swear, it's her attitude towards mothering that makes all the difference, I really do. She decides what's happening and when – her pups simply fall into line, every time.'

'You've got your hands full?' asks Melissa, nodding towards Rosie and Socks, patiently sitting whilst I chat.

'I have, but then not so much. They're pretty pro at mothering, so it's a joy to have pups in the house for twelve weeks. I'll be lost when this litter go.'

'Have they each got homes?'

'Yes, I've a waiting list.'

'I see ... if there is ever one who doesn't find a home, would you give me the nod? I know Verity is always saying how Floss came from you, many moons ago ... and she's wonderful.'

'She did, and she is, but that's down to our Magnus' handling and training too; I can't take all the credit for the dog. She's a definite beauty is our Floss, despite her now gammy leg.'

'Nasty incident, wasn't it – on one of the main roads?'

'She walks with a clunk, but she's coping well; it'll take more than a car bumper to knock that lassie off her stride.'

'If there's ever one that doesn't find a home, remember us.'

'Sure. I'll add you to the list when I get back. It'll be one of these girlies next,' I say, gesturing to the pair of bitches calmly awaiting my command.

'Such lovely dogs.'

'Calm temperaments, whether it be sheep or little ones,' I add, sensing a fourth family member for Melissa's clan. 'And don't forget the offer of a chat or a cuppa, to give you a bit of a break; I'm home most parts of the day. And if I'm not what you need, but one of my three girls is, then you're more than welcome to walk a dog and stretch your legs along the coastal path. They'll happily listen while you have a rant or a bloody good cry.'

'I will, thank you, Heather. I meant to ask Isla when I called in at the gallery, but Tabitha was present, so I didn't like to. But any news regarding her cookery book being published? She hasn't mentioned it since I took those still shots for her – the ones with Natalia, Ned's ex-girlfriend, as the model.'

I hesitate before saying anything, knowing Isla's playing it down a little. 'Well, she's secured a contract with a small publisher on the mainland. They're currently working through the edits together, but I'm keeping my fingers crossed – it'll be out for Christmas, despite the timings being fairly tight.'

'Wonderful news, but is she not happy? I'd be singing it from the rooftops!'

'I think it's more daunting than anything for her – she doesn't know what to expect, so she's keeping it under her hat for now.'

'Pass on my congratulations, won't you? But I'm sure it'll be just fine. And what about you? A little birdy tells me you've received a certain batch of cookies, made only by the fair hands of one special gent.' Melissa gives me a coy smile and gently rubs my forearm to show she's teasing.

'My word, I see the grapevines are healthy down at the allotments!' I exclaim, instantly blushing and feeling very self-conscious.

'You know what the men folk are like down there, Heather. They pretend not to be yapping about others, but they love to spread a bit of news – they can't help themselves. And yours is definitely good news. Kaspar is a lovely chap – one in a million.' Melissa steps closer and whispers, 'Has he told you about my little incident when I first took over my plot?'

I shake my head, intrigued to hear more, but still slightly panicked to think others have been talking. Though once Mungo hears a whisper, he has to wheedle more out of folk; it's simply his manner.

'Exactly. Kaspar's a true gent. I bet he won't utter a word either, because he'd prefer to save my blushes. Don't worry, nothing intentional – purely accidental on my behalf – I got my clothing snagged on the wire fencing whilst chasing a stray goat. Anyway, to cut a long story short, I ended up flashing my underwear to all and sundry. Thankfully, Levi and Kaspar saved my reputation by capturing the troublesome animal. Honestly, you both deserve the good things in life.'

'Ahhh, Melissa – that's lovely of you to say.' I give a giggle, charmed by her light-heartedness.

'Anyway, I'll be heading off now, as this little one will need feeding soon, but I'll see you around. I might drop by for a cuppa one of these days.'

'No worries, honey. Focus on you, and this little boy will be as happy as Larry.'

We depart as quickly as we met. My two dogs instantly pick up the pace and we trudge back home for a warm cuppa and a plain shop-bought biscuit.

Tabitha

I pause the film partway through, grab my notebook and jot down a detail or two about the mannerisms of the actor playing Scrooge, in the scene where he's chastising the visiting charity people entering his counting house.

'How many more times?' asks my mum, looking up from her own work.

'Sorry, I know it's tiresome, but I really want to get this role right, Mum. Ebenezer has put a lot of faith in me. He could easily have given the main part to Mavis, or even Old Reg,' I say apologetically.

'You've watched three different film adaptations today,' she adds. 'It's supposed to be your day off. Hardly relaxing, is it?'

She's right; I'm sending myself crazy, trying to absorb every nuance uttered by actors who have played the role previously.

What Mum doesn't understand is that an acting role is like taking an exam; you need to immerse yourself in study beforehand if you're to deliver the goods.

'I can see why Ebenezer carries that battered old book around with him – it's too precious to put down if it contains all his performance jottings,' I say, more to myself than my parents.

'He's got nothing better to do than parade it around, that's why!' mutters Dad, reclining in his armchair and staring aimlessly at the paused screen shot. 'It can't be normal for a director to be this demanding of amateurs?'

'Doh, yeah! This is how he's risen through the ranks in his profession – I need to learn all I can from him, Dad. We might be amateurs but we can adopt professional attitudes, can't we?'

'Is this film your final bit of research?' asks Mum.

I shake my head. 'I'm researching Dickens after this. I want to gain an insight into the context and the creation of his original novella.'

'Is it truly necessary, love?' she asks. Then adds, 'You'll be dedicating hours to learning your lines soon.'

'If you don't catch up with some of your friends soon, you might be heading down the same route as this Ebenezer geezer!' offers Dad.

'Phuh! No chance. You'd think I'd know this story inside out, given the number of times we've watched it as a family. But the more I read the book and browse the script, the more I'm discovering what each actor brings to these film adaptations. It's fascinating!'

'Humbug!' mutters Mum, receiving a chuckle from Dad, before returning to her own task.

'Ah, Mum, you're too funny!' I say, releasing the pause button on the TV and grimacing at my mum's sense of humour.

Chapter Twenty-Three

Saturday 24 September

Callie

'Callie, could I have a word, please?' asks Jemima, standing on the doorstep of the tradesman's entrance, as if she's been looking out for me.

'Sure. Anything up?' I ask, crossing the cobbled courtyard and walking briskly away from The Orangery.

Jemima is standing in front of my granddad's old front door; it's been two weeks since it was installed here, but it still brings me up short.

'Not really, just wanted a quick chat,' she says.

I smile, but now I know there's something up, because this isn't Jemima; we might be cousins, but we've never bothered with regular catch-ups.

Jemima leads the way through the corridors with their gleaming white wall tiles and scrubbed floors, passing through the old kitchen now used by the hotel and straight out towards the posh bit. This section of the manor makes me nervous, with the amount of tartan, tapestries and crystal hanging above our heads.

'We'll use the library, to save time,' she says, indicating the oak door.

Further along, in the main hallway, I spy the hotel reception, with guests checking in.

Jemima politely holds the door open for me. She's looking well today – more her usual self – as I enter and head straight for the couch. I'm guessing this won't be a quick chinwag, in which case I'd have preferred to stand, nod, possibly agree, then swiftly leave. Though she'll have to walk me back to the exit, because I don't venture into the manor often enough to know my way around.

'Anyway, some things have been brought to my attention and I was wondering if I needed to be concerned or not,' she begins, settling herself on the couch opposite.

Her warm smile suggests I shouldn't worry – but I do, always.

'Such as . . .?' I wait. I want to hear the details before answering.

Jemima takes a deep breath. 'Ned's received a couple of letters in recent weeks regarding your curt behaviour, some tardiness, and instances of rudeness towards customers. I know Isla mentioned these complaints to you briefly, a while ago, but you didn't flag anything in particular as a cause for concern. So, I was wondering if the situation with Pippa has eased a little.'

'No!'

She blinks rapidly, taken aback by my sharpness.

'I mean, no,' I repeat, making an effort to soften my tone. 'Nothing has changed. The situation has definitely mellowed in recent months, but we don't get along, you know that.'

'We all got along as children.'

'Nah, we didn't. Being the eldest, I was always the one left in charge while you pair moaned and whined until your parents collected you. I can hardly say it was a pleasure, babysitting family.'

Jemima shifts in her seat. I continue, before she interrupts trying to soothe troubled waters that run deeper than Loch Ness.

'There's just the two years between you and me, but a gap of four years with Pippa. We've nothing in common.'

'You have me.'

I stare – what trick is she trying to pull on me? 'I don't think you count.'

'Maybe I should. You see, I recall things very differently. As a child, I remember being excited to share time with both my cousins; we'd visit the park, we'd be excited to go on the swings, the slides and the roundabout. I think we even ventured out roller skating one time, and we often walked the coastal road, just the three of us.'

Mmmm, given the height of the coastal drop – how did we ever survive? I wonder.

I smile. Jemima's always been a glass half full kind of girl, and Pippa's the glass half empty type, whereas I'm more concerned about the quality of the glassware I'm using – rapidly followed by the repayment terms needed, if I pay by credit card!

'Jemima, where's this leading?'

She shuffles on the couch for a second time, before coming clean. 'Pippa seems in a better place at the moment, she's enjoying life getting to know Levi. Ned and I are preparing for the baby, so I just wanted to check up on you. How are you doing?'

Bloody hell, how do I get out of this one? Well, it's like this, Jemima. You fell into money and married the guy. Pippa obtained her freedom on the roads of Shetland by delivering bread in a mobile van and hooked up with a local taxi driver. And I'm stuck in your artisan café, selling cake all day, shuffling credit card bills each night, and living alongside my parents who, as you know, aren't a barrel of laughs, even on a good day.

'Fine. Just fine,' I say quietly.

'Pippa might have made some huge mistakes in the past, but I think she's turned over a new leaf in recent times.'

'I'll believe it when I see it.'

'It runs deep, doesn't it?' she asks, tilting her head and scrutinising me.

'You of all people know what she's like. She stole the honesty box money from the allotment's Veggie Rack store and sabotaged a pumpkin, purely to get one over on you. Don't be fooled – you're hardly her best buddy, Jemima.'

'You're right, she did do those things – for those exact reasons. But I'm sensing you've something on your mind, and a problem shared is a problem halved.'

'I don't think that's any of your business, Jemima. I don't ask you about your private life, cousins or not.'

'Callie. I'm trying to help.'

'Really?'

'Yes, really!'

'I . . . I . . .' I stand up before my brain is in gear. I'm as surprised as Jemima to find myself standing over her, looking down at her seated position.

I'm as tetchy as hell. The end of the month is fast approaching, and I'll need to settle more bills. I've no gracious words to declare, no witty comeback to make – and worst still, I can't even storm out because I have no idea which way to turn along the tiled corridors. I continue to stutter, my brain whirring in search of something to say, and then it arrives.

'Not all of us find ourselves in your fortunate position in life. Some of us budget, week in and week out, purely to afford the basics in life, so please spare me the lecture. And now . . . I'd appreciate it if you'd walk me back to the tradesman's entrance.'

There, I've said it. Not as eloquently as I'd have liked, if I'd only had more thinking time, but there's no taking it back. I certainly hadn't intended to spill my woes on the library floor for her and Ned to pick over when they find a spare minute. And given the look of surprise etched across Jemima's features, there's no denying that she heard.

'Certainly but . . .'

'Jemima, I'd quite like to return to my work, please – I'd hate for Isla to be left alone struggling with the early morning orders for the artists.'

Jemima slowly responds, her composure is rattled, her movements slow; that's taken the wind out of her sails. 'This way.'

We walk in silence through the rabbit warren of corridors. I sigh when we reach the tradesman's door, refusing to be distracted by thoughts of our granddad. I don't wait for Jemima's pleasantries. I yank the door and it opens freely – which is another of Jemima's achievements, I reflect bitterly.

'Callie, if there's anything I can help with . . .' Her words fade, before she adds, 'Please, you only have to say.'

'Sure.' My answer is automatic, verging on sarcastic.

'I mean it.'

'Of course you do. But it's so easy being the one offering the help, when you aren't the one needing it – or the one obliged to accept it.' Bloody hell, the truth always comes out.

Jemima nods; she gets it. She was there, once upon a time.

Heather

I traipse along the driveway of Harmony Cottage, making my way to the pony paddock that stretches alongside it. The Shetland pony's face appears over the wooden gate to watch my slow approach; he's jet black and adorable.

'Morning, my lovely,' I call, knowing full well I sound as daft as they come. 'Are you ready for our date, looking forward to a mucking-out session?'

The pony simply burrs his lips in reply. How many years have we done this? It has to be nearing fourteen; Isla was just a nipper when she started having riding lessons. And every day since, I've either seen, cared for or thought of this cheeky boy with his rotund belly and stumpy legs. I unlatch the gate and the pony moves back, allowing me through. I dip my hand into my jacket pocket, retrieving a few goodies, which Jutt snaffles with a fluttering top lip.

'Life would be so different without you, old boy.'

I joke that Isla should allow him to leave our little family and take up residence elsewhere, enabling small children to ride him every day, but she won't hear of it; deep down, neither will I. I keep testing her, purely to strengthen her resolve to keep this fine boy. Who knows? He might still be here when the next generation are old enough to cling tightly to his mane and enjoy a plod along the lane.

Isla does what she can, offering lessons to children in the area, but he's not ridden half as much as he used to be. Though he's still in his prime. I'm hoping Isla doesn't move him to pastures on the Lerwick estate, alongside the alpaca paddock, as I'd miss my daily chats with this peerie fella.

We traipse across the paddock, and pick up our conversation from yesterday. I ready myself to do my daughter a giant favour by mucking him out whilst she's still at work. Isla's excellent with her husbandry tasks, but today I need a physical, outdoorsy chore to ease my second date nerves. Mucking out is the perfect job.

'I'm like a giddy schoolgirl. According to Ellie, "I'm a serial first dater" – through no fault of my own, I'd like to add, Jutt.'

I dated in my younger days, of course I did, but this is different, very different. Back then, I was an impressionable young woman; I wore my heart on my sleeve, had only one dream, and found myself agreeing to like anything Jimmy was into, purely to oblige him and appear compatible. I cringe when I think back on the hours I spent chatting to a pair of legs in oil-stained overalls protruding from beneath the chassis of a car while he tinkered with an exhaust. Did I really class that as spending quality time with my boyfriend? Had I nothing better to do with my time?

'Yet now, a fully fledged mother of two young women, with a busy life and more commitments than I care to count – tonight's date with Kaspar seems ideal.' I stare down at the pony keeping pace alongside me; as we near his stable, his ears are twitching as he listens. 'I've come into my own as the years have passed, don't you agree?'

I want to giggle, because this pony has listened to me chuntering on for years and never once shunned my nonsense – be it trouble at home, daft arguments within the family, or parental nightmares.

'I'll show an interest in whatever his hobbies are, I'll ask questions, and draw out more information as the night goes on. And not purely for the sake of securing a third date. If getting to know each other doesn't work, then the relationship simply doesn't work, does it?'

It seemed vital when I was younger to have plenty in common, but now life's taught me that opposites certainly do attract. And more importantly, it's the connection and chemistry that support a healthy relationship, plus interests outside the partnership to maintain a happy balance. I've learnt that from our Isla, when she dated that no-hoper, Lachlan. She tried to live in his pocket, morning, noon and night, only to be used – and, dare I say it, emotionally abused by his game playing.

The pony comes to a halt as I open the tiny storage shed and collect the shovel and broom, before continuing. 'The poor girl gave up her friends, her nights out, all on the off-chance that he'd be free and wanting to spend time with her. Thankfully, she never gave you up, Jutt – which is a blessing.'

Funny how my household has always stuck by their animals, refusing to neglect and rehome anything – from a goldfish to guinea pigs or ponies. We've always shown a true sense of responsibility towards them, and yet others haven't been so loyal towards us. 'My girls' father treated us with less respect in his so-called efforts to be a family man,' I tell Jutt. 'The dog upped and offed, leaving me to raise his pups – ironic, in view of my chosen career, don't you think? I blamed myself for years afterwards, for having been so naive in my choice of mate.'

I grab all the necessary equipment before starting, making the task easier. I chat away happily to Jutt as I work. 'It's good to see my daughter keeps her tackle spick and span – it shows a level of maturity and discipline. It's surprising how well our Isla has turned out; there were times in the past when I worried like crazy, but she's proving to me there really was no need. If anything, in recent weeks, it's our Ellie I've been more concerned about. I'm not too keen on some of the attitudes she's displaying regarding other people's looks – her comments are instant and pretty disparaging.'

My phone begins to ring. I tug it from my pocket, to find an unknown number flashing across my screen. Do I answer or not? My heart suddenly plummets; I bet this is Kaspar cancelling tonight's arrangements.

'Hello?' I say, sounding as bright and cheerful as I can, whilst expecting the worst.

'Hello? Is that Heather?' asks a male voice.

It doesn't sound like Kaspar.

'Yes, Heather speaking.'

'Hi, it's Jock McHaddit from the butcher's . . . I was wondering if you were doing anything tonight?'

OMG! I peel the phone away from my ear, stare at the unknown number as if checking for something, and then return it to my ear.

'Actually, I'm busy tonight.'

'Ah, right, tomorrow maybe?'

What the hell? Be nice, Heather, it takes a lot to call and ask.

'I'm so sorry but I'm not free this week.'

'Is next week good for you?'

Heck! Why did I say that? Do I really want another night hearing about the 'Butcher's Bargains' when a brisk walk past the window would be preferable? Though, to be fair, I haven't walked that way since our first date, for fear of being spotted. Where's this phone call popped up from?

'Actually, Jock, I've started to get to know someone else, and I'm a little uneasy getting to know two people at once. I know others do it, but that really isn't me. I like to keep things simple, if I'm honest.'

'Oh, I see. Anyone I know?'

I bristle at his question; given that we live in close proximity, the answer is, 'Probably.' But I don't wish to be drawn on the subject, so I keep it vague. 'I'm not sure, Jock.'

'OK, I'll see you around then . . . when you're passing maybe . . . we've got a great deal on brisket this week.'

'Sounds lovely.' I tap the screen quickly, ending the call, for fear he might launch into reciting a meat-feast list.

'Close shave there, Jutt, my boy!' I say, patting the faithful pony on his rump.

Which gives me the heebie-jeebies, knowing that 'prime rump' is probably on the 'Butcher's Bargains' list.

I've made a decent start with clearing the dirty straw bedding and have trundled my filled wheelbarrow several times to our manure pile, when my phone rings again. I cringe; please, not Jock again.

I retrieve my phone, to find a different unknown number displayed. Don't say this is Kaspar.

'Hello?'

'Hi there, is that Heather?'

'Speaking.'

'Hi, it's Irvine, we met up for a drink the other week. I was wondering if you're busy tonight?'

'Hello, Irvine, good to hear from you,' I say, composing myself to answer with another kindly rejection. 'Tonight, as in *tonight*?' Is short notice the new norm? Personally, if I were a bloke, I'd give a little notice – a few days, at least.

'Yeah, I thought we could grab a bite to eat and—'

I interrupt him before he finishes. 'I have to be honest, Irvine, I'm out on a date tonight.'

'Really?'

I hear his questioning tone and my hackles rise, so I quickly add, 'Yes, a lovely gent, he called a few days ago and gave me plenty of notice. Which allowed time for me to check my diary and suggest a convenient night out, without it being suddenly sprung on me.'

'Oh, like that, is it?'

'I share my life with others, and I have responsibilities, so I can't always drop everything at the prospect of a last-minute date. I need a little planning time.'

'I'm not a planner, Heather. I'm a ball of energy, a man who lives life to the full, twenty-four seven, and goes after what he wants.'

'I see, well, that doesn't quite work in my life. I have a basket of newborn pups and their nursing mum to care for, two young women to consider, and elderly relatives who rely on me.'

The line goes dead.

Was I too harsh, or too honest? Am I proving to be picky – or even too difficult to date?

'Oh well, Jutt – if Kaspar phones and cancels me at the last minute, I've definitely burnt my bridges elsewhere.'

The pony grazes from his freshly filled hay net as I continue to shovel and sweep the remnants of last night's bedding.

When my phone rings for the third time, I literally raise my hands to the heavens. Can I not get peace and quiet for an hour to complete one simple task?

I pull my phone from my pocket to find our Magnus' name flashing on the screen.

'Yep, what's up with you?' I say, knowing it'll be a fleeting call, it always is with him.

'Heather, have you any idea where my mum is?'

'No.' Instantly, alarm bells ring. 'I'm assuming she's not at home?'

'Nope. Dad has called, saying she went out first thing this morning and hasn't been seen since. I wondered if she'd dropped by yours for a cuppa and cake ... but if you haven't seen her then I can't imagine where she's got to.'

'Are you at the farmhouse?'

'Yep, just arrived. I've checked all the rooms – you know what they're both like.'

'And you're sure she's not there?'

'She's nowhere to be found. Her coat has gone, plus her out-door shoes and that big brolly.'

'OK. Take a look at the calendar on the kitchen wall above the dog bowls. Is there anything pencilled in?' I wait, listening to his muffled footsteps as he walks across their kitchen.

'No. Today is empty.'

'What about a week today?' I ask, knowing she's made mistakes before now.

'Nope, that too.'

'I'm as flummoxed as you. She's pretty good at saying what her plans are, and she hasn't mentioned anything in recent days.'

'Have you seen Floss today?' asks Magnus.

'No. Is she missing too?' A sudden rush of warmth fills my heart for one of the first dogs I ever bred.

'Yep. Which gets me thinking.'

'Right, I'm coming straight over. Give me ten minutes.' I end the call, and kick my mucking-out routine to the kerb. 'Sorry, Jutt old boy, but our Isla will have to carry on from this point. Duty calls.' I give the pony a hearty pat on his neck and dash off, heading for the farmhouse.

As I hotfoot it down the uneven driveway of Harmony Cottage, I recall our Iona's usual Saturday routine. A bit of cleaning – if she feels up to it. A trip to the local shop – if she feels well enough to walk. And several chapters of a library book – come rain or shine. Magnus' phone call might have been panicked, but a disappearing act on our Clyde, or an unexpected invite in the local vicinity, aren't usually on her agenda! And what did he mean about Floss being missing as well? It's Iona who's missing, isn't it? None of it makes sense!

I'm not aware of when I started to cry – on the phone or reaching the end of the driveway – but the sheer confusion rises within me like a torrent of waves dashing against the black rocks.

Tabitha

'How much work have you done?' asks Rabbie, picking up my script copy from beneath the countertop.

We're enjoying a quiet moment during my Saturday rush.

'I guess more than you have?'

'I've done nothing, other than having a quick chat with Aileen to check how she's planning on playing it. She's only really got the one scene, so I don't want to clip her wings by overshadowing her performance with mine, but she's happy keeping it simple. But this . . .' he waves my annotated script at me, 'is something else.'

'Stop it, I'm simply taking pride in my role – giving it all I've got. You should try it,' I playfully jest, before peeling away to answer a customer's question. 'How may I help you?'

I busy myself with the lady and her questions about a specific allergy and goat's milk; I can't help noticing Rabbie going through my script, his eyes wide and eyebrows twitching at various points.

'Impressed?' I ask, my tone slightly flirty, after finishing with my customer and returning to the counter area.

'I'd say so. Do you fancy marking up my script like this one?'

'Not a chance! That little masterpiece took me all day on Tuesday to complete – and every night since, to read and digest.'

'You need to be careful, or soon you'll be turning into Eben-ezer. We'll be seeing you as his natural successor when he retires as director.'

'Phuh! I doubt that very much!'

'Honest, you'll be there with your own battered ledger, making pencilled notes about each of us actors during auditions and casting. Putting little marks against our names for each error we make or session we miss.' Rabbie carefully stashes the script beneath the countertop, before heading over to greet a new group of customers.

He's pulling my leg, but his tone sounds fairly serious – as if he's not entirely happy with my actions. Did he secretly want the main lead? Or are my efforts making him feel inadequate about his role?

Hmmm, interesting.

There's no sign of animosity for the remaining hour. Rabbie serves customers and answers questions as gleefully as I do. But try as I might, I can't shake off the nagging suspicion that I've picked up on something earlier – something Rabbie might not wish to discuss.

'Was it a childhood obsession or regret that led you to join the am-dram group?' I ask, a short time before he's due to clock off and return to his bell boy duties in the hotel.

'Neither, to be fair. I always auditioned for the school plays, remember? My parents were both enthusiastic about the local group in their younger days. They're for ever reminiscing about past shows, the laughs backstage – in fact, that's how they met.'

'Sounds romantic,' I say, swooning slightly at the prospect of young love blossoming on the stage.

'Not really. My dad split his trousers on the opening night of *Singing in the Rain* – my mother happened to save the performance, and his blushes, by having safety pins in her purse. The rest is history, as they say,' explains Rabbie, digging out his dicky bow and attempting to thread it under his collar without a mirror.

'Here, you're making a right hash of that,' I say, automatically reaching across to correct his skewed collar.

'Cheers.' There's a sudden flush to his cheeks, and I hastily retract my hand.

That's the second time today I've felt something between us. I'm not sure if it's a flirty vibe. Maybe not? But I'm definitely not the only one sensing it.

'Sorry, your collar was turned under.'

'No worries,' he says, averting his gaze and busying himself collecting his belongings from beneath the counter. 'Will I see you on Thursday?'

'Yeah, sure. I never miss a session, especially not now.'

'Cool. See you later.'

Heather

'Can you imagine how embarrassed I was when I opened the front door?'

Isla starts ranting at me before I've had a chance to remove my coat and explain.

'He arrived bang on eight – and he'd even brought you flowers!'

She gestures to the draining board where a colourful bouquet stands upright, the stems submerged in a bowl of water. Now I feel guilty, as well as exhausted.

'And then he stood on the doorstep, gawping at me as if he'd knocked at the wrong house. I felt so sorry for him, Mum. He was all dressed up. I've only ever seen him wearing his yellow waders, but not tonight. He looked lovely, he'd really made an effort, and you didn't even bother to call him to cancel.'

'Hang on a minute! I didn't do it on purpose; I had an emergency. How would you feel if your sister went missing? On second thoughts, don't answer that one, but I'm sorry.' I throw my handbag and keys on to the table, before looking Isla squarely in the face. 'I panicked when Magnus said that Floss was missing too. And yes, I can imagine how embarrassing it was for you to open the door and have to explain that your mother had gone AWOL. And yes, I admit it, I hadn't actually mentioned to Kaspar that you're my daughter. You don't mention everything on the first date. I didn't lie, I simply said I had two daughters, but that was all. Our conversation that night wasn't about you!' I'm fraught, tetchy, and now bloody annoyed to arrive home and receive an ear-bashing from Isla.

'I gathered that, by the look on his face, Mum! Poor Kaspar got the shock of his life – he didn't know whether to ask for you or order his morning latte!'

'I'll phone him. I'll apologise and explain everything. I didn't do it on purpose, you know. I had a family emergency, which it wouldn't kill you to ask about!'

'Is she back home?'

'Yeah, but you still don't seem very concerned. God help us when I'm that age and go on a jolly in the middle of the day and don't come home.'

'We'll be fine,' says Isla, before adding, 'which is more than I can say for Kaspar – his face fell, he looked so sad. I'll never be able to serve him again without seeing that doleful expression. I've never seen him without a smile, until tonight. I'm sure he thought I was lying on your behalf and you didn't want to go out – he probably imagined you were hiding in the broom cupboard instead.'

'I'm truly sorry you had to deal with such an awkward situation, but seriously – give it a bloody rest. I've had enough for one night.'

'Where did she go?'

'She walked the coastal path all day, by the sounds of it. Though Floss walked alongside her all the way, hobbling along on that clunky leg of hers.'

'Ahhh, Mum, that's so lovely.'

'I know, people saw them together – going around in circles, lapping the coastal road – and thought nothing of it, so they didn't bother to enquire if she was OK.'

'You know why that is, don't you?' pipes up Ellie, calling from the front room.

'Yes, I know, I'm not stupid.'

Isla pouts, unsure what her sister is referring to.

'Marina,' I mouth silently.

Isla nods sympathetically, showing a mature understanding for her tender years.

'The poor woman must have walked that road a million times these last thirty years, in search of comfort. Our Magnus was beside himself when we spotted her shuffling along, head bent, shoulders rounded, with Floss at her side.'

'Don't, you'll make me cry,' says Isla, her hands fluttering to her mouth.

'You can imagine how we felt then?' I say, opening the fridge to grab a much-needed glass of wine. 'Physically, she was fine in herself ... just not ... coherent on her recall – it was as if she didn't know she'd even been out, which is not like our Iona. She's a bit forgetful of late, a bit hit and miss on details, but that's just her age, surely? It happens to the best of us, at one time or another.' I avert my gaze, sensing that our Isla's not fooled by my casual tone.

'And next time?' asks Isla, confirming my thoughts.

'I'm worried we won't find her ... and that dear dog won't have the stamina to accompany her.'

'Floss isn't old, Mum.'

'She's old enough – but after that road accident a few months ago, she's not fully fit; she's still recuperating. Between me and you, I can't see her ever running the sheep as she once did.'

Isla raises her eyebrows. 'Don't let Magnus hear you saying that about either his mum or his beloved dog.'

'Exactly. I think things will change up at the farmhouse after today. I do the best I can, given the time I can spare, but Iona needs more than that – and Clyde too, if I'm honest,' I say, sitting down at the scrubbed table to take a sip of my vino. 'Oooo, now that tastes good.'

Isla pushes my phone towards me. 'Call Kaspar.'

'It's quarter to ten, you don't call folk at this time of night – they'll think there's been a death in the family.'

'Please, do it for me,' whispers Isla. 'I can't bear to think he might believe you stood him up. He deserves better than that, Mum – as would you, if the tables were turned.'

Chapter Twenty-Four

Sunday 25 September

Callie

'Firstly, I want to apologise for yesterday, you must have felt ambushed by my sudden request for a chat. Sorry, Callie. I handled it badly and as a result you ... well, you were rightfully upset,' says Jemima, sitting on a couch opposite me in the manor's library.

I flush with sheer embarrassment; I want the sofa cushions to literally open wide and swallow me whole.

'I don't know what to say,' I mutter, staring into the tea cup cradled in my palm, as if that's any explanation for my actions and rudeness yesterday.

'You might want to start at the beginning.' Her tone is soft, urging me to speak.

But I fear I can't. The very thought of coming clean to someone who would never have behaved as rudely as I did is going to be mortifying.

'I'd run my credit card to the max, so I applied for a second one. I didn't think there was a hope in hell of being accepted by the company, but I was. It arrived within days, and the credit limit was fairly high, so I carried on. My intention was to use the lower introductory rate on the new card to shift the balance on the first card, which was obviously at a much higher interest rate. I worked out I'd be better off if I upped my monthly payments but ... well, that didn't quite happen, because things cropped up, and before I knew it the special introductory rate on the new card expired, leaving both credit cards on the same APR rates.'

Jemima is nodding. I know she's not going to comment, it isn't her style. She'll let me talk, without judgement, and say what needs to be said once she has all the details.

'Then I did the worst thing possible ... I applied and was accepted for a third card. And so I kept going.' I fall silent, sip my cooling tea and wait.

'How many have you got now?' she asks, shifting her position on the couch.

'Seven, maybe eight. I've had more, but I cleared those balances so I cut them up. I reckon I might have had twelve at one point. I simply juggled the various companies and banks. Paying this one, postponing payment of that one. Calling another to discuss the minimum payment and negotiate a delay in a penalty fine being issued or further action being taken,' I say, knowing I could go into much more detail. But what's the point?

Jemima gets the picture. 'And then Grandpop died?'

'Yep, I was gutted. I loved the old bugger to bits but ... oh my God, this sounds awful.' I fall silent, not wanting to continue, but knowing I must if I'm going to win her trust. 'I just thought any little legacy that he'd left me would help. I wasn't after his money, but even a couple of hundred pounds would have enabled me to get one or two of the companies off my back for an extra month. But it didn't turn out that way.'

'No, because he didn't include you or Pippa in his will.'

'Now do you see why I felt needled that you ended up with ... well, what you rightfully deserved, I'm not saying you didn't, but still, it hurt. I felt we'd been disowned by him ... disinherited by his actions and ... oh, there's no bloody excuse for what I did. There really isn't, Jemima.'

I know that, regardless of how strapped for cash Jemima has

been in her life, she'd never have sold our grandparents' posses-
sions. I did, in the blink of an eye.

'You sold Nanna's engagement ring instead?'

My jaw drops. How does she know?

'Pippa told me,' says Jemima softly.

There's no anger or irritation in her voice, simply kindness,
which I don't deserve.

'When you asked for the ring, was that your intention?'

'Of course not! Bloody hell, how ruthless do you think I am?
I know how much Nanna loved that ring; she wore it every day
of her life for sixty-odd years . . . but I was desperate. I thought,
well, kidded myself really, that she wouldn't want it sitting in
a jewellery box for ever and a day. Nanna was more practical
than that, wasn't she?'

'She certainly was thrifty. She cut coupons from the news-
paper, saved plastic bread bags to wrap Grandpop's allotment
sarnies . . . but come off it, Callie, who are you trying to convince?
She wouldn't have wanted her engagement ring sold, if that's
what you're implying.'

Jemima looks rattled now – see, everyone loses patience with
me eventually.

'Don't you think she'd have preferred that I benefit from the
money?' I ask.

'No. I don't. She'd have expected you to come to one of us, to
share your worries, so we could support you, rather than some
miser getting his hands on a piece of jewellery which, let's face
it, secured the union between her and Grandpop as the first step
towards making our existence even possible.' She finally draws
breath, before adding, 'And that's what makes me so mad – that
you'd be fickle enough to allow Nanna's ring to leave the family.'

'When did Pippa tell you?'

Jemima considers. 'Not straight away. I believe she pondered what to do and the best way to handle it, before mentioning it to me.'

'She grassed me up then?'

'Come now, be honest. You argued, you told her, and she bit back at you for selling a family heirloom. Both Pippa and I would have treasured the ring if Grandpop had given it to either of us, instead of you, after Nanna's death.'

'I wasn't given it after Nanna's death. I asked for it when we cleared out his apartment at the Happy Days sheltered housing complex. So if she's told you anything else, she's lying – as ever.'

'That's exactly what she told me.'

I don't answer, there's no point.

'I'll fill you in on the ending, then it might help you to see Pippa in a different light. She retrieved Nanna's ring from the antique jeweller you'd sold it to.'

'No,' I gasp. 'Did he charge her?'

'Course he did, he's in business.'

I wait, wanting her to continue without me having to ask how much Pippa paid.

'If you're interested, she had to pay him fifteen hundred quid.'

'No way! He gave me just eight hundred.'

'I know, Pippa said.'

I put my tea cup down; some dregs remain, but the tea's cold. 'What's she planning to do with the ring now?' I ask, wanting to fish for all the information I can get, but knowing I don't have any right to be consulted, in view of my recent conduct.

'Well, that's where she surprised me. Pippa asked if I would accept it . . . for safe keeping.'

'You've got it?' Knock me down with a feather.

'I was reluctant at first, but Pippa insisted that I look after it and make sure it stays within the family. I have no issue with you or her borrowing it, if you want to – I don't believe it should be mine but enjoyed by us all.'

'I asked for it, Pippa paid for it, but you've got it?'

Jemima gives a tiny chuckle. 'That sounds wrong, somehow, but it's entirely factual. Though . . .' she pauses, before waving aside her next remark.

'No, go on.'

'Well, actually, Pippa isn't out of pocket. Ned and I wanted to ensure that her good deed for the family was recognised in a fitting manner.'

'So you gave her the money?' I can't believe what I'm hearing.

'Not quite. It all happened in a roundabout manner . . . in a way that was acceptable to both parties, given the circumstances.'

'And has Pippa asked to wear or borrow the ring since?'

'No, actually, she hasn't. But if she does, who am I to argue? I haven't worn it either, for that matter.'

'See what I mean? Sitting in a jewellery box gathering dust. I knew it would be.'

Jemima tilts her head. I know what she's about to say before she opens her mouth.

'The reality is, we know it's sitting in *my* jewellery box gathering dust until it's needed, Callie. And not in the possession of some stranger who doesn't know its history or the decades of devotion it symbolises.'

Ouch! I flinch at her words. Though I deserve them.

Heather

'I am so, so sorry,' I say for the umpteenth time, as we sit on a bench overlooking Lerwick harbour.

Kaspar is more forgiving of my actions – my daughters not so much. If I have to hear one more time, from either of them, how rude my behaviour was, I'll scream. It's become a constant refrain in our house – whether halfway through our dinner, watching the soaps, or each time I casually mention his name.

'You don't need to say anything more – you've apologised, and I believe you,' says Kaspar.

'I don't want to mess this up,' I admit, as his hand reaches for mine. 'I seem to have a knack for messing things up, or so my daughters keep telling me.' I also don't wish to be rebranded a serial first dater, but that's another issue.

'You haven't messed up, Heather. I like you, a lot. You make me laugh, and I hope to get to know you better,' he says, sounding charming rather than awkward.

I can relax; he believes me.

'The lady who went missing – she's your sister?'

'Yes, but she's much older than me. I was a late surprise for my parents, so the age gap is quite telling now we've reached this stage in our lives. It's strange, because in recent years I haven't noticed the age difference so much. But now it feels like when I was a small child; I was attending primary school and she was raising her own family – that seemed an incredibly large age gap, which closed as the years went on, only to reappear now.'

'I have no siblings, but I understand how frightened you must have been . . . helpless.'

'Exactly. I kept thinking, what if she's fallen over, banged her head, or worse . . .?' My words fade.

I take comfort as Kaspar squeezes my hand. A silent gesture, from a near stranger, yet it shows more understanding than I've received from my nearest and dearest. How is that possible?

'Your brother, he'll sort out a carer or a nurse, maybe?'

'He's my nephew, actually. No, I'm not sure that's the kind of care they need. I think it's more subtle than that. Magnus is so busy with the sheep and alpacas, he hasn't had the opportunity to see and hear everything that goes on at the farmhouse. I think they need more of a network around them, to observe and step in when little issues arise, taking it day by day. I suppose a woman's touch is needed, around the clock, rather than a big burly bloke breezing in when he's got a spare moment. And Magnus is already juggling so many other commitments.'

'We try our best.'

'Oh yes, he gives it his all. He's done very well over the years, managing to cope, but the next few years are going to be telling for both my sister and her husband. I'm not so sure the situation is going to ease before it gets worse.'

'Your Magnus is not with a partner?'

'Yeah, but Verity has her own decisions to make. I thought she'd have decided by now, but apparently not. I suppose the prospect of additional responsibilities, when you'd quite like to be loved up and nest building, isn't the fairest thing to expect from a relatively new partner.'

'I think about the future too. I'm here on my own, just me . . . active and very capable now, but in time, who knows? I might need help, or maybe I could be useful to someone else, if they are in need.'

I nod. I get where he's coming from. I scour the harbour front and note the various boats moored there; some of the masts are tall and elegant, while others are stubbier and squat. If I were a boat, I'd want to be the former rather than the latter. Maybe it's not the boat but the skipper and crew that make the difference. Who knows?

'None of us are getting any younger, are we?' I say absent-mindedly.

'No, and I believe none of us get out of here alive either!' he says, with a cheeky grin. 'Which is why I try my best now. I try to find a good person, a loving woman, who makes me laugh, and then we share our time together. Does that make sense?'

'Kaspar, it makes more sense today than it did yesterday.'

'Perfect, so let's put this gloomy talk behind us and enjoy our time together. Yes?' He gives my hand a final squeeze.

I warmly return the gesture. I've got a funny feeling that I'm no longer in the serial first daters club, which will be headline news back home.

We sit on the bench overlooking the harbour for ages, probably the longest time I've spent in years. And we simply talk.

We talk about the passing boats, the rolling waves, his job navigating the ferry. We talk about my girls, our childhood memories, and the souring of past relationships. And just when I'm becoming conscious that we've nothing left to talk about . . .

He kisses me.

Not a polite peck on the cheek, as he did at the end of our first date. But a full-blown 'I like you and I want to know you better' kiss, the kind I haven't had in years. A kiss that takes me by surprise and yet doesn't, as his closeness and lingering gaze are clearly apparent. A kiss I've been secretly dreading, having forgotten how to kiss a man. I've been fearing the basics of intimacy, in case I mess up the magic of the moment by not responding in the right way. But when his lips gently touch mine, I welcome his gesture. I let go of my fear, cease thinking and simply react in the moment. Our moment.

Callie

I'm fuming. To think I told Pippa about Nanna's engagement ring in confidence and she went behind my back and sought it out. For what? Just to make me look and feel worse than I already did? Or to suck up to Jemima? Either way, she's got a nerve – and then what? Gifting the ring to Jemima. As if she needs any more good luck or wealth! The Lerwick Manor estate and Ned's inheritance have both landed in her lap in recent months. My God, when you think about it, money always goes to money, doesn't it? Never to those who need it the most.

'Morning, Callie! Jemima came looking for you earlier,' says Isla as I walk into The Orangery, already late for my waitressing shift.

'I've spoken to her, thanks.' I don't miss a stride but walk straight through to the rear, in a hurry to stash my jacket and handbag.

I'm not expecting the Spanish Inquisition from Isla. She doesn't need to know my business – though I'm sure Jemima will share a few choice snippets with her when she's ready to confide in someone.

I hang my jacket on my designated coat peg.

I wonder if Pippa haggled with the jeweller over the price of the ring? To think he gave me eight hundred, yet sold it to her for a grand and a half – what a rip off! Our Pippa must be rolling in it, if she can find that sort of money.

I return to the front of house, to find Isla is not alone.

'Speak of the devil,' I say, knowing it'll push Pippa's buttons, just as Jemima prodded mine.

Isla and Pippa cease their morning chat and glance over towards me.

'Me?' says Pippa, as if it would be anyone else.

'Yes, you! Jemima just mentioned Nanna's engagement ring ... were you not going to mention it to me?'

Her cheery expression fades, to be replaced by a pensive stare. 'Not really, given that you weren't in the equation any longer. You had it, you sold it, and now someone else is looking after it ... what's the difference?'

'It would have been nice to know, that's all. I told you everything in confidence, and then what ... you hawked your way through Lerwick, seeking it out?'

'Pretty much. The small detail you're forgetting, Callie, is that she was our nanna too. If you didn't want the ring, surely your first port of call should have been me or Jemima, not some stranger with an eye glass and a wodge of notes.' Pippa's tone is defensive.

I glare at Pippa, and she glares back.

Isla's expression is one of shock. 'Ladies, ladies, it's none of my business, but surely this isn't the way to conduct a family conversation. If you want to take five and have a chat, I'll bring you each a coffee over. But this . . .' she gestures between our frozen stances, 'is not how family should behave.'

Neither of us answers. We're staring each other out, like we did as children. Though if I remember correctly, I rarely won.

'What's it to be – call it quits or coffee time?'

'Quits,' I say.

'Coffee,' mutters Pippa.

Isla looks between us. 'I could have predicted that one.'

I make the decision for us. I grab my pinny from beneath the counter, swiftly tying it round my waist, signalling my choice.

'Excuse me,' I say to Isla as I reach for the bottle of cleaning spray and a cloth, currently blocked by her legs.

She steps aside cautiously, as if expecting me to pull a stunt on her or my younger cousin. I pretend neither of them are watching me as I head towards the rear of the café and begin the first task of the day: wiping down tables.

When I next look up, Pippa has gone; I expect she's busy filling her mobile bread van with baskets of fresh bakes, preparing to head out on the open road for the day.

'Here, I've made you a drink,' says Isla kindly, placing a fresh latte on the serving counter. 'Want to talk?'

'Nope.'

'OK, but shout if you do.' With that, she turns on her heels and takes her drink into the back room, leaving me alone with my thoughts.

Can you imagine the look on her face if I'd told her the truth?

Thousands of pounds in debt. Selling Nanna's ring saved me from a potential disaster; I was able to pay off a chunk of debt to a company that was threatening serious action. Would Nanna have wanted me to keep her ring in a jewellery box, untouched for years? I'm not sentimental, never have been, but I get why my cousins are so hurt. I just don't want to discuss it, for fear of having to come clean to everyone.

Boy, what it must be like to have as much money as you need. I don't mean wealthy, but enough to be comfortable from one week to the next. A simple existence such as my parents have created – though at this rate there's little hope I'll ever emulate their achievement!

Chapter Twenty-Five

Saturday 1 October

Ebenezer's ledger

What I wouldn't give to play Scrooge one final time! Bah humbug! Tabitha's trans-
formation and acting skills need to convince her audience that she's a cold-hearted
miser. With the warmth she bestows on others, I'm now doubting my casting choice.
But if she plays it too well, she might fall foul of the dramatic muse and end up
re-enacting the role, day after day – like the rest of us.

Callie

My irritation towards Pippa simmers for an entire week. As I
watch Magnus and Floss practise herding the alpacas around
their paddock, my anger and emotions boil over when I spy
Pippa heading over on her day off.

'Hi,' she says, leaning on the fence a little way along.

'I still can't believe you told Jemima I'd sold Nanna's ring!' I
sneer, unable to let the subject drop.

'Which is what you should have done, but chose not to, Callie.'

'I had good reason,' I mutter.

'Really? Maybe you'd like to enlighten me, because it must be
one hell of a good reason to sell Nanna's engagement ring behind
our backs,' retorts Pippa, shifting her position against the fencing.

I hesitate. Pippa wouldn't get it, even if I tried explaining.
She'd sneer and pout, call me a liar, accuse me of being selfish –
and I'd have to reveal more about myself than I want to – so
what's the point?

'I knew you wouldn't be able to come clean. That's the problem with you, Callie – you always expect everyone else to drop into line with your plans, when you can't actually justify your actions. It's like when we were little and you always took charge of the sweet money on trips to the local store. It wasn't because you were any more trustworthy than us, simply that you were the eldest and the adults thought it best. But you milked it for all it was worth, and even when we arrived at the shop, you chose our sweets – you never allowed us to hold our own money. No, you had to be in charge of every single penny.'

I squirm at the memory; she's not wrong. Boy, how I wish I could go back to those days and keep a tight grip on my money. My life would be so different from what it is now. I chase my tail every day of the month; the only glimmer of hope is the morning of pay day when, for a couple of hours, I'm filled with optimism for the month ahead. Though as soon as I sit down to tackle my budget, I realise I should have worked an extra hundred hours if I'm to survive the month ahead. The very next day, I'm back on the treadmill: juggling debts, shuffling card payments and stuffing envelopes into my handbag for 'safe keeping'.

'Has the cat got your tongue?' asks Pippa.

Lost in my own thoughts, I'd almost forgotten she was present. 'No,' I say, staring mutinously in the direction of Magnus and Floss in the paddock. If I ignore her, she'll hopefully lose interest and leave me alone.

'Callie?'

I look over, give a sigh, awaiting her next jibe.

'Are you OK?' Her tone has changed; the edginess has gone.

'I'm fine.'

'Come on, I know you're not!' Her hand slides towards mine, and gently takes hold. 'Tell me.'

I don't answer, nor do I look up, as my eyes fill with tears. I can't let her see me upset. I've told Jemima, but Pippa doesn't need to know. She'll mention it to her mum, and she'll mention it to my dad, and then the whole family will go around in circles, asking, questioning, talking and judging, because that's what happens in our family. Everyone judges, without actually knowing the facts or asking a single damn question.

'Just stop it, will you? I've had enough!' It feels like a dam has broken within, as I snatch my hand back from her gentle hold. In an instant, I am a mess of snot and tears, still fuelled by a gush of anger, while my cousin stands frozen with shock, staring at the meltdown before her.

'OK, I hear you,' she attempts to reassure me. 'But whatever is going on ... surely I can help in some small way. This isn't the Callie I know. You're usually bubbly and bright, but this ... this isn't you.'

'Isn't it? How would you even know?'

'Callie, I know you, for God's sake, we're family.'

I look up and stare into her bright-blue eyes. 'What does that even mean?' I shake my head at the utter nonsense. 'It means we share DNA – it means nothing more. All the crap that your mum spouts about "standing together as family" is utter tosh. You've become closer to Jemima in recent times, through working here, but I'm not convinced that you'd choose to be friends with her outside of the gallery.'

Pippa shrugs. 'What can I say? She's grown on me.'

I snort.

'Don't dismiss my answer, please. I'm being honest. I rarely spoke to her before Granddad died but now, yeah, I think I would choose her as a friend. Likewise, with you, as well.'

'Now I know you're lying.'

'Am I?'

'Pippa, you don't even have the time of day for me. You curl your lip whenever you see me, growl if I ask you a question, and berate me if I go anywhere near that damn mobile bread van of yours. So please, you're not fooling me with your sickly-sweet comments.'

'Did I pinch the honesty box money from *you*?'

'Err no.'

'Did I sabotage *your* pumpkin in order to knock you down a peg or two?'

I shake my head, wiping my tears on the cuff of my cardigan.

'I did those things to Jemima, but we've still been able to salvage the basics of a relationship. So there's hope for you and me yet.'

'What are you saying?' I'm confused.

'Maybe . . . we could try to build a bridge or two?'

'Why would you even want to?'

'Just because . . . I can.'

Pippa looks genuine; she sounds authentic, but we all know that Pippa can tell porky pies the minute it suits her.

'What? Are you recalling all the fibs I've told?' she asks, watching my reaction intently.

I give a tiny nod.

'I don't blame you, but honestly . . . I've changed since being with Levi. He's taught me that I'm allowed to be the version of me I want to be. No lies, just one hundred per cent authentic Pippa, who does as she wishes – and that's me. I'm not living within the limitations imposed by others any more; I do what I feel and say what I choose. Like it or lump it, this is me!'

My God, how liberating!

I doubt I'll ever be able to muster such honesty, or have the confidence to make a similar declaration. Though I suppose if Pippa can do it, maybe there's hope for the rest of us!

Tabitha

'I can't thank you enough,' I say, looking into the large mirror at the reflection of Callie standing behind my chair.

The corner of my mum's kitchen on a Saturday night is hardly a conventional beauty salon, but it's the best I can do.

'I'm sure it's been a long and tiring day for us both, but at least we have wine.' I lift my glass in a mock toast.

'I'm happy to help. I only hope you aren't disappointed,' says Callie, taking a sip of her wine and tilting her goblet towards the mirror, as if to clink with mine.

It took a few minutes to rearrange the kitchen, dragging the family-sized table across to the countertop, providing a suitable work station for Callie's vast supply of products and styling equipment. We've pinched the lounge mirror from over the mantelpiece and propped it up against the splashback of the cooker. It feels a lot like those Sunday nights as a child when my mum would suggest a little tidy of my fringe before school the next day, and a bath towel would be swiftly draped around my shoulders. It's an experience from which I'll never recover; I still shudder at the memory of her scissors repeatedly clipping my fringe, shorter and shorter, '. . . because I just can't quite get it level.'

'I haven't a clue what I want to look like. I simply know what I need to portray . . . if that makes sense?'

'You'd be surprised how many brides say something along those lines for their wedding day make-up practice.'

'Ahhh, interesting. So maybe treat my vagueness in the same light?'

'Sounds good to me. Let's hear the "must haves".'

It takes me a few minutes to outline the role of Scrooge: his miserly character, his rudeness, sour temperament and, most importantly for Callie, his frosty persona.

'As you can tell, I've studied his character a lot since being awarded the role. I want to give the best rendition of Scrooge that Lerwick . . . no, that Shetland has ever seen! But I can only do that with your help.'

'Right you are. Can I tie your hair up into a top-knot and make a start on cleansing your skin? And then let's just see what I'm working with, shall we?'

Heather

'I'd like a quick word with you, missy,' I say, marching up the staircase.

I've arrived home after a lovely date with Kaspar, determined to confront Ellie as she gets ready for bed.

'Now is not the time, Mother!'

Her voice has an edge to it; but I plough on, regardless.

Isla appears in the doorway of her bedroom. 'Are you pair OK?'

'No.' I shouldn't snap, but I do.

'Yes!' says Ellie, flouncing across the landing in her towelling robe.

'Ellie, I don't know how long this has been going on for, but I'd have thought you'd have the courtesy to mention it to me.'

'What? In the same way you discuss your new relationship, you mean?'

'That's different.'

'How?'

'It just is! So instead of you having a mature conversation with me, I'm informed by Levi Gordans . . . during the taxi ride home.'

'Because Levi's such a fountain of knowledge, isn't he?' she quips sarcastically.

'You've missed my point. Levi's a decent guy, more like! One who's not afraid to speak up if he sees something amiss. Do you know how embarrassed I was to find out in such a manner?'

Isla is caught between us, glancing from one to the other, quickly coming up to speed. 'Are you dating someone?' she asks Ellie, surprise etched across her features.

Now there's a novelty, not even telling her sister.

'She is – and do you know who?' I ask Isla, turning my attention back to Ellie.

Ellie's eyes widen, as if daring me to speak.

'The chef from Lerwick Manor Hotel,' I say, addressing my words to Isla.

'The tall one or the beardy one?' she asks, turning to her older sister for confirmation.

'Theo, the beardy one.'

'But he's . . . way older than you.'

'Thanks a bunch, Isla – I'll return the favour for you, one day!'

'Hey, don't take it out on her.'

'Yeah, don't snap at me!' says Isla, still peering at Ellie.

'He's thirty-one actually!' spits Ellie, her defences rising by the second.

I watch Isla's reaction; her eyes widen, her jaw drops.

'Great stuff, Isla! Side with Mum, why don't you? It's fine for Mum to be dating a bloke ten years younger, but it's not OK for me to do the same, but a few years older? Slightly hypocritical, seeing as we met through the same dating app.'

This is news to me. When did she create a profile?

'I'm not siding with anyone, but I reckon Mum's situation is better than yours. Hang on a minute . . . Theo?' Isla stops short, her brow furrowing deeply.

I remain quiet, despite my inner rage. I want Ellie to hear Isla's response; maybe it'll make more sense, coming from her sibling, than the lecture it will sound like coming from me.

'Isn't his girlfriend pregnant?' Isla drops her bombshell.

'What?' I blurt, eyeing Ellie up and down, suddenly suspicious of the way she's swaddled beneath a towelling robe.

'Not me!' screeches Ellie, annoyed by my silent insinuation.

I'm totally confused, if not her – then who?

'Now that's just plain wrong, Ellie!' Isla exclaims. 'They've only just broken up, and she's what . . . seven months?'

'Eight, actually. And she's his ex!'

'Eight months pregnant and he's starting afresh with you? My God, talk about history repeating itself!' I retort, my mind cart-wheeling as awful memories from my own pregnancies swirl in the midst of this drama. 'And you have the nerve to compare your situation to mine!'

'That's just plain *ick*,' says Isla, her lip curling in disgust.

Isla's final exclamation lingers in mid-air, as if floating around the three frozen figures on the landing. I lower my gaze to the floor; I can't face seeing Ellie's hurt expression. I don't want to witness her reaction, see her response, and face the fracture this conversation has just created in our family portrait.

'Did you just say "ick"?' demands Ellie.

Isla gives a faint nod, suggesting that her choice of word has surprised her as much as her older sister.

'Thanks a bunch, Isla. Well, thanks for the chat, ladies, but I'd like to go to bed now, if you don't mind.'

'Ellie, I didn't mean . . .'

Ellie's bedroom door slams; a full-stop to end Isla's sentence. I remain frozen.

'Mum, I didn't mean to say that.'

'I know, sweetheart. I get where you're coming from. I feel the same way.'

'Why wouldn't he want to support an ex-partner if she's having his baby?' mutters Isla. 'Surely his focus should be on his unborn baby – not dating my sister.'

I chew my lip for a few seconds before speaking, knowing that Ellie is definitely listening in on my reply.

'Precisely. Relationships hit rocky patches at all stages of life – me and your dad proved that – but to actively start dating just weeks before the birth . . . well, I'm shocked.'

'Why's Ellie even getting involved?'

'Who knows, Isla? She's a fully grown adult, so there's little I can do about it. I'd like to discuss the situation with her, but if she refuses, that's her right as an adult – I can't make her. Though I'll be hoping that the values I've taught her in life come through, and she's true to herself. I'd much prefer she was dating someone who was at the same stage in life . . . regardless of the age gap. Now I know why she didn't say anything.'

'Mum, but what if he . . .?'

'Isla, I can't do anything about this. There are three grown women in this house and we have to respect each other's choices.'

Isla looks at me, and her big puppy-dog eyes take in and recognise my pain. 'Are you OK?'

'No, not really. But I'm not in control, sweet. I must allow Ellie to live the life she chooses.'

'Ah, Mum.' Isla's tone makes me want to melt.

'I'm making a cuppa – do you want one?' I ask, gesturing downstairs.

Isla nods and we traipse down the staircase.

'How was your date with Kaspar?' she asks as we enter the kitchen.

'Lovely. You were right, the man's so kind. Such a gentleman.'

I close the kitchen door, for fear that Ellie might overhear and misconstrue any conversation, assuming it to be about her.

I have no intention of discussing Ellie's situation further; I need to have faith.

Tabitha

After three long and fairly laborious hours for Callie, Scrooge finally appears; I don't recognise myself.

'That's amazing,' I say, not wishing to move my mouth in case I ruin the effect.

She's added prosthetics to my cheeks, nose and jawline, creating a stubbly chin and an evil-looking nose.

'I wish I'd covered the mirror before you started now, so we could have had a grand reveal. It's utterly amazing!'

'It's frightening what you can do with moulded latex, glue and decent make-up.'

'I reckon my own mother wouldn't know me!' I say, peering into the mirror and inspecting my new look.

'Imagine yourself in a suitable, wiry grey wig – and I think you're done.'

'Callie, I can't thank you enough. Is this something you could reproduce easily on performance night?'

'I can, now that we've had a play around with the various options. It took a while to get going, didn't it? There was lots of time wasted, matching skin tones and selecting the right fits, but it'll take a fraction of the time now we know which prosthetics provide the overall look.'

I can't believe my eyes, but I want a second opinion.

'Mum! Mum! Come in here for a minute?' I holler, hoping my voice reaches the lounge.

We hear the lounge door open as my mum responds to my shouting, chuntering as she gets nearer.

'What is it you're wanting now ... *Aargh!* My God, that is freaky. Tabby, is that really you under there?'

'How old do I look, Mum?'

'You look like the director chap, but without the fancy frock coat and white hair!'

Chapter Twenty-Six

Thursday 13 October

Heather

'Mum, I hear what you're saying, but surely the heart wants what the heart wants. Go figure!'

I hadn't expected my morning cuppa to be accompanied by such a deep conversation over the breakfast table. There are days when I'm relieved that Isla is at work incredibly early; it can't be much fun witnessing our bickering.

'Ellie, you're hardly at the same stage in life as this boyfriend of yours? Plus, he'll have additional responsibilities in a few short weeks, when the baby arrives. You don't want to be the obstacle stopping them from being together as a family. Isla said he and his ex-girlfriend have only been separated for a matter of weeks – they might just need time to sort their issues out.' I can hear the plea in my voice, and it's not sounding good.

'You're quite happy for me to be dating a string of younger men then?'

'Unattached men and truly single – yes!'

'Who will dump me when it suits them, play away behind my back, and be more interested in their car's souped-up exhaust system than in my happiness.'

'Some men might be more interested in their souped-up car than in you, but not all twenty-something guys will treat you like that.'

'Ah, I see, just the ones I've met so far!'

'Ellie, you're taking such an emotional gamble.'

'No more than you! Is Kaspar at the same stage in life as you?'

And that's the end of our discussion; she's not wrong, but I have a wider experience of dealing with men. They are not all the same. I might not have had many partners, but I've got older brothers, numerous brothers-in-law and, of course, our Magnus – who's been my rock through thick and thin. Growing up in a household of females, my girls have very little if any experience of even sharing the house with a man, let alone having a relationship with a fella. In a way, having such close ties to our Magnus, the ultimate good guy, won't teach my girls much about the average relationship.

Of all the situations and conflicts I've imagined having with my girls, I never thought that a guy replicating their father's behaviour would cause the biggest stand-off this house has seen. I feel out of my depth even arguing the point. I'll just have to keep my fingers crossed that her older man proves himself as worthy as my younger man is doing.

'We can't keep going around in circles, Mum,' says Ellie softly. 'Theo wants to meet you, he wants to get to know you and Isla – maybe that's a way to ease some of this tension.'

I shrug.

'What? You're dismissing that idea before thinking it through?'

'No, I'm concerned about the situation you're becoming embroiled in. In my book, his actions speak louder than his words ever will.'

'Fine. Well, don't complain that you haven't met him then. The offer was there, but you rejected it. It's more than Kaspar has offered to do.'

'Isla knows him.'

'And me?'

She's got a point. Ellie didn't grace us with her presence at the annual allotment festival; too busy meeting up with her older guy.

'Would you like to meet Kaspar?'

'Funny that, Mum – I just asked you to meet Theo, and you rejected him with a line about actions and words. Maybe the same applies to me. I'll wait a while, thanks, and see what this Kaspar guy turns out to be like, before I pass judgement.'

Tabitha

I'm so tired.

The last thing I want to do is go to my weekly am-dram session at The Garrison, but I know I must drag myself there. Ebenezer has sent out strict instructions that everyone must attend; he's going to explain the details of the performance once, and once only. I've no doubt that I'll be glad I put the effort in, once it's over, but right now – nah, I could easily go home and veg in front of the TV. Is the pressure of a principal role curbing my enthusiasm? Have I bitten off more than I can chew?

I grab a fish supper on the way into town and settle at a table to 'eat in'. Going home would be too much of a rush, plus too much of a gamble – I might sink into a comfy armchair and just stay put. I tear a hole in my chip parcel, allowing just enough space to prod my chips in the covered tray with my little wooden fork. Steam rises, along with a tempting smell of warm vinegar and lashings of salt. I begin to eat in a mechanical fashion, stabbing chips while I stare out of the window at the passing traffic. It's fairly busy outside, yet calming to watch – I've got nowhere else to be yet, just filling time, as well as my stomach.

'A penny for them?' says Rabbie, appearing at my table.

'Hello, I didn't see you arrive.'

'I know, ignored me completely, you did. Can I join you?'

I gesture to the three spare seats.

'How are you?' he asks, tearing a hole in his chippy parcel.

'I feel drained, juggling the soapery and the theatre.'

'Jack something in then.'

'Truth is, I love doing it all – even Ebenezer's skits, which are a sodding pain at times. If I scaled back my involvement with the theatre – what would I have? Just my basic Thursday nights. But surely, life's meant to be lived to the full, to gain maximum enjoyment.'

'So don't change anything then,' advises Rabbie, a puzzled expression on his face. 'You can't have it both ways, Tabs.'

I hear what he's saying, but I enjoy doing the homework in preparation for a role; digging into the context, the character research. Not to mention the enjoyment of one-off occasions like the make-up Callie did for me the other week.

'That's it,' I mutter to myself, then explain to Rabbie. 'I actually did more than usual the other weekend – I probably overstepped the mark, on top of a busy working week.'

'There you go then ... you need to pace yourself, otherwise you'll burn out completely.'

I watch him eat a couple of chips, before asking, 'And you?'

'Me what?'

'How are you coping with your new role at the hotel, your Saturday stints in the soapery, and then working on your Bob Cratchit?'

'My job is more physically demanding than mentally draining. I'm running up and down the grand staircase a hundred times a day in my bell boy role, as there's no lift. Add that to the leg work as a waiter, back and forth from the kitchens. I'm used to it, plus it gives me head space to think about the theatre role; I can be reciting my lines and going through my stage directions, whilst I'm charging around all day – it works for me.'

'And that's what matters, finding what works for each of us,' I say, prodding my final few chips before attacking the battered fish.

'Aileen says that . . .'

'*Aileen says*,' I mutter under my breath.

Rabbie ceases talking and stares at me. 'Well, that's rude. She speaks so highly of you.'

Instantly, I feel ashamed. He wasn't supposed to hear. I wasn't supposed to be jealous.

'Sorry – like I said, I'm tired.'

'Mmmm, if you say so.'

'No, seriously, tell me what Aileen says during your private rehearsal sessions.'

'Actually, she's invited you over to join us. So don't get all defensive and mardy – there's nothing going on.'

'I never said there was, did I?'

'Your offish manner did.'

Rabbie stabs and eats several chips with the wooden fork, his gaze never leaving mine; I can see the cogs whirring as his expression shifts. He doesn't understand my reaction – and nor do I.

And that's where we leave it: an awkward truce over the remains of our fish and chips.

'Will you liven yourselves up before I have to start issuing penalty points,' demands Ebenezer, glaring at the fifteen of us all slumped on the front row. He's attempting to explain his vision for the production. 'What's wrong with you all?'

Nobody answers him. Instead, we each exchange a brief glance with the person on either side. I suspect everyone's flagging slightly; the nights are drawing in, the clocks will change soon, and the recent excitement of casting has faded as we become aware of the hard work involved in learning lines and memorising stage directions.

'Our opening night will be on Christmas Eve,' he continues, 'befitting the novella's setting and nearly matching the time frame too. Our usual seven thirty evening performance should be a full house – I'll expect nothing less. We'll advertise it as a "must see" performance in preparation for the perfect family Christmas.' He stops, stares at each of us in turn as if checking we're listening, before continuing. 'I'll expect every single one of you to be word-perfect on the night, none of these dilly-dallying excuses "Oh, Ebenezer, I've been busy with other things, sorry, sorry, sorry!" *Boohoo*. I want the very best that you can deliver, nothing short of excellence. Any questions so far?'

Rabbie's hand shoots into the air. 'Are there any other performances?'

'Not until after Christmas – which is why I want maximum ticket sales for the opening night on Christmas Eve . . . no half-filled auditorium, like I'm told in previous years, spread across two different nights. We'll sell the Christmas Eve tickets and only then make provision for another evening if . . . *if* . . . we can generate demand for another full house based on the eagerness of the audience to witness what the opening night's audience enjoyed!'

'Sounds a bit daft to me,' mutters Aileen, into my right ear.

I give a tiny nod, hoping Ebenezer didn't catch my movement. Then I cautiously raise my hand.

'Yes!' answers the director.

'Could we have a charity donation added to the ticket price? Say five per cent to go to a local—'

I don't even finish my sentence before Ebenezer begins to bellow.

'Are you serious? Do you know how much revenue we need to raise to fund this theatre for a year? Have you any idea?'

'Errr . . . no,' I splutter, shocked by his outburst. 'People will happily give a tiny bit extra at Christmas for a good cause.'

Several cast members are nodding in agreement with me.

Ebenezer's expression slowly morphs from agitated to thunderous, as he says, 'Charity ... begins at home!'

And that is his final line of the night.

Callie

'The guy on table five wants four double brandies,' instructs a waitress, tapping her pen on the bar counter impatiently. I grab four brandy balloons from beneath the bar, locate the correct optic and pump the rim of each glass – twice, for a double.

'Come on,' mutters the waitress as I'm partway through her order.

'I have to wait between shots, otherwise the optic hasn't quite refilled,' I say, taking her remark to be aimed at me. I don't want a customer complaining his doubles aren't true measures. I repeat as necessary, before placing the glasses on a tray, then begin adding the cost to table five's bill via the till screen.

'Any chance of being served tonight, or are you on a go-slow?' demands a male customer, waving his twenty-pound note before my eyes as I peer at the till screen, attempting to complete my task.

'Certainly, what would you like?' I'm trying my best here, yet nothing is good enough.

Jayden called at the last minute, asking me to fill a shift at a private awards party, and all I've had so far is narky comments from staff and impatient customers. I wouldn't mind, if they were justified. But so far tonight, I've completed an hour on cloakroom duty whilst guests were arriving, before being moved to assist with the bar, working alongside a barman who moves at a glacial pace. I've no idea where anything is kept, can't locate the prepped lemon slices, and I'm pretty sure we're running out of ice cubes. The customer gives his order and I begin locating optics and wine measures in a bar that is low on stock and hasn't been fully prepped for a busy shift.

'A bottle of bubbles for table three, please,' calls another waitress, from the far end of the bar.

'Three flaming sambucas for table ten, when you're ready,' calls a waiter.

It's been non-stop so far – and there are still two hours to go. I'm impersonating a manic octopus behind this bar; my arms reaching in all directions and pumping optics, measuring liqueurs, removing corks and still seeking the lemon slices. My list of tasks and drinks are arriving faster than I can produce results, and the other barman keeps hinting he wants a fag break. There's not a cat in hell's chance that's happening, when this entire bar is about to grind to a halt because we're running low on clean glasses – and yet the glass collector is nowhere to be seen!

I quickly grab an ice bucket, fill it partway with ice and thrust a bottle of bubbles in at a jaunty angle, before signalling for it to go! I'm running around like a fool, getting nowhere fast. My heart is beating rapidly, my nerves are jangling, and I can't locate the sambuca bottle. All this for an extra few measly quid to help make an additional payment to another card while a different card company increases their interest rate, wiping out my contribution from this shift!

'Aren't the sambucas poured yet?' moans the waiter, returning to the bar.

I could stay schtum. I could; but I won't.

'Excuse me, I'm hardly standing here painting my sodding nails, you know! I haven't stopped since the moment I arrived. You might be walking back and forth from the restaurant but I've clocked up a marathon distance in this small space whilst tending this bar. So please, wind your neck in and wait for two seconds while I pour your drinks!'

The look of shock etched upon his face makes time stand still.

I know my next action before my brain has a chance to inform the rest of my body. I might appear to be the general dogsbody, but I'm not.

'In fact, pour it your bloody self!' In one action, I whip off the bar apron tied around my waist and thrust it over the bar counter at him. 'I'm going home!'

I lift the bar's hinged countertop and saunter through, as if I haven't a care in the world, though metaphorically I drag behind me a hefty but invisible chain of debt, which weighs me down every moment of every day.

I stride through the bar, under the watchful gaze of every waiter. There is no disguising the fact that the bartender has just 'walked'. I'm heading for home with my head held high.

By the time I reach my car, I'm in tears. But there's no going back. I'm angry, frustrated and downright tired of all the demands; I'm trying my hardest to dig myself out of a hole. All this effort, and still I feel like I'm simply treading water.

I *am* trying. I'm not asking to be bailed out. I'm not asking daddy to sort out the bills. I'm taking full responsibility for my actions and am doing my best to swim, not sink.

I jam the car into gear and trundle out of the car park, heading for home. I'll make an excuse for being back before my intended time, sneak off to my room and have a well-deserved cry. Tomorrow, I'll deal with the fallout from tonight and begin searching for a new job, one where I can have a little bit of routine rather than being a jack-of-all-catering-trades for fifty pounds a shift.

I navigate the winding roads, my mood switching from anger to triumph.

Good for me, I took back control and showed them where to shove their job – though Jayden will definitely be docking my night's wages after that spectacular hissy fit!

Chapter Twenty-Seven

Wednesday 19 October

Heather

I grab my morning cuppa, don my towelling robe, and cosy up on the sofa to snuggle with a pup, Sherbert. I try to choose a different baby each morning, knowing that every day is a day nearer to them leaving us. I want to instil all the love that I can before they leave me for their for ever homes, hoping that a tiny bit of my love remains lodged within their DNA. Call me stupid, I know DNA comes direct from their parents, but I like to pretend that my love can be transferred by osmosis. Each and every fur baby I have bred and loved so dearly appears in my precious album of 'puppy love' – my girls joke that I love that particular album more than I love their own baby album, but that's not quite true; though it's a close runner-up.

The sable-coloured pup nuzzles into my chest, sending shivers down my spine. The smallest of actions, yet evoking the warmest of feelings in a single moment in time. Ah, how I love dogs; they can convey in one simple move what humans fail to convey with a thousand words. That tiny wet nose, those padded paws pushing against my warm skin, and the cutest pink nose.

I have unconditional love for my girls – have done since the very first moment I knew of their existence, even before their arrival in this big bad world – but my pups, well … my pups are a whole new level of love. I have planned their existence from the day of conception – which I can't quite say about my girls – but hey, both are blessings. I've chosen the time, the place, the mate and, thankfully, the care and attention my three adult bitches have received before, during and after giving birth. My dogs receive the best care and attention in the world because, that way, they produce the very best pups – and I continue to prioritise their well-being after the pups' eventual departure. If anyone dared to label me a 'puppy farm', I'd see them in court.

The pup settles against the warmth of my chest whilst I indulge myself in musing on the miracle of life. The miracle that takes the tiniest of cells and joins it with another's, to create a new life. If I could keep the pups longer than twelve weeks, I would. But logistically, that's the max. For ever homes want their pup as soon as possible, so twelve weeks is the time frame I must adhere to.

I choose a loving home, one that will protect and provide for their every need. Who doesn't want a for ever home? A family to love and cater for your every need, enjoy your company every single day they are blessed with your presence, and treasure the memories of you for a lifetime. Boy, if only humans could find that so easily, we'd be sorted! That's my goal with this dating malarkey – to find my for ever home, and share it with another.

'Who have you got?' asks Ellie, sloping in with her morning brew.

'Little Sherbert,' I say, checking it's the purple-collared pup.

'She's going as a pair with Sheba.' Ellie flops into the armchair, curling her legs beneath her.

'Ahhh, you've been listening!' I hold the pup a little closer, knowing that tomorrow she'll be bigger than she is today.

Ellie watches me for a moment.

'What's up?' I ask, conscious that my girls are for ever watching what I'm doing or saying.

'Are you going to contact the dog breeder man?'

I shake my head.

'Oh, Mum, why not?' she moans.

'Because I think one dog breeder is enough for any family. It's my work, it's my pleasure, and I don't want it to be the basis of my relationship. It seems too logical to make a pairing. I want a relationship where differences come together through our hobbies, families, work situations; it'll bring new interests into my world, rather than rooting me in what's already familiar.'

'OK, then the great outdoors man?'

'You really aren't taken with Kaspar, are you?'

She shakes her head.

'Be honest, why not?'

'I can't imagine you staying here if you seriously hook up with him.'

'Ellie, it's a date, nothing more. Just a few drinks, or dinner, or a day out, spending time together and getting to know each other's likes, dislikes and quirks. That's it, I'm taking this pretty slowly. I'm not getting married a week on Saturday!'

'You'll leave, won't you? I assume there'll come a point in his life when he will want to return to his homeland. And you'll be torn between him and us. And having been on your own for all these years, before finally finding someone you care for – you'll follow him.'

'Is that your only concern?'

Her eyebrows flicker. I've tried to step back from Ellie's situation; if I rant, she'll want Theo more – with any luck it might have fizzled out before his bairn is born.

'I think you're ahead of the game, Ellie. I've spent a few hours in his company, and you're worrying about stuff like that.'

'It could affect our entire family.'

'It might. But the chances are slight, Ellie. And anyway, would it be so wrong to leave Shetland?'

'Mum?'

'No, seriously, Ellie. I was born here, raised here and reared my own children here. How much of this big wide world have I denied myself by following tradition and remaining in Shetland?'

'See. And that scares me, Mum.' Ellie's gaze glistens and sparkles with looming tears; she's truly worried.

'Ellie, if I'd attempted to predict my future, I'd never have achieved anything; I'd have scared myself half to death – first of all, I'd never have believed myself capable of raising two beautiful daughters single-handed, now would I?'

'I imagine not. But I don't want to be dashing on a plane to see you every Christmas and birthday, either.'

'Surely knowing someone is happy in their world erases such issues?'

'I suppose so. But your life is here with us, and not in some foreign land.'

I shake my head. 'Maybe not, Ellie. Just like this little pup, maybe I should go further afield, across the waters. Who knows? I might have been denying myself an exquisite adventure my entire life.'

'Please don't! Contact the dog breeding guy instead.'

'No, Ellie. I'm not dictating what you do, am I? What will be, will be. I'd have a houseful of dogs if I hadn't let my babies go to their for ever homes, spanning this big wide world. If that's where fate takes me, so be it. And on that note, I'm going to get dressed and start planning the day ahead. Running errands for my older sister and then a date with Kaspar.'

'Urgh!' Ellie pulls a face.

I unfurl from the corner of the sofa, return my snuggling pup to her litter, and straighten the front of my robe. Pepper glances up, as if checking in on her wriggling brood.

'I hear you, Ellie. In that case, I'll ask Isla to curl my hair this evening.'

'I don't know why you insist on involving her; you said you wouldn't.'

'I did, but she appears to be more mature about my situation than I'd given her credit for – which is surprising, isn't it?' I say.

I rub my daughter's forearm in a gesture of reassurance as I walk past. Her troubled expression isn't lost on me as I walk out of the lounge.

Callie

'Any luck?' asks Isla.

I'm perched by the log burner, finishing my lunch and browsing the local paper for part-time work. It has been nearly a week since I walked out on the Jayden job. He hasn't been in touch, but I haven't received any pay for that last shift, so it figures.

'Nah, nothing that allows me to keep working here,' I say, folding the newspaper repeatedly. 'Maybe something will turn up by word of mouth from the guys around here?'

'I'm sure it will,' says Isla, collecting my dirty plate.

'I can do that,' I say, indicating my crockery.

'No worries, you've another ten minutes, and I'm on my way to clear those,' she says, gesturing towards a neighbouring table.

'Are you looking for extra work?' asks a lady customer sitting nearby.

'I am. I'll pretty much consider anything, as long as it's local and organised efficiently.'

'My father lives in the Happy Days sheltered housing complex, they're always looking for extra help there. The staff seem to come and go at a rate of knots, so they have difficulty filling certain shifts – especially the twilight shift.'

'Thank you,' I say, appreciating her input.

Isla moves away, intent on clearing the other table.

'You're welcome. It's not everyone's cup of tea; but from what I've seen of the "helpers", as they're called, they're not required to carry out any personal care. It's more a matter of fetching, carrying, overseeing while dinners are being served, or assisting with leisure activities. It's not hands-on or specialised nursing, more a case of extra staff needed at certain times of the day.'

'My granddad had an apartment there, a year or two ago. He loved it. I'll drop by after work.'

'My dad loves it too. He's got a better social life than I have,' jokes the lady, finishing her coffee.

Tabitha

'Afternoon, Isla, what's going on here then?' I say, nodding towards the group huddled at the rear of The Orangery.

I spy Dottie, Mungo, a sickly-looking Jemima – and one other woman, dressed in a neat navy suit but with flamboyantly wild hair.

'Wedding planner,' whispers Isla, head down, as if pretending she's not actually speaking to me.

'Top secret, is it?'

'Something like that,' she mutters.

'Don't say any more then. But why? It was never going to be a long engagement, surely?'

'Exactly. Dottie doesn't want any fuss, but Jemima's not well enough to assist her in organising even a small wedding,' adds Isla, frothing the milk for my latte.

'I see. For October, is it?'

'Nah.'

'November?' I ask, peering at the group.

'Nope.'

'Christmas?'

'Mmmm-hmm!' mutters Isla, staring fixedly at her coffee machine.

'Really? What about the Yule Day celebrations – won't it clash?'

'Cancelled,' hisses Isla, from the corner of her mouth.

'My God, really!'

'Shhhhhhh,' she hisses fiercely. 'I didn't say a word, remember. Which also, by the way, puts a stop to me holding a book-signing event or launch for my cookery book.'

'Well I never! But that's sad news about your launch. The Yule Day celebration was so popular last year – I thought it would be an annual event. So I gather the wedding is . . .'

'Christmas Eve!' says Isla, carefully pushing my prepared latte across the countertop.

'That figures. The same night as my opening performance then,' I say, making a mental note not to pursue Dottie for tickets; she'll have more important things to think about. 'Cheers, thanks for this.' I pick up my drink and head for the seating area, a short distance away from the wedding planning.

I'm delighted for Dottie and Mungo, but a stray thought niggles at the back of my mind. Ebenezer won't be happy to share the limelight with anyone on Christmas Eve – least of all a wedding party on the Campbell estate.

'I'm glad you've dropped by,' says Aileen, interrupting my thoughts and sliding into the armchair opposite mine. 'Any ideas for Mrs Cratchit's costume?'

'Second hand, and tarted up with ribbons – that's how Dickens describes it,' I say.

'Does he?'

'Err, yeah, have you not read the scene?'

'Only in the script . . . I don't read the classics,' says Aileen, shifting uncomfortably in her seat. 'Rabbie said you'd know.'

'Did he now?' I perk up at the very mention of his name.

'Yeah, he reckons you could help me in town by visiting a few charity shops and picking up a few bargain dresses too.'

'Really?' I chuckle at her nerve, despite my stomach clenching. I'm afraid of what else I might hear. 'I'm playing the lead role, so is anyone assisting me?'

'Phuh! You don't need any help, do you? Rabbie says you're all sorted, with your research, your script notes – and I've no doubts your costume too.'

'Mmmm, I'm thinking of asking Ebenezer for one of his frock coats. What do you think?'

'Err, good luck with that venture,' says Aileen.

'How are your practice sessions coming along?' I ask, out of habit rather than interest or even niggling curiosity.

'Pretty naff, to be honest. With the best of intentions, we get distracted every time.'

'What?' I snap, my tone surprising both Aileen and myself.

'Yeah, don't get me wrong, I'm grateful for the help. But Rabbie gets distracted, then I follow suit, and before we know it . . .'

I zone out; I can't listen to this. I don't want to hear anything that will unsettle my current crush – even if my feelings don't progress any further than 'liking' – in my head Rabbie's officially off-limits to others. I don't wish to hear about Aileen being his leading lady in more ways than one.

I'm hearing Aileen's speech in disconnected sound bites – 'endless chatting', 'such a laugh', 'time simply flies by' and 'get to know him better' – together, the sum of the parts equates to much more than I care to acknowledge.

'Tabitha?'

'Yeah.' I stare, agog, as Aileen peers intently at me. 'Are you OK, honey?'

'Sure. I was distracted by . . .' I look around for a valid excuse and spy Dottie and Mungo's wedding planner closing her file, before the group stand to bid their farewells. 'Oh, look sharp!' I say.

Aileen follows my gaze, heeds my warning and instantly stands up. 'Shout if you need a hand with your costume, Callie,' she says, reverting to her role and feigning work by wiping my table to cover our chit-chat.

'*Likewise*,' I mutter, sipping my latte to extinguish my flaring jealousy.

Callie

I've decided to seize the day. What have I got to lose?

I stand before the locked doors of Happy Days and press the button. It takes me straight back to the days when I visited Granddad in his tiny apartment. Not that I visited him frequently, but it was often enough to know the routine that every guest has to sign in at reception on arrival.

I peer through the toughened safety glass; the tiny squares of wire ignite an urge to colour them in, like wasting time in maths class with graph paper. The reception desk isn't far beyond the doors. I can see the cheery receptionist is on the telephone; she's noticed me, glances up and nods while she ends her call. I wait a moment before hearing the muted buzz of the security door as she presses the button on her desk.

'Good evening, how can I help you?' she asks, smiley and overly perky for this time of night.

'I'm looking for extra work and heard that you're sometimes seeking additional helpers. I was wondering if there are any vacancies?'

'There are always vacancies here,' she says, rolling her eyes. 'Can I ask you to complete this application form? You'll need some basic checks done against your name, and you'll have to provide references, but if you return everything to Matron, she'll assess your suitability.'

I wait patiently while she shuffles to a cabinet on the far side of the reception, locates the right drawer and retrieves an application form. 'There you go. It's pretty straightforward – there are no trick questions.'

'Thank you. My granddad, Thomas Quinn, used to live here, so I know a bit about the complex.'

'I suggest you pop that detail in somewhere; it always helps to know if there's a connection, and Matron might look more favourably upon your application. The pay is basic, but there's a lot of satisfaction and enjoyment to gain from working with the older generation.'

I'm walking back home in no time. The application doesn't seem a lengthy document, two pages at the most; if I start filling it out tonight, I can hand it in as I pass this way tomorrow evening.

I walk faster, increasing my stride. Happy Days came up trumps for Granddad, so who knows? Maybe this will prove to be the job for me!

Chapter Twenty-Eight

Friday 28 October

Tabitha

'Hi, Tabby, how are you?' calls Verity, sauntering into the soapery just before lunchtime.

'Good, thanks. This morning has been a bit slow. You?' I look up from my counter where I'm busy jotting down notes.

'Meh, so, so,' she says, browsing the nearest shelves, picking up a soap bar and smelling it, before reading the label then replacing it and selecting another.

'Like that, is it?' I say, pushing my written work aside, sensing there's a purpose to her visit.

She flashes me a brief smile, before saying, 'It's just one of those days when you wonder what you're doing.'

'I know those days,' I say, grimacing. 'They creep up on you without a word of warning, forcing you to battle through the day feeling melancholy and out of sorts. Thankfully, I'm usually as right as rain the very next day.'

'Exactly that!'

'Anything I can help with?' I say, taking in her appearance. There's nothing amiss – she's well presented, as always, in a casual style of tunic and leggings, with artfully tousled hair and make-up.

Verity diverts her attention from my products and comes to join me at the desk. 'I'm not sure. I just fancied a wander over to have a sniff and a browse – a break from The Yarn Barn and . . . and . . . all my thinking.'

'Thinking? Now that's dangerous!' I jest.

'Sitting in there, knitting away, between customers – I can't help it though. You've probably sussed that my year here is nearly up, so I need to decide what I'm doing?'

'Torn?'

'Yes, torn. I know what I want, but I can't have it all . . . not here, anyway. My three lads have their own lives in the Midlands – and then there's Magnus.'

I simply listen; I sense that's what she needs.

'Yet the thought of going back home and . . .' Her eyes well up with tears, forcing her to fall silent. 'See? That there.' She gestures to herself, as if I hadn't seen the tears or heard the crack in her voice.

'Difficult choices. But "that there" means something, Verity. Your mind may be looping back on itself whilst you're knitting, which is annoying as hell when you want a break from thinking about stuff, but the deep connection you've made with Shetland must be comforting in some respects?'

She nods. 'You're right, it is. The last year has been truly amazing – what with meeting Magnus, and The Yarn Barn taking off. But I didn't come all this way with the intention of staying for ever. It was supposed to be a gap year from home, to test and establish a transferable business format that I could take home with me. But . . .' She shakes her head in a downcast manner.

'But . . . look what happened!' I say, treading cautiously, not wanting to undermine her worries but also trying to point out some positives. 'You met Magnus!'

She gives a big sigh. 'I certainly did.'

'Do you mind me asking what the alternatives are?'

'We either take the next step by moving in together, or we decide to call it a day and I go home to my lads.'

'Either way, you keep your business in some form.'

'Absolutely. But there's so much to think about in relation to my lads; my parents aren't getting any younger, either. And then there are Magnus' parents to consider too. His mum, Iona, went walkabout the other week, which has highlighted her need for more support.'

'There's a lot stacked up on one plate then?' I say, hearing the enormity of her decision in her tone. 'Though it all boils down to one decision, really.'

'Yeah, and no one's rushing me to make that decision, but it's looming over me.'

'And on melancholy days, such as today, it crowds out all other thoughts, I suppose,' I add, recognising my own behaviour.

'Yep, so that's me. What are you up to there?' she asks, pointing to the jottings in my notebook.

'Oh, just something I'm working on,' I say nonchalantly, dragging my pad of paper back to a central position on the countertop. I hesitate, before confiding, 'Actually, I'm concocting a brand-new soap for a very special occasion.'

'The big occasion I witnessed being secretly booked the other week, by any chance?' asks Verity, with a little giggle.

'The very same one, though I do think the details are wheedling their way out into the public domain.'

'I don't understand the secrecy, myself. They can have a small wedding; no one's going to be offended by the lack of invites, are we?'

'I said that to Isla. I think Dottie wants it all planned and in hand before announcing anything – though you know the Yule Day celebrations aren't happening this year?'

'Yeah, Jemima mentioned they're holding a one-day Christmas Market in early December. Which simply confirms that The Orangery and the courtyard are being used for the other, smaller event at around that time.'

I nod, giving a gleeful smile – she's got it!

'Anyway, having proved my worth with a sandalwood balm, Mungo asked if I could create a little something as a wedding favour, a token gift for the ladies who'll be invited. And I've come up with this.' I turn my notepad around to show her a doodle of a flower design. 'I've called it Dottie's Delphinium Delight, which I'm hoping will be pale blue in colour, to match her eyes. I just need to figure out if I can create a suitable delphinium shape for a mould, or if I should leave it as a simple bar of soap.'

Verity's expression melts before my eyes. 'That's lovely,' she swoons.

'Thank you.' I'm relieved and delighted by her reaction. 'I've put a lot of thought into it.'

I've been researching the symbolism and meaning of delphiniums all morning, and the more I read the more the idea is taking shape. Apparently, they symbolise devotion, ardent attachment and strong bonds – which I think sums up Mungo and Dottie's relationship perfectly!

Callie

'Could you tell us why you are interested in working with our elderly residents?' asks the only man on the panel of three.

I pause; it's questions such as this which always trip me up in interviews. I want to be honest, but I know they want to hear more than, 'I need a reliable job to earn money to pay off my stupid debts.' I've had to leave work early to attend this interview, so I'm hoping the effort pays off.

'My daa was once a resident here, and he loved his time living in his little apartment. He downsized his home after my nanna died, as he'd go days without using certain rooms, and the bills can be pretty hefty living on your own. Being here gave him a new lease of life; he was surrounded by people twenty-four hours a day, and he knew that if his health declined there would always be care available. It lifted his spirits in those final two years. He still missed his wife, but he was able to enjoy life, right up until the end, thanks to the facilities and staff here.'

I fall silent, hoping that sounded sincere – though I suspect my answer sounded utterly cheesy. I can only speak from the heart; I don't have any control over their decision.

'That's lovely to know, Callie. Here at Happy Days sheltered housing complex we like to think we offer a good balance – our aim is to provide independence coupled with care. Our residents may be elderly, but there's a lot of life flowing through these corridors,' adds the male interviewer. He turns to Matron, sitting on his left, and mutters something inaudible.

'Did you visit regularly?' she asks immediately, peering at me over the top of her specs. She already knows the answer, but obviously wishes to hear it from me.

'No. Not as much as I would have liked. Which makes me doubly keen now to do what I can to brighten the days of the other residents who supported him in his final months. Something always cropped up – an event, or an emergency at work – and I'd cancel, knowing he could fill that time with bowls, history discussions, or pottering about on his allotment plot. I feel guilty now, but back then I knew he wouldn't be sitting alone, with no one for company. There was always so much he wanted to do – and so many things to be involved in.'

'Old Tommy was a treasure around these parts. He generously shared fresh eggs from his chickens with his neighbours, and often donated his home-grown vegetables to the kitchens. He was renowned for his pumpkins, utter monsters they were, and the chefs would make a special soup out of them. It would be on the menu for days – and not a drop would be wasted,' beams Matron, recalling the memory.

'See, that there, that's what I want to be able to do. To offer a snippet of someone's life back to an elderly person's family – it lets them know that their relative was valued, cared for and loved as an individual whilst living here.' I'm as surprised as Matron to hear my intention voiced in this manner.

She delivers me a succession of swift, bouncy nods. 'And your family?'

'I live at home with my parents. It probably seems strange, in this day and age, but I'm an only child, so it makes sense. I have two cousins in the area, but that's it – we're a pretty small family, to be fair.'

'I can see from your application and references that you waitress at Lerwick Manor Gallery – we've forged close ties in recent months. They very kindly donated a beautiful wrought-iron Christmas tree for our enjoyment last Yule Day, and they've sent us some beautiful cakes and pastries at holiday times throughout the year,' explains Matron.

'Yeah, they're like that. They have a true community spirit; looking after and supporting everyone is central to their vision.' I have no idea where these phrases are coming from, but the voice in my head sounds a lot like our Jemima.

'And your other reference is from Magnus Sinclair – he gave you a glowing report.'

'Thank you. I feel he knows me well, as we work with the herd of alpacas kept on the estate,' I say, feeling relived that my references were suitable.

'Have you any additional questions for us?' asks the lady on the far end.

'Can I ask what my duties may include?'

'Of course. It's the twilight shift, half six until half ten, which is very much an overseeing role. Our residents can enjoy their evening meal in our dining room or have it delivered to their apartment. Many choose to sit with others, make it the social event of the day, and then enjoy time in the communal lounge or participate in the timetable of activities. We need the helpers to assist in whatever way is needed.'

'It might be an evening of board games – where things can get a little heated and very competitive. Residents need assistance sometimes with the basics, such as keeping score, or fetching escaped dice, or simply making up the numbers in a game of Scrabble. Or a resident might wish to go for a quiet walk, view the stars, take a turn about the garden – we try to accommodate their wish for independence and not treat them like children by saying tomorrow, during the daytime, would be better. We want helpers who can venture outside with them, but who won't invade their quiet time, respecting their wish to reflect or recall happy memories.'

'Every shift can be different, which is a bonus, as the nature of the role is fairly fluid. One night you might be serving coffees, the next refereeing an argument over a card game – it's a case of adapting to requirements,' explains the lady.

'Sounds lovely,' I say, wondering if they'd consider accommodating thirty-somethings in a complex of apartments.

'Anything else?' asks Matron.

I shake my head. 'No, that's it from me.'

'Thank you, Ms Quinn, we'll be touch in due course.' She stands and gestures towards the door.

I thank them repeatedly before leaving the room.

I trot down the staircase towards the main reception, my fingers firmly crossed; I *really* want this position.

Heather

'Why would you want to go anywhere else?' asks Kaspar, as we walk hand in hand around the high wall of Fort Charlotte. 'To leave here would break my heart.'

I stop walking and tug his hand, turning him to face me. 'Are you serious?'

'Yes. This place, the people, the land – it has it all. Why go elsewhere when it is all . . . what's the saying? On your doorstep? Am I right?'

'Yes, that's the saying. But what about the intrusions: the difficult weather, the harsh realities of living in a small-town community. I'm not getting any younger, Kaspar. Life would be easier on the mainland, surrounded by . . .' My words falter on seeing his expression. 'What?'

'You have rose-tinted spectacles on; you are not seeing the true beauty here in Shetland. It is glorious, right here. Why would you want to go away? Here is your home – you've found your for ever home.'

'For ever home,' I repeat – the term I use so frequently for my pups. I always stress to potential owners that they should think in those terms. And yet, I'm doubting my own location? I've known nothing else. My history is here. I've raised my children here. Cared for relatives and supported my friends. But if I were one of Pepper's pups, am I in the right home? Could I answer the question I've always demanded of others when considering homing a dog, for the next twelve or thirteen years?

'Heather, you have made a life for yourself here. You are searching for home, when it's under your nose already,' whispers Kaspar, tenderly stroking my cheek. 'I am grateful to be here. The people of Shetland, they welcomed me when others elsewhere turned their backs or gave me the cold shoulder. Here the people opened their arms. They welcomed this stranger, Kaspar, to their island. I knew no one when I arrived, but now, I have found my true home in their homeland. I am a lucky man. My search has ended.'

His words ignite my tears. How can he be so passionate when I'm blind, like a newborn pup.

'You are unsettled. This is a time in your life when you are seeking answers for this and that. But seeking answers only clouds your view. Enjoy. There is so much beauty all around – you will see it in time.'

I nod, quickly wiping my eyes and feeling daft.

'It's like dating. You seek, you put yourself through lots of difficult situations, but then you must trust your heart. Kaspar, he trusts his heart in this land.'

His poetic turn of phrase goes straight to my heart. He's so right.

'I worry that my life has been too small, here in Shetland. Have I achieved all the things I wished for, growing up?'

'Small – yes, maybe. But you have built a valuable, precious life here. Treasure it, don't waste it seeking something you can't grasp . . . chasing after shadows.'

Precious life, now there's a point. It seems my beau is a philosopher as well as a poet.

After our walk around Fort Charlotte, we find a quiet pub and settle down in the lounge area with a couple of drinks. Kaspar's not flash, he's not out to impress a date but is as down to earth as I could hope for.

'Do you want children?' It's the one question I'm nervous about asking him. It sounds such a personal question and yet, if we're on different pages, what's the point in continuing?

'I've always thought I would like little ones, they are so cute and adorable, but I don't know if they are in my future. You?'

'Me?'

'Would you like more little ones? Yours are big now, but you might want more children.'

I'm taken aback by him turning the question on to me.

'I can't imagine having any more, if that's what you're asking. I haven't had the easiest of times raising my two. There were many occasions when I thought I'd let my daughters down by being a lone parent; I've struggled to provide the foundations for a secure family unit.'

'But still, it might be different in the future. A new baby would have a different upbringing given your maturity and situation – so you might experience other pleasures regarding motherhood.'

'I've enjoyed being a mum, please don't think otherwise, but it hasn't been easy. I would have chosen a different path than the one I had, that goes without saying, but I've enjoyed my daughters. We've created many memories, laughed endlessly, even when the times were tough. I would have preferred them to grow up in a two-parent household, that's all. They've missed out on other things. They haven't been raised within a relationship, so they haven't had the other influences or opportunities a second parent would have given them.'

'I see, but they wouldn't have witnessed your strength either, seeing what you have achieved single-handed. They might need those skills themselves, one day.'

Kaspar's right. As much as I compare my situation to other families, my girls have strong characters; they've seen the life I've lived and the sacrifices I've made to provide for them both. They never went without the basics: plenty of love, time and my undivided attention. They've never shared me with anyone else, only each other, and they've never witnessed the horrible abusive situations some children experience.

'I shouldn't be so hard on myself,' I say, seeing his gentle gaze assessing my reaction. 'I panic now they're entering relationships. They've never lived in a house where they've witnessed a full-time relationship. They haven't seen the good days, the making up after arguments, the thoughtful surprises, a couple living together in mutual love and respect, and the small everyday stuff that occurs between two adults who care for and protect each other. My daughters are under the illusion it's all flowers, chocolates and expensive dates, when the reality is laughing together, washing up after Sunday lunch, supporting each other after a crappy day at work, or the tenderness of gestures shared whilst watching TV. I worry they might be unable to cope with the everyday normality of relationships once the initial fireworks have died down.'

'I understand. It is simple: a relationship should enhance your life not detract from your happiness. That is my goal. Better to be alone, if your world is made sad by another.'

'Exactly. My girls probably don't understand that concept. They haven't learnt by watching two parents – so how will they know?'

'They will learn by talking, and by taking their time with new relationships.'

'And how easy is that?' I say, recalling my own hasty mistakes with their father.

'As easy as this, me and you – we're taking it slowly and we talk endlessly – you're setting the right example for your daughters.'

'Thank you, Kaspar – time spent with you is like coming home to a safe harbour after a long stint on a turbulent sea.' I snuggle beneath his outstretched arm and inhale his warmth.

'I take that as a compliment . . .' His words fade as his face lowers, his mouth finds mine, igniting an inner spark the second our lips touch.

I have no words to describe the warmth, trust and respect that flows freely between us each time we connect. There's no rush, no inner doubts, no second-guessing our intentions towards each other; we are simply two people who wish to enhance each other's lives.

Chapter Twenty-Nine

Saturday 5 November

Ebenezer's ledger

I can't go on for ever – retirement beckons my soul and spirit. I'll need to choose a protégé to secure the fortunes of this theatre company if it's to survive. Rabbie's a talented actor. Kenzie could be moulded. Freddie's a waste of space. And Tabitha . . . she's got a fighting spirit!

Heather

'What are you doing?' asks Ellie.

I'm carrying the wicker laundry basket around the lounge, plucking random items from surfaces and shelving, and collecting them in the basket.

'Clearing up. I've got families coming around, every hour on the hour, to meet and greet their new pup. And you, missy, need to do me a huge favour,' I say, snatching at two Mother's Day cards I really should have put away in March. But I love seeing them, so I've kept them out on show.

'What now?'

'When the first family arrives, I want you to take the boy pup upstairs and . . .'

'Mum, that's dishonest.'

'No! It's not! They asked for – and paid a deposit for – a girl. They have been rewarded with a beautiful girlie with bright eyes, a juicy wet nose and a big soppy heart. What they don't need is a tug on their heartstrings, thinking the only boy in the litter is

homeless. I promise you, one of them will snap him up like that!'
I click my fingers before her nose, emphasising my point. 'I'm
not having arguments or cash hastily bandied about. That little
boy will have a loving home ... I'm just not certain yet where
that'll be, but it's purely geography, nothing more.'

Ellie mutters something under her breath.

'What was that?'

'Nothing! Except we all know where the little boy pup will
remain ... here, alongside his mummy. You daren't admit it, but
we all know – we're unofficially a four-dog family!'

I stare at the child I raised.

'That's totally untrue. I'm not harbouring desires to keep him.
I have girlies. I have daughters. I run an all-female establishment
here, no boy's bits allowed.'

Ellie lifts her chin, as if questioning my statement.

'Don't give me the "yeah, right" chin gesture.'

'Admit it. We won't think any less of you. In fact, I might
respect your honesty – especially after the sanctimonious lecture
I received the other week about not having the pure heart of a
dog! That was a low blow, Mum.'

I gulp. I do feel guilty each time I recall my words. But then
I feel angry when I remember her cutting remarks. I want my
daughter to date decent blokes, not these player-types I see
flaunting their 'big dick' watches, their designer gear and flash
cars. I only hope this Theo guy who's currently paying her so
much interest is a decent sort at heart, despite what I've heard
so far. I want my future son-in-law to have a proper grounding
in this world, with honest values and a good soul – though the
chances of that happening, when my elder daughter appears so
superficial, are pretty slim.

Tabitha

'I'll need you to take charge of customer sales – freeing me up to pick and pack the internet orders,' I say to Rabbie, the second he appears for his weekend mini-shift.

'Sure. Has it been this busy all morning?' he asks, scanning the huddled customers browsing the shelves. There'll be no time today for theatre chat or practising lines, as we've done in previous weeks.

'I've been run off my feet since I opened,' I say, before adding, 'I placed a few sale items on my webpage, as loss leaders, hoping to ignite a wave of Christmas orders, which has more than done the trick. It's gone crazy. I'm yet to complete yesterday's orders.'

'Feast or famine, eh?' says Rabbie, cutting the conversation short to attend to a customer's query.

I'm grateful that he's proved to be so reliable each week; I haven't had to put up with any no-shows or late arrivals. Yesterday, when I saw the interest and orders generated by my webpage, I knew I could rely on him to hold the fort, allowing me time to prepare each parcel for posting. Good job we organised this little arrangement weeks ago – I'd be up the proverbial Swanee if we hadn't.

I grab several packing boxes from my supplies, swiftly folding and tucking the flat-pack cardboard into sturdy shipping cartons. They are not the prettiest of containers but definitely recyclable – and one hundred per cent reliable when efficiently secured here and there with brown parcel tape. It's the goodies and prized ingredients inside that my customers are counting on, not the packaging. I stifle an inner giggle; that little description could also be applied to my Saturday helper – though the memory of his taut six-pack whilst sunbathing before the *Romeo and Juliet* skit still makes me shiver. But it's his inner qualities I'm keen to learn more about: dedication, loyalty and an upbeat spirit appear to be his main ingredients, with top notes of humour and creativity. Though if Aileen's comments are anything to go by, I'll have to rein in my interest and prepare myself for acting the gooseberry at Thursday night's am-dram session. Not that they wouldn't make a lovely couple, I like them both individually ... simply not as a pairing who are likely to cross my path on a daily basis.

I keep one ear cocked, listening in on Rabbie's conversation, whilst I print the order sheets and address labels: 'soothes irritations', 'provides naturally occurring vitamins A, C and D' and 'helps by not stripping away the skin's healthy bacteria'. He's certainly got the patter and has listened when I've explained the benefits of goat's milk soap – no doubt using his acting skills to the max in this role.

If he gets overwhelmed with questions or sales, I'll step in. But for now, he's in the spotlight and working that floor beautifully.

'You're quite the showman, aren't you?' I say.

Rabbie's final customer has just left, with a satisfied smile and a bag full of goodies. Customer sales have been non-stop for the entire two hours, whilst I've focused solely on my website orders.

'I try my best. This isn't really my thing, but I've learnt my script and can deliver the necessary lines about your products. No different to my Cratchit role, really, is it?'

'No, it's pretty much the same,' I say. 'It's all about showcasing the product and fulfilling the customer's needs.' Though I can't imagine he and Aileen have been focusing on his sales patter as much as their Cratchit scene.

'You're a full-time actor then, really?' he says, with a chuckle.

'I wish! Though what I do here isn't fake or pretend; I truly believe in my products – it's not as if I'm trying to con folks out of their money.'

'I get that – your passion shines through.'

I smile; I'll take that compliment.

'Did you get all your orders sorted?' he asks, eyeing the clock. His time is nearly up.

'I did, thanks to you. Thirty-six orders ready and waiting, with more coming in each hour. I might have overdone it with the loss-leader soaps, but it'll be worth it in the long run.'

'Do you want me to fetch you a coffee before I dash off?'

'Would you? Otherwise I might not get a chance until closing.'

'Sure. It's the least I can do. Latte?' He's halfway out of the door already.

Wow, he didn't hesitate! Acting like the helpful employee? Or is he showing his true colours? I haven't forgotten the allotment festival day, when he flashed me numerous smiles. But that was before his countless practice sessions with Aileen.

Aileen.

Doh! How stupid am I? He simply needs a reason to visit The Orangery, no guessing as to why!

Callie

I head into the rear storage area the second Isla says I'm free to go. I don't waste a minute putting my new uniform on, ready for my first shift. I close the door, yank at the pull cord and swiftly change: from waitress to care helper in less than five minutes.

The aqua-green and white stripes aren't to my liking, but the colourful tunic will help me adjust my mindset and transform myself into the friendly carer Happy Days requires. And I can sport the same black trousers – which will save on time and laundry.

I've got fifteen minutes before my new shift starts. It'll make for an extended workday, but this is better than having an awkward one-hour gap between finishing one shift and starting another. That would be the pits. I'd have just enough time to get home, make a cuppa, before dashing out of the door to clock in at Happy Days. This way, I can move seamlessly from one role to the other.

I stuff my dirty waitressing uniform into my holdall and exit the storage room.

'Oooo, look at you, ready and raring to go,' sings Isla, tidying the final few items before locking up. It's rare that she is on lock-up duty, given her very early starts.

'Thank you, it's my first shift. I'm praying they want to play games all evening and drink tea – I'll be adept at making as many cups as they wish.'

'I'm sure you will offer them so much more, Callie. You undersell yourself, every time.'

I blush. She's right, I do, but that's because I'm disappointed in myself.

'There's a couple of slices of gateau going begging. Do you want to take them along?'

'Could I? That would be a nice gesture.'

'Sure. There's nothing wrong with them. I expect one of us was a bit heavy handed, and the toppings are a bit squashed,' explains Isla.

'Thank you, I appreciate that. It'll break the ice and give me a way in with the staff conversations.'

'No worries, I'll box them up for you.'

'Are you sure you don't mind?'

'Nope. In all honesty, I wouldn't have put them on display for tomorrow because they look a bit wonky – you know how it is, we eat with our eyes before our bellies.'

I give a giggle, she's so right.

This is what I like about Isla; she's got more common sense than others far older than her. I wait as she disappears into the chiller fridge, returning moments later with a cardboard box, fixing the lid in place.

'There you go!'

'Thanks, Isla – I'll explain that it was your idea, not mine.'

She shrugs; that's how unaffected she is by compliments. She has so little sense of ego. I smile ruefully – I could learn a lot from her.

Rarely have I embarked on a new adventure and been this excited. The prospect of helping others has ignited such enthusiasm that I hope it lasts far longer than my first shift.

I knock on the main entrance doors, giving a tiny wave to the reception lady inside. She activates the door release immediately.

'First shift, is it?' she asks, as I remove my gloves and prepare to sign in.

'It certainly is, I'm looking forward to it. Fingers crossed, I'll be asked to participate in some fun and games.'

'There's a good chance it's bingo tonight, so they'll be squabbling for sure. You'd best have your ears finely tuned because if more than one person calls "house", there's not a hope in hell they'll share the winnings. You'll be called on to adjudicate – and you'll be wishing there was a VAR system in place before the night is through.'

'Surely not.'

'Are you kidding? Be prepared, that's my advice. Because when the jackpot stands at eight pounds fifty pence for a full house, the atmosphere in the dining room is tense; they're not likely to take kindly to a "sleeper" who isn't alert and listening to the bingo caller.'

I stand aghast and stare.

'A word of warning, don't let them talk you into being the bingo caller, either – they'll try and pull that stunt, but they'll expect you to know all the lingo. Bless you, Callie. You haven't a clue, have you?'

I shake my head.

'You'll need your wits about you tonight, so don't fluff it up!'

'I won't,' I say, reassuring myself more than answering her.

'Ahhh, lovey, it's not too late to call in sick if you want to. Matron hasn't seen you yet!'

'I can't call in sick, I've just arrived!'

'Phuh! You're a brave one.'

'I'll be fine . . . I think,' I mutter, as I scribble my signature in the staff book.

Heather

'Hello, please, come on in,' I say, a bright smile adorning my face while my heart sinks a little at the thought of my first pup leaving our nest.

The family of five from Fetlar clamber through my front door. Parents and their kiddie-winkies all cluster in the hallway, waiting for me to lead the way into the lounge.

'Your pup has a pink collar,' I tell them. 'I've been calling her Marble, as you requested, so she's getting used to her name. Please make yourselves at home, sit on the floor if you wish, ask any questions that come to mind, and I'll fetch us a cuppa in a while, once the pups are settled in your presence.' I know that my practised lines will avoid any mishaps or misrecognition, making sure each family bonds with the right pup. 'This way, if you would.'

As I open the door to the lounge, I ready myself for the tearful moment I usually have to hide.

Soft exclamations of '*ahhh*' fill the air from five voices, and I swallow back the emotion that instantly clogs my throat. It gets me every time, without fail.

I'm used to seeing the pups each day, but to hear a new family setting eyes on them for the first time makes my heart sing.

Immediately, the children drop to their knees, and little hands stretch out towards the large basket of babies; Pepper looks on cautiously as inquisitive fingers touch tiny paws and noses.

The mother automatically steps forward in an attempt to halt proceedings.

'It's fine,' I assure her. 'It's a natural reaction, Pepper's fine . . . she's seen this all before. She's very much a family pet, used to children and adults. My own daughters are always handling and petting her babies; we can't help ourselves.'

Both parents relax on hearing permission being granted.

'Marble is yours now, not ours.' I repeat such sentiments every time, more for myself than the new family, but my words hit their mark on seeing the parents mellow, able to enjoy their collection visit.

Once the family are seated on the carpet, playing with the five pups, but paying special attention to their little pink-collared darling, I disappear to make tea and dry my eyes. I can't help it. Seeing the love and joy created by a young pup is simply the best reward I could receive for the sleepless nights, the silly worries and the time spent raising a healthy litter.

As I flick the switch on the kettle I know that young Marble is going to be utterly spoilt in the years to come. I can just tell, and I love it!

'Mum! Can we come down yet?' Ellie wails from upstairs, her voice floating down over the banister.

I won't admit it, but I forgot to call them down some forty minutes ago, when the American family left. I was so bowled over by their emotional attachment to little Sherbert and Sheba that I quite forgot my own children, banished upstairs to a bedroom where they've been nursing the tiny boy pup. Isla had only been home from work for ten minutes when she was ushered upstairs to Ellie.

'Yes, the coast is clear,' I say, not letting on.

I hear their thumping footsteps; they both sound like baby elephants, thundering downstairs.

'How did it go?' Ellie enters the lounge, cradling the boy pup to her chest. Ah, bless her.

I'm flopped in the armchair, sipping my coffee and pretending to have remembered my own litter. Pepper glances at me graciously; I swear, she knows everything.

'Fabulous, though the second but one family arrived late, and the American family turned up early, so there was an unscheduled meeting, but it went well. There's nothing wrong with that, except it lengthens the process – and they rarely stay in touch, despite promising they will.'

'Any concerns?'

I shake my head. 'Nope, not a single one. They'd all been thoroughly vetted before completing their questionnaires. Marble's family has been waiting for eighteen months, so I'm thrilled they've finally got a pup. You wouldn't think people would wait, would you? Especially nowadays, in this "want it now, buy it now" society, but they do.'

'That's down to your reputation as a breeder though, Mum, give yourself some credit,' says Isla. 'That's like me questioning why the artisan café is so popular – week in, week out. The secret is my dedication and Gran's recipes. It's not rocket science, is it?'

'I suppose not. Though eighteen months is a long time to wait for a pup, Isla.'

She shrugs. 'They know her breeding and temperament are worth waiting for, if they want the right dog for the next twelve years.'

I want to cry; that's possibly the nicest thing anyone has ever said to me.

'How did Pepper cope, saying goodbye to five babies in one day?'

'Like the top dog she is,' I say, looking towards my beautiful Pepper. 'They must feel it, mustn't they?'

Isla nods. 'Though I suppose that's one more reason to keep the little boy.'

I shake my head. Is nobody listening to me?

'Stop saying that. I just haven't made my mind up. In my heart of hearts, I know I have to get his for ever home right. No ifs, no buts, it has to be perfect. The little chap nearly didn't make it into this world, so I want him to be looked after and cherished as much as we cherish Pepper.'

My voice cracks; it's been a tough, emotional day, meeting all the families. And now, finally, the tears flow.

Chapter Thirty

Thursday 10 November

Callie

I rap on the back door, as Magnus instructed earlier, and wait. I'm about to knock again, having had no response, when the door handle turns and an older lady stands before me, her greying fringe sweeping the top of her spectacles.

'Hello, I'm Callie. Magnus has made arrangements for me to complete a few hours,' I say, unsure if the lady expected my early evening arrival.

I was surprised when he'd asked for a chat earlier today. But he did give me a glowing reference for the job at Happy Days – and after my first shift went so well, it seems logical.

'Yes, yes, come on in. I'm Iona, Magnus' mum – Clyde's in there. You only have to knock, then step inside, everyone else does,' she says, ushering me inside the warm kitchen. 'Magnus did say. Though he only mentioned it this afternoon.'

'Yes, same here. I work at the gallery and he dropped by this morning asking if I wanted a few extra hours' work? I've nipped home first to change. I'll arrive earlier than this in future, I promise.' I'm conscious that home helps don't usually arrive at gone seven o'clock, but my waitressing uniform was hardly practical.

'He said an hour tonight, and then to make arrangements for a regular Monday or Tuesday, is that right?' asks Iona, leading me through to the lounge. 'Clyde, this is the young lady Magnus mentioned earlier.'

'That's right, I'm usually off on those days. Hi there, nice to meet you,' I say to the elderly fella in front of the plasma TV, watching snooker.

Boy, is it hot in here. I glance at the roaring coal fire. I'll need to dress for the tropics, at this rate.

'How you doing?' Magnus' dad replies, before switching his attention back to the onscreen action.

'Now he hasn't given me a list of tasks you're prepared to do, or anything,' continues Iona, straightening her specs.

'General house work, is what he said to me earlier.'

'In that case, can you do a dust and polish in here, then a quick whizz round with the vacuum?'

'Sure. Just show me where you keep your polishing rags.'

'Under the sink, lovey. Would you like a drink before you start?'

It takes a fair amount of time to dust their lounge, given the number of ornaments and general clutter lining their mantelpiece, hearth and every flat surface – making the job somewhat laborious. I'm mindful that they're both seated a few feet away, enjoying their evening TV, while I sidestep around their lounge, spraying and wiping as I go.

They seem a nice couple, very friendly, and they make me a cuppa, which I drink as I work. I can't see that Magnus is paying me to sit around and chat, so I keep busy.

'Where do you keep your vacuum?' I say, after some forty minutes of polishing.

Iona pushes herself up from the armchair to show me the cupboard under their stairs.

'Will you just be doing downstairs when you come?' she asks, as I unwind the cable and search for a plug socket.

'I believe I'm being led by you, Iona. Whatever you want me to clean – whatever makes life easier for you both. If you want me to clean the bathroom but not the bedrooms, that's fine by me. I'm happy as long as you are.' I turn the vacuum on, drowning out the snooker commentary. 'I won't be a minute!' I mouth to Clyde.

My intention is to zip around the carpet in record time, but with the number of throws dangling from sofas, small coffee tables to manoeuvre and rugs to move and replace, it takes much longer than I anticipated. As I push the vacuum, I can hear the grit making its way through the powerful machine towards the collection canister; it's been a while since this job was last done.

Within fifteen minutes, having asked each of them in turn to lift their slippered feet in unceremonious fashion, allowing me to vacuum beneath, I press the 'off' button and return the dulcet tones of the snooker commentary to the lounge. 'There, all done,' I announce, much to Clyde's satisfaction.

I wind the cable around the handle notches and deliver the vacuum back to its rightful place under the stairs.

'It's just after eight o'clock, so I'll leave it there for tonight,' I say, happy that I've gone a little over time; I'd hate Magnus to think I was skimping on the job. 'Is it Monday or Tuesday you'll be wanting me next week?'

'Monday, please. Maybe you could clean the kitchen for me on your next visit,' says Iona, fetching her purse from the sideboard.

'Is ten o'clock OK for you?' I ask, making a note on my phone.

'It is. How much do I owe you?' she asks, her fingers poised over her unzipped purse.

'I believe Magnus is dealing with that side of things. We've discussed a weekly payment via online banking – I just need to jot my hours down and agree them with you,' I say, surprised by her actions. 'I've done the hour tonight, and it's a maximum of two next Monday.'

Iona seems surprised, but thankfully closes her purse.

'Night, Clyde! Have a good weekend,' I say, waving as I leave the lounge.

Iona follows me to the back step. 'And that's it. You'll be doing some cleaning each visit?'

'I will, see you Monday.' I bid Iona good night and make my way along the path towards the front of the farmhouse.

I'm not entirely sure if Magnus has explained it badly, or whether his mum has forgotten half the details, but either way, they seem a nice couple. And with the generous hourly rate offered by Magnus, it'll go some way towards easing my situation.

Tabitha

I stand centre stage, opposite Kenzie, staring at her blank features.

'Err, umm ... mmm,' she mutters, unable to recall her next line from the scene where Belle and Scrooge share a past memory.

I'm giving it my all, knowing that Ebenezer is listening and watching my every move. I want to hear his praise; it matters to me that I can outperform myself as Aunt Em in the previous production, despite playing a role I didn't expect. I'm not chasing standing ovations here at The Garrison, it's more a sense of pride and self-worth.

The rest of the cast are either peering from the wings or watching from the stalls, scattered amongst the two front rows, surrounding a disgruntled Ebenezer. I witness the growing panic in Kenzie's eyes; the cogs are turning feverishly. I'm willing her to have a lightbulb moment – to remember the first word, kick-starting her memory, and the rest of the line will flow – but it doesn't happen.

And now, given her wide-eyed stare, I'm unsure if she even knows what scene this is.

'You fear . . .' I whisper the opening of her line, hoping she hears me and can complete it.

Kenzie's gaze widens further before she lowers her eyes to the stage, seemingly paralysed at the realisation that not only do I know my own part, but her lines too.

'No more!' cries Ebenezer, jumping up from his seat. 'I can't bear this shambles any longer. Don't you know Belle's lines, Kenzie?'

Kenzie turns to answer, her chin wobbling. 'I do . . . it's just that I can't remember them as quickly as Tabby here.'

'*I can't remember them as quickly* . . .' mimics Ebenezer, now on his feet and storming towards the front of the stage. 'We'll warn the audience of that then, shall we?'

I cringe at his lack of sympathy. Whether Ebenezer can see it or not, I'm close enough to be aware of tears welling in Kenzie's eyes. Not only is she embarrassed by her failure to deliver her lines, but being belittled in front of the entire cast isn't what she'd envisaged for her Thursday night. I imagine she's taking my whispered prompt as a put-down too.

'Forget it! Move on, next scene!' rants Ebenezer, swiftly riffling through his script notes and dismissing Kenzie from the stage.

'I'm sorry,' I say, as she passes me.

'Are you?' she quips.

Her words to me sting as much as Ebenezer's to her. I seek out her gaze once she reaches the safety of the curtained wings and is comforted by others. But she averts her eyes, denying me any connection.

I run down the foyer stairs, once we've been dismissed at the end of the session.

'Kenzie!' I call, racing to catch up with the figure ahead of me. 'Kenzie, wait!'

'What?' She stops and turns – her tone is harsh and impatient.

'Hey, I just wanted to say don't take it to heart – you know what he's like when things don't go his way. Ebenezer can be a right task master when he chooses.'

'You're no better, Tabby! You never miss a chance to shine, do you?' she spits back at me, venomously.

'That's uncalled for. I was trying to help. Sometimes I find if I manage to remember the first word, the rest of the line follows – I wasn't trying to put you down. You know me better than that, surely?'

Kenzie raises her eyebrows quizzically.

'You seriously think that was my attempt to show you up and undermine your role?'

She doesn't answer, but continues to stare.

'Wow! I didn't see that coming,' I say.

'You're only interested in sucking up to Ebenezer, ensuring you have the best roles!'

I glance around the empty foyer, unsure whether to laugh or cry, seeking backup. After all I've done over the years to help and support others – I'm now hearing what they truly think of me.

'I'll show you how unsupportive I am . . . I was about to offer you my time this week to go through our scenes at yours, my mum's, or in the soapery – you choose. That's how underhand I am, Kenzie.'

She shifts her stance, brushing her dark hair back off her face.

'Because my main focus around here is making everyone else look utterly shite while I lord it over you as star of the show!'

There's a heartbeat between uttering my final word and my hand fiercely pushing the brass plate on the exit door. Kenzie doesn't utter a word as the door swings closed behind me.

Heather

I close the front door. The silence of the house hits me, and I burst into tears.

'I knew you'd do this,' says Ellie, coming down the staircase with the boy pup in her grasp.

'It gets me every time. You should have seen how happy the little girl was! She kept singing, "Skye's coming home."'

'I could hear her from upstairs; she was chuffed to bits to get her hands on her pup. Though twelve weeks is a hell of a long time to wait when you're that age, Mum.'

'It is, but she'll have her best buddy for thirteen years, so the wait will prove to have been worth it.'

'Here, this little pup wants you,' says Ellie, handing over the wriggling boy.

I rub noses with my remaining little one; mine is as wet as his. 'And then there was one,' I whisper.

'Mmmm, I can't see you letting him go any day soon,' says Ellie, traipsing into the kitchen.

As I enter the lounge, returning the boy pup to the snug warmth of Pepper's basket, she gives me a knowing look. They're all assuming that we'll soon have our first permanent male in residence, but they've got me quite wrong. I've no intention of introducing a male – pup or otherwise – as a permanent feature to our home. I can hear Ellie fussing in the kitchen, making tea, so I settle in the armchair and stare at the near-empty basket in which Pepper and her son now stretch out. Was it really just twelve weeks ago that I sat here on the floor, panicking and timing the arrival of six wriggling pups? Cringing as our Magnus did the necessary, and then failing at my attempt to dramatically rub life into this little pup's limp body. How the weeks have flown – so much has happened in such a short time. I wonder what the next few will bring.

'Here you go!' says Ellie, offering me a steaming mug of coffee.

'Cheers.' I take a grateful sip.

Ellie snuggles into the corner of the sofa, folding her legs beneath her. 'A penny for them.'

'Nothing much, just pondering how much has happened, and so quickly. The pups arrive and are now virtually gone; you and this Theo guy; me and Kaspar ... then there's Lachlan's trial looming on the horizon. It makes me wonder what else will pop up.'

'Phuh! He needs to be sent down for a long time for what he did. It'll allow our Isla to move on if he's sent away.'

I stare at her over the rim of my mug. 'Do you think she's still hankering after what could have been?'

'Maybe. She was totally smitten, Mum. You don't forget your first love, do you?'

I raise an eyebrow. I didn't, but then I have two daily reminders of mine. Jimmy Creel was a definite Lachlan in the making, if ever there was one.

'My parents warned me about your dad, you know.'

Ellie looks up, surprised.

'I reacted in the exact same manner as you. A "wide boy" was the term they used, back in those days. Flash and gobby, but I wouldn't listen. I thought I was old enough to know better, old enough to make a choice. Old enough to fight my corner and dedicate my entire life to the few simple promises he made after a drunken night in town.'

'And?'

'And he let me down. Told me what I wanted to hear on every occasion. Then shipped out, chasing other women, when I said I was expecting.'

Ellie points to herself, and mouths, 'Me?'

I nod. Not a conversation I planned on having, but one that's possibly long overdue – and necessary, in the light of recent events. I've always shied away from the full details, sketching out the basics of our situation, wanting to protect my girls from the harsh realities of life.

'And Isla?'

'He wanted the best of both worlds; he'd play the field with other women, then drop by to play daddy and head of the house, when it suited. I didn't learn my lesson, did I? Our Magnus never had a good word to say about Jimmy, not one. He warned me, just as much as my parents did – but I knew best, of course. Still knew best the second time around, two years on, when you were tearing around on a tricycle and our Isla was on the way. I didn't know whether to be angry that I'd fallen for his charms yet again, or delighted that my little family would be complete.'

'And Dad?'

'Ah well, I'm not sure he knew what to say to the locals when the news broke. I know he was sporting a couple of black eyes for several days, and our Magnus had busted knuckles, but we never discussed it. You know how Magnus is; his business remains his business.'

'He never!' She gasps, shocked at what I've just told her.

'I suspect he did.'

'Violence isn't the way to go, but I suppose blokes will be blokes.'

'Exactly. Deep down, I was rather taken by his protectiveness towards me. He'd have done the same for their Marina, God bless her.'

'And afterwards?'

'Nah. Yee dad packed up and left. He saw Isla, the day after she was born, bought you a dolly from the local shop, if I remember correctly, and then disappeared to the mainland to set up home with a woman from Glasgow.'

'And that's it?'

I nod. 'Which is why I'm concerned for you – Theo isn't as unattached as he might wish to be, seeing as there's a little one on the way.'

She looks upset.

'I've never hidden the truth, and yet you seem surprised, Ellie.'

'I am. I haven't really thought about it in context before now. The git! You had two children with him, and yet we rarely hear from him?'

'Don't. He's your father, whatever else he's proved himself to be over the years.'

'Phuh! That's not a father. Our Magnus has done more for us over the years than he ever has.'

'I agree, and he's never asked for anything in return, which is why I've always dashed back and forth when he needs me to help Iona and Clyde.'

'Do you reckon Verity will stay in Shetland?'

'I do hope so; Magnus will be gutted if she decides to return to the Midlands.'

'Which means you won't be needed as much up at the farmhouse, if she's there permanently.'

'There's that, but I'll still drop by for my sister.'

'It'll give you more time to spend with Kaspar,' she mutters tentatively. 'You really are quite smitten with him, aren't you?'

I give her a knowing look. 'We're taking it slowly, but all good things come to those who wait!' I say, before sipping my drink.

Everyone has a niche to fill. Isla's world is filled by her wonderful baking, Magnus' by his farming and general good-guy status. And me? I glance at the sleeping dogs, cosy and settled, wrapped together as one. I have my place here in this tiny world, but is there more out there waiting for me?

My life was once full, brimming with anticipation and excitement; I enjoyed juggling the hectic demands made on me by my two girls, numerous relatives, and litters of newborn pups. But now, each commitment is fading away as life changes.

My past, even my present, seems radically different to what might be awaiting me in my future.

Chapter Thirty-One

Thursday 17 November

Heather

'Your hair looks nice, Iona,' I say, stepping into my sister's warm kitchen.

She isn't one for pampering. But still, her fringe looks much better framing her face, rather than covering her glasses.

'I can't find it anywhere, and I've looked all over,' she says, not hearing or accepting my compliment.

'Sorry, I didn't quite catch that, Iona. What have you lost?' I ask, as my sister continues to stare around her kitchen with an expression of bewilderment.

'My necklace. You know the one that Clyde bought me when we got married?'

My ears prick up. It was nice for its time, a simple gold necklace with a sturdy lobster clasp, which must be eighteen-carat gold, nothing less. Quite a gesture, since they hadn't two pennies to rub together at the start of their married life.

'When did you last have it?' I'm not wanting to cause any distress or panic.

'Now let me think,' she says, leaning against the countertop, her index finger pressed to her lips.

I can see the effort; her brow is crumpled and her gaze is lifted towards the ceiling. 'I definitely had it in the shower, but was that this morning? Yesterday morning? I remember feeling it when I was soaping my neck, and then . . . I can't really say.'

'Let's have a look, shall we?' I reach out a hand, wanting to ensure it isn't around her neck and she's having a senior moment.

My sister leans forward, as I lift her hair away from her nape, expecting to see the all-too-familiar glitter of gold. Nothing, just freshly bathed skin.

'When did you take it off?' I ask her.

'Clyde? When did I take it off?' calls Iona, through the open doorway into the lounge.

'How should I bloody know . . . you usually take it off when you go to the hairdresser's.'

'Yes, I went the hairdresser's on Monday morning. I always take it off, in case they snip through it, you know . . . by accident. But where did I put it?'

'Where do you usually put it?' I ask, my gaze scouring the kitchen countertops.

'She leaves it bloody anywhere,' comes a gruff voice from the lounge. 'Side of the bath, top of the toilet cistern, on the kitchen window ledge, side of the bed . . . that's half the problem, she never knows where – it can lie there for days.'

Iona shakes her head, rolling her eyes to the ceiling, conveying how many times she's heard this particular complaint over the years.

'Don't you go shaking your head, you know I'm right!' calls Clyde.

I want to laugh, the synchronicity of their actions and comments has a comedy value to it, but I suppose that comes with spending a lifetime together. Iona gives me a wry smile, knowing his bark is worse than his bite. We continue to search: the kitchen, bathroom, lounge and their bedroom – without luck.

'No doubt it'll turn up when I'm not looking for it, that's what usually happens. Tea?' she asks, flicking the switch on the kettle.

And without fuss, my sister moves on to the next task. Sadly, I can't. I draw out a chair from her kitchen table and plonk myself down, my eyes continuing to scan every surface, even the red-tiled floor.

'How's your morning been, Heather?'

'Ah, well, that's why I've dropped by. I took myself off to the Sheriff Courts earlier, I wanted to attend the hearing for that toerag Lachlan.'

'Today, was it?'

I nod, before cautiously continuing. 'Clyde, do you want to come through to have a listen?' I shout, turning towards the lounge doorway.

'I can hear ya,' he replies.

Iona stops halfway through her task, the perfect tableau of tea making: line of empty cups, milk jug in hand beside a boiling kettle.

'I won't beat around the bush. He was found guilty and given five years for causing Niven's death by dangerous driving whilst under the influence of drink.'

'Just drink?' calls Clyde.

'Yes, his barrister said there wasn't any evidence of illegal drugs in his system, just alcohol.'

'Just alcohol?' repeats Iona.

'He's going to prison then?' asks Clyde.

'Yes, like I said, for five years, Clyde.'

'Is that all?' The pain etched on Iona's face says so much. I wanted to be the one to tell her. But at the same time, with every step I took to reach the farmhouse, I was dreading it – knowing what it would mean to her.

'They took into consideration that he'd left the scene and had a load of points on his licence for speeding.'

'He'll be out before too long, if he behaves himself!' says Clyde, appearing in the open doorway, as I suspected he would.

'That doesn't seem right ... for taking a life, I mean.' Iona directs her comment to Clyde, who makes his way across the kitchen towards his wife. 'To think that's all ... someone might have got for our Marina. We've had ...'

She doesn't finish her sentence, but I know her omitted words, and I understand the sentiment: 'a lifetime's sentence'.

'I know, pet.' Clyde gently rubs her back, in a loving and soothing fashion. Not a man of grand gestures but as solid as a rock.

I avert my eyes as they stand together, each reading the other's sorrow. I'm not sure if it's their pain I can't bear to witness, or their sheer devotion.

'Don't upset yourself, lass.'

I can't tear my gaze away for long, knowing their grief isn't solely their affair, but it touches us all. Marina was their daughter, but my niece. As well as being a little sister, a granddaughter, a cheeky cousin, a smiley best friend – so young, yet she meant so much to so many. The ripples of grief resulting from such a tragedy continue to spread – extending far wider and running far deeper than anyone would ever guess – and the pain endured by the whole family seems endless.

'I'll never understand how these things happen. One minute you're busy building a life, raising your children, being a happy family, and the very next minute ...' Iona's sadness breaks as tears roll down her cheeks. She turns away, pours the milk into the waiting cups and reaches for the sugar bowl.

The happy domestic tableau is broken.

As Iona busies herself with her tea-making task, Clyde steps away and joins me at the table. I run my fingers across the scrubbed surface of the knotted wood. It seems like only yesterday that I sat here, little more than a child myself, tears streaming down my face, without a single word of comfort to offer them, but believing that my silent presence was all they truly needed from me. From that day forth, nothing else would matter. Their world had changed for ever; no sentimental verse, no flowers or symbolic gesture would mean as much to them as my presence. And on that fateful night, I vowed to always be there for them. I wasn't going to disappear on them following the funeral, rarely to be seen after the sympathy cards were stashed away, avoiding the mention of her name, glossing over her birthday, her anniversary, ignoring the arrival of silent milestones Marina would never reach. I'd done the only thing I could ever do for them both, and that was to show up and be present every day.

Clyde and I exchange the briefest of glances; we've been here many times before.

The boiling kettle rudely interrupts our moment. In no time, Iona delivers three steaming cuppas, depositing them on the table beside our idle hands, and slumps down into another chair.

'Anyway, this necklace,' says Clyde, after a sip of his scalding cuppa.

'Bugger it. What does any of it matter … that lad just got five years. Is that all Niven's life was worth?' asks Iona, batting away Clyde's opening sentence.

I send him a gentle smile for trying; he always has.

'It's cruel, but I wanted to be the one to tell you,' I say, watching as Iona focuses on her cuppa. She's doing that internal monologue trick of hers – pressing her 'emotional reset' button. It'll take a minute, though Lord knows how she does it.

'His parents are decent folk too, you know,' adds Clyde, working his own 'reset' button in his own manner.

'Poor buggers, having to sit through that, knowing the likelihood was that he'd be found guilty.'

'They were composed throughout, but his mum lost it when he was asked to stand to hear the verdict. Heartbreaking, it really was. I've known them for a few years, because of our Isla's connection to him.'

Iona's head shoots up, her eyes wide. 'Yes, I forgot. Does she know?'

'She's working today. I'll tell her when I pick her up later. I doubt she'll be surprised. I've no doubt it'll dredge up some emotions and memories of that night, but she'll be fine. She's a tough cookie.'

'Poor lassie. She can't go blaming herself, not like she did last Christmas,' says Iona, with considerable force.

'It's not easy though, is it?'

We all fall silent again. I'm not relishing the task of telling Isla, but needs must. I know that after a few tears, followed by a quiet evening at home with me and Ellie, she'll go to bed in a better place. Which is far more than I imagine that young man will be doing, hearing his cell door clang shut for the first time, somewhere on the mainland.

'You did the right thing by going to the trial – someone from the family needed to,' says Clyde. 'Our Magnus didn't go then?'

'No, I asked him not to, Clyde.'

'Right decision, lassie,' he says, nodding slowly before giving a huge sigh.

'I went because I needed to see justice being done. Deep down, I couldn't help but wonder . . .'

'Aye, that's what I keep wondering each time Niven's name is brought up. Was he responsible or not?' says Iona, putting down her mug. 'We'll never know, not now.'

'It's not worth torturing yourself over, pet. We've endured enough over the years,' says Clyde, patting her forearm.

'If it's any comfort, I think it was him,' I say quietly, glancing between the pair. 'If you think about it logically. He walked every-where, all his life, and how many times did he say "I only drove once"? I must have heard that line hundreds of times but never ventured to question him further. I always felt inclined to cheer him up, because the sadness hung heavy around his shoulders.

But can you imagine living with the guilt? Knowing you'd caused someone's death – you would behave like that, wouldn't you?'

Iona visibly gulps.

Clyde gives a curt nod. 'Our Magnus thinks the same too. I'm not so sure, but as Iona said, we'll never know now.'

'Would it have eased your pain knowing?' I ask him.

'Probably not, lassie. Which is why I can live with the knowledge I have.'

'I think Niven paid a price, living with his secret – maybe that was enough of a sentence?' I suggest.

'Exactly, I wouldn't want it on my conscience,' says Iona, before picking up her mug and swigging her tea.

Callie

'Please allow me to try, Jemima. If it fails then so be it, but without trying we'll never know.'

I'm twanging those heartstrings, good and proper, which I sense is working. I see her expression begin to soften. I quickly continue, before she can reassess my proposed plan.

'Carpe Diem, he's as quiet as a mouse, stands perfectly still, never bites or chomps clothing, and will affectionately nuzzle anyone who shows him some interest. Now, he'd be a perfect choice.'

'And you honestly think the elderly folk will benefit from a visit?'

'I know they will. Heather has taken her dogs in before now; you should hear them talking about it for hours afterwards, and then telling their relatives on visiting days. It might only be an hour, but the impact and connection is immeasurable. Imagine having owned pets all your life, but then spending your retirement without any.'

Jemima eyes me cautiously. She's looking well today, with a slight glow to her cheeks and a perkier disposition. There's so much more I want to say, but I'll be over-egging the custard if I do. Worst-case scenario would be to undo the progress I've made with her so far. This looks like a winner to me.

'He'll need a companion to ensure he doesn't fret about leaving his herd,' she says, eventually.

'That's fine, Mungo said he could hitch the trailer to his car . . . there's room for two or three.'

'I'll agree to two alpacas, but three handlers.'

'Sure. I'm happy with that . . . Karma or Serendipity?' I ask, not sure I'd wish to take any of the others off site.

'Karma. The two of them often buddy together, and they'll happily interact with each other if they're a bit fearful of the unfamiliar environment.'

'A one-hour visit then?'

Jemima nods. She still seems fairly cautious, but willing to go ahead, so I push on, securing every detail I can. 'So, let's say I have a word with the manager and see if we can arrange something next month – perhaps in the run-up to Christmas?'

'You'll need to check that Aileen can cover the café.'

'I already have, and she's agreed in principle.'

Jemima's expression cracks into a smile. 'You've thought of everything, eh?'

'I want this to happen, so yeah, I have. I've grown quite fond of the residents, and I'd like to give something back, even if it's simply a one-off visit – I know they'll love it.'

Heather

'How did she take the news?' asks Magnus, piling hay bales from his truck into the alpaca barn.

'Not well, but I was expecting it. Reopens a can of worms, doesn't it?'

'In many ways, for many people,' mutters Magnus.

'And you?'

'Me? Just glad I didn't go, to be honest. I'm torn between what Lachlan did and not fully understanding Niven's involvement in my sister's death. I didn't trust myself to sit quietly, so Verity also suggested I stay away.'

'Wise woman.'

'Yeah, she is.'

'Oh, so you do know?'

Magnus throws down his straw bale before standing tall, eyeing me in the process. 'Sure. Best day's work I ever did. Why, don't you think that shows?'

I shrug. As open as Magnus can be, he rarely discusses his private life. One false move and he'll close up tighter than any clam.

'Seriously, Heather, are you expecting us to drift apart then?'

'Not so much drift ... but she has commitments elsewhere. And let's face it, Magnus, you're not one for showing your hand as such, are you? I'm slightly fearful that you'll play those cards so close to your chest that you'll lose a bloody good woman, should her sons start needing her. She feels undecided between here and the Midlands, as it is.'

Magnus purses his lips, grabs another bale and throws it down on to his half-built pile.

'Get my drift?'

'I get it. She's loving it here in Lerwick, the lads are doing well back home, and her business is jogging along nicely. What more can you ask for?'

'We both know life only does that for so long, Magnus. Every time we think we're sorted, along comes the unexpected – ready to blow that pretty picture to smithereens. Yeah?'

'I suppose you're right.'

'So?'

'So what?'

'Are you going to continue jogging along as you are, or are you actually going to make an honest woman of her?'

'Phuh! I think it's the other way around in our case, don't you?'

'Yeah, I was trying to be tactful. Your future needs defining.'

'Oi, I think you need to sort out your own backyard before you come around here making suggestions for me, Heather,' he says, with a jokey tone. 'What's this I'm hearing about Kaspar?'

'That's it, turn the tables on me, why don't you?' I say, before adding, 'He's nice.'

'Nice? He's more than bloody nice, Heather. He's the equivalent of Verity, from what I know.'

'We're taking it slow. I'm having issues with our Ellie around dating and age differences. She's rattled my cage with a couple of things lately, and I'm questioning my own bloody judgement. You know how it is?'

'I sure do.' He drags the final bale from the back of the truck and throws it on to the pile, before jumping down to tidy the stack. 'You need to focus on you and let Ellie start taking care of herself. She's not stupid; you've brought her up to have sound morals and values, so let her prove her worth. She'll be her own woman, regardless of what you say or think.'

'But that's my baby,' I mutter, more to myself than him.

'That might be so, but she's got to live her own life someday. So it might as well be now – when you're around to support her, if it goes wrong.'

I glare at him from beneath my furrowed brow. 'Damn you, man. Why have you always got the right turn of phrase? You always know the words to change my bloody mind, regardless of the topic or situation – or our sodding ages.'

He laughs, giving the wall of straw bales a final pat. 'Just a family trait I have – and sadly, you don't! Come here.' He wraps a brotherly arm around my shoulders and gives me a giant hug. 'Now quit moping, Kaspar's a top bloke, you should be grateful – especially given your age.' Magnus flinches, knowing he's rattling my cage.

'You cheeky sod! I'll get you back.' I peel myself from beneath his embrace, faking annoyance, but he's right, as always. 'Anyway, has your mum found her necklace yet?'

Magnus stops and looks at me sternly, all signs of our jokey banter gone in an instant. 'I didn't know she'd lost it.'

'She took it off to visit the hairdresser's . . .'

'In case they snip through it,' adds Magnus, having heard that line throughout his life.

'Exactly, but she couldn't find it earlier. Your dad was suggesting it could be . . . what's wrong?'

His features have instantly darkened as he hangs on my every word. 'And now she can't find it?'

'No. Hasn't she said?'

'Not a word.' Magnus pulls his phone from his pocket and begins tapping the screen. 'What day was this?'

'She went to the hairdresser's on Monday morning, and I spoke to her earlier today.'

Magnus stares at his phone.

'What are you checking?'

'I've organised different days for each helper to attend the farmhouse.'

'Oh!' My heart instantly sinks.

'Oh, exactly.'

I watch as Magnus swipes rapidly, before peering intently at one screenshot and expanding the details to read. His gaze flickers up to meet mine, before his shoulders drop and he expels a sigh.

'Who?' He doesn't answer, but he bites the inside of his cheek as if mulling over the information, so I continue, 'If it's the woman with the whiney voice, I won't be surprised; I thought she was dodgy from the off, despite her references being immaculate.'

Magnus shakes his head. 'Nope. We're not that lucky.'

'What do you mean . . . lucky?'

'No sooner do you solve one issue than it causes another. Callie.'

'Callie . . . what?'

'Callie. She had perfect references too – from me!'

The name hangs between us as I catch up with his meaning.

'No way!' I insist.

Magnus grimaces.

'Are you sure?' I ask, as he turns the screen towards me, showing the rota.

'If Mum took it off for the hairdresser's and hasn't seen it since . . . then only Callie has entered the house since. She completed her visit on Monday, then Mum called her in for an extra visit on Tuesday, as she couldn't wait till next week for the rest of the upstairs to be cleaned thoroughly.'

'There must be some mistake.'

'Do you think?' The sarcasm drips from his tongue. 'I'll have a quiet word, methinks.'

'Magnus, think before you act, please.' My stomach suddenly goes twitchy and nervous at the very thought of him mentioning the missing necklace.

'What's there to think about? I'll ask if she saw it while she was cleaning. If she changed the beds and vacuumed the rooms, she's been through the entire house en route to the washing machine. She might have spotted it. I can only ask.'

'Shall I come with you?'

'No, Heather. I'm not accusing her – just asking whether she's seen it.'

'Tread carefully, please.'

'I will. Not a word to anyone, right?' he adds.

I nod. 'It's bloody typical, you think you've sorted a situation and then something like this happens and ruins it for everyone. I felt a sense of relief, knowing that the Lachlan and Niven case was over – and then this occurs.'

I feel selfish even thinking it, but if Callie doesn't continue with the role, I'll need to squeeze some extra time out of my week, which I really wasn't banking on.

Chapter Thirty-two

Monday 21 November

Callie

I walk the length of the farmhouse driveway, with my nerves rattling in my throat. I haven't heard a whisper from anyone since Magnus spoke to me. I was expecting my shift to be cancelled. I've checked my phone several times this morning; there are no missed calls, and no text messages. My greatest fear now is that, on arrival, they'll ask me to leave – which will be totally humiliating. I'm on the verge of tears as it is. Every stride I take towards the farmhouse feels one step closer to potential disaster.

When I get closer to the farmhouse, I scour the frontage for clues, but nothing looks any different to my last few visits. There is the usual swathe of mud on the left, leading to Magnus' sheep barns, and the mud-splattered crazy paving peels off to the right, towards the sprawling brick farmhouse. Inside, I know I'll find Iona and Clyde sitting cosily in the lounge, a real fire blazing, plasma TV on, living out their retirement in comfort. On any other day, I'd make a fresh cuppa, ask which task Iona wants doing first, and waste no time getting stuck in. What today will bring is anyone's guess.

My legs feel like lead as I approach the farmhouse. My pace slows and my nerves increase. I really don't want any unpleasantness, arguing or upset. I need this job. I like this job. Christ, like my Happy Days shifts, I actually think I'm good at this job.

I once felt that way about my beautician work – making people feel better through massage, manicures and pedicures – but this job has a more personal element to it. I'll miss helping Iona and Clyde if they refuse to let me into their home. What if Carole, the other carer, is already doing an extra shift?

I turn around and stare back along the driveway in the direction from which I've just come. If Magnus dismisses me, I'll be dashing back along this stretch in less than five minutes – I'll die of shame!

There's no way I'll be able to hide it from my parents if I'm back within thirty minutes and stay home all day; they know I've taken on extra work. I can see this being a disaster just waiting to unfold before me.

I head around to the rear kitchen door. I rap loudly on the wooden panel, as usual, though turning the handle and opening the door feels so awkward. I must act normally, I remind myself; I've done nothing wrong.

'Hello, it's Callie!' I wait by the open door, my head cocked to one side, listening for their answer.

The kitchen is as warm as ever, thanks to the faithful old Aga on the far wall.

'Hello, lassie. Come on in, and shut the door, don't go heating the street!' says Iona's chirpy voice from the lounge. 'Would you mind a shopping task? It'll save our Heather a trip or two.'

Her usual manner. Not what I was expecting!

I step inside, wipe my feet, close the back door and head into the lounge. I find the scene just as I had imagined it: a content couple in the throes of watching snooker, halfway through their cuppas – the beginnings of their new day.

I glance around the lounge, checking that a third party isn't lurking in the nearest armchair: it's empty. You could knock me over with a feather. What is their game? If Magnus truly thinks I've taken Iona's necklace, why are they allowing me to continue cleaning for them? Or have they found it, but they don't like to admit it? Either way, this feels much like an ordinary day – as all my previous shifts were.

Iona busies herself finding paper and a pen.

'A new tournament or a repeat?' I ask Clyde, whose gaze is fixed on the green baize.

'The 1985 World Championship – Davis and Taylor, my favourite,' mutters Clyde, seemingly unbothered by my presence.

I stare at the plasma screen, feeling snookered myself after being roundly accused of pocketing something that wasn't mine. I'm not as relaxed as I used to be. I'm agitated, feeling nervous still, but less so than walking up the driveway. Do Iona and Clyde suspect me of being a thief – or simply Magnus and Heather? I can't ask straight out. Surely.

I follow Iona into the kitchen. She's peering into the freezer, deciding which items to add to her shopping list. My gaze slowly scours each worktop, praying that I spot a glint of gold poking out from beneath a cookery book, a tea towel or a chopping board.

Nothing.

'Has your necklace been found?' The question leaves my lips before I have a chance to put my brain into gear.

Iona whips around to face me. 'No, lovey, it hasn't. I didn't know you knew about that.'

'Magnus mentioned it,' I mumble, softening the tone of his 'mention' considerably.

'Clyde reckons I've dropped it down a plug or a drain, but I doubt I have.'

'I assume you've retraced your steps for that day?'

'Yep, my hairdressing day, it was.' Iona continues with her task.

I do likewise, my gaze dropping to drift along the kitchen skirting boards, hoping against hope to see a sliver of gold lying on the red tiles.

Again, nothing.

'Right, I think that's your lot,' announces Iona, closing the freezer door firmly and handing me the double-sided list. 'Clyde, have you got cash for this shopping?'

'In here, I've put it on the mantelpiece,' calls Clyde.

Iona gestures for me to go and collect it. How can they suspect me if I'm being trusted with their cash? I go back into the lounge and Clyde points to the mantel, where some notes have been stuffed under a trinket ornament acting as a paperweight.

I collect the notes and replace the trinket on the shelf.

'Twenty, forty, sixty pounds. OK?' I say, counting the notes out before him, not that he's watching me. 'I'll bring you the change.'

'Sixty pounds. Correct.'

I fold the three notes and wrap the shopping list around them, before stuffing them in my pocket.

'Any jobs need doing en route?' I ask Iona, returning to the kitchen.

'My library book could do with renewing ... would you mind?' Bless her, she looks almost guilty for asking.

'Of course not, I'll drop by the library before heading to Tesco.' I collect the set of hessian shopping bags from beside the shoe rack and organise them inside one of the larger ones.

'Here's the library book. You'll be OK getting a taxi back?'

'Sure, I'm happy walking there, Iona. It's a nice morning.' I stop short of suggesting it'll clear my head of my recent worries. 'Right, I'll see you in a little while. Call me if you think of anything else.'

'I will, lassie. Thank you. I'll have a cuppa on the go when you return.'

I leave the warm kitchen, make sure the door is shut securely behind me, and let out a deep sigh – a sense of freedom, plus relief that all remains well.

'Oh, hello, it's you!' His deep voice makes me jump.

Magnus.

'Hi, yes, it's me. I'm heading to the shops, plus the library,' I say, pretty sheepishly. His presence instantly unsettles me. 'I've got a list, and sixty pounds.' The sudden need to mention the exact details reflects my unsettled state. It's on the tip of my tongue to ask if he honestly thinks I'd steal from his parents, but I bail; I can do without adding to his feelings of annoyance. I need this job more than he realises.

Magnus gives a curt nod, before stepping briskly around me and opening the rear kitchen door, closing it firmly behind him.

I take several deep breaths to steady my nerves for the umpteenth time this morning, before traipsing off along the driveway.

Surely life isn't supposed to be this stressful?

Tabitha

'Again!' I say, from the armchair in Aileen's front room.

'Are you serious?' asks Rabbie, looking put out at my request.

'You fluffed your lines, Rabbie – there's no room for error. If Ebenezer were here, you wouldn't question it,' I say, having spent the afternoon walking them through their scene. 'Do it again, for one last time, but with a full-blown embrace on greeting – a warm exchange, and not the pretence you were both doing earlier.'

Rabbie eyes me cautiously. 'Aileen, are you OK with that?'

'Sure.'

Aileen steps back, away from Rabbie, returning to her original stage markings. He exits the dimensions of the Cratchits' dingy front room and prepares to re-enter, pretending Tiny Tim is on his shoulders.

'Bob Cratchit, where . . .' begins Aileen, dashing forward from her cooking hearth, wiping her hands on her imaginary apron.

I sit entranced. It's mesmerising to watch a scene take shape and spring to life before your eyes. The tiny nuances we've worked on during our practice time have made a considerable difference to both actors.

Within seconds, the imaginary Tiny Tim has been removed from his father's shoulders, and the actors warmly embrace and kiss.

I sit staring.

Enough.

That's all. Call it quits! A peck would have done!

'Th-that … w-was p-perfect!' I stammer, unnerved by my sudden fit of jealousy.

Both actors release, continuing the scene and their lines. But I'm stuck fast, confused by an embrace that didn't involve me.

Chapter Thirty-Three

Callie

'Jemima, could I have a word?' I call across the cobbled yard.

I've dropped by to assist Mungo with putting the alpacas away. But on seeing Magnus' truck parked alongside the barn, I've decided against it.

'Sure.' Her eyes sparkle with intrigue – or is this the pregnancy bloom she is so rarely able to muster?

I dash ahead, ready to hold open The Orangery's heavy door, with Jemima in tow. I wave a brief greeting to Isla, who is working alone, before heading towards the furthest couch. I don't wait for Jemima to settle before I begin.

'If someone asked you straight out, without rhyme or reason, if you'd seen a particular gold necklace, how would you take that?'

'First, I'd want to know when I was supposed to have seen it. And then I'd want to know why they were questioning me?'

'That's exactly what I asked them,' I say triumphantly. 'But they got all shifty, and simply repeated their questions.'

'OK. So maybe they had a reason for being so cagey. Did this conversation take place here?' asks Jemima, glancing around, despite The Orangery being empty.

'Yes and no. It happened here, the other morning. But it's not about here. It's something entirely separate.'

'I see, but still, I would have expected them to outline the full details.' Jemima falls silent and watches me. Her brow is puckered, her lips slightly pursed, and her gaze is soft.

Can I trust her? Should I say more?

'Callie, you seem upset.'

Typical! One word of kindness and tears flood my cheeks. I can be angry at folk, I can shoulder their insinuations, yet one iota of compassion towards me and I turn into a blubbering mess.

'Oh, Callie. Here, take it. It's clean.' Jemima digs a folded paper hanky from her pocket.

I gratefully accept the offering, dabbing at my cheeks. I don't attempt to speak; I'll only hiccup my way through, and Jemima won't understand a word.

'How about you start from the beginning and tell me everything?' She settles herself into the couch, readying herself for whatever I'm about to say.

I take a deep breath. 'Magnus has asked me if I've seen a gold necklace belonging to his mother. She took it off in the farmhouse last Monday, and hasn't seen it since. I visited that day, and the next, but I swear I didn't see any gold necklace. I was in and out of bedrooms, dusting and hoovering, the entire time.'

'And you've told him this?'

'Yes, straight away. He simply stood there in silence, staring at me, as if waiting for me to change my mind and admit to something I haven't done.'

'Did he say anything else?'

'He didn't have to – it was quite clear what he was thinking. "She's taken it but isn't admitting to it." Later, I phoned another lady who helps out at the farmhouse – her name's Carole – and asked if he'd spoken to her? She knew nothing about it.'

'I see.' Jemima bites her bottom lip. 'Did you see the necklace?'

'No!' I almost wail the syllable.

'OK, I believe you. How did Magnus leave things with you?'

'He said, if I should discover it, he'd like it returned.'

'Did he really?'

'Yes, he might as well have said, "You have it at home, I expect you're now feeling guilty, so bring it back in the morning." I saw Heather the next day, and she looked as guilty as sin when she spotted me – so I left the subject alone. They've only questioned me about it, as far as I know – no one else.'

'Are you upset at the accusation, or the fact that they've only asked you?'

'Both. But more so that they've instantly decided I'm the culprit. I'll probably lose my cleaning shifts now. And if the matron at Happy Days finds out – then I'll lose my shifts there too. So I'm buggered – and through no fault of my own.'

'When's your next cleaning shift supposed to be?'

'Not until next week, as I went earlier today, but I can't have this hanging over my head. I'm half expecting them to cancel me before then, in light of what Magnus believes about me.'

'Have they ever cancelled before?'

'No. But now they think I'm a thief!' My voice cracks as the realisation hits home.

'Callie, what a horrible situation to find yourself in.'

'If I'd worked there longer, they'd know me better, but after such a short amount of time – they've jumped to a hasty conclusion.'

Jemima looks away, glances back and then turns to view the serving counter where Isla is wiping down surfaces, preparing to close.

'Would you like me to say something on your behalf?' she asks gingerly.

I'm shocked out of my skin. She may be my own flesh and blood, she might have offered me a job when I was in dire straits and needed employment after my beautician work went to the wall, but this – Jemima speaking up for me! I could only be more shocked if it were our Pippa suggesting it.

'It might help . . . it could ease the situation.'

'We've never had anything of the sort happen here. You've

worked alongside Isla and Aileen for long enough – and there are constant opportunities, with the non-stop flow of artists and customers passing through the café every day. If you were a thief, surely we'd have had reason to suspect something in the time you've been here.'

'I've never taken anything.'

'I might speak to Magnus – or would you prefer it to be Heather?'

'Heather, please. She might be more obliging – I'm not sure Magnus would take kindly to his business being discussed at the gallery.'

'OK, leave it with me.' Jemima rises awkwardly, with the aid of a hefty push on the sofa arm. 'This certainly gets in the way at times,' she says, indicating her belly, 'or is it the low sofa cushions?'

I'm taken aback by her kind gesture, so I miss the humour in her remark.

'Thank you, Jemima. I just needed to tell someone: I certainly didn't expect you to commit yourself.'

'I get it. You're mithered by the insinuation – and yeah, why shouldn't you share your troubles, Callie? Try not to worry. And let me know if Magnus cancels your shifts in the coming days.'

'I will, thank you.' I give her a quick sideways hug, to accommodate her growing bump.

It feels alien to be hugging our Jemima, but surprisingly good after the unexpected kindness she's just shown me.

Heather

'I don't see the issue, Mum. The other pups left two weeks ago, yet he still hasn't got a home,' says Ellie, as if I hadn't noticed. 'You've got the details of seven families, and you admit that two of them are perfect. It's hardly rocket science. Though he's hardly a cute puppy any more – he's fairly big now.'

'Ah, you make it sound so easy, don't you?' I retort, staring at the paperwork scattered across my dining room table.

'It is. You call the first family. If they say they've already reserved another boy pup, or have already collected one from somewhere else, then it's job done. You simply phone the second family, as it's their lucky day. Isn't that the system you yourself introduced?'

'I'm just not sure, Ellie.'

'I saw you earlier at the kitchen sink, wringing your hands and muttering to yourself. And I thought, I bet she's mulling over the situation with the little boy pup. You're making it more difficult than it needs to be. It's easy.'

'Is it now!' I snap, letting my emotions get the better of me. The dilemma of the homeless pup, the missing necklace, and even arranging another date with Kaspar, are all hanging over me.

Ellie raises her eyebrows. 'And you reckon you're so professional where your pups are concerned. Oh, Mum, just get on with it. Or admit you don't want him to go. It's obvious!'

'How wrong you are!' I storm out of the dining room, leaving my scattered paperwork to be dealt with later.

I hear the door slam behind me. Was that me, or did Ellie just conclude our conversation with a hefty slam of the door? I stomp upstairs, much like our Isla does when she's in a mood. It's not that I mind my girls chatting about things behind my back. What I mind is them both assuming they know everything I'm thinking or planning when it comes to my own pups. Correction, Pepper's pups.

I'm crossing the landing to my bedroom, when I hear our Isla calling me.

'What, Isla?'

'I said, are you OK?' comes the muffled reply from her bedroom.

I knock but don't wait for an answer before popping my head around the door. 'Not one hundred per cent,' I say, pulling a stupid expression for fear of exploding – either in anger or tears.

'Little boy pup?'

I nod, my daft expression still in place.

'Want a hand?'

'Well, your sister said that, twenty minutes ago, but I've just stormed out on her because she reckons I want to keep him.'

'Don't you?' Her eyebrows lift in a questioning manner.

'Look, who doesn't want a cute pup in the house? Which breeder wouldn't give their right arm to let Pepper keep one from every litter, but I can't do that. Three bitches around here is enough.'

'Yeah, plus the three dogs – so that's six in total!'

A bubble of laughter bursts from my chest. 'I didn't mean . . . us three.'

'Yeah, well, you aren't trying to complete your proofreading against a backdrop of sniping from downstairs,' she says, closing her cookery book project on her computer. 'Come on, let's "go and do", as Jemima says when there's a nasty task to complete.'

'It's not nasty, I just don't want to regret my decision, that's all.'

We go downstairs to find the dining room has been vacated by Ellie. I'll make a point of apologising in a little while, but first I need to complete the task, with Isla's help.

'This is the boy paperwork pile?' she says, settling at the table beside my chair.

I nod, pushing the questionnaires towards her.

'I take it the top one is the main contender?'

I nod again. Isla lifts the first piece of paper and reads it thoroughly. I'm liking this attention to detail; it's not a side I usually see of her. She's definitely matured in recent months, since joining the Campbells at the manor, but I'm seeing her in a whole new light. I can see there's more than a touch of Jemima's influence here.

'And the issue is?' she asks on finishing.

'They're a lovely family who've been waiting six months. Nice people, with two children, a back garden, no other pets, and previous experience owning a Sheltie; apparently, the mother had one as a teenager.'

'Sounds perfect.'

I give a slight tilt of my head.

'You'll have to say it aloud, Mum – I'm not a mind-reader.'

'Here. I pass her the second family's details. They've been waiting just two weeks less than the other family.' Again, I watch Isla skim through their details.

'There's hardly anything to choose between them, Mum. Both have children, gardens, experience with grooming a dog, so that won't be a surprise. I can't see how you could pick these people over the first family. He'd be lucky to belong to either.'

'I should choose, and just be done.'

'No, you shouldn't "just be done". I've never seen you like this over one pup before, so come on – what's really the matter?' Isla stares at me, the papers held aloft in each hand.

I slump back in my chair, staring from one family's details to the other's. I need to be honest, because my girls are starting to question my ability to do this role.

'Neither is good enough for this little one.'

Isla's jaw drops. 'Are you serious? These are both perfect families – you couldn't have asked for better.'

'Not for this little one. You weren't here. You didn't witness the first three being born and then . . . nothing happened. Nothing for ages, in fact. Pepper didn't panic, she remained calm, despite looking as if she was struggling. And then, when the contractions subsided, she nursed the first three arrivals. There was something about being here and seeing her whelp. I could sense that she was asking for help; I just knew there were more pups to come. I called Magnus and he came and did . . . well, you know. And that was this little pup, number four. Then the final two simply popped out like magic.'

'It wasn't the easiest of all the births you've witnessed, but all was well in the end.'

'Yeah, but . . .' I need to continue talking, otherwise I'll swallow it down yet again. It's an idea I just can't get out of my head. 'He's the only boy in the litter. The only ram in the herd, the only bull in the field . . . the only cockerel in the hen house.'

Isla rolls with laughter at my words. 'Seriously, are you alright?'

'That's our Magnus.'

'What?' And now, she's totally confused.

'Magnus, he's spent his life surrounded by us women, looking out for us in any way he can, and when I needed him, he didn't hesitate. He never hesitates. I think this little boy pup belongs to Magnus, they're one and the same.'

A tear plops on to the back of my hand and I look down, as surprised as Isla to see I'm crying.

'Oh, Mum! Is that what you've been thinking?'

I give a teary nod; finally, I've said it out loud.

Isla gently rubs my shoulders before addressing the two sets of paperwork, now lying on the table. 'Well, these families can both wait, Mum – it's just a matter of time before you deliver them each a boy pup.'

'And Floss?'

'Floss is getting on in years, Mum – she doesn't move as well as she used to after that accident, does she? She'll soon knock this little one into shape.'

I nod; I feel lighter for sharing my thoughts.

'You've got your work cut out, convincing our Magnus though,' says Isla.

Chapter Thirty-Four

Sunday 4 December

Ebenezer's ledger

Every ticket sold!!!! Not a penny to spare for those godforsaken charity folks. It'll be a full house for our opening performance on Christmas Eve! This could be my finale!

Tabitha

I spend half my morning making the lye for my new creation: Dottie's Delphinium Delight. The other half is spent open-mouthed, staring at the glorious decorations a team of professionals are installing in The Orangery.

'I thought last year's creation was like a winter wonderland, but this is something else,' says Nessie.

She's joined me in the soapery's doorway to admire the festoon of sparkly garlands and giant baubles being secured high above the plush couches and coffee tables.

'Though don't tell Isaac there's mistletoe,' she teases. 'He'll only panic!'

We both laugh, thinking back to her wayward advances from last year.

'They've never done all this purely for a one-day Christmas market? It's for the wedding too, isn't it? You can't tell me they're installing festive decorations now, only to remove and replace them for the Christmas Eve wedding?'

'You're right. Though what they'll do about converting The Orangery into a wedding chapel for the day is beyond me – you'd hardly want the tables and chairs stacked in a corner, now would you?'

I grimace. 'I've no doubt it's all in hand. Jemima might not be organising it, but she's chosen the wedding planner, so it'll be top-notch and quality. Though she'll have had the baby by then, surely?'

'Speak of the devil and she shall appear!' I exclaim, as Dottie emerges from the tradesman's entrance.

'Hello, ladies, how are we both?'

'Good, thanks. How's Jemima coping?' I ask, knowing that her due date is nearly upon us.

'That lassie has had a time and a half of it. The sooner that bairn gets here the happier I'll be,' says Dottie, beaming at the very thought of a Campbell baby.

'Are you going to let us in on your wedding secrets?' asks Nessie, giving her an encouraging smile.

'We want a small and intimate wedding – none of this "boom, boom" music malarkey. We're having The Orangery for our wedding venue, with the wedding reception in the manor's ball-room – and then we'll be retiring as such, and calling it a day.'

'No evening do?' I ask, not sure I fully understand.

'No, lassie, the day will be long enough for us. A quiet evening in a nice hotel will do us nicely. It'll only make us crabbit if the celebrations go on towards midnight.'

Nessie and I glance at each other and chuckle.

'Oi, none of your sauciness, either. Behave yourselves,' quips Dottie playfully.

'Bridesmaids?' I ask.

'No. As long as I have Ned to walk me down the aisle, I'll be happy.'

'You're having a nice dress and a bouquet though, surely?'

'Of course, but it's of my own choosing and style ... these modern dresses aren't for me.'

'And Mungo?' asks Nessie. 'Is he going with tradition?'

'He wouldn't have it any other way. Levi's his best man, with both of them dressed in their best bib and tucker.'

'It should be lovely, Dottie – I can't wait to see you as a blushing bride.'

'Dorothy Tulloch, now there's a name I never thought I'd hear!' she says, bidding us a goodbye and darting into The Orangery to inspect the decorations.

Nessie and I exchange a glance.

'I only hope everything goes according to plan,' she confides, 'and they get the best wedding day ever.'

'And have a few years to enjoy it together,' I say.

Callie

'Heather?' I call out from behind the counter the second I spy her enter The Orangery.

Isla turns swiftly, eyeing me cautiously. The café is busy, and I'm supposed to be serving afternoon tea for a table of ten, having completed an alpaca trek.

Heather doesn't look surprised, which suggests she knows about my previous conversations with Magnus and Jemima.

I quickly dispose of my tray and make my way around the counter before Isla can stop me. 'Sorry to grab you,' I blurt out. 'But I wanted . . .' I don't finish my sentence. Instead, I guide her towards the log burner, an area of the café which is much quieter. I have no intention of others overhearing our conversation, giving rise to speculation and more gossip. I'm aware of Isla throwing me a strange look as I take a seat.

I don't waste time sugar-coating it. 'I assume Magnus has mentioned that his mother's necklace has gone missing?'

Heather goes to speak, thinks twice about it and nods.

'I just wanted to say to you what I said to him. I didn't see it on either of my days. I haven't touched it, moved it or put it anywhere for safe keeping, either inside or outside the farmhouse.' I fall silent and watch her reaction. I'm embarrassed at the necessity of having to say it so plainly.

'Look, we're asking anyone who's been helping out at Iona and Clyde's if they've seen it, so there's no offence meant. I'm sorry if Magnus came on a bit strong,' says Heather, shifting in her seat. 'I understand he explained as much to Jemima; apparently, she knows of the situation too.'

'I see, so you've asked Carole?' I say, watching her reaction.

Heather licks her lips before answering. 'I haven't asked anyone, I've left that to Magnus.'

'Why not?'

Heather inclines her head. I think she's stalling for time. I continue, not wishing to sound and act passive-aggressive, but I'm not having this situation blow up in my face. This has hung over me now for weeks. I need the extra cleaning shifts, and I won't be palmed off with excuses when I know they haven't spoken to anyone else.

'Just me then?' My question hangs over us like a November fog rolling in off the North Sea. I refuse to jump in and erase the tension, purely to make her feel more comfortable, when I've been made to feel like a common thief.

'Callie, I'm sorry, but Magnus works long hours – it's a difficult time, farming in winter. I assume he spoke to you first, as you'd done a double shift on the exact days, but please don't think that—'

I don't let her finish. 'Well, I do think. It seems I've been targeted – probably not what you wish me to say, but that's what it looks like to me, Heather. If it wasn't meant to look that way, maybe you and Magnus should have approached both of us on the same day. But I know Carole hasn't been spoken to – or even had a text – because I've asked her.'

'You have?' Heather's expression is a picture.

'Well, thanks a bunch, Heather.' I stand up. I hadn't planned on being so curt, but I've said my piece. I need to leave the conversation and return to my work. There's no point continuing.

'Everything OK, ladies?' asks Isla, cautiously approaching with a freshly made drink for her mother.

'Yes, thank you,' I say. 'I'll leave you to explain, Heather.' I move away from the pair, trying my hardest not to stomp, dash or even lower my head, as that would suggest guilt. Right now, I have the urge to cry. But I won't. Because I need to deliver a fresh round of drinks to my afternoon tea guests in a short while.

I have no reason to cower away from the accusations being flung at me. I haven't taken that necklace, I haven't done anything wrong – not even helped myself to a biscuit without asking. And to think they haven't had the decency to even speak to . . . The Orangery door opens wide. I look up, grateful to have a customer to distract me: Pippa, my younger cousin.

'Hello,' I say cheerfully, probably with a little extra gusto than is usual in our terse relationship.

Pippa stops, turns around to look behind her, before smiling at me. 'Hello, yourself. Wow, what a greeting!'

I really wish I'd paused for a second before opening my mouth but, hey, I'm upset.

'Not really,' I protest. 'Your usual, is it? How were the bread deliveries today?'

'Please.' Pippa continues towards the counter and digs in her trouser pocket for change. 'I've just arrived back. But I'm freezing, so I wanted a drink before I unload the wicker baskets from Rolly.'

'How's Levi?' I say, busying myself making her hot chocolate with sprinkles.

'Are you alright?'

I glance over my shoulder as I work the coffee machine, to find her watching me.

'Yeah, why?'

'You never greet me like that – and you never show an interest in me or Levi.'

'Sure I do.'

Pippa shakes her head.

I return my attention to the jug of frothy milk. Bloody hell, is no one going to give me a break today?

'The decorations look fabulous – were these put up this afternoon?' asks Pippa, viewing the Christmas garlands.

I tap the jug to disperse the bubbles and swirl the warm frothy milk into the prepared mug. Pippa stands watching as I reach for the arty metal template and dust a festive holly design with chocolate powder.

'Yeah, it's taken the company most of the day. They're coming back tomorrow to decorate the courtyard. There you go, on the house,' I swiftly say, not meeting her eye.

Pippa jiggles her handful of change, eyes me cautiously, before speaking.

'Now, you might not want to admit it, but you and I know this . . .' she waves a hand back and forth between us, 'this, never happens between us. I won't ask for a third time, but what I will say, if you need me, just shout, OK?'

My gaze flicks upwards to meet hers.

'Thank you, Callie,' she says, picking up her drink and walking towards the nearest sofa.

I give her the smallest of nods. That interaction wasn't difficult, or as strained as our usual attempts at conversation. Maybe there's a silver lining to recent events, after all.

Chapter Thirty-Five

Saturday 10 December

Tabitha

'I can't believe how busy it is!' exclaims Rabbie, dashing past me on his two-hour stint.

I'm frantically restocking today's star buy: Mistletoe Magic, a pure white bar of soap, containing glittery flecks of gold, which is selling faster than Isla's warmed buttered bannocks. It's a custom-made soap, especially for today, to complement the winter wonderland extravaganza staged in the gallery's cobbled courtyard. The whole place has been transformed by swathes of mistletoe, garlands of holly and ivy, candle lanterns and the giant wrought-iron Christmas trees crafted by Nessie, aptly decorated with unique baubles hand-blown by Isaac – around which the Shetland Choral Society are gathered singing carols.

'Can you believe it? I thought the Campbells offering us a Christmas market day was baloney, to head off any complaints about lost trade from the cancelled Yule Day celebrations, but this ... well, this is quite unbelievable,' I say, glancing around at the swarms of customers piling into my soapery. 'And it's been constant all day, since opening.' My hands busily unpack and stack the bars as I speak. 'Though if Crispy duck and Pancake waddle in seeking warmth again today – there's no telling what I'll threaten to do with a rich orange sauce!'

'Next year, they'll be opting for a Christmas market plus Yule Day, so watch out!'

I feverishly nod. Is there anything the Campbell couple can't achieve when they set their minds to it? Be it business, allotments, livestock or hospitality – they've got the Midas touch in all areas, plus they're the sweetest people whilst grafting to make their business a success. Talk about living the dream! I wish we were all that lucky.

My gaze lifts to observe Rabbie answering a customer's query about my range of balms. I've spent days wondering how he and Aileen are getting along: are they able to focus on their scripts or have personal matters got in the way? I've shied away from asking Aileen, for fear of her confirming their couple status in person or via social media. I suppose I'll know when I see their performance onstage at The Garrison. I'll need more than pan-stick stage make-up to muster a brave face if their kiss is more than acting.

'Do you mind me nipping out to grab a hot drink?' asks Rabbie, breaking my train of thought. 'I'm frozen to the bone despite wearing this woollen jumper. Everyone seems happy browsing for a second.'

'Sure!'

He turns, strides away, before swiftly returning. 'Are you?'

'What?'

'Sure? You sound narked. Do you want anything fetching?'

I shake my head, realising that my thoughts of him and Aileen are hardly charitable. Nor any of my business. I shouldn't inter-fere but focus on my own livelihood. I'm struck by a sense of déjà vu. Is this air of foreboding truly going to overshadow my festive cheer? Or am I unknowingly rehearsing the opening scene in Scrooge's counting house?

'Tabs?'

'Just go!' I hiss, not wanting to continue this conversation.

Furthermore, I don't wish for Freddie or two charity collectors to enter the soapery as Rabbie swiftly departs.

Heather

I enter The Orangery in search of mulled wine and festive nibbles, after a long day assisting Nessie and Isaac in the forge, only to find two lengthy queues: the usual one for hot beverages and another, spanning the length of the conservatory, organised by a diligent Pippa, leading to our resident author, Isla Henderson. She looks quite the part, seated behind a decorated table, with hardback books stacked on either side and a pleasing grin fixed in place as she signs the title page for each happy purchaser. Quite amazing to think that this is my daughter! My little girl, who once had unruly curls, a toothy grin and an aversion to the printed word, actually has her name on the front cover of a book with my mother's trusted recipes inside.

'How's it going, Heather?' asks Verity, sidling up next to me.

'Amazing. I feel quite emotional,' I say, gesturing towards Isla. 'My mother would never have imagined this – her bannock recipe available worldwide, and as for Isla signing these copies . . . well, it seems surreal.'

'She's done well. The queue hasn't faltered in length all day – I hope she's got more stock stashed out the back.'

'Believe me, she has. Talking of boxes . . . have you received an unexpected gift box today?' I don't like to ask, for fear of offending her if she hasn't.

'You too?' asks Verity, a genuine look of shock adorning her kindly features. 'You do mean Callie's present, don't you?'

'Yes! Well, you could have knocked me over with a feather – gift wrapped, with a glittery bow and everything. Nessie didn't know whether to thank her or laugh!'

'Nessie too?' she asks. 'Talk about surprised; we're pally but not on that level. I felt awful accepting it, so I'll pick her up a little something in return.'

'That's exactly what we said after she'd left the forge. Isaac said he wouldn't bother – they're tightening their belts, money wise. You've heard their news, I take it.'

'Moving in together? Oh yes, they'll be settled by Easter.'

'And you . . . any news?'

'News?' Verity seems almost baffled by the question.

'You and Magnus, any further forward on that front?' I ask, hoping to hear better news.

'*Weeeell*,' she draws out the word, 'you could say that. They reckon that ninety per cent of life's happiness or sadness comes from just one decision, don't they?' she says, a cheeky smile adorning her features.

'And?' I know my workload will increase if I have to start managing the rental of Harmony Cottage, as I used to do before Verity arrived.

'I've done lots of soul searching in recent weeks, but I can't imagine my life without Magnus. What we've found in each other is precious. I love my three lads to bits, but sooner or later they'll be off in search of their own lives. If I lost Magnus, I'd be throwing away the chance of a lifetime. Which always results in regret.'

'It does,' I say, urging her to put me out of my misery.

'Keep it under your hat for now, I wouldn't want to take the shine off Dottie and Mungo's day – or the Campbell baby, when it decides to arrive – but yeah, I'm staying. It means a house move – into the farmhouse, to live alongside Magnus' family. Your sister and brother-in-law have acquired daily carers, but it'll be easier with the two of us caring for them in the coming years.'

'Excellent! I've got the perfect moving-in gift for you both!' I squeal, in delight.

Tabitha

'Hi.'

I glance up whilst finishing my end-of-day cleaning routine. Half the lights are switched off and my freshly mopped floor is still damp.

Rabbie is leaning against the soapery door, watching me.

'Hi, yourself,' I reply. 'Has your bell boy shift finished already?'

He peels himself away from the doorjamb and enters, gently nudging the door closed with his foot. 'Yep. Are you going to spill the beans or what?'

I shrug, a poor attempt to act dumb.

'OK. I'll start. Today, you were lost in thought and snappy when I asked a simple question. I happened to mention it to Aileen when I collected a coffee, and she reckons you've been like that for—'

'Sorry,' I butt in. 'Honestly, I am. It's none of my business.'

'What isn't your business?' Rabbie leans against my countertop, peering intently at me. His gaze is direct and questioning as my cleaning routine falters.

I instinctively glance towards the closed door, as if expecting Aileen to appear and take centre stage.

'Tabs? Talk to me.'

'I simply can't.' If I cared a little less then maybe I could, but I can't.

Rabbie begins to nod – a definite, assured nod – as if he knows what lies behind my words.

'Let me run this past you then. Aileen reckons you think she and I have got something going on! How absurd is that?'

I baulk at his honesty.

'Only an amateur would suggest such a thing. OK, so our script includes an onstage kiss – which we've ceased practising, by the way, as it feels wrong in her mum's lounge. But a seasoned pro like yourself would never venture down that road, would they?'

I don't answer. In an instant, my thoughts seem utterly foolish – childlike and, as he suggests, totally amateurish.

'Here.' His upturned hand reaches across the countertop for mine, narrowly missing the display of Mistletoe Magic, then he leads me around the bulky obstacle until I'm at his side. He stands straight before me. 'I didn't want it to seem as if I was sucking up to the leading star, so I held back. But surely you noticed the slip-ups I made on festival day, I couldn't take my eyes off you . . .' He falls silent, his free hand reaching up to move a strand of hair caught on my lashes. 'While all the time you were thinking that me and Aileen . . .'

I nod.

He shakes his head.

I wait. My breath quickening in my chest.

He waits. His gaze roaming my features, drifting between eyes and mouth.

Within seconds, his face has blurred as my eyes close and I feel the touch of his lips warming mine.

'Bob Cratchit is not supposed to kiss like that!' I jokingly protest, as we finally drift apart from our embrace.

'Especially not Scrooge!' mutters Rabbie.

Chapter Thirty-Six

Thursday 15 December

Callie

'Thank you, Mungo. I couldn't have done this without your help,' I say, as we unhook the trailer's rear door to reveal the tethered alpacas – one fawn coloured, the other russet – standing shoulder to shoulder.

'Away with yee, lassie. You'd have found a way, I'm sure. Anyway, let's hope these boys don't behave as badly as a goat Melissa once hired for her allotment plot.' He begins to chuckle. 'I won't be happy if they do a repeat performance, so let's make haste and get these boys unloaded.'

I don't ask for further details. But his grey beard keeps jiggling, so I assume he's tittering to himself about Melissa's ordeal. We walk backwards, easing the rear door down into its ramp position. I quickly step up into the trailer. Both alpacas eye me cautiously as I begin spreading a little straw on to the metal ramp, hoping it encourages them to walk down it.

'Here's Isla,' calls Mungo as her car draws into the car park and she finds a free space.

'Perfect, the whole gang is here then,' I say, untying the two rope leads and slowly coaxing the boys to follow me.

'Steady now, fellas . . . there's nothing to worry about,' soothes Mungo, in a husky whisper, as both alpacas inquisitively sniff the air before venturing down the ramp.

'Going well, I see,' says Isla, approaching at a cautious pace. 'I suppose I could have bought some baked goodies, I simply didn't think.'

'Never mind. So far, so good!' I say, as we circle the tarmacked car park.

I glance up and see several expectant faces lining the large lounge window, carefully watching our arrival. Carpe Diem and Karma stand majestically as Mungo and Isla quickly lift the ramp and secure the trailer.

'Good lads. You know, don't you?'

Their ears prick up and twist at the gentle tones of my voice. I always feel honoured to be one of their handlers, but even more so today, given the experimental nature of our visit. I'm trying not to pin my hopes on this becoming a regular occurrence, but if everything works out nicely and the residents feel a therapeutic connection with these timid creatures, who knows where it might lead?

'Which way?' asks Isla, blushing under the watchful gaze of a crowd of elderly residents.

'Around to the rear garden, which is through that gate at the far end,' I say, gesturing towards the back of the car park. I walk slowly; I'm trying my hardest to take my time and not panic the boys. But I'm excited to see the reaction they cause too.

As we cross the car park, making our regal procession towards the gate, I notice the faces in the lounge window have disappeared. I imagine the residents are making their way towards the large conservatory at the rear, overlooking the garden.

A familiar figure greets our arrival in the garden, 'Hello and welcome,' says the manager, speaking in such a hushed tone, I can hardly hear her. She's clearly anxious not to spook our two VIP guests this evening.

'Hello,' I say, leading the alpacas towards the main patio where a semi-circle arrangement of chairs has been organised. 'They're more than happy, as long as they can see each other.'

'Everyone is so excited to meet these . . . are they llamas?'

'No, they're alpacas,' corrects Mungo.

He is following behind, carrying an assortment of bags and dried food; a blatant bribe, in case we need to settle or calm either animal.

'Llamas look similar but are very different,' he declares.

I want to giggle at his brisk explanation but it's sufficient answer for now, until my actual talk begins. A steady flow of residents, togged up in coats and scarves, make their way into the garden from the conservatory; selecting the best seat is their priority amongst the excited chatter and pointing.

'If you're happy to begin, I'll introduce you, Callie,' the manager continues, not querying Mungo's brief answer.

I note that Isla is setting out a few rope leads to be used in our demonstration, and Mungo has found a prime spot in which to park himself, in anticipation of a nice cuppa.

'That'll be great,' I tell her. 'We'll stick to the plan we discussed yesterday. Both animals are happy enough and seem calm, so the petting and stroking session can go ahead.'

I take a deep breath and smile at my audience, hoping that nothing changes for either alpaca, forcing us to curtail our plans.

'How did it go?' asks Jemima as we unload the alpacas from the trailer on arriving back at Lerwick Manor.

'I nearly cried about a million times, that's how well it went!' I exclaim. 'The residents absolutely loved them to bits; they couldn't stop staring and reaching out to stroke them. The two alpacas stood as still as statues. It was quite a sight to see. I didn't want the session to end, if the truth be told.'

I'm aware that I'm gushing, but I can't help it. I'm still on a high from the experience I've enjoyed.

'Same here,' says Isla. 'The residents' faces were a picture – they couldn't get enough of stroking them, breaking away briefly before lining up for a second or third petting session. Half of them ignored the tea trolley and mince pies – they were too interested in our lads.'

'That's amazing, well done,' says Jemima, a beaming smile adorning her features. 'And Mungo?'

'He had the best time,' I say, leaning in to avoid being over-heard. 'He has more friends there than he has here, so he was in his element catching up.'

'Along with a bit of showing off regarding his alpaca knowl-edge – he soon chirped up when it was time for the Q and A,' adds Isla, with a giggle.

Jemima laughs, her large bump jiggling.

'That's Mungo! He always makes out he's not interested in being involved. But given half a chance, he's up front and centre stage, directing the action.'

Tabitha

'Gather round, gather round!' orders Ebenezer, beckoning the cast over. 'We have just nine days until our opening night, so I expect everyone to play their part and make the most of tonight's rehearsal. I can only promise one more meeting, which will act as a dress rehearsal, before the actual performance night.'

There's a muttering from the various cast members. I'm eager to begin, knowing that I've worked myself into the ground for this one role and I need to make the most of the opportunity afforded to me.

'I want to see everyone give it their all tonight, then we can look forward to the curtain rising on a full house on Christmas Eve!' he calls, before shooing us away to our places.

I stand in the wings, awaiting my cue, watching as Bob Cratchit settles himself centre stage at his clerk's desk, warming his frozen fingers against the puny flame of a stubby candle. Rabbie looks great in his Cratchit costume, which he's put together from odds and sods found in a local charity shop.

I'm not entirely sure what came over me the other afternoon in the soapery. It appears that single kiss has ignited something inside – a turmoil of emotions I wasn't expecting. In my past, I've never been one for following my gut reaction. I may have been bold in pursuing my acting dreams, but I've never shown a similar determination when it comes to love.

Standing here now, I'm not so sure if I like this actual guy – or simply the thought of a guy in my life. I've enjoyed Rabbie's flirty smiles, the free-flowing banter we share on Saturday afternoons, but do I want a closer friendship, or more, from Rabbie? Or was it just a spark of jealousy towards Aileen, resenting her for being awarded the role opposite Rabbie that I truly wanted?

Ebenezer claps his hands; this is my cue.

I stroll on to the stage.

As I enter my counting house, in character as the looming figure of Mr Scrooge, I hear the sound of door chimes tinkling overhead.

The narrator reads, 'Marley was dead . . .'

Chapter Thirty-Seven

Thursday 22 December

Callie

'How are things?' asks Jemima, waddling through The Orangery in search of a fresh loaf for the hotel kitchen.

'As awkward as hell. Every time I touch or dust something, a voice in my head whispers, "Don't pinch it, Callie." Nowadays, I'm glad when my shifts are over at the farmhouse. Every other week they ask me to iron, yet this week Iona suggested I dust instead. That, in itself, made me ten times more suspicious . . . did she change my task, hoping I'd trip up and pinch something else?'

'Now you're being utterly ridiculous.'

'Am I? Am I really?'

'Yes, and you know it. Iona asked you to dust because you did the ironing last week, instead of shopping. The woman is allowed to change the tasks in her own home.'

I want to believe her, truly I do, but I don't! I cried on the walk back home, drying my tears only when I reached the garden gate, knowing that my father would ask questions if he caught any sign of tears.

'I think I might hand in my notice to Magnus,' I say.

'Are you joking? And convince them that being guilty has forced your hand? Not bloody likely, Callie. You listen to me, you'll stick this out, you'll make the most of it, and when the truth comes to light . . . you'll be there doing your job. You'll be able to hold your head up high. You've got nothing to run away from. Nothing at all.'

I glance up at her; if only she knew. If only Jemima could see the folder under my bed, crammed with credit card statements, boy, she'd have taken a different tack.

'What?'

'What's what?' I ask, losing the drift of our conversation.

'I don't know, something in your expression told me that there is something. Callie, is there something you're not telling me?'

Oh my Lord, now she's asking. What the hell do I say? Do I admit just how bad my debts are? There's no denying it, pawning a gold necklace would go a long way towards covering my repayments this month – and maybe next.

'Callie?'

'What?'

Jemima peers at me, as if I'm a looking glass and she can read the truth in her reflection.

'There is ... there's something you're not telling me. Has Magnus said more? Has Heather been to speak to you?' Jemima's voice rises a pitch or two. And now, she's worried.

'Look it's nothing, I'm fine.'

'Fine? Fine never sounds great. I use "fine" when I'm not fine and Ned's digging for the truth. So please don't brush me off with that one, Callie.'

Do I stick to my guns or confess? Tell her the truth about how much money I owe, or lie?

'Callie? *Please!*'

'I've been stupid. But I've been making headway, paying off my debts, month by month, and that's why I'm so worried about them sacking me. Where else am I going to find a cleaning job that fits in with my Orangery hours, where Verity can pop across with a message about extra hours if needed, and where I get to be home within fifteen minutes of finishing the shift? I'm gutted, if I'm honest.'

'Why haven't you said anything before?'

'Doh, because I shouldn't have allowed it to get so wildly out of hand. I feel stupid for having landed myself in this situation. Now, when it's crunch time, I can't even save my own bacon but have to rely on my younger cousin to have a quiet word on my behalf. Which I'm grateful for – but seriously, Jemima, I haven't much to crow about.'

'Callie, we all have bad times in life. Look at me, I had to take a sabbatical from my job in order to address my anxiety issues after Mum died, and then Grandpop too. If you need a loan to ease the pressure, just say.'

I hear what she's saying; her kindness shines through.

'Sadly, my troubles are self-inflicted. More a case of trying to make myself happy – and doing the exact reverse, in the long run.'

Jemima tilts her head in order to capture my gaze. Her green eyes shine with concern.

'Look, you don't have to tell me your business, but I'm here if you need to talk. OK?' she says, rubbing my forearm gently. 'My working days are becoming slightly sparse as this bump grows. And Ned's insisting on re-allocating my tasks. So please, just shout.'

'Thank you,' I mumble. It's all I can muster; I'm grateful, but I've said too much as it is.

She flashes me a sympathetic smile and bids me goodbye.

'Bye,' I reply, humbled by her genuine offer of help.

And in a flash, she's off, heading across the cobbled courtyard. Typical Jemima, as solid as a rock, there for everyone in need, and briskly heading towards the next item on her 'To-do' list.

I wouldn't describe myself as a jealous person – I might get miffed when I feel cheated or don't reap the rewards I feel I've earned – but right now, watching my cousin head off, I'll admit she has everything I would like in life. Jemima's done alright for herself and still retained her down-to-earth nature.

Who knows if I could have done that?

Tabitha

'I always find it daunting when the rest of the cast are absent,' I whisper to Rabbie.

We grab our coats, waiting to accompany Ebenezer from the theatre after the dress rehearsal.

'Me too! He scrutinises us more than is necessary,' Rabbie agrees. 'He's slightly less obnoxious when others are present.'

'Exactly . . .' I shush, as Ebenezer returns from backstage.

'Ready?' he asks, glancing suspiciously between the pair of us, as if we've just performed the best version of our scene, without him present.

'Sure,' I say, buttoning my coat.

'Rabbie, can you grab the ghost light please?' asks Ebenezer, straightening the stage curtain and ensuring it is left pristine.

Rabbie heads off to the right of the stage, collects the ancient lamp, plugs it into the socket, before trailing the electrical flex across to the middle of the stage. There's a yank on the lead as he walks a tad too far.

'Careful! You'll pull the wires from the plug, doing that,' scowls Ebenezer, looking thunderous.

I want to laugh. That's why I never race to be the one in charge of the ghost light; there's always someone moaning about how you've done it wrong.

'Sorry . . .' Rabbie's continued muttering is barely audible. He steps back, slackens off the lead and switches the lamp on. The tiny flame-shaped bulb illuminates the stage with its faint glow.

Ebenezer watches, as if mesmerised by this simple act. 'Come on, we're wasting time here,' he says, leading the way along the aisle towards the main entrance doors, his keys jangling in his hands.

I quickly follow him, not wishing to be left behind – or worse still, locked in. I shake my head; what a ridiculous idea, when Ebenezer is accompanying us.

'What are you saying, Ebenezer, do our acting skills suck?' asks Rabbie, giving me a cheeky wink behind our director's back.

'I wouldn't say I've been enthralled by tonight's rehearsal, but there was a definite improvement.'

Rabbie lowers his head. He knows what to expect from Ebenezer – as do I.

But still, I can't help asking, 'What more can we do between now and Saturday?'

'Put your heart and soul into it. Try to live up to Dickens' true intentions when he created his characters,' replies Ebenezer, sharply.

I don't comment, but suppress my irritation that Ebenezer rarely praises me for anything I contribute to the company.

The frosty night air bites at our cheeks as we leave and Ebenezer performs his routine, double checking the heavily chained padlock and rattling the handles for good measure.

He turns and delivers his parting shot. 'Let's hope you get it right on the opening night.'

Heather

'Hello, it's only me!' I holler, poking my head around the kitchen door and wait as usual.

The answer is spoken by a new voice in the farmhouse: Verity's.

'In you come, don't wait on the step; otherwise you'll be heating the street before you know it, Heather.'

Nice one, Magnus!

I struggle to enter, juggling the weight of my basket. I kick off my shoes, as is my custom, and pad through to the lounge. I've trodden the scrubbed tiles of this farmhouse floor a million times, yet something is different, very different, this time. I feel a different warmth about the place, I sense it before even reaching the lounge door, knowing that the scene beyond has changed.

For ever.

'Hello, how are we all?' I say, bustling in.

I find my sister and brother-in-law, as always, in their favourite spots. Magnus is in his armchair, his socked feet resting on the hearth; Floss is lying beneath his outstretched legs, and Verity is knitting in a rocking chair. Picture perfect in every way.

A jumble of responses – 'good', 'can't grumble' and 'fine, fine' – greets my entrance.

'It's toasty in here,' I say, as the wall of heat from the coal fire hits me.

'Warmth is never something we go short of in this place,' mutters Magnus, in his sleepy manner. 'What's in the basket?'

'Wouldn't you like to know?' I say, churlishly, holding the basket tighter in my arms, as if teasing, but pleased that he has asked.

'Do you want a cuppa, Heather?' asks Verity, immediately winding her knitting around the needles and popping it down on the coffee table, before standing up and stretching out her shoulders.

'I will, but I've a gift . . . a sort of house-warming present, not that you need this place any warmer than it currently is,' I joke, flapping my hand at my reddening face.

All four expectant faces turn and view me, which is pretty much a first for my brother-in-law, Clyde.

'Anyway, I know how much the lovely Floss is adored, but I know in my heart of hearts you'll find a place for this little boy!' I plunge my hands into the basket and retrieve the plump blue-collared pup. My actions are quick, maintaining the element of surprise, but also to prevent me from changing my mind and quickly scurrying away from the farmhouse.

Squeals and gasps fill the lounge, and instantly I know I've made the right decision.

Verity leaps forward, arms outstretched to take the pup, in a heartbeat. Magnus retracts his socked feet from the fender and stands up, stroking his doting Floss, as she awkwardly lifts herself to sit tall.

'I know what you'll say, there's plenty of life in the old dog yet, and I agree there is. But this is a new chapter for you guys, and I believe this little pup's rightful place is here with you, especially as Magnus helped him into the world, so to speak.'

'Actually, Pepper was the—'

'We don't need the details, thanks,' I say, quickly raising my hand. 'Witnessing it was bad enough, I don't need a recap.'

Verity visibly winces, before turning to Magnus, still clutching her new baby.

'Any chance you could hold him a bit tighter, Verity? Nah, I didn't think so!' jests Magnus, striding across the room to me.

'Heather, thank you so much. He's adorable,' squeals Verity, burying her face in the pup's soft sable fur.

'I take it we're keeping him then?' asks Magnus, giving me a wink while Verity isn't looking.

'Yeah, little Cass.'

'Cass?' asks Iona, from her armchair.

'Cass?' repeats Clyde.

'Cass it is!' sighs Magnus, giving the pup a gentle but firm head rub. 'Floss and Cass ... aye, it goes. Come here, old girl, come and meet your new buddy.'

We watch as the faithful old dog comes on command, and Verity lowers the wriggling pup to meet her nose. Floss gives him a sniff ... once, twice ... and then a large lick, causing his entire head to lift and drop with the forceful action.

'He's in. He's got her seal of approval,' mutters Magnus.

Chapter Thirty-Eight

Friday 23 December

Tabitha

'Tabby, quick, get up!' A frantic hand rattles my shoulder, arousing me instantly from my sleep.

'What time is it?' I ask my mother, whose face is currently inches from mine. I take in her frantic expression, wide eyes and mouth agape. 'What's wrong?' My urgency to know the time disappears.

'It's just gone two in the morning. You're needed at The Garrison.'

'The Garrison? *Whaaat?*'

'Quick, get up!'

I'm up, dressed and dashing out of our front door in record time, with the intention of running to the theatre. Once I'm on the street, all intention is gone.

I stop dead. And stare.

It is absolutely freezing outside, but the sky above Lerwick is a beautiful orange against a backdrop of starry black. A stunning effect – if only it were a stage backdrop, clever artwork or a new curtain design – but the air is filled with burning embers floating on the chilly breeze like fireflies, drifting far and wide.

This is nothing short of an emergency.

'What the hell!' I don't know what to do – run towards the theatre or run for help? We've never discussed such a disaster; the round robin system we use when a rehearsal is cancelled seems pointless now, with flames flickering into the night sky.

'Well, go then!' calls Mum from the doorstep, wrapping her towelling robe about her frame. 'Mind you stay clear!'

I run off, attempting to figure out what role my mother intends me to perform, other than standing and staring, offering condolences to myself and every other member of the cast, because it doesn't take a genius to work out that this does not look good. In fact, this looks like the absolute worst-case scenario of all!

As I near The Garrison, the blue neon lights of the emergency services add a crazy pattern of flashing lights to the night sky's vivid orange glow. I didn't know Shetland had so many emergency vehicles; they are parked everywhere, with their hoses and ladders criss-crossing the vicinity. The fire crews are beavering away to save a building with flames licking through a gaping hole where the roof once was.

A crowd of people stand on the street corner watching, their breath billowing in the cold night air, their silhouettes highlighted in stark relief against the unfurling drama.

'Rabbie, what the hell has happened?' I ask, making a beeline for the first person I recognise.

'Can you believe it! Ebenezer reckons the ghost light may have fused and the soft furnishings caught alight ... with the upholstered seating and the drapery, there's enough to fuel an almighty blaze.'

'Has anything been saved?'

'From the production? Who knows – probably nothing.'

'Are you serious?'

'Sure, would you have ventured inside to rescue a box of props or the costume trunk?'

'No, but there's a fire curtain ... surely that helped to save something.' I glance around, looking for Ebenezer.

'It would only save a section of the stage – it's anyone's guess what remains in the wings and backstage.'

'He must be gutted.'

'He? All of us, surely?' adds Rabbie, his tone edged with disappointment.

'I suppose it's all gone?'

'Doh!' comes his reply.

I give him an offended glance, the last thing I need from Rabbie is a *doh*! I'm no moron.

'Brrrrr, I'm freezing. It's cold enough to snow,' he mutters, zipping his jacket to his chin.

'Ebenezer!' I call, as the solitary figure drifts by, head low, shoulders bent.

'Ah, Tabitha!' he replies, looking startled to see me.

'Catch you later, Tabs,' mutters Rabbie, as Ebenezer makes his way over.

'Yeah, later,' I say, as Rabbie jogs off towards another group of onlookers.

'Is there anything we can do or save?' I ask.

'The fire crew said there's very little left of the auditorium. Despite the fire-retardant seating being slower to burn, it does finally succumb to the flames, along with the curtains and carpets.'

'And backstage?' I ask, eager for good news.

'Who knows? By now, the props and costumes might be smoke damaged, or ruined by water.'

'Don't say that – we've got a day to rally round and salvage what we can.'

Ebenezer shakes his head, bestowing a pitying look upon me.

'Don't look like that, it *can* be done. That infamous line "the show must go on" has never been more apt than now!'

'Like the Christmas performances of 1980, 1995 and 2020 – this one's cancelled too. But never fear, I have my faithful ledger – details of past, present and future performances are all safe and sound.' There's an acceptance of fate apparent in his tone.

'That's not the attitude to have,' I protest, my voice cracking with emotion. 'How are your crappy pencilled notes going to help us overcome this?' I add.

'Everything's gone, Tabitha. I'll post notices around town tomorrow, letting everyone know the performance is cancelled, and we'll refund their tickets after Christmas.'

'Please don't. We need to call in some outstanding favours, appeal to the community for help and support – we can turn this around, Ebenezer – honest, we can!'

'Let it go. Accept when you've been dealt a losing hand,' he says, dismissing my determination.

'What, like you do? Skulking around town, cradling your battered ledger, denying the community spirit, bad-mouthing good hard-working people, putting others down when they're filled with ambition and joy? No, thank you! The day I act like you, Ebenezer, is the day I give up the ghost!' My words astonish me, let alone him; I didn't realise I carried such anger within me.

'I'll say good night to you, Tabitha,' says Ebenezer sternly, before striding away.

I remain on the corner, as others mill around me. My gaze is fixed on the burning remnants of our beautiful little theatre, and slowly my heart breaks. Memories from my childhood, early teenage years and recent weeks, all go up in smoke and drift like a million burnt embers caught on the night-time breeze.

Heather

My visit to the cemetery was always going to be a difficult task, and last night's snowfall hasn't helped. It's taken me a while to traipse from my parked car, each step seems treacherous, with the crunch of snow beneath my boots. It might look picturesque, with the headstones and memorials standing tall and proud beneath a blanket of white, but it's freezing cold. I turn my back towards the sea view, bracing myself against the bitter winds coming in off the open water.

'Niven, old chap,' I say, removing the holly wreath from my hessian bag. 'I'm never one to miss an anniversary, and I couldn't have forgotten yours.'

I crouch beside the granite stone, with its simple inscription, and brush the snow away before leaning my simple offering against his headstone. The vibrant satin ribbon flutters in the breeze while the tiny toy robin nestles amongst the berries. A posy of fresh flowers wouldn't have survived, given the blustery weather.

'I have no idea if you were responsible for our Marina's tragedy that night, but I imagine you paid a heavy price for your silence, if you were. I appreciate you must have been scared, often isolated by your decision, but you didn't deserve to leave this life in the way you did, that fateful night.'

I stand up, straighten my coat and look out across the North Sea, its waves rolling beneath an unspoilt horizon.

'Lachlan's been put away for what he did to you, Niven. I'm not sure if that would have brought you any comfort or caused you further misery, but I thought you ought to know.'

So much has changed in one year, and yet nothing ever does – the waves keep on rolling, the sun continues to rise, and the stars shine down each night.

'Other news is the little theatre on Market Street burnt down last night – which is terribly sad. Dottie and Mungo finally get married tomorrow – it's taken them long enough, hasn't it? Ned and Jemima's baby is long overdue – I'm sure the midwives will call her in as soon as Christmas is over. Our Clyde's doing well, though Iona's found herself in a pickle of late. Her gold necklace, the one she always wears, has gone missing . . . she presumes lost for ever. I wish I knew who has it, or who took it. Then I could return it to her and ease her fraught nerves in time for Christmas. She reckons one of her carers has taken it, but it simply doesn't add up. Why that particular young woman – when she's had plenty of opportunity elsewhere and nothing has gone astray. Ah well, Niven . . . listen to me, rabbiting on about nothing, as always.'

I touch the headstone for a final time, my fingers lingering on the inscription, before stepping away, intending to head for home.

I swiftly turn back, having forgotten, and whisper, 'Merry Christmas, Niven.'

Tabitha

I awoke this morning to find a thick layer of pristine white snow covering Lerwick – hardly surprising, given the plummeting temperature in recent days.

In contrast, on entering what remains of The Garrison alongside Ebenezer and Rabbie, I discover thick blackened charcoal covering every inch of the theatre. Gone are the elegant proscenium curtains, the fancy gilt-edged plaster panels decorating the side walls; not a speck of burgundy velvet remains. There's nothing left of the auditorium.

'Be careful what you touch, you won't want this on your hands or clothing,' mutters Ebenezer, leading the way along the charred aisle, as firefighters continue to dampen down the rows of raked seating.

Myself and Rabbie have been asked to accompany him inside, to see what we can salvage from behind the stage; it appears that the fire curtain has done its job in some respects.

'What's that?' asks Rabbie, pointing towards the stage area.

We turn, our gaze following his gesture. Where the stage once stood, there is now a ribcage of blackened struts, held upright by structured metal joists. On one flaky, peeling and blackened beam, protruding from the stage, sits a marbled base with a metal prong lifting towards the empty void of the spotlight.

'I believe that could be the offending object, so please don't anyone touch it. I think the insurance company is requesting fire crews dig a little deeper, to establish if it might have been arson or not,' explains Ebenezer, his voice cracking with emotion.

'Arson? Are you joking? Clearly, those are the remains of the ghost light.'

'Maybe . . . it seems logical. How many times did we comment on the electrical flex being overstretched? Hundreds. Hindsight is a wonderful thing, eh?'

As wrecked and damaged as our little theatre is, it seems ironic that we are staring at the simplest of objects, knowing it might have played a frightful role in snuffing out our opening night.

'I'm sorry, but that's not happening!' shouts Ebenezer.

We're sitting at a table in the back room of The Douglas Arms. Word of the disaster has reached cast and crew of our am-dram community, and we've gathered to commiserate with one another and work out what to do next.

'If you think I am going to kowtow to the likes of Ned Camp-bell . . . you've got to be joking!'

'I'll ask him then,' I say, unperturbed by our director's out-burst.

'Phuh! Over my dead body. Have you any idea of the impact his recent acquisitions have had upon the local community? Well, have you?'

I cringe as all eyes around the table turn to me; Aileen, Rabbie, Old Reg, Deacon, Kenzie, Mavis and Freddie watch in stunned silence. I'm not sure what he means by 'acquisitions', but I'm assuming it's to do with the recent opening of The Lerwick Manor Hotel, or even the stables gallery – or maybe, at a stretch, Ned's association with the allotments . . . I'll bluff till I'm sure.

I don't think a shrug is the answer he was looking for, but it'll buy me some time to work out a proper answer.

'Some of the businesses in our local vicinity have had their trade cut – slashed, in fact – because the likes of Ned Campbell have opened up an arts and crafts gallery, which has wiped out passing trade. How many of yee sitting here spend at least one day a week up at the gallery, browsing the gifts, watching the artists and smelling all the pretty soaps and things . . .' His voice has a mocking tone, which touches a nerve.

'Oi, the soapery is my pitch, so don't you knock it!' I interject, defending my livelihood.

I see the flash of surprise in several people's eyes; I might want to rein in my crabbit ways and be a bit more conciliatory, if we're to find a solution to our desperate situation.

'I'll tell you something for nothing, Ned Campbell and his ventures have changed the shape of this town,' moans Ebenezer, his index finger pointing in my direction, punctuating every word. 'And not necessarily for the better.'

'I disagree!' The words spill from my lips before I can stop myself. Hearing the gasps and seeing the wide eyes staring at me, I'll have to think on my feet. And fast. 'The Campbell family have always contributed to this community and the surrounding area. If you start with the allotments, from decades ago, the land was donated so locals could grow their own food during wartime. The family didn't take it back once the war was over; they've allowed others to use the land for a minimal charge – fifty pence a week, I believe the council charges. That money doesn't return to the Campbell household, but goes direct to the council.' Having made my point, I move swiftly on. 'And with the opening of the gallery in the old stables, there's been a revival of the traditional arts and crafts, which has seen an influx of visitors, keen to sample and take up new hobbies, thanks to the initiative. So please, don't knock the Campbells for their hard work and tenacity.' I fall silent, expecting an answering tirade from Ebenezer.

The lowered heads around the table slowly lift and twist, scrutinising Ebenezer, who appears speechless and a little shell-shocked that one so young could produce such an outburst.

Ah well, I've blown it now. I'll take the consequences, come what may. If he wishes to demote me . . . well, let him – the performance won't be taking place now, anyway. Though I suppose it'll help him to stamp his authority on our little troupe, if I'm ejected from the cast.

'Please, take a seat. We're intrigued by your request for a meeting,' says Ned, gesturing towards the meeting table.

It's bang on three o'clock, and they've squeezed me into an already busy schedule.

'Thank you. I wanted to ask a favour. I want to be straight with you both, no dropping hints or subtly trying to win you over, but rather putting my cards on the table, so to speak, and asking outright.' I settle myself opposite Jemima, giving my words time to sink in.

'Now you're scaring me. Should I be worried that we're going to need to replace you as an artist in the gallery?' asks Jemima, looking both intrigued but also slightly panicked. She sits forward in her chair, her bump looking decidedly round.

'No, nothing of the sort. I know The Orangery is booked for Dottie's wedding reception, but can the theatre company use your alpaca barn for a performance of *A Christmas Carol* on Christmas Eve?' I quickly draw breath, before continuing. 'You won't have to do a thing. Me and the cast will organise everything. We'll clean the barn, deliver and lay out chairs, build a stage ... and even remove the snow from the driveway to make sure there are no accidents. You won't know we've been.'

There, I've said it aloud. My words are floating free – out there in the universe – what will be, will be. No more discussion, just a straight answer.

'Sorry?' says Ned, looking alarmed, his brows shooting up into his hairline.

'What a relief!' sighs Jemima, who was obviously fearing the worst, despite my reassurance.

'The rest of the company are prepared to throw the towel in but ...' I choke unexpectedly, that was not supposed to happen! I plough on, my voice all squeaky and distorted with effort and emotion. 'I've given too much to this production to abandon the play now. I've learnt my lines, encouraged and helped other cast members to learn theirs, spent night after night rehearsing and sewing costumes – I don't think I should be expected to jack it all in because of a disaster.'

'A pretty major disaster, may I add,' says Ned.

'Yeah, but you can't let that stop you in life, can you? You wouldn't!' I draw breath, blushing slightly at having put Ned on the spot.

'You're quite right, Tabitha.' There's a slight chuckle to his tone.

He's being dead honest with me, as he and Jemima have achieved so much in recent years. They aren't quitters. They're the backbone of this tight-knit community, leading the way, showing folk how it's done. And their success boils down to the basics: hard graft and determination.

I've been ballsy enough to say exactly what I think, and to ask for exactly what I want – which will hit a nerve with this pair.

Ned glances at Jemima. She simply smiles, before rubbing her bump.

'Tabitha, I can't really argue a case against it. It's yours if you want it. As you can see, we have our hands full at the moment with the forthcoming arrival, plus Dottie and Mungo's wedding, but we're happy to support you in any way we can.'

I want to cry – but don't, thankfully.

'I owe you the biggest favour ever for this!' I squeal in delight, jumping up from my seat. 'The theatre company are not going to believe that you've been this generous to us. I can't wait to tell Ebenezer, especially after his comments about . . .'

I fall silent, scrambling to regain control of my chattering self, whilst unceremoniously returning my chair beneath the table, creating theatrical mayhem with the coffee cups amidst my excitement to leave.

Chapter Thirty-Nine

Tabitha

'He said what?' asks Ebenezer, his face contorted in surprise.

'Ned said it's ours if we want it.' I fall silent, basking in the glory.

'B-but h-he ... I-I-I would never have asked ...' stammers Ebenezer.

'Well, *I* did. And now we'd best get a wiggle on if we're to move all the backstage equipment from here to the new venue,' I say.

It's a shame the guy can't manage a simple 'thank you' for the favour we've been so generously given.

'There'll be little help once we arrive at the manor, because it's Dottie and Mungo's wedding tomorrow. Plus the snow is going to hinder us somewhat.'

'Are you quite sure?' Ebenezer asks, still unable to believe this turnaround in our fortunes.

'Ned said he'd call in a favour or two from the estate tenants. He'll organise a tractor to clear the floor of the alpaca barn and quickly lay a fresh layer of straw. A bit of extra manpower won't do any harm, will it?'

'Of course not.' Ebenezer suddenly moves in a frantic manner: turning left, then right before twisting back to me as if about to speak, but doesn't.

'Are you OK?' I ask, despite it being clearly apparent that he isn't.

'Never in a million years would I have thought Ned Campbell might allow us to use his property.'

'You judge him too harshly, Ebenezer. He's a decent guy who has tried his best to support and strengthen the community spirit, at every opportunity. The Campbells aren't cold-hearted business people – they truly care about what happens here in Lerwick.'

'I may have been a little hasty in my judgement,' he concedes.

'You have indeed. But I've no doubt you can put that right from now on. So, what's it to be – costumes and props first, or move that spare lighting rig? It's rather bulky,' I say dubiously.

'Can you make a start organising the props? I'll instruct a team to dismantle the spare rigging – we won't and can't take it all, but we should be able to salvage something from the smoke and water damage.'

I don't linger but dash off in pursuit of the wooden trunks in which we store some costumes. I can't help taking a sneaky peek over my shoulder to observe Ebenezer in his continuing state of surprise and shock. I watch him spring into action, his renewed enthusiasm belying his years. His battered ledger is nowhere to be seen – this is a time for action, not words!

It takes six hours to pack, transfer by van and unpack the basics needed for our one-off performance at Lerwick Manor. I didn't realise we had so much clobber for one production. I stand up and stretch my tired back, surveying the scene before me.

A forklift truck is manoeuvring bales of straw on to the freshly hosed and scrubbed floor, while a farmhand cuts the ties and spreads the bales out evenly. Another farmhand from a neighbouring estate is counting and moving stacks of chairs into line against the far wall, ready to be arranged in neat rows. The makeshift stage is coming to life, thanks to the drapery currently being hung from the rafters, tastefully tied back with the alpacas' leading ropes.

'How's it going?' asks Rabbie, appearing as if by magic.

'So-so. And you?'

'I think the mini lighting rig is now secure. Though Ebenezer's having kittens in case the bulbs become too hot and set fire to the rafters,' he adds, with a wink.

'Seriously, don't joke about that – Ned would never forgive us!'

'Don't worry, they won't. The fuses would blow first,' he reassures me. 'The sound system has been wired in and Ebenezer's about to test it.'

Right on cue, an ear-piercing screech comes from the large black box that houses the speaker system.

'One, two. One, two. Testing,' comes Ebenezer's breathy voice.

Rabbie and I swiftly exchange a glance before both turning away to hide our smiles; we shouldn't be taking the mickey, but it's hard not to when our director is so awkwardly full on with everything he does.

'You'd think he'd take a day off once in a while, wouldn't you?' jests Rabbie.

'There's no fear of that – it's twenty-four seven with Ebenezer.'

'Maybe you should suggest it, Tabitha?'

'Hardly! I'm his least favourite person in the company, these days.'

'I doubt that very much, he's always singing your praises. He might not let on, but he really appreciates you.'

'Do you think so?'

I stare across to where Ebenezer is tapping the mic head and repeating his infamous 'one, two, testing' routine.

'Why's he always so snappy with me then?'

'He probably feels threatened by your talent, not to mention your organisation skills – and you know how he likes to lord it over everyone, keeping us all on our toes.'

I shudder at the thought of all those black marks in Ebenezer's ledger, glance at Rabbie for reassurance and then shrug off the compliment. 'Nah, pull the other one, it's got bells on it.'

'Are you two going to stand there all day, or is there a chance you'll pull yee bloody fingers out and get some work done?' Ebenezer's harsh tones blast out over the speaker system, loud and clear.

'Your microphone is working perfectly, Ebenezer,' I shout, giving him a big thumbs-up.

Rabbie doubles over in laughter. 'Come on, Tabs, let's get a move on – otherwise we'll find ourselves sacked.'

'Now, that I'd like to see,' I joke, collecting a pile of printed programmes from the packing trunk. 'Catch you later, Rabbie.'

'It's Bob Cratchit to yee, Mr Scrooge!'

'Humbug to you, Bob Cratchit.' I blush profusely, busying myself with the suddenly urgent task of straightening the programme edges.

Rabbie lingers. 'Maybe I'll catch you for a drink later . . .?' He pauses, turning it into a question and waiting for my answer.

'Yeah, that'd be good,' I say hesitantly. Then, more firmly, 'Great. Lovely.'

Rabbie leaves me mired in a world of my own embarrassment, feigning close attention to my pile of performance programmes.

Chapter Forty

Saturday 24 December

Heather

I'm taken aback at how emotional I feel today. I've been invited to plenty of weddings and commitment ceremonies, and yet I've cried three times already whilst getting ready. I don't know if it's my hormones or the fact that a true love story reaches fruition today. Six decades of unrequited love will be dispelled for ever with those tiny words 'I do' . . . and here I go again, this can't be happening to me! Every time I think of those two lovely people, and I do genuinely class Mungo as such . . . well, once you get to know him and can look past his obsession with security and his gruff nature.

'Are you not done yet?' asks Ellie, dashing from her bedroom into the bathroom and attempting to pinch my position in front of the spotlit vanity mirror.

'I . . . just . . . can't . . . stop!' I blubber, grabbing for a swatch of toilet roll and dabbing my eyes.

'You'll need to sort yourself out before you continue with your make-up, so scoot up; I can only see half my face.'

I do as asked, because she's right; I'm wasting my time even trying here. I plonk myself down on the edge of the bath and dry my eyes.

'Can you imagine what they're going through, if I'm like this?'

'I'd rather not,' says Ellie, slathering her face with primer.

'Oh, Ellie, don't be heartless. They've known each other for a lifetime, yet never admitted to each other that they both felt more. How romantic is that?'

Ellie pulls a face. 'Mum, they have the prospect of sharing dementia, care homes and incontinence with each other. If they'd fessed up earlier in life, their days could have been filled with holidays, children and hot sex!'

'Ellie!'

'Oh, sorry, I forgot it's Saint Dottie's wedding day, we're not allowed to mention such things.'

'You, young lady, have a mind and mouth like a sewer at times; I don't know where you get it from.'

'I wonder.' Ellie raises her eyebrows sarcastically, whilst dabbing foundation on to her cheeks.

The cobbled courtyard looks like a Christmas film set, beneath a layer of crispy white snow. We enter The Orangery to the glorious sound of the choir singing carols, whilst clumps of snow fall from our shoes. I'm not one for going to church or participating in religious worship, but I defy anyone not to be moved by the sight before us. Gone are the comfy armchairs, sofas and coffee tables, while the counter area is hidden by a highly decorated screen depicting an old master painting. A red carpet runs from the glazed doorway and turns sharply right, creating an aisle between the rows of covered high-backed chairs, each with a huge satin bow in a deep rich red, all very Christmassy and festive amidst the professionally crafted luxurious garlands, glass baubles and fairy lights.

At the rear of The Orangery, where the roaring log burner is usually the focal point, stands a carved wooden arbour entwined with holly and ivy, framing a smiley registrar lady. She stands alone, nodding to guests as we enter and settle; Mungo isn't present, as yet, which is a little concerning. There'll be hell to pay if he doesn't arrive before the bride. In the centre of the arbour hangs a decorative wreath of mistletoe – which, I assume, is festively symbolic and also fitting for today's ceremony. A piano and an adult choir with their master are gathered in a semi-circle on the left-hand side of the aisle, and a table decorated with a linen cloth and floral spray completes the picture on the right-hand side.

'Where are we sitting?' asks Isla, indicating left or right.

'I assume . . .' I pause as I spy the placard.

Choose a seat not a side, we're a family once the knot is tied is declared in scripted font.

'There's your answer.'

'I say the back row, as there'll be lots of friends who are closer to them than we are,' says Isla, ushering Ellie in first to sit beside two other guests.

I take the aisle seat and immediately spy familiar faces, sitting nearer the front, in their best bib and tucker: Verity and Magnus, linked arm in arm; Melissa and Hamish, minus the baby who is probably being babysat and truly spoilt by doting grandparents; Nessie and Isaac, affectionately holding hands, alongside a smartly dressed Pippa whose other half has his best man duties to perform, first and foremost. And finally Kaspar, looking dapper in a dark-brown double-breasted suit, complemented by a fresh haircut and an ultra-close shave.

The slightest glimpse of him still takes my breath away, despite the time we've spent together – which excites and intrigues me when I think about a potential future together. It might seem odd to others that we've arrived separately at the same event, but it's our way of taking control of our blossoming relationship. We're not suddenly joined at the hip, living in each other's pockets twenty-four seven – call it conscious dating, or simply maturity, but we still have our independence from each other. I wanted to accompany my daughters, and Kaspar wished to attend with his closest friends from the allotments. While I'm staring at his back, Kaspar turns about, as if sensing my presence, and gives me a hearty smile that reaches as far as his eyes. I return the gesture, as my heart instantly melts. There'll be plenty of time for us to catch up during the wedding reception – or not, if we're both busy chatting, or seated with others.

'It all looks very beautiful,' I say, eyeing up every inch of the venue. 'You wouldn't believe it was a coffee shop only yesterday.'

'What's with the old painting?' says Ellie, gesturing over her shoulder towards the elaborate dividing screen.

'Oh, that. I had to ask when it arrived yesterday,' says Isla. 'Apparently, it's "The Wedding at Cana" where the water was turned into wine, one of Dottie's favourite paintings,' she explains, before discreetly chuckling, 'Mungo's hoping it'll happen here too. Ned warned him that his wine cellars had better remain intact! Though to be fair, the Campbells are footing the bill for most of this – and given how generously they've stocked the bar, nobody will go without. Though Ned did say he'd confiscate Mungo's keys if the cellars were raided. You can imagine his reaction to that!'

I watch Isla as she chatters away about the goings-on and realise I like my daughter. I like her very much. She's not your average girl ... err, woman, but something a bit special. She happily helps others, she easily converses with both young and old, she shows kindness to all God's creatures, and despite some pretty rough times growing up she truly cares about other people. I hear her words, but I'm observing more than listening. I truly like what I see.

'Now what are you crying about?' she asks, a look of surprise flitting across her cheery expression.

'Nothing, my sweet. Happy tears.' I quickly find a tissue and dab beneath my eyes. What am I like?

We sit quietly chit-chatting for another ten minutes, before the composed and careful steps of Jemima are heard as she enters The Orangery. She is wearing a beautiful cream and fern corsage, pinned to the front of her smart navy coat dress. Maternity wear for formal occasions isn't always flattering, but she looks stunning as she carefully settles in the opposite row to ours, across the aisle. I would have expected her to choose a front-row seat – though I know she's been involved in the intricate planning for this event, so I won't be questioning any of the finer details.

I nod, smiling politely, as she returns the gesture. Her bump looks huge today – though it's hardly the thing to say – and I can see she's not looking comfortable, seated on a hard-backed chair.

'Not long now,' I say in a cheery tone, when she looks up and catches me staring.

'I'm so far past my due date, I'm doubting I was even pregnant when it was first confirmed,' she sighs, shaking her head in disbelief.

'The baby'll be here before you know it,' I add, before shutting up; I've literally run out of clichés to spout, so I politely turn back to our Isla.

I remember being at that final stage with her. If standing on my head would have proved doable or comfortable, I'd have attempted it in a heartbeat. Not that it was necessary; pre-eclampsia and an emergency C-section put an end to my misery. I'm not wishing that on Jemima, but it was a one-way ticket towards maternity and a swaddled newborn.

'Where's Mungo?' hisses Isla, raising her hand to cover her mouth and hiding her question.

I shrug.

'If Jemima is here, it must be about time to start. Ned told her not to rush but to arrive just a few minutes before him and Dottie,' she adds, staring around me to view Jemima, still shuffling in her seat.

'Can you imagine if he's done a runner?' scoffs Ellie, leaning around Isla to speak to me.

'I'll give you what for in a minute, young lady, making such a cruel suggestion,' I snap in a whispered tone, adding a mother's glare for good measure. I seriously don't understand her thought processes at the minute.

'You'd have to get in line behind Dottie, Mum. Can you imagine her reaction?' says Isla.

I want to laugh, but it's no laughing matter.

'Ah look, it's started to snow again,' whispers Ellie, pointing towards the windows.

The choir change from festive carols to a glorious toe-tapping, happy-clappy version of 'Oh, Happy Day', causing infectious smiles and gentle swaying to break out amongst the guests.

'How great is this,' squeals Ellie, jigging happily alongside Isla and me.

'But where is Mungo?' asks Isla, more urgently this time, turning to view the glazed door.

I shrug; I've no idea, but I can't imagine anyone is going to complain about his lateness with such vibrant music entertaining us. If this is an insight into the wedding schedule, we are in for a treat of a day. How marvellous!

The glazed door swings open, admitting a blast of cold air . . . and Mungo. He dashes in, straightening his cravat and stamping snow from his brogues, with a harassed Levi in tow, dressed for the occasion in his traditional kilt, his hand rammed in his one pocket as if securing the most precious items: namely two wedding rings.

'I l-lost my bloody car k-keys,' stammers Mungo, his Tulloch kilt swinging with each step. He looks around at our expectant faces, all turned to view his arrival. 'The bloody things had slipped down the arm of the chair.'

I want to laugh out loud. Of all the things to delay Mungo

on his wedding day, it was his beloved keys. Was that their mini protest at the change occurring in his life?

Mungo slows to a rapid walk, and his kilt straightens itself; he spies the registrar and mumbles an apology. Levi straightens his black jacket and sporran, before joining his trusted friend at the decorated arbour.

To watch an elderly gent prepare himself, in the final few minutes before the love of his life walks through the door, is an honour and privilege few around these parts have seen. Mungo is as nervous as a lamb; he rakes his hand through his freshly trimmed hair, tugs at his wiry beard and turns to his trusted buddy several times, for words of encouragement.

I could cry, again. I can almost sense what he must be feeling, having waited so long for this moment to arrive. To have watched from afar, to have witnessed Dottie's trauma and grief over many years, to have known deep down that she was 'the one' whilst holding back for fear of rejection – or worse, ridicule from others – only to have reached this precious day . . . the day when he and his Dottie are officially joined in matrimony. Ah, I can't be anything but jealous of such a wonderful union. I can only hope and pray that this, one day, will happen for me.

Amidst the disruption, I haven't noticed that the choir has fallen silent, allowing the piano to grace the final moments as we await the bride's arrival.

The glazed door creaks open, I turn to view a delightful image. A piper in full regalia enters, followed by the bride and Ned.

Dressed from head to toe in a cream bejewelled gown styled like a Charleston girl, with a dropped waistline and fringed hemline, Dottie makes her entrance, complete with an elaborate peacock feather secured to a beaded headband, and a cream fake-fur stole wrapped about her shoulders.

My hand reaches to my mouth, stifling a gasp. She looks beautiful. Gone is the octogenarian, gone are the years of experience and maturity etched deep within her skin, and before us stands the most elegant bride upon the arm of Ned Campbell. Her piercing-blue gaze is fixed steadfastly on her bridegroom's back, and there's a gentle smile caressing her lips. She knows. How the hell does she know he was late? I want to laugh. I want to call out to Mungo that his ticket is up, because she knows! But I don't. Instead, I watch as Dottie and Ned have a final conversation, a last-minute giggle, their heads close together, nattering and sharing smiles, before they begin the final walk behind the piper, as he and the choir join their talents for 'Amazing Grace'.

As they sweep past, I fight the urge to weep. I glance towards Jemima, knowing she would have wanted to play a more pivotal role than her condition will allow.

We sit in silence as the registrar begins the ceremony. Ned steps aside after giving Dottie an affectionate peck on the cheek and Mungo a hearty handshake, to sit down on the first row. Dottie and Mungo stand opposite each other, gazing into each other's eyes. They look so in love, it is quite touching. Just goes to show – true love knows no boundaries, and love sees no faults, no creaking bones or weathered wrinkles.

Levi steps up as the couple prepare to exchange wedding rings.

I glance towards Jemima; she returns my gentle smile before her face drops in an expression of shock and anguish. What's wrong? I spot her sudden reaction; her head drops forward to view the slate floor . . . and a puddle appears around her feet.

No! This can't be!

Jemima's mouth circles into a perfect 'o' as her stricken gaze meets mine.

'I'll be back in a second,' I whisper to Isla, thrusting my packet of tissues at her for safe keeping.

'Mum, where are you—?'

I raise my finger to my lips, before tiptoeing to Jemima's side. 'I think we'll take a little walk, shall we?'

'I can't.' She gestures towards the wooden arbour and the happy group beneath.

'I don't think you have much choice, Jemima. They'll understand – now come on, let me help you up.'

'Heather, this isn't supposed to happen today.'

'You don't get to decide when *this* happens,' I whisper, placing an arm around her shoulder and quietly ushering her out of The Orangery under the quizzical stare of my two daughters.

We cross the snowy cobblestones in silence, Jemima taking tentative steps as if expecting a baby to appear by magic, any second, with no labour necessary. I simply guide her, knowing that she needs to be comfy and not sitting on a hard wooden chair. She might have hours to wait, but at least she'll be relaxed for the labour ahead.

I shouldn't compare her to one of my expectant mums, but you never can tell what's in store at this stage. There have been many occasions when I thought I had time to collect the girls from primary school, only to return and find a litter of pups cleaned and sleeping within a thirty-minute window. Other occasions, I've waited entire evenings for the first pup to show, and then subsequent ones have taken an age. It's always better to be safe than sorry – with any delivery, human or canine.

'I can't believe I've missed their big day,' says Jemima, in a despondent tone.

'You haven't missed it, you saw the majority of it,' I say, though five minutes more would have seen the most important part, but never mind. 'With a newborn to cradle, Dottie's going to forgive you anything.'

Jemima laughs, just as a raucous round of jubilant clapping and cheering issues from The Orangery.

'Ahhh, they're man and wife,' mutters Jemima.

I gently usher her through the newly refurbished tradesman's entrance, closing the door behind us and muting the wedding celebration.

'Which way is it?' I ask, faced with a rabbit warren of tiled corridors.

'The nursery is upstairs, in our private quarters,' she says, her hand reaching for the familiar walls of the manor for additional support. 'Everything is laid out, ready and waiting.'

Ordinarily, there would have been other people to help from this point – the smiling receptionist, plenty of friends, as well as some family – but due to the wedding arrangements, the hotel has no guests staying and the only other people available are the caterers preparing for the wedding reception to be held in the ballroom. I make sure we creep past without disturbing their duties.

We make slow progress, Jemima wincing and flinching as we totter forward. I try to distract her with soothing talk, but my mind is racing ahead, imagining what the next few hours might hold. The Campbells haven't installed a lift yet, so a mountain looms ahead of us as we take it a step at a time up the grand staircase.

Chapter Forty-One

Callie

'Callie, could you inspect the table and check that each place setting has the correct cutlery?' asks the catering manager.

I head off as she directs someone else to follow suit, checking the glassware.

I don't mind it being a working day, I'm not as close to Dottie and Mungo as others are; I would have hated for Isla to feel obliged to support the outside caterers with their task, instead of attending the wedding herself. I methodically work my way around each side of the beautifully decorated table situated in the centre of the ballroom. The linen is pristine white, the cutlery polished to perfection, and the floral displays and candelabras add height and sophistication to the overall finish. As I note the occasional missing fish fork or dessert spoon, I see there's a hive of activity going on all around me. The cake table has been decorated with a festive garland and now, Isla's beautiful wedding cake is being carefully unboxed and assembled by two nervous waitresses, each holding their breath whilst settling the second tier on top of the bottom layer. The string quartet are tuning their instruments in the corner, gathered around the piano, and the new duty manager, Stella, is drifting in and out between the ballroom and her reception desk.

My phone rings, which isn't the most convenient time to answer. I slyly ease my pocket open, sneaking a peek at the illuminated screen: Iona.

What does she want? I definitely explained that I wouldn't be free today to drop around for any last-minute cleaning chores before Christmas.

My phone continues to ring, but I ignore it, mouthing a hasty 'Sorry' to the woman who is circling behind me checking the glassware.

My phone falls silent, so I quickly switch it to vibrate.

I fetch the missing cutlery items and position them next to the place settings, making sure everything is perfectly aligned, before continuing with my inspection. I've only completed a few more place settings when my phone starts to vibrate in my pocket. I'm going to get into trouble if the catering manager sees me, but I sneak another glance at the illuminated screen. Iona again. She's either sat on her phone and is ringing me in error, or there's a real emergency going on.

'Excuse me, I'll be back in a second,' I say apologetically to the waitress inspecting the glassware.

I head out into the hallway and dig my phone out of my pocket; I have no option but to return Iona's call. I can't settle, thinking she might need help – and I can't concentrate on work, with my phone constantly vibrating.

I tap the screen and wait.

'Hello, Callie, is that you?' Iona's tone is eager.

'Yes, Iona. Is there anything wrong? You've called me several times and I need . . .' I don't finish my sentence.

'I found it. We found it.'

'Found what?' I ask.

'My necklace.'

I hear her words; they register, but I hold back in case there's another meaning. Maybe she means a different necklace and not the gold necklace I've been accused of stealing.

'Which necklace?' I ask gingerly, not daring to hope, as my breath catches in my throat.

'My gold one,' answers Iona.

The gold one? She definitely said it.

'Anyway, I need to see you as soon as possible, because I need to apologise for what's been said—'

'Where did you find it?' I ask, rudely interrupting her flow.

'I'll explain when I see you. Please come over,' she begs, 'and then I can explain everything.'.

'I can't at the minute, Iona. I'm busy with Dottie and Mungo's wedding reception today. I'll drop by when I can – but it won't be this afternoon, or even later tonight.'

'The sooner the better. Bye.'

I tap the screen, ending the call. The relief that hits me is totally unexpected; tears gush from nowhere, surprising even me. I knew the truth would come out eventually, absolving me of any blame. I hadn't ever touched the necklace, so I knew I had nothing to fear. It was all well and good thinking that, but working under a cloud of suspicion has been a slog, these last few weeks. Knowing that people were talking behind my back, pointing the finger at me, assuming I was the culprit – it was so unkind.

'Are you OK, Callie?' asks Stella, appearing from her rear office.

'Absolutely fine, thank you. In fact, never better,' I say cheerfully, despite the tears pouring down my cheeks.

Heather

It didn't take long to organise a fresh set of clothes for Jemima, once we'd conquered the grand staircase. I felt somewhat pressured, seeing past generations of Campbells lining the walls and glaring down at us as we manoeuvred the future generation, unborn and currently snug in Jemima's belly, into the waiting nursery.

The room is exactly as I'd imagined. A large airy space, with adjoining bathroom, so perfect in every detail – from swinging crib to colourful mobiles, pastel-painted furniture and a sturdy rocking chair – that it could have been lifted straight from a stage play of *Peter Pan*. The only thing missing is Nana, the Newfoundland dog, but the large wooden rocking horse in the corner, complete with its red leather saddle, dappled paintwork and flowing mane, more than makes up for the omission. It all creates the perfect setting for the arrival of this much-anticipated bairn.

In the centre of the room a huge double bed is ready and waiting, and Jemima gratefully settles herself against the pillows, once she's changed into a nightgown and robe.

'You've done this out beautifully,' I say, admiring the decor.

'Ned was born in here, so I wanted a home birth – but things might change, you never know.'

'So true, you can't plan for everything.'

I can't find her slippers anywhere so ask where I'll find a pair of socks.

'It seems ridiculous but I haven't seen my feet in weeks, so there's no hope that I'll be able to . . .' she trails off, as I retrieve a pair of warm woollen socks from the nearest drawer.

'I was exactly the same. Here . . . let me.' I work my finger and thumb inside the first sock.

If anyone had told me I'd be performing such a motherly task on the mistress of Lerwick Manor, I'd have laughed. Though Jemima is so refreshingly down to earth that I don't think twice before placing her foot on my thigh, just like I did when my girls were little, and easing the sock over her petite toes.

'There,' I say, pulling the woollen heel to match hers snugly. 'All done.'

'Thank you, Heather. I do really appreciate it. I've caused you to miss the wedding too. I'm so sorry.'

'No worries, Jemima. I'm happy to help. I think we did well to sneak out without anyone clocking us.'

'Ned will be worried when he realises I'm not sitting on the back row.'

'My girls will bring him up to date, I'm sure. Now, can I get you anything while we wait for Ned to join us?' I ask.

'I still can't believe my waters broke right in the middle of their wedding vows – how embarrassing! I suppose it's a waiting game from now on.'

'It sure is. There's no hurrying bairns, they're like pups – they'll arrive when they arrive, and be what they'll be, so there's no point anticipating . . . girl or boy?'

'We don't know what we're having; neither of us wanted to know. A surprise is always nice, I think.'

'I agree. And names too.'

Jemima nods and I stop talking before I put my foot in it. I've done so well thus far.

'I suppose you've played the waiting game lots of time with your dogs.'

'More times than I care to remember, to be honest. Though they are always different. Our Socks never has two pregnancies the same. And Rosie, well . . . she's so hit and miss with whelping, I daren't leave her on those final few days. Pepper is the easiest – though even she had a problem last time. One of the pups got himself stuck fast and . . . aargh! I shouldn't be talking like this in front of you. All will be fine, and your midwife will be here in no time.'

'Did you need to call the vet?'

'Actually, no . . . erm . . . oh, I shouldn't have said anything.'

'No, it's fine. Did you?'

'No, because our Magnus is pretty handy at delivering lambs, pups and anything else that needs attention in the midwifery department. So he obliged, and everything was fine in a jiffy.'

'Always handy to know – though I doubt he'll be so obliging should our midwife need assistance.'

We both laugh at the very thought – and horror – of such a prospect.

Without a word of warning or a knock, the door bursts open and in strides Ned, in a state of fluster and panic.

'Are you OK? I couldn't believe it when Isla told me. Has the midwife been called? Do you need anything?'

'Ned, please. I'm fine. Heather has taken good care of me – we just thought it best to leave the ceremony without causing any fuss. Though I'm sorry to have missed their vows.'

'I'll call the midwife right away,' says Ned, heading for the door, obviously needing something to do.

I gently pat the pillow, gesturing for Jemima to lie back and rest.

'Ned!' calls Jemima, after doing as I suggest.

Ned abruptly stops at the door, his expression conveying his deep devotion veiled by apprehension.

'We'll have ages yet.'

Bless him. It might be advisable for him to grab a bite to eat and expect the unexpected as bairns, like puppies, rarely arrive suiting our time frame.

Tabitha

'Ladies and gentlemen, if you'd kindly take your seats for tonight's performance,' announces Ebenezer, in uncharacteristically dulcet tones, over the sound system.

I quickly pull my unruly wig over my own hair and secure it with hairgrips. I'm grateful that Callie has applied my make-up as she'd promised to do weeks ago. Personally, I can't imagine Scrooge having brown hair, a replacement wig rescued from the debris, but I'm not about to argue, tonight of all nights. The whole company has pulled together, putting in extra effort and working doubly hard to make sure the performance can go ahead tonight – in spite of all the setbacks and difficulties we've encountered.

'Five minutes till curtain,' calls Freddie, dashing through to the improvised backstage area, as if his voice doesn't carry the additional few feet.

The buzz of excitement has been growing all afternoon. Never in my wildest dreams did I think we'd pull this stunt off. It's one thing to ask the Campbells for a favour, but an entirely different ball game to actually move an entire production from The Garrison to our makeshift theatre, by mucking out, cleaning up and unpacking every item of kit and costume. If I'd realised that we would finish barely an hour before the performance, I'd probably never have entertained the idea in the first place But there's no going back now.

'Are you ready, Scrooge?' asks Rabbie, appearing in his finest Cratchit apparel.

'I certainly am, Bob Cratchit.'

'Remember, you've got this, OK?'

'As if I doubt myself!' I jest, still unsure whether our bantering will ever lead anywhere.

The sound system suddenly gives out an awful squeal, causing the entire cast backstage to cover our ears and glare at one another.

'What's the fool doing?' says Rabbie.

'It's enough to clear your sinuses, isn't it?' I say, slowly peeling my hands away from my ears, for fear of a second audio attack.

'Ladies and gentlemen, we are about to commence our performance. But first, we do have a very special announcement,' says Ebenezer, his voice carrying clearly around the barn.

'What's he doing?' I ask, knowing he's gone off track from his usual opening speech.

'Announcing his retirement as director, I hope,' scoffs Rabbie.

'It's with the greatest pleasure that I hand over to our bride of the hour, Mrs Dottie Tulloch, who would like your attention for a moment or two. Dottie – the stage is yours.'

'What the hell?' mouths Rabbie, fiddling with his flouncy cravat.

'Hello, good evening and welcome,' says Dottie, her tinny voice zipping around the rafters. 'It gives us – my husband and I – enormous pleasure that you are able to join us on this our wedding day.'

There's a titter of laughter, a couple of *whoop-whoops* and some applause.

'But today, I'm hoping that the nicest gift is yet to be delivered. Mr and Mrs Campbell send their deepest apologies but they won't be joining us for tonight's performance, as a certain little baby seems to have chosen today to make their appearance. It gives me the greatest of pleasure to welcome each and every one of you to this unique performance, on what I hope will be a truly memorable day here at Lerwick Manor. So without further ado, I ask you to put your hands together to welcome the very talented actors from The Garrison Theatre, here for one night only, purely for our pleasure.'

The audience expels a huge round of applause and cheering as I picture Dottie handing over the microphone and carefully making her way down the steps.

'Did Dottie say the baby was already here?' I ask, to no one in particular.

'No, it's on the way. I assume Dottie wants it to arrive before midnight, to share her big day!' says Rabbie.

'It's a really late delivery – Jemima's gone over her due date,' I add, looking at the assembled cast, none of whom seem particularly interested.

No one answers me. Instead, they close down into their own

mental space for a last-minute attempt at reciting those pesky lines that plague us all.

'Are we getting this show on the road, or shall we wait another week?' complains Ebenezer as he struts through the backstage area and spies us all in a world of our own.

I bite my tongue; there are times when this guy truly gets my goat!

'Break a leg, everyone,' I call to those nearest to me.

I receive a mumbled response and a couple of back slaps in return.

'Good luck, my darling – I'll see you in Stave One,' says Rabbie, with a cheeky wink as he runs from the wings, getting into position behind his high desk for our opening scene.

My darling – wow, there's a new one. If I didn't know better I'd be thinking that Bob Cratchit has fallen for Scrooge, in a strange twist of fate.

I squeeze into the wings and watch in awe as the curtain rises, the stage lights lift and the spotlight picks out Bob Cratchit, bent double over his desk, frantically warming his frozen fingers against the puny flame of a stubby candle. I'm lost in a world of am-dram, where the odds can be against us, yet we give it our all.

This is my cue.

With the sound of door chimes tinkling overhead, I enter the spotlight as the narrator reads, 'Marley was dead . . .'

Chapter Forty-Two

Sunday 25 December

Callie

'Merry Christmas!' I call, bright and breezy, entering the residents' lounge dressed in a Santa suit with a large hessian sack of presents slung over my shoulder. 'Have you all been good?'

'I'm not on the naughty list!' calls one elderly dear, sitting by the window.

'Excellent, I'll have a present for you then,' I say, lowering my sack of gifts to the floor in front of the fireplace and settling myself in a large armchair.

'I'm definitely on your naughty list!' jests another elderly lady. 'But I wouldn't have it any other way – not now, not ever!'

A titter of laughter fills the air and a fluttering of sporadic applause follows the lady's outspoken remark, while I subtly attempt to readjust my fake white beard, which is itching like crazy. The Santa suit is definitely two sizes too big, and the heavy sack feels like I've strained my shoulder carrying it, but the joyous expressions on their faces makes up for that.

'Santa, I'm sorry but your official elves are delayed elsewhere. But the staff are happy to help distribute the gifts for you,' says Matron, playing along with the act.

I delve into the large hessian sack and retrieve a beautifully wrapped present, complete with a satin bow.

'First gift from the sack is for . . . Bertie!' I announce, offering it to the nearest staff-elf to deliver, before repeating the process.

'The second gift is for . . . Louisa!'

I wave my goodbyes in a hearty, slightly overexcitable manner, slinging my empty hessian sack over my shoulder, and leave the residents' lounge. I'm absolutely exhausted, I could do with a lie-down to recover.

'That was some show!' says a male voice, causing me to jump.

I whip around, to find Magnus and Heather sitting in the reception area patiently waiting.

'No one volunteered for the role, so I thought why not? It's hardly taxing, though they were a tough crowd to please,' I say jokily, removing my fake but annoying beard. Delivering my own barrelled brush gift sets amongst my gallery friends had been far easier but somewhat less rewarding.

'We're very impressed,' says Heather, standing up to greet me.

'I realise you're busy, but can we have a minute of your time?' asks Magnus, stepping nearer.

'Sure. I think the dining room is free for the moment.' I gesture over my shoulder towards the nearest room. 'Shall we?'

They follow my lead into the vacant room. I'm suddenly very aware of my costume, and wish I'd taken a moment to change, as they both seem fairly serious.

'Before Magnus speaks, can I ask how Jemima is?' asks Heather, glancing between us.

'She and Ned are on cloud nine; she had a healthy baby girl in the early hours of this morning. I'm not sure Mungo expected to spend his wedding night pacing the landing of the Lerwick Manor. But Dottie wasn't about to be anywhere else but there, ready and waiting.'

'Wonderful news!' exclaims Magnus.

'Delighted for them all,' adds Heather, her eyes glistening. 'Wish them well from us, won't you?'

'I will,' I say, happy to deliver good news.

'Which brings us to the reason why we're here,' says Magnus.

I notice his tone isn't as bright; his manner has mellowed a tad or two.

'We need to apologise to you for an awful mistake we made. Iona has found her gold necklace in her "bits and bobs" drawer in the kitchen.'

'You know how she's been of late, all absentminded – putting the milk carton in the tumble dryer, and the washing-up liquid in the fridge. We wrongly accused you, when the necklace hadn't left the farmhouse at all but was sitting in a drawer, just waiting to be found,' explains Heather, before biting her lip. 'We're so sorry.'

I don't know what to say, but what I can't do is be blasé and say, 'That's OK, folks – no worries.' I can't pretend and let them off the hook – their accusation hurt me deeply, because it showed what they thought of me.

I say nothing, but give a brief nod.

'We realise there is nothing that will make this right, but saying sorry might go some way towards making amends, surely?' says Magnus, his gaze searching mine for a response.

'It does, thank you. And I'm grateful that you've taken the time to come here to speak to me – especially on Christmas Day of all days – but I can't flick a switch and return to how things were before I was wrongly accused. You never imagined the others were involved, just me – that stings too. I've had plenty of opportunity to steal from The Orangery, to help myself to the other artists' takings, or put my hand in the till at the various bar venues I've worked in recent weeks. But nothing – I've never taken a single dime. And it's been a struggle in recent months, honestly it has. I'm learning not to hold grudges, but right now I can't brush it under the carpet and say never mind, what's done is done – in time I will, but not right now.'

'That's understandable, Callie. In the meantime, can we rely on you to continue your shifts at the farmhouse?' asks Magnus, his manner relaxing somewhat.

It's now my turn to bite my lip. 'I'm not sure that I want to.'

They exchange a fleeting glance on hearing my answer.

'When the necklace was missing, I couldn't very well leave because that suggested I was guilty as charged, but I need to focus on what's good for me right now. I'm delighted that Iona has her necklace back and all is well, but I think I'll be asking for more shifts here rather than continuing at the farmhouse. Sorry. I hate to disappoint people – especially when you've both been good enough to apologise in person.'

'No hard feelings, I hope. We've done well, working together with the alpacas – I wouldn't want that to change, Callie,' says Magnus, extending his hand.

I take it and give it a warm squeeze, before offering Heather an apologetic smile. 'Nor me. I think we've got our work cut out, with Jemima's future plans for the herd's breeding programme. I hear she was enquiring on the mainland about a super-stud called Tarragon, to help perk things up a little.'

'She's probably on the case right now as we speak,' jests Magnus.

'I doubt it very much,' offers Heather, her wry smile suggesting Magnus has forgotten about the new arrival.

Tabitha

The doorbell rings in the middle of our Christmas dinner, causing my mum to huff and puff at the untimely interruption.

'I'll go!' I say, sliding from my seat at the dining table.

I reach the front door, unable to identify the caller from their blurred outline through the frosted glass.

On opening the door, I'm utterly shocked.

'Ebenezer! Please come in. To what do I owe the pleasure?' I should have recognised his brocade frock coat and white hair.

'I won't step inside, thank you. I wanted to bring you a small gift, as a way of saying thank you for all your hard work yesterday and the day before . . . and, in addition, to your stunning performance last night. You played the part down to a T – nailed it, in fact. A perfect portrayal of Scrooge . . . not easy, under the circumstances.'

I listen, still in shock, as this is the most I've ever heard him say in one breath – plus I believe I heard praise being issued, which rarely happens.

'Anyway, less babbling . . . this is for you.' He hands me a gift, wrapped in brown parcel paper, after which he instantly turns on his heels.

'Are you not waiting for me to open it?' I call, as he's already halfway along our driveway.

'No need, no need. There's a letter enclosed – please read it carefully!' he calls, reaching his parked car.

'Merry Christmas . . . and thank you.'

'Merry Christmas to you, Tabitha.' With that, he slams his car door shut and turns the key in the ignition.

What a strange man he is. I turn the gift over, pulling away the line of Sellotape. I peel back the wrapping a fraction . . . and gasp. I don't need to reveal the entire object to know what it is: Ebenezer's battered ledger, detailing a lifetime of experience in the theatre!

Heather

'Evening,' I whisper, entering the nursery to be greeted by calm and tranquillity.

Dottie is sitting in the rocking chair, her watery gaze fixed upon the bundle cradled in her arms.

'Evening,' she softly replies. She doesn't look up, doesn't take her eyes off that tiny rosebud mouth. Why should she?

I cross the floor to view the sleeping babe; there's no chance I'll get a cuddle on this visit. Dark fluffy hair frames her sleeping features, with a row of dark eyelashes resting on snow-white cheeks. She's definitely a Campbell, complete with Jemima's dark locks.

'How's she doing?'

'She's perfect, the best Christmas present I have ever had,' coos Dottie, still not looking up.

I get it, honestly, I do. I'm the same with a basket full of pups; I want to absorb every single moment, each tiny breath and snuffling noise. I can't imagine Dottie will move far from this crib in the coming months.

'And Jemima?'

'Enjoying a little sleep in her own room.'

'Good for her, that's exactly how it should be.'

'Gives me a chance to get my cuddles in.'

She's the picture of contentment, gently rocking back and forth: a new granny in every sense of the word.

'Have they named her yet?'

'Cecelia Dorothy, after Ned's mum and . . .' her sentence fades, as she glances up and beams that cheeky smile of hers.

The queen bee of Lerwick's allotment association finally holds the baby she's been waiting a lifetime for – I'm almost overcome with emotion at the sheer thought of how much love this child will receive.

'How wonderful. You must be thrilled.'

Dottie gives the swaddled baby a gentle squeeze, causing her to nuzzle and slap her lips in her sleep.

I reach down and stroke her cheek, so soft and plump.

'I'm going to leave you to it, Dottie. Shout if there's anything Jemima needs,' I say, knowing that a longer stay will result in nothing more; both babe and Dottie are quite content.

'Will do, Heather.'

I cross the nursery floor, heading for the door, when she calls my name.

'Yeah.'

'If Kaspar's making any of his condensed milk cookies, they'd be sure to lift the new mum's energy levels,' says Dottie, her twinkling gaze looking up at me for the first time.

'Sure, I'll pass on the message.' I gently close the door behind me.

Boy, she's a minx; she never misses a trick.

Epilogue

Saturday 1 April

Tabitha

'What in God's name are you doing with that?' asks Aileen.

She watches as I awkwardly manhandle the wooden ladder, resting it against the interior wall of the now-vacated library building; they've opted to move up the road, having outgrown these premises, formerly the church of St Ringan.

'I want a permanent reminder, if nothing else,' I say, testing my foot on the bottom rung, before confidently grabbing the hammer and nail from the polished countertop beside the prepared photo frame.

'Seriously, woman, you'll cause yourself – and me – an injury if you do a Freddie in here; there'll be no saving you with a soft landing enabling you to gambol down a grassy embankment. Please let me call your Rabbie to do that task. You'll break your neck for sure.'

'Break my neck, break a leg – it's all said in jest when linked to drama!' I mutter, holding the nail in my teeth and armed with the hammer as I gingerly begin to climb each rung, much to Aileen's dismay.

When I reach my desired height – slightly higher than Freddie ever dared to ascend in our infamous Shakespeare skit, but significantly lower than the ornate wrought-iron railings – I begin to hammer the nail into the wall, hoping it holds fast. Once done, I give it a firm wiggle: perfect.

'Aileen! Can you hand me the frame, please?'

'This one?'

The frame appears in mid-air at my side, but accompanied by Rabbie's not Aileen's voice.

'What are you doing?' he demands.

'Thank you,' I say, taking the proffered frame. 'Like I said last night, I want his letter up on the wall as a permanent reminder.'

'Aileen, correct me if I'm wrong, but surely Tabs here and the rest of our company currently have a permanent reminder each time we pass the shell of The Garrison Theatre. She'll be showcasing us her new ghost lamp next.'

'Funny you should mention a ghost lamp, Rabbie – I'm expecting delivery tomorrow, ready for Thursday night's session.'

'Surely you need only take a little walk, Tabitha, to see why reigniting that superstition is foolhardy,' says Aileen.

I'm not listening to them; as the new creative director of our am-dram group I'm allowed to decide what direction we steer this company in. Ebenezer's Christmas letter, now framed and hung upon the wall of our temporary home, will assist me.

I gingerly climb down the ladder, my knees slightly knocking, for fear of falling.

'Looks good, doesn't it?' I ask the sceptical pair.

I receive a nod from my dear friend and a comical expression from my now-boyfriend.

Our first date had to wait. We delayed until our Cratchit and Scrooge roles had departed, like ghosts – or much like Ebenezer after his Christmas delivery to my house. We've seen and heard neither hide nor hair of him since that day, so I can only believe the letter tucked between the pages of his battered ledger.

'I suppose it does look rather impressive,' Rabbie concedes, adding, 'Though you can't read it, way up there.'

'Who needs to read it? I know it off by heart.'
Rabbie smiles as Ebenezer's inky scrawl fills my mind.

Dearest Tabitha,

This is possibly the hardest letter I've had to write, as it
signals the end of my career spanning some seventy years
in theatre. From the age of ten, I've trodden the boards and
repeatedly hoped to break a leg in the finest performances
imaginable. But now, it is my time to depart, pack away
the face paint, divest myself of the costumes and frock coat,
and fade into my retirement.

Anything worthy of note within my career has been
included in my ledger . . . I don't make notes on individuals,
as many have construed over the years – you now have
proof of that. Read my notes, learn from my mistakes,
Tabitha, and enjoy your life within the theatre. I sense you
believe your dream lies elsewhere, but I truly believe it is
here in Shetland – make the most of local talent, and create
many dreams rather than chasing one.

I came to Lerwick with one intention: to end my days,
knowing that I had saved a much-loved theatre for the generations to follow. I couldn't secure the future of a big West
End theatre, but I could rescue a small local affair. The fire
was unfortunate, but fire is necessary if a phoenix is to rise.
And so I have succeeded – through you, dear Tabitha – in
securing The Garrison's bright future. Shine bright, shine
often, and light the way for all who follow!

Your everlasting friend,

Ebenezer

Heather

I've never ventured inside The Cabbage Patch social shack before, so I'm taken aback by the interior: a vast wooden structure consisting of bare beams, joists and floorboards. Previously, I've had no reason to attend the Lerwick Manor Allotment Association's general meeting, but now that we're officially a couple, I want to support Kaspar during the forthcoming season. Not that he needs my help where his allotment is concerned, but I still want to show willing. The decoration is minimal, with several untidy noticeboards detailing long-forgotten undertakings, and a strand of red bunting pinned to the edge of the tea counter, complete with a hissing urn and an old coffee machine.

We stand at the back, my arm slung through his, behind a horde of people seated on row upon row of white patio chairs and the occasional low-slung deckchair. I recognise many people from the local community and the surrounding areas. I could name the majority and provide a little potted history for most. Likewise, they could do the same about me and mine. Thankfully, my little family is happily plodding along without igniting gossip. My Isla's baking talents continue to blossom and her recipe book is selling nicely. Our Ellie's coping well after her break-up with Theo, though it was for the best and hardly unexpected, given his circumstances.

The door opens and a small group of newbies flood in, each one a little furtive in their manner, not wishing to tread on any toes or step out of line in a room full of experts – barring me.

Levi walks along the rows; he hands out a pink flyer to each attendee. It doesn't appear as if refusal or lack of interest qualifies as an excuse not to receive the offered literature.

'Thank you,' says Kaspar, holding the agenda before us like a shared song sheet.

I scan the committee's agenda of discussion items: annual allotment festival date, bonfires and waste disposal, prohibited keeping of cockerels, stolen tools, security/personal safety, rules and regulations – and, finally, AOB.

There must be eighty people squeezed inside this shack: sitting or standing around the edge, waiting for the meeting to begin.

Ting, ting, ting.

A teaspoon is rapidly tapped on the side of a mug by Dottie, and the raucous chatter fades to silence. Mungo stands tall behind the trestle table to address his audience.

'Welcome to the Lerwick Manor Allotment Association's first meeting of the year. I'd like to introduce the committee for those new members joining us, starting with myself, Mungo Tulloch, as chairman, then Jemima Campbell as treasurer, Dorothy Tulloch as secretary, and Levi Gordans as deputy chair. There are many more committee members, all of whom you can rely upon in our absence – you'll find their details pinned to the noticeboard. Now, let's get down to business.'

Bang on cue, the shack door creaks opens, admitting a solitary male in a chunky knitted jumper and heavy walking boots. Strapped about his chest and torso is a sturdy baby carrier, complete with a sleeping infant. Ned's fleeting nod towards the top table is taken as his apology to the entire room.

'By tradition, we always hold a meeting in April – despite it being a no-go month for us while we await finer weather. But this month gives us ample opportunity to get ready for the growing season ahead, and to plan for the September festival. The first item on the agenda is to choose the date of our annual festival. Now, I need a show of hands in relation to dates. Is there any objection to a public vote? We can organise a secret ballot, if folks prefer, but like dear Old Bill used to say, "I hate wasting time on the unnecessary." Anyone?' Mungo's gaze scours the room for an indication of a hand or a twitching eye. 'Good, that settles it – a public vote. Last year, we held the festival on the third of September, so I propose either the second or the ninth, this year – what's it to be?'

After a flurry of hands, a rapid count by the committee and numerous allotmenteers, agreement is reached on the earlier date. I watch in bewilderment, as the minutiae of allotment life play out before my eyes. Who'd have thought Mungo would be so forthright in his decisions, that Dottie would take a back seat, and that Jemima and Levi would happily undertake such time-consuming yet rewarding roles on behalf of us all, the allotment owners?

'Moving on,' says Mungo, peering at his agenda. 'Bonfires and waste disposal . . .'

I tune out as he begins to outline the difficulties encountered in recent months, with instances of fly tipping on the car park and chemical damage to the environment; no doubt Kaspar knows all about such things. My gaze roves around the room, noting various people: positioned near the front is Melissa, gently rocking baby Noah in his pushchair, which is good to see. Jemima's looking healthier these days – a picture of contentment, seated at the committee table. Dottie is attentive and eagle-eyed, as always, watching the tiny cherub nestled against Ned's torso. Levi actively supports his buddy Mungo, whilst occasionally sending a loving smile in Pippa's direction; new adventures are bound to occur now they're living together at Harmony Cottage. The trio by the doorway, Callie, Nessie and Verity, are nervously signalling to one another that they haven't a clue what's going on; they're probably asking themselves, 'Whose idea was this?' From what I've encountered in recent months, since being with Kaspar, they're in for a whole load of fun, and a very steep learning curve!

Callie seems happier of late, juggling her waitressing shifts with alpaca treks and weekly stints at the Happy Days sheltered housing complex. Nessie and Isaac are simply passionate and as loved up as any young couple can muster, be it at home or in their forge. And Verity has found peace and security within the farmhouse, alongside our Magnus – apparently, she's promised never to fill the freezer with home-made lasagne!

'And finally, that brings us to any other business!' announces Mungo, bringing me back from my daze.

Lord knows what the outcome of the previous agenda points were, but I'm sure Kaspar will enlighten me later.

'Is there any other business? No? Nothing? In that case, I'd like to ask Jemima if she would do the honours by introducing some new recruits who have recently became allotment holders. Jemima?' Mungo takes his seat.

Jemima stands, as requested. 'Where are they?' She peers at the audience, seeking particular faces. 'Ah, there you all are! Yes, on behalf of Lerwick Manor Allotment Association I'd like to offer a warm welcome to Callie, Nessie and Verity – these ladies, along with young Isla, who's holding the fort back in The Orangery, are taking on Old Bill's allotment plot – number 13 – now that it's vacant again. And a grand job you'll make of it too, I'm sure. Though please learn from my mistakes … never throw away comfrey tea, never waste a drop of water, and always wear gloves when handling a compost heap. If you're not sure why then please come and ask me, I'll put you straight!'

There's a healthy roar of laughter and a round of applause from the gathered members who remember Jemima's untimely arrival.

Jemima waits for quiet to return to The Cabbage Patch, before adding, 'It gives me the greatest pleasure to wish you all a happy, healthy and productive new allotment year! There's more than just nettles and mare's tail growing on our plots; we have life-long friendships blossoming and sprouting everywhere – as proven, season after season, by our past, present and hopefully future members.'

Acknowledgements

Thank you to my editor, Kate Byrne, and everyone at Headline Publishing Group for believing in my storytelling and granting me the opportunity to become part of your team.

To David Headley and the crew at DHH Literary Agency – thank you for the unwavering support. Having a 'dream team' supporting my career was always the goal – you guys make it the reality!

Thank you to my fellow authors/friends within the Romantic Novelists' Association – you continue to support and encourage me every step of the way.

A heartfelt thank you to the Shetlanders for providing such a warm welcome whilst I holidayed in Lerwick, Shetland – who would have thought that this little girl's dream of visiting the top of the weather map would result in a series of books!

A huge global thank you to my readers across the social media platforms who answered my request for alpaca, dog and pup names.

Ginger – @loriliquidamber; Bramble – @san_mcn11; Fern – A. Sorrells; Rosie – K. Jenkinson; Socks – S. Penrose; Pepper – A. Fowler; Skye – @lisaalpacaallwood; Cass – J. Dey; Marble – C. Scott; Emily – S. Elmer; Sheba – H. Wroe; and Sherbert* – L. Lindsay.

A surprising thank you to every GCSE pupil to whom I taught Dickens' *A Christmas Carol*. Whilst teaching, I'd never have imagined this book would be part of my future life; maybe we had a 'silent, unseen spirit' observing from the corner who already knew our fate!

Unconditional thanks to my family and closest friends, for always loving and supporting my adventures – wherever they take me.

And finally, thank you to my wonderful readers. You continue to thrill me each day with your fabulous reviews and supportive emails. I'm truly humbled that you invest precious time from your busy lives in reading my books. Without you guys, my characters, stories and happy-ever-afters would simply be daydreams.

---

* Sherbert's name was originally chosen by a small child, many moons ago, hence the additional letter in the spelling.

Don't miss more feel-good reads
from Erin Green, coming soon!

SUMMER DREAMS
AT THE LAKESIDE COTTAGE

and

CHRISTMAS WISHES
AT THE LAKESIDE COTTAGE

REVIEW

from Shetland, with love

An uplifting novel about how friendship
can blossom in the most unexpected places...

Available now from

REVIEW

Taking a Chance on Love

The perfect feel-good, romantic and uplifting read –
another book from Erin Green sure to warm your heart.

Available now from

REVIEW

Bookends

When one book ends, another begins...

Bookends is a vibrant new reading community to help you ensure you're never without a good book.

You'll find exclusive previews of the brilliant new books from your favourite authors as well as exciting debuts and past classics. Read our blog, check out our recommendations for your reading group, enter great competitions and much more!

Visit our website to see which great books we're recommending this month.

Join the Bookends community:

www.welcometobookends.co.uk

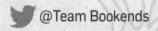 @Team Bookends   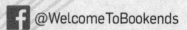 @WelcomeToBookends